WELCOME TO SHOWSIDE

CREATED BY IAN McGINTY

FOR

CHARLIE

WELCOME TO SHOWSIDE

Written By

Ian McGinty
& Samantha "Glow" Knapp

Art By

Ian McGinty

Colors & Letters By

Fred C. Stresing
& Meg Casey

The Best Hoodie in the Universe
Written by Ian McGinty & Art by Carey Pietsch

Hot Chocolate, Cool Ghost
Written by Ian McGinty & Art by Carolyn Nowak

What's in the Box?
by Kate Leth

All characters copyright Ian McGinty, First Edition May 2016, Published by Z2
Comics New York New York. Publishers Josh Frankel And Sridhar Reddy

Boo's New Pants
written by Fred C. Stresing
& Art by Katy Farina

Showing Showside: the Show!
written by Fred C. Stresing
& Art by Meg Casey

8 Bit Kit
written by Fred C. Stresing
& Art by Michael Knepprath

Cool Ghost Visits Beezlebob
by Fred C. Stresing

Buff Boo
written by Meg Casey
& Art by Maddi Gonzalez

The Mayor's... Millions?
written by Fred C. Stresing
& Art by Caitlin Rose Boyle

Frank's Weekend
written by Kara Love
& Art by Joey Weiser

Teenomiconathon
written by Kara Love
& Art by Jen Bartel

Cool Ghost Memorial Service/BBQ
written by Meg Casey & Fred C. Stresing
with Art by Patabot

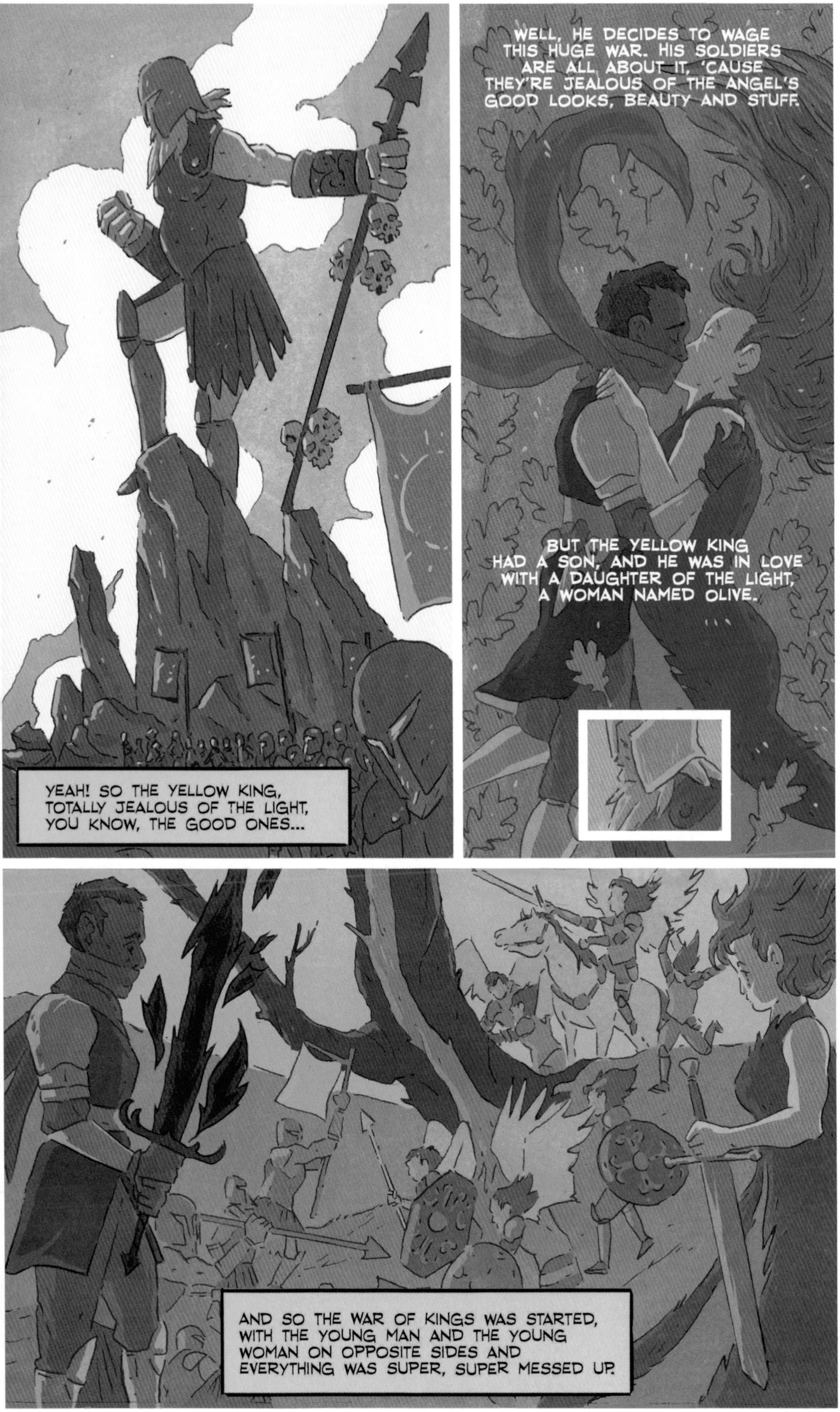
YEAH! SO THE YELLOW KING, TOTALLY JEALOUS OF THE LIGHT, YOU KNOW, THE GOOD ONES...
WELL, HE DECIDES TO WAGE THIS HUGE WAR. HIS SOLDIERS ARE ALL ABOUT IT, 'CAUSE THEY'RE JEALOUS OF THE ANGEL'S GOOD LOOKS, BEAUTY AND STUFF.
BUT THE YELLOW KING HAD A SON, AND HE WAS IN LOVE WITH A DAUGHTER OF THE LIGHT, A WOMAN NAMED OLIVE.
AND SO THE WAR OF KINGS WAS STARTED, WITH THE YOUNG MAN AND THE YOUNG WOMAN ON OPPOSITE SIDES AND EVERYTHING WAS SUPER, SUPER MESSED UP.

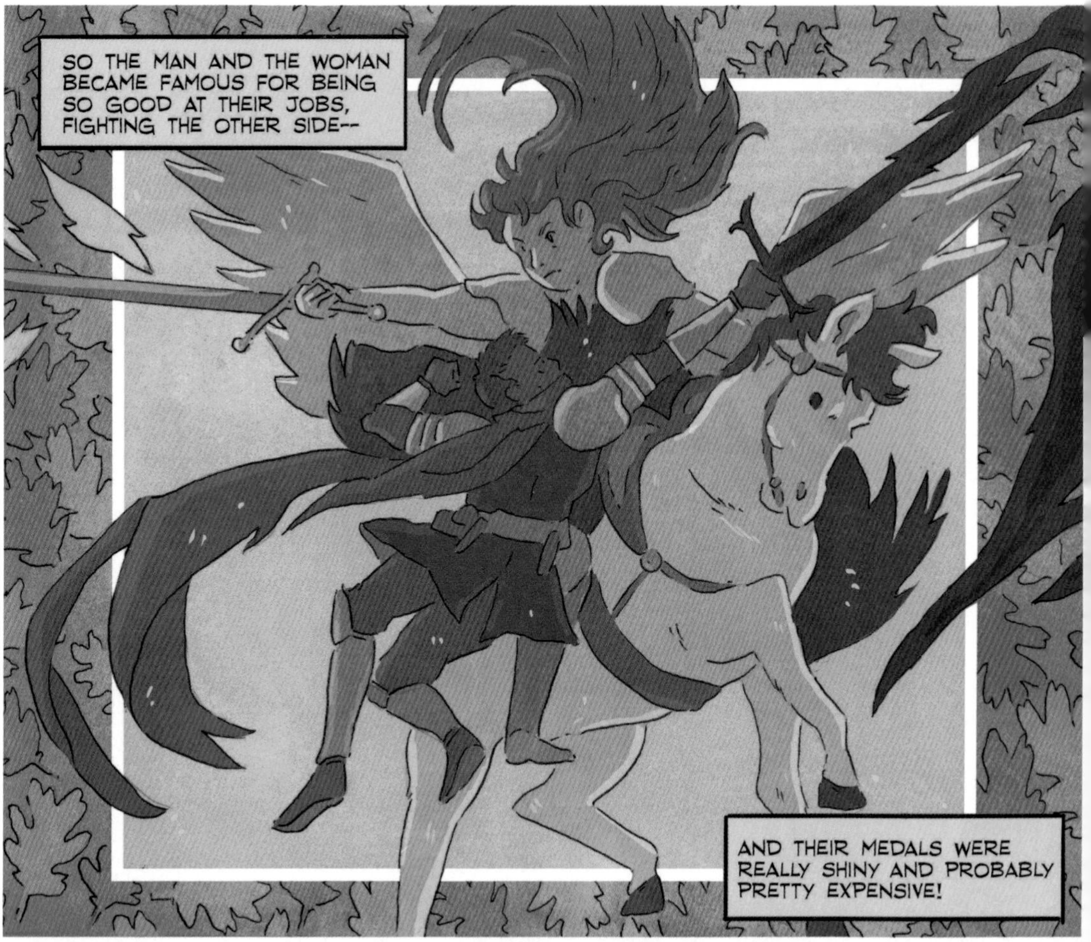
SO THE MAN AND THE WOMAN BECAME FAMOUS FOR BEING SO GOOD AT THEIR JOBS, FIGHTING THE OTHER SIDE--
AND THEIR MEDALS WERE REALLY SHINY AND PROBABLY PRETTY EXPENSIVE!

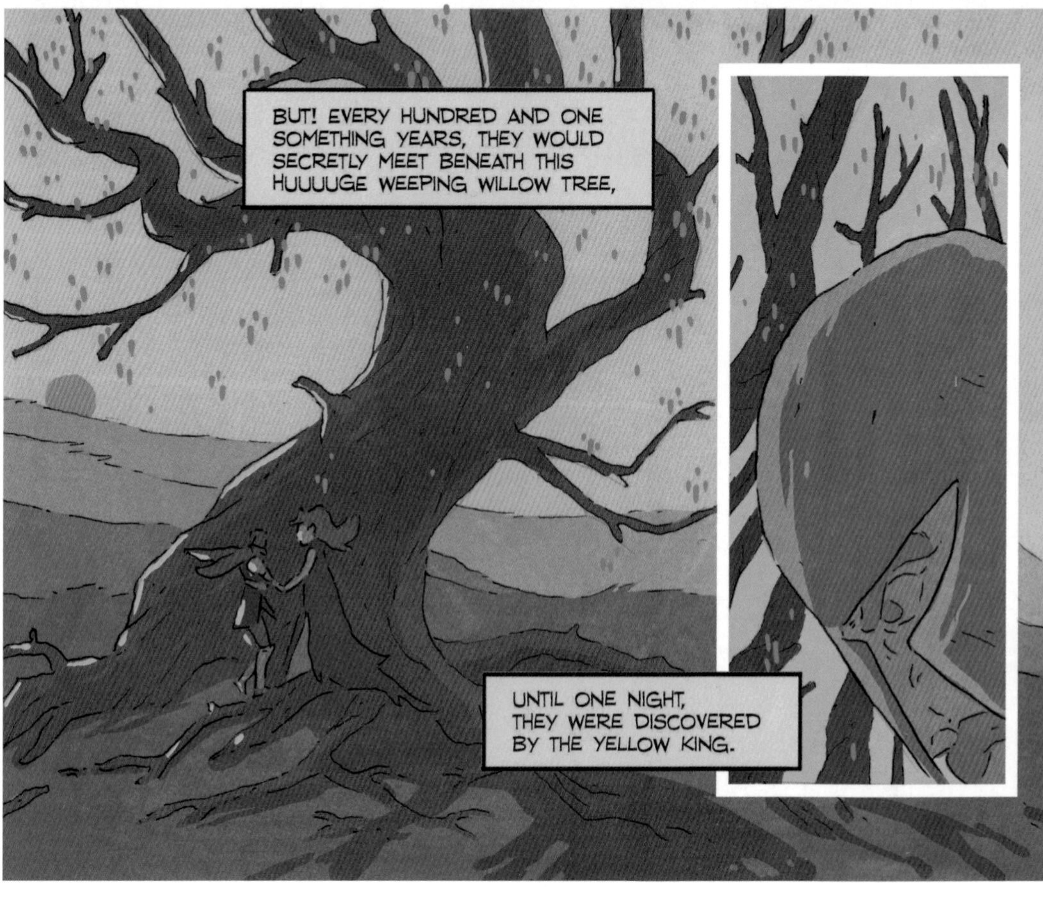
BUT! EVERY HUNDRED AND ONE SOMETHING YEARS, THEY WOULD SECRETLY MEET BENEATH THIS HUUUUGE WEEPING WILLOW TREE,
UNTIL ONE NIGHT, THEY WERE DISCOVERED BY THE YELLOW KING.

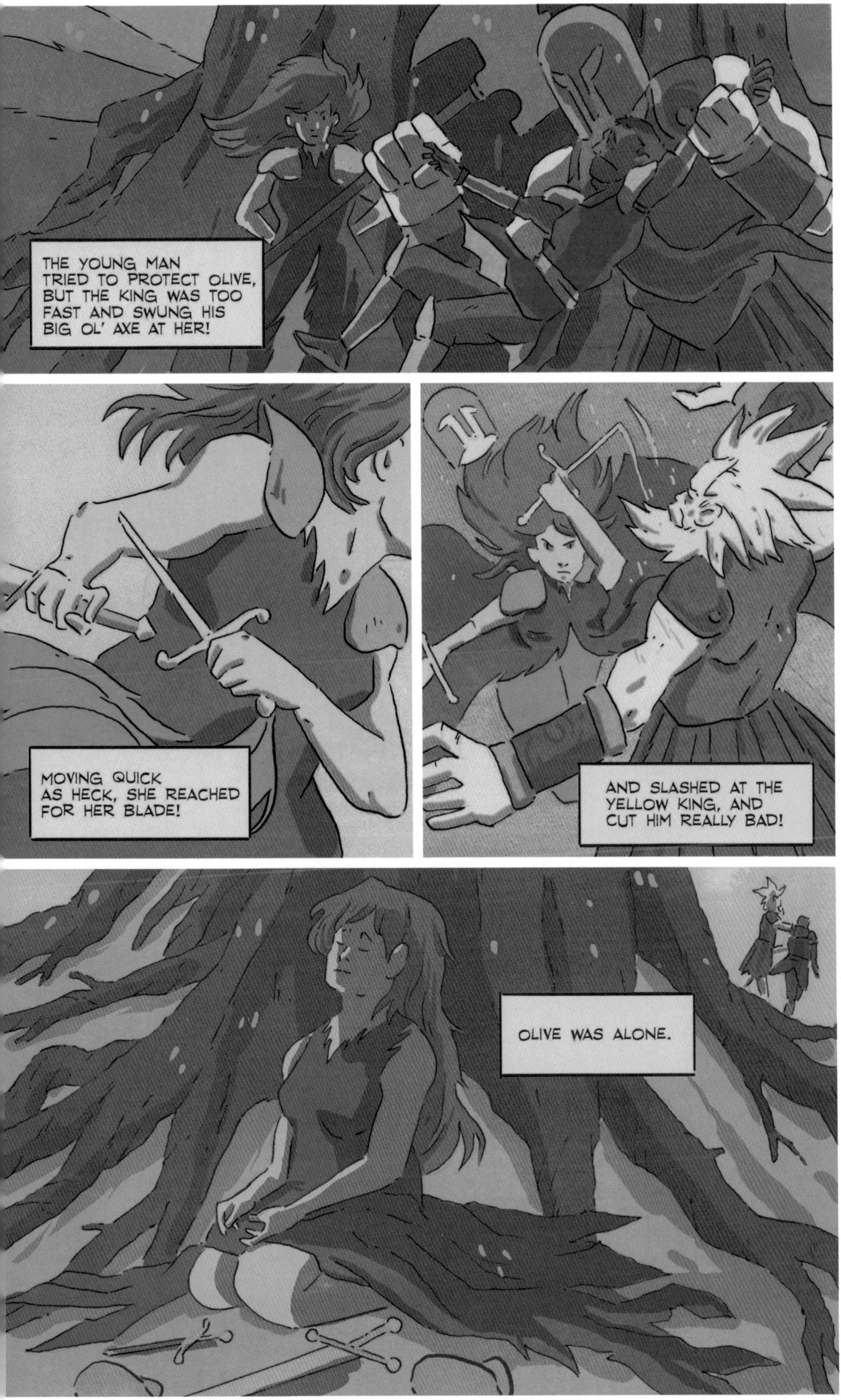
THE YOUNG MAN TRIED TO PROTECT OLIVE, BUT THE KING WAS TOO FAST AND SWUNG HIS BIG OL' AXE AT HER!
MOVING QUICK AS HECK, SHE REACHED FOR HER BLADE!
AND SLASHED AT THE YELLOW KING, AND CUT HIM REALLY BAD!
OLIVE WAS ALONE.

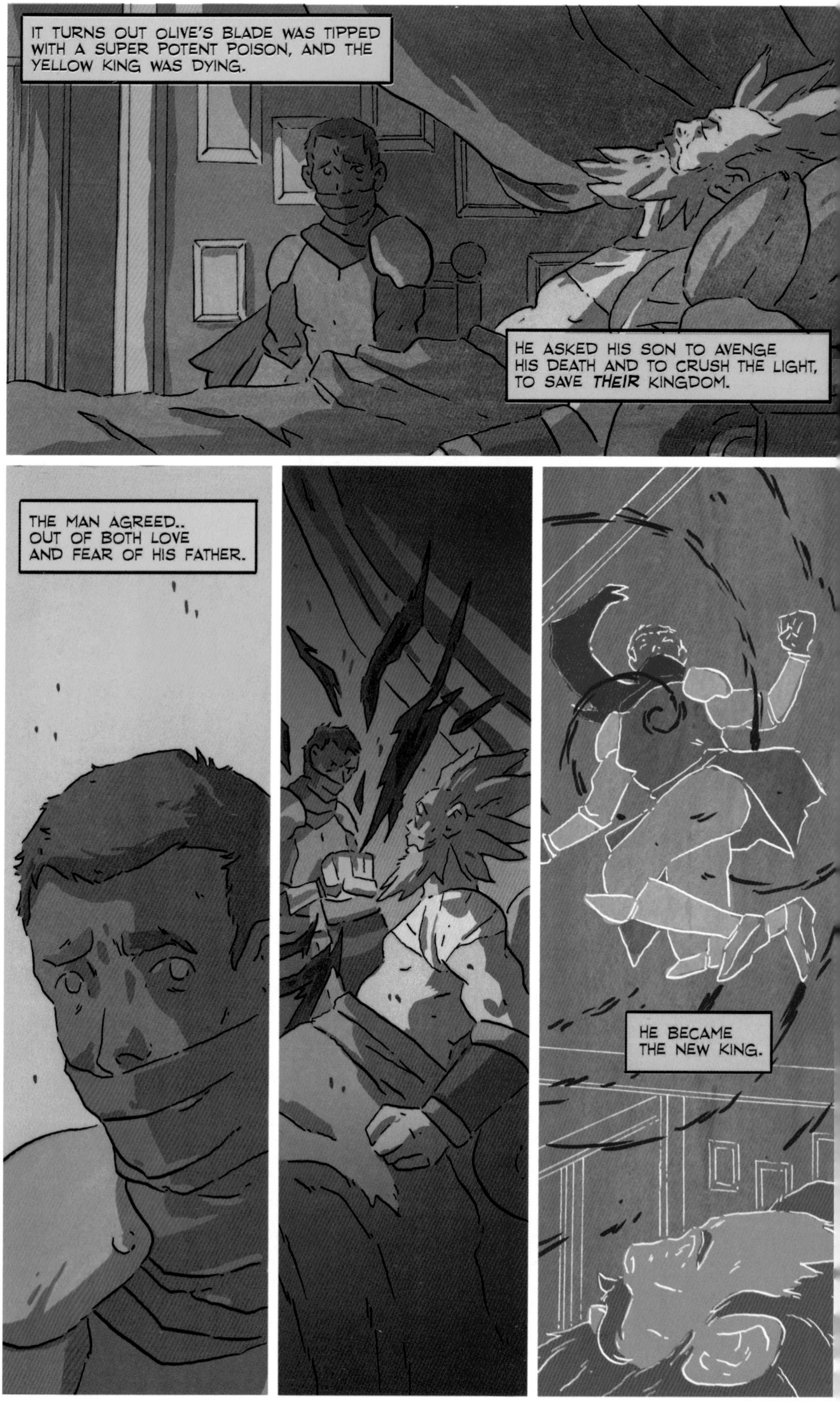
IT TURNS OUT OLIVE'S BLADE WAS TIPPED WITH A SUPER POTENT POISON, AND THE YELLOW KING WAS DYING.
HE ASKED HIS SON TO AVENGE HIS DEATH AND TO CRUSH THE LIGHT, TO SAVE THEIR KINGDOM.
THE MAN AGREED.. OUT OF BOTH LOVE AND FEAR OF HIS FATHER.
HE BECAME THE NEW KING.

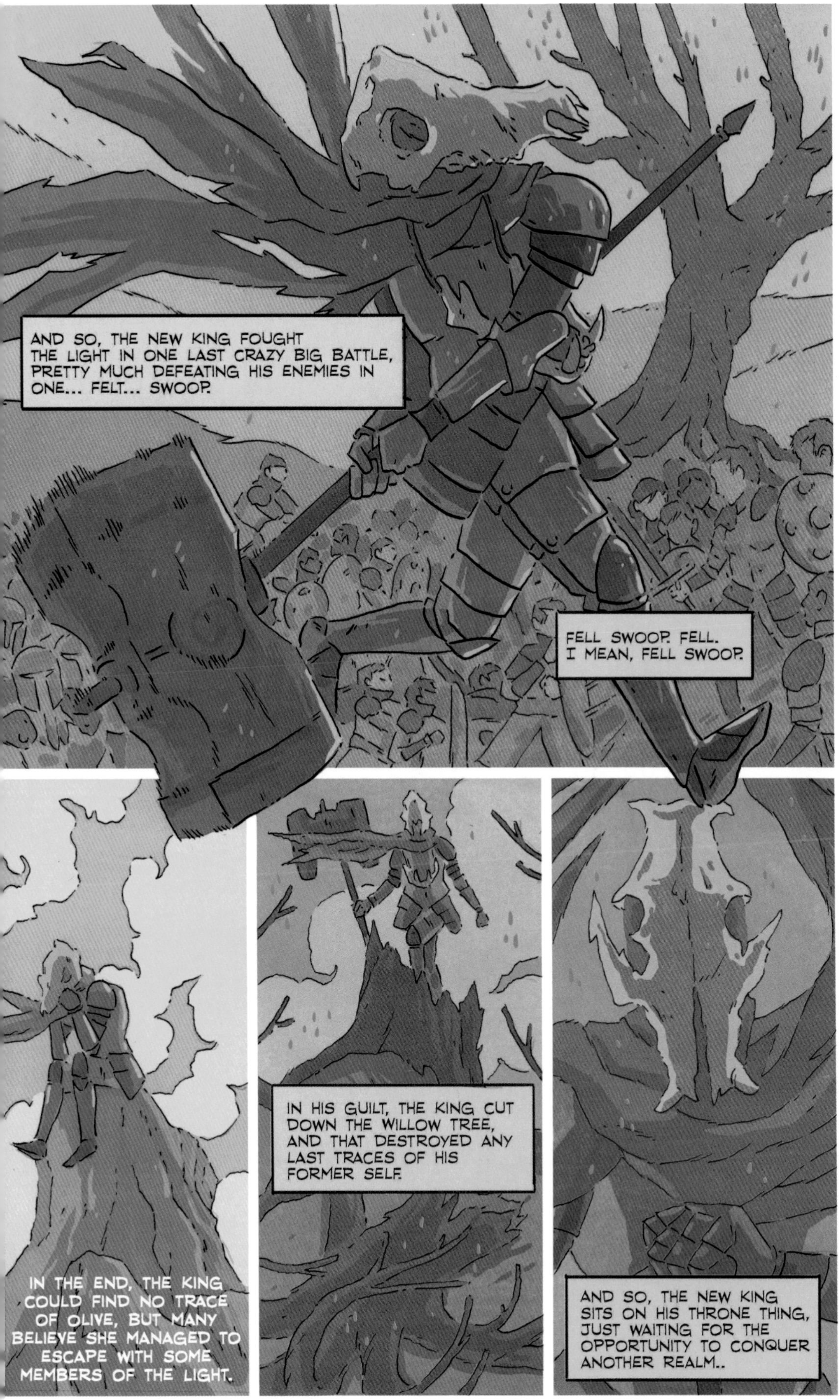
AND SO, THE NEW KING FOUGHT THE LIGHT IN ONE LAST CRAZY BIG BATTLE, PRETTY MUCH DEFEATING HIS ENEMIES IN ONE... FELT... SWOOP.
FELL SWOOP. FELL. I MEAN, FELL SWOOP.
IN THE END, THE KING COULD FIND NO TRACE OF OLIVE, BUT MANY BELIEVE SHE MANAGED TO ESCAPE WITH SOME MEMBERS OF THE LIGHT.
IN HIS GUILT, THE KING CUT DOWN THE WILLOW TREE, AND THAT DESTROYED ANY LAST TRACES OF HIS FORMER SELF.
AND SO, THE NEW KING SITS ON HIS THRONE THING, JUST WAITING FOR THE OPPORTUNITY TO CONQUER ANOTHER REALM..

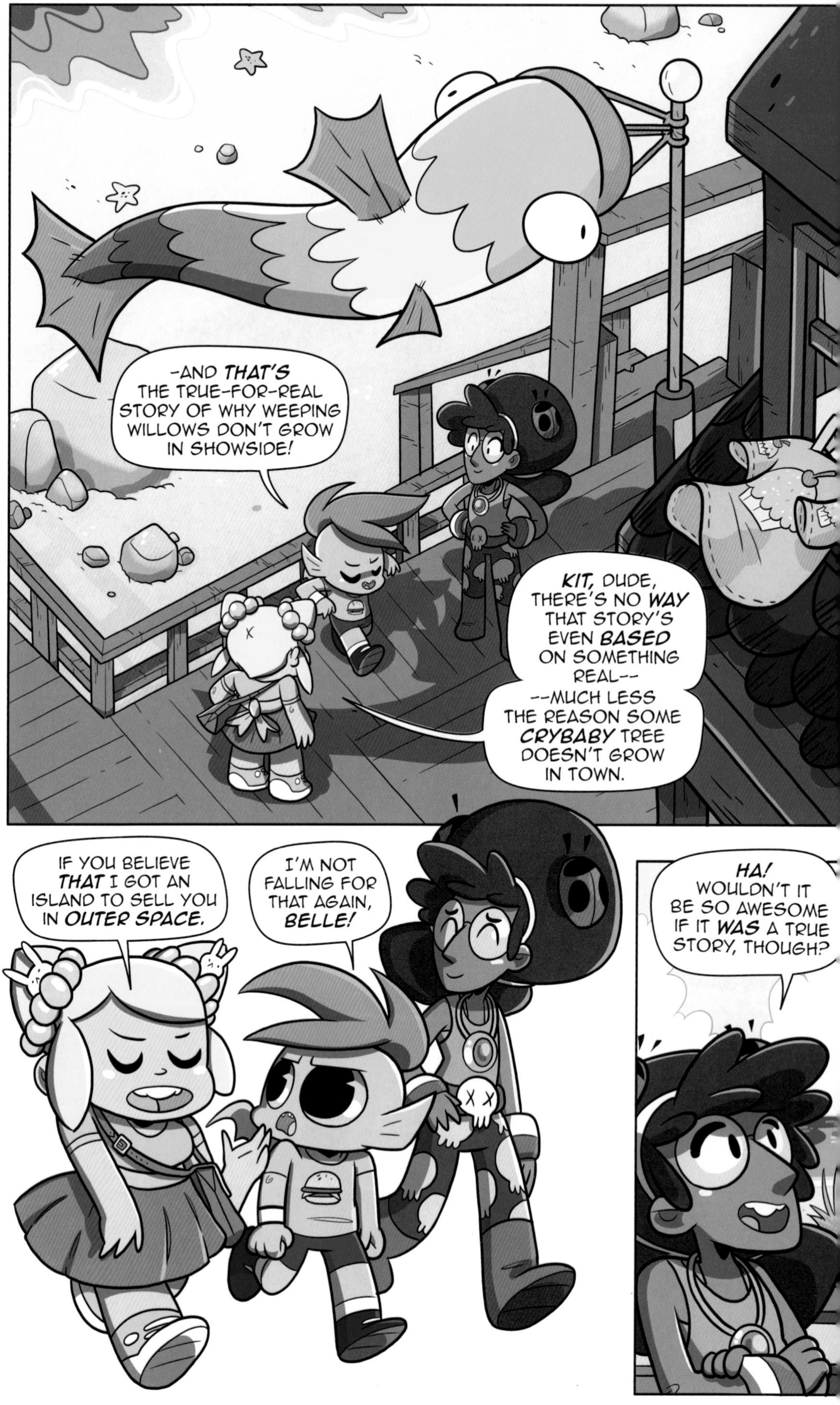
-AND THAT'S THE TRUE-FOR-REAL STORY OF WHY WEEPING WILLOWS DON'T GROW IN SHOWSIDE!
KIT, DUDE, THERE'S NO WAY THAT STORY'S EVEN BASED ON SOMETHING REAL--
--MUCH LESS THE REASON SOME CRYBABY TREE DOESN'T GROW IN TOWN.
IF YOU BELIEVE THAT I GOT AN ISLAND TO SELL YOU IN OUTER SPACE.
I'M NOT FALLING FOR THAT AGAIN, BELLE!
HA! WOULDN'T IT BE SO AWESOME IF IT WAS A TRUE STORY, THOUGH?

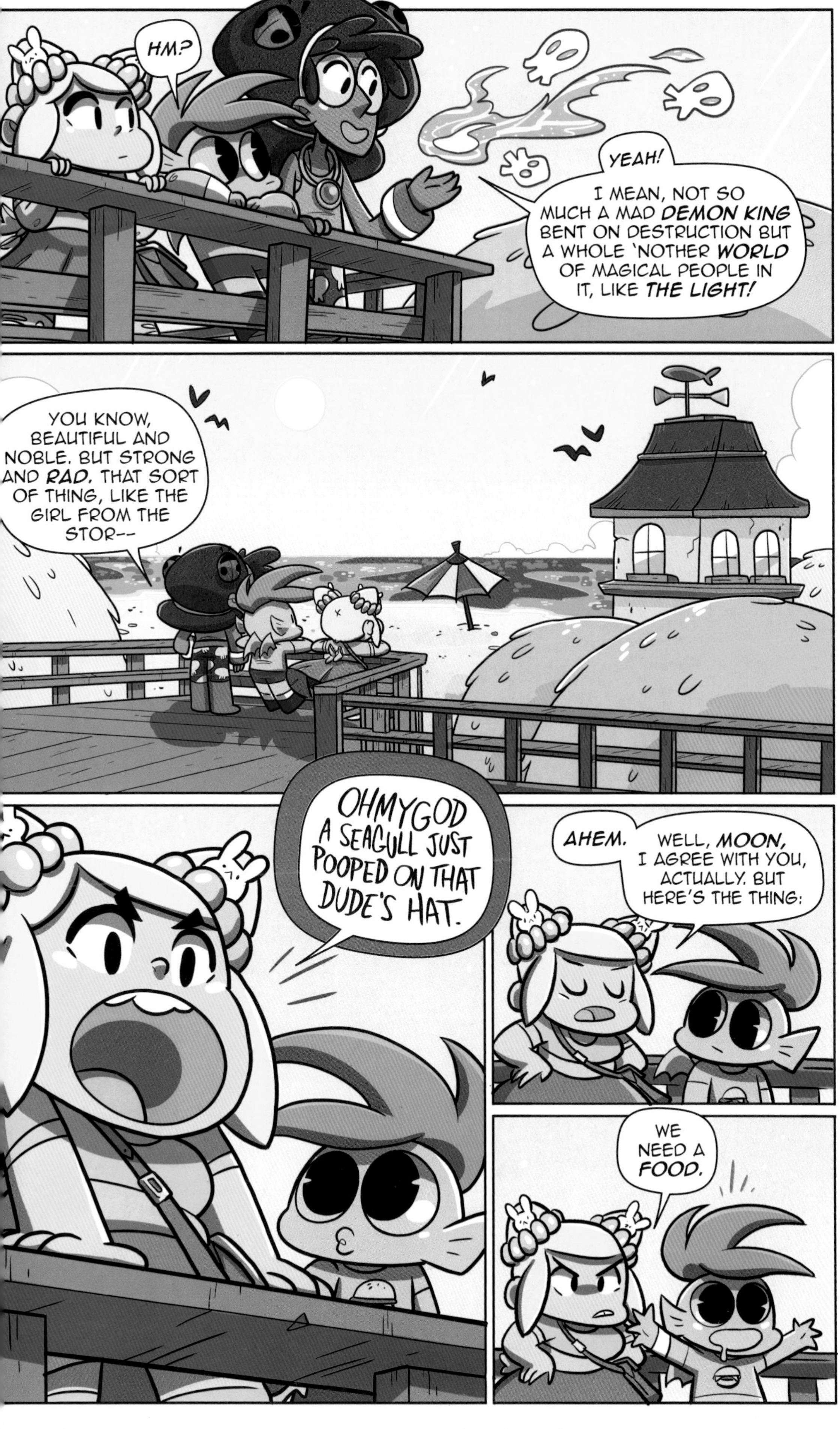
HM?
YEAH!
I MEAN, NOT SO MUCH A MAD DEMON KING BENT ON DESTRUCTION BUT A WHOLE 'NOTHER WORLD OF MAGICAL PEOPLE IN IT, LIKE THE LIGHT!
YOU KNOW, BEAUTIFUL AND NOBLE. BUT STRONG AND RAD. THAT SORT OF THING, LIKE THE GIRL FROM THE STOR--
OHMYGOD A SEAGULL JUST POOPED ON THAT DUDE'S HAT.
AHEM.
WELL, MOON, I AGREE WITH YOU, ACTUALLY. BUT HERE'S THE THING:
WE NEED A FOOD.

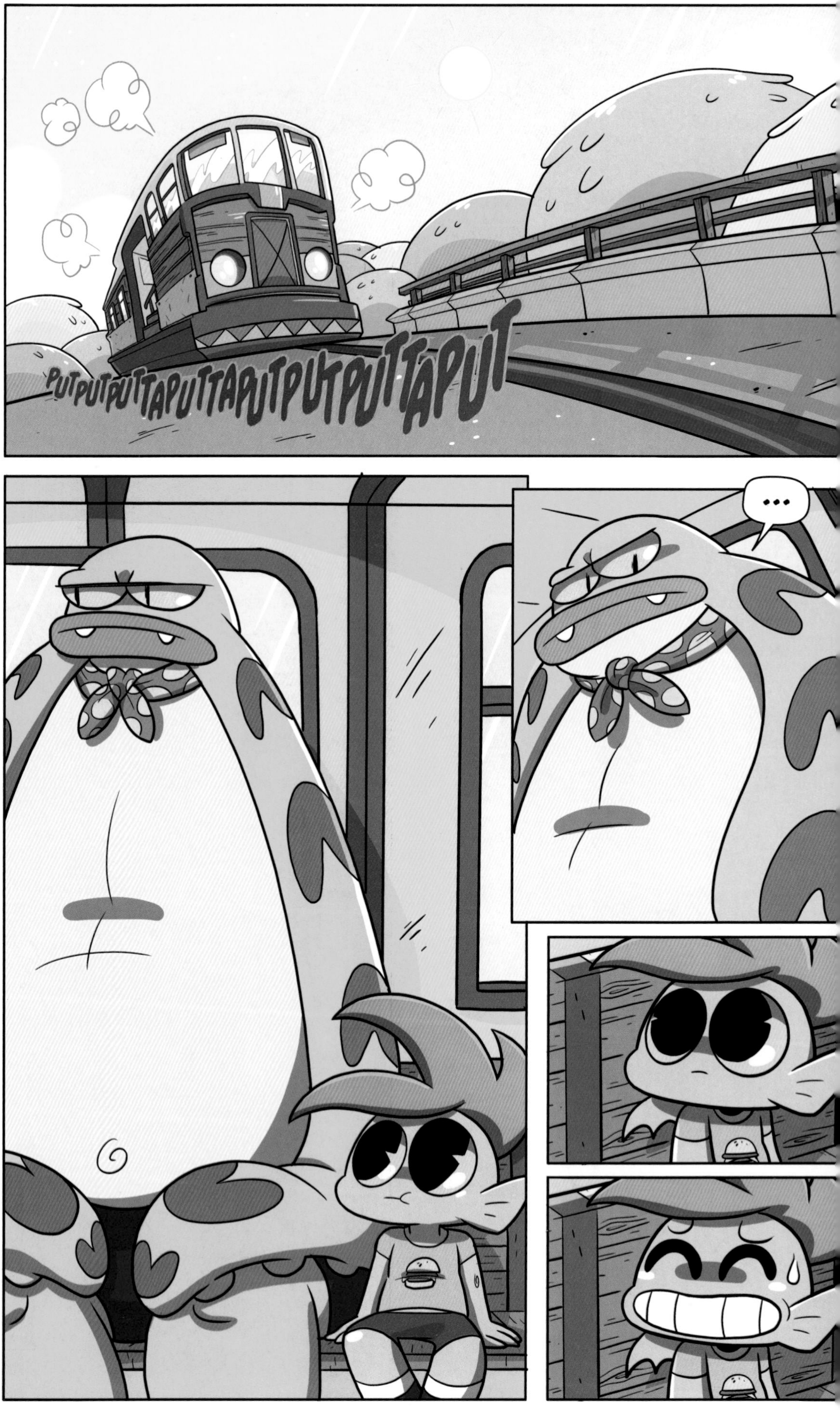
PUTPUTPUTTAPUTTAPUTPUTPUTTAPUT
...

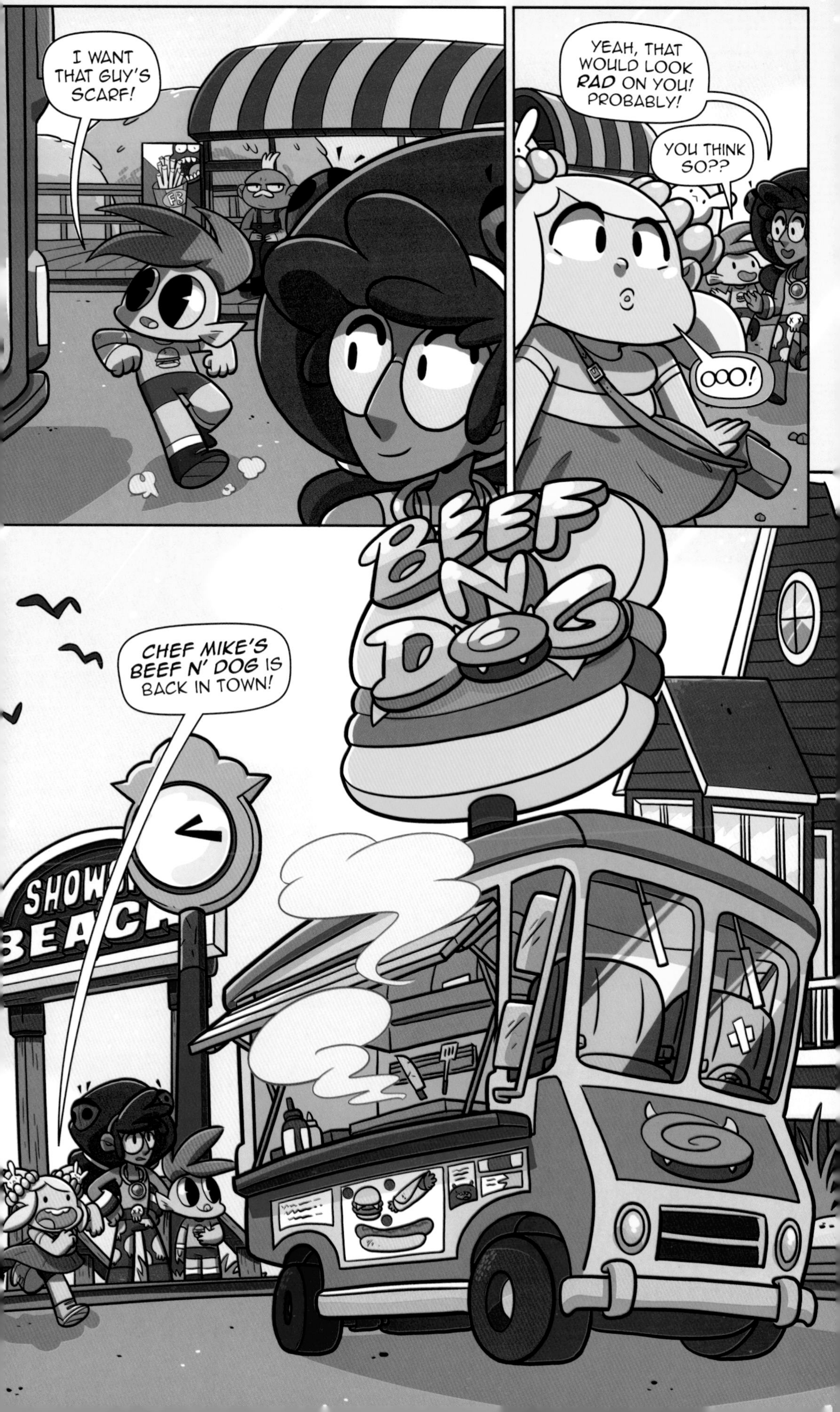
I WANT THAT GUY'S SCARF!
YEAH, THAT WOULD LOOK RAD ON YOU! PROBABLY!
YOU THINK SO??
OOO!
BEEF N' DOG
CHEF MIKE'S BEEF N' DOG IS BACK IN TOWN!
SHOWS
BEAC

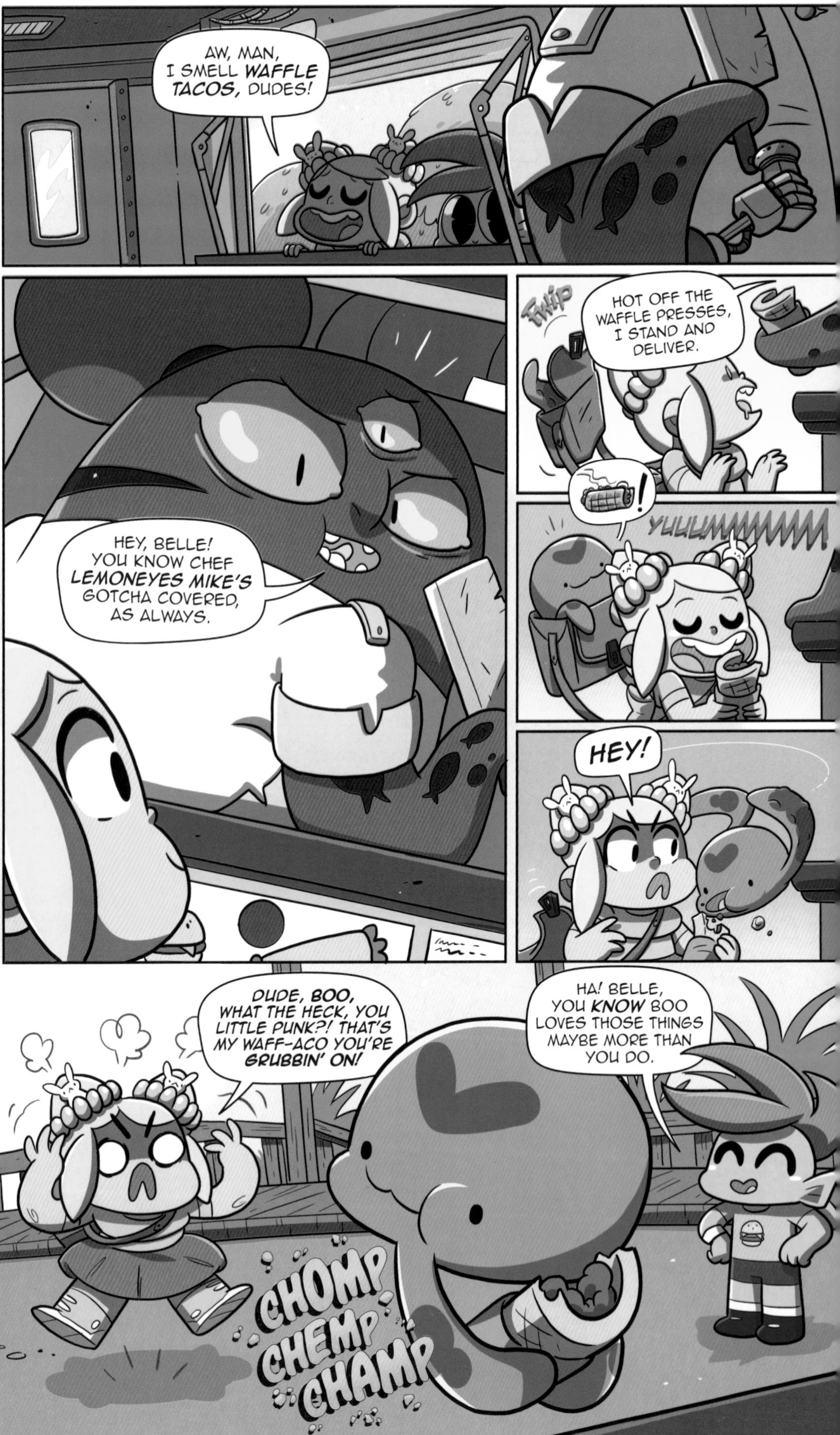
AW, MAN, I SMELL WAFFLE TACOS, DUDES!
FWIP
HOT OFF THE WAFFLE PRESSES, I STAND AND DELIVER.
HEY, BELLE! YOU KNOW CHEF LEMONEYES MIKE'S GOTCHA COVERED, AS ALWAYS.
!
YUUUMMMMMM
HEY!
DUDE, BOO, WHAT THE HECK, YOU LITTLE PUNK?! THAT'S MY WAFF-ACO YOU'RE GRUBBIN' ON!
HA! BELLE, YOU KNOW BOO LOVES THOSE THINGS MAYBE MORE THAN YOU DO.
CHOMP
CHEMP
CHAMP

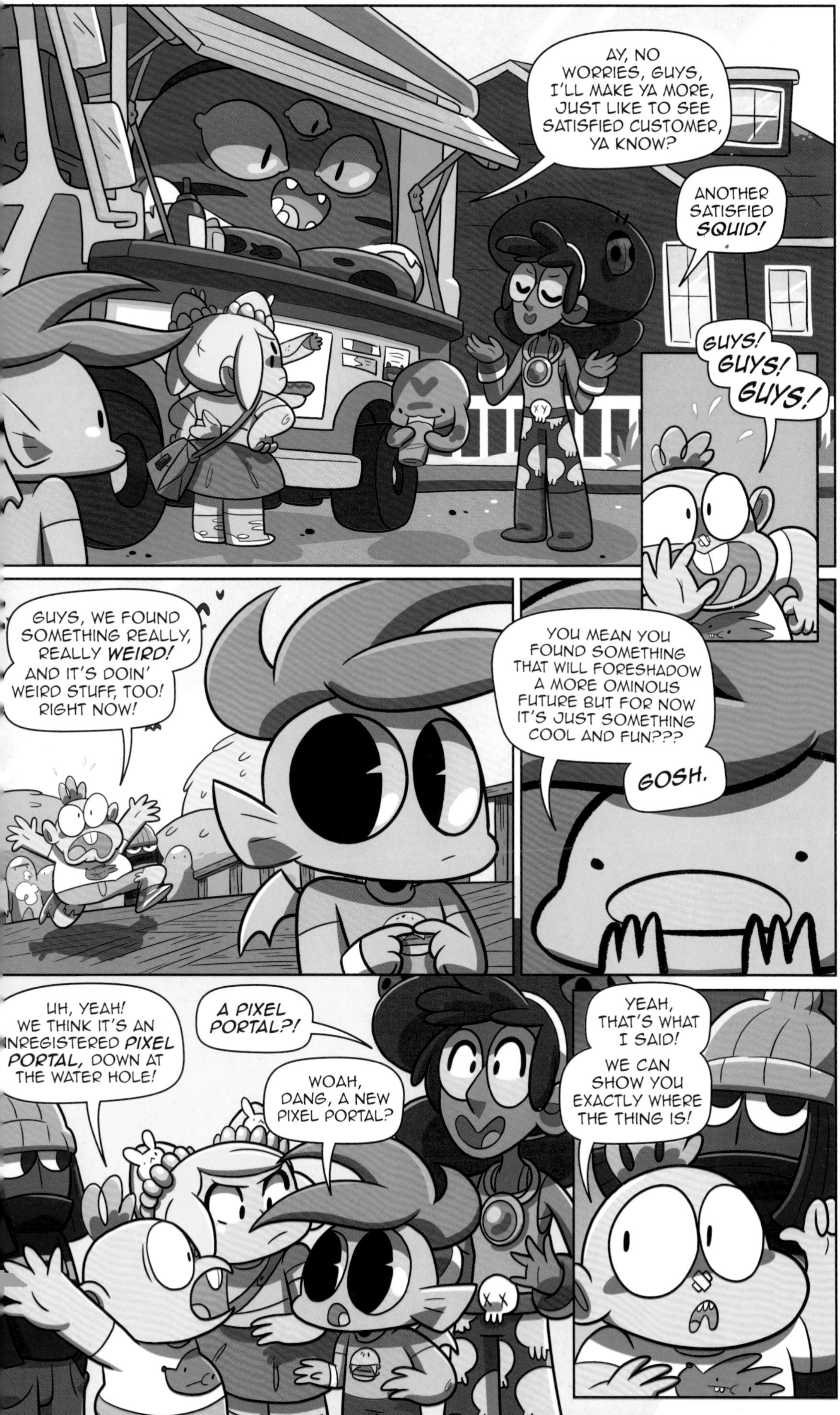
AY, NO WORRIES, GUYS, I'LL MAKE YA MORE, JUST LIKE TO SEE SATISFIED CUSTOMER, YA KNOW?
ANOTHER SATISFIED SQUID!
GUYS! GUYS! GUYS!
GUYS, WE FOUND SOMETHING REALLY, REALLY WEIRD! AND IT'S DOIN' WEIRD STUFF, TOO! RIGHT NOW!
YOU MEAN YOU FOUND SOMETHING THAT WILL FORESHADOW A MORE OMINOUS FUTURE BUT FOR NOW IT'S JUST SOMETHING COOL AND FUN???
GOSH.
UH, YEAH! WE THINK IT'S AN UNREGISTERED PIXEL PORTAL, DOWN AT THE WATER HOLE!
A PIXEL PORTAL?!
WOAH, DANG, A NEW PIXEL PORTAL?
YEAH, THAT'S WHAT I SAID!
WE CAN SHOW YOU EXACTLY WHERE THE THING IS!

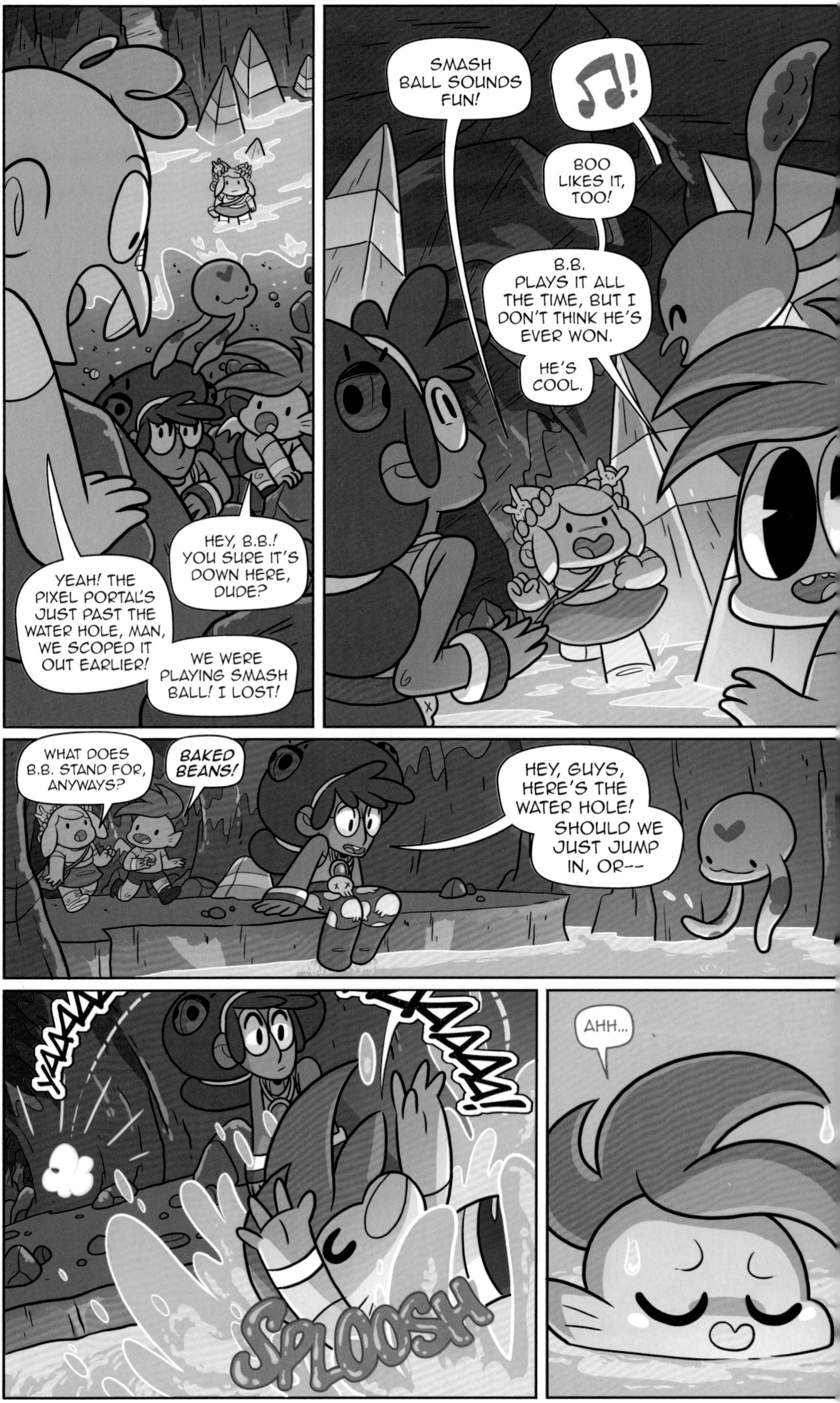
HEY, B.B.! YOU SURE IT'S DOWN HERE, DUDE?
YEAH! THE PIXEL PORTAL'S JUST PAST THE WATER HOLE, MAN, WE SCOPED IT OUT EARLIER!
WE WERE PLAYING SMASH BALL! I LOST!
SMASH BALL SOUNDS FUN!
♫!
BOO LIKES IT, TOO!
B.B. PLAYS IT ALL THE TIME, BUT I DON'T THINK HE'S EVER WON.
HE'S COOL.
WHAT DOES B.B. STAND FOR, ANYWAYS?
BAKED BEANS!
HEY, GUYS, HERE'S THE WATER HOLE!
SHOULD WE JUST JUMP IN, OR--
SPLOOSH
AHH...

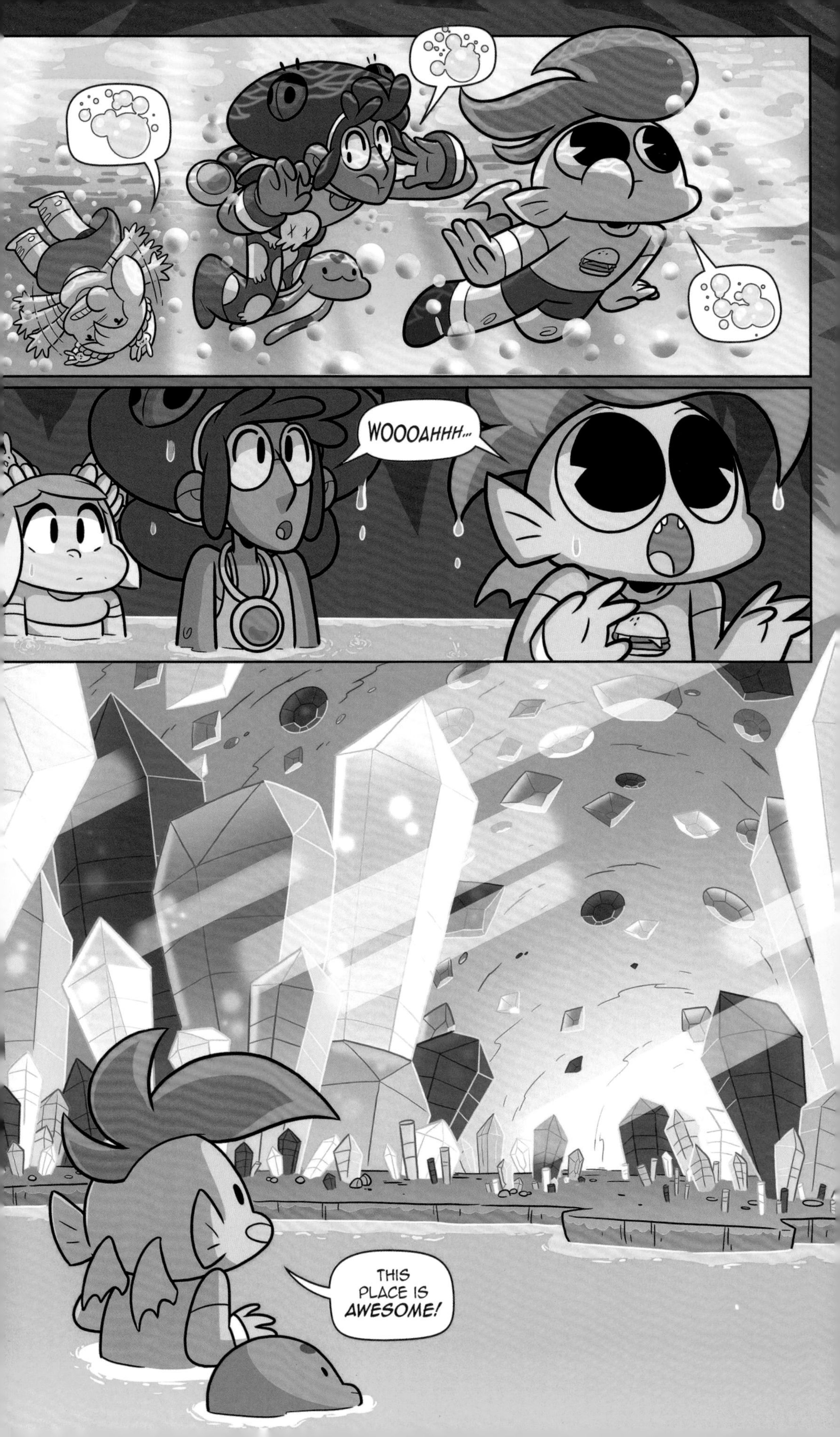
WOOOAHHH...
THIS PLACE IS AWESOME!

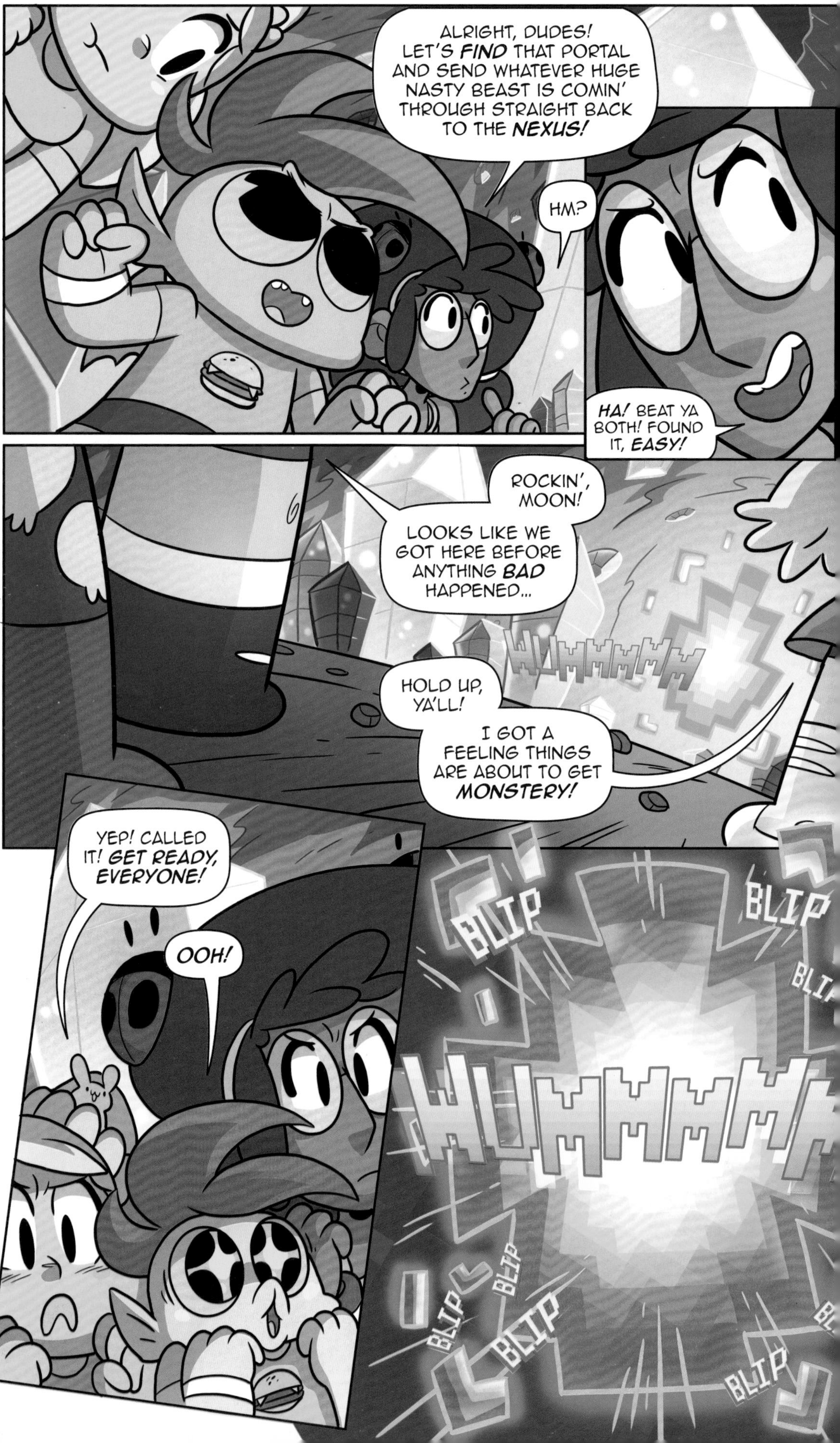

ALRIGHT, DUDES! LET'S FIND THAT PORTAL AND SEND WHATEVER HUGE NASTY BEAST IS COMIN' THROUGH STRAIGHT BACK TO THE NEXUS!
HM?
HA! BEAT YA BOTH! FOUND IT, EASY!
ROCKIN', MOON!
LOOKS LIKE WE GOT HERE BEFORE ANYTHING BAD HAPPENED...
WHMMMMM
HOLD UP, YA'LL!
I GOT A FEELING THINGS ARE ABOUT TO GET MONSTERY!
YEP! CALLED IT! GET READY, EVERYONE!
OOH!
BLIP
BLIP
WHMMMMM
BLIP
BLIP
BLIP
BLIP
BLIP

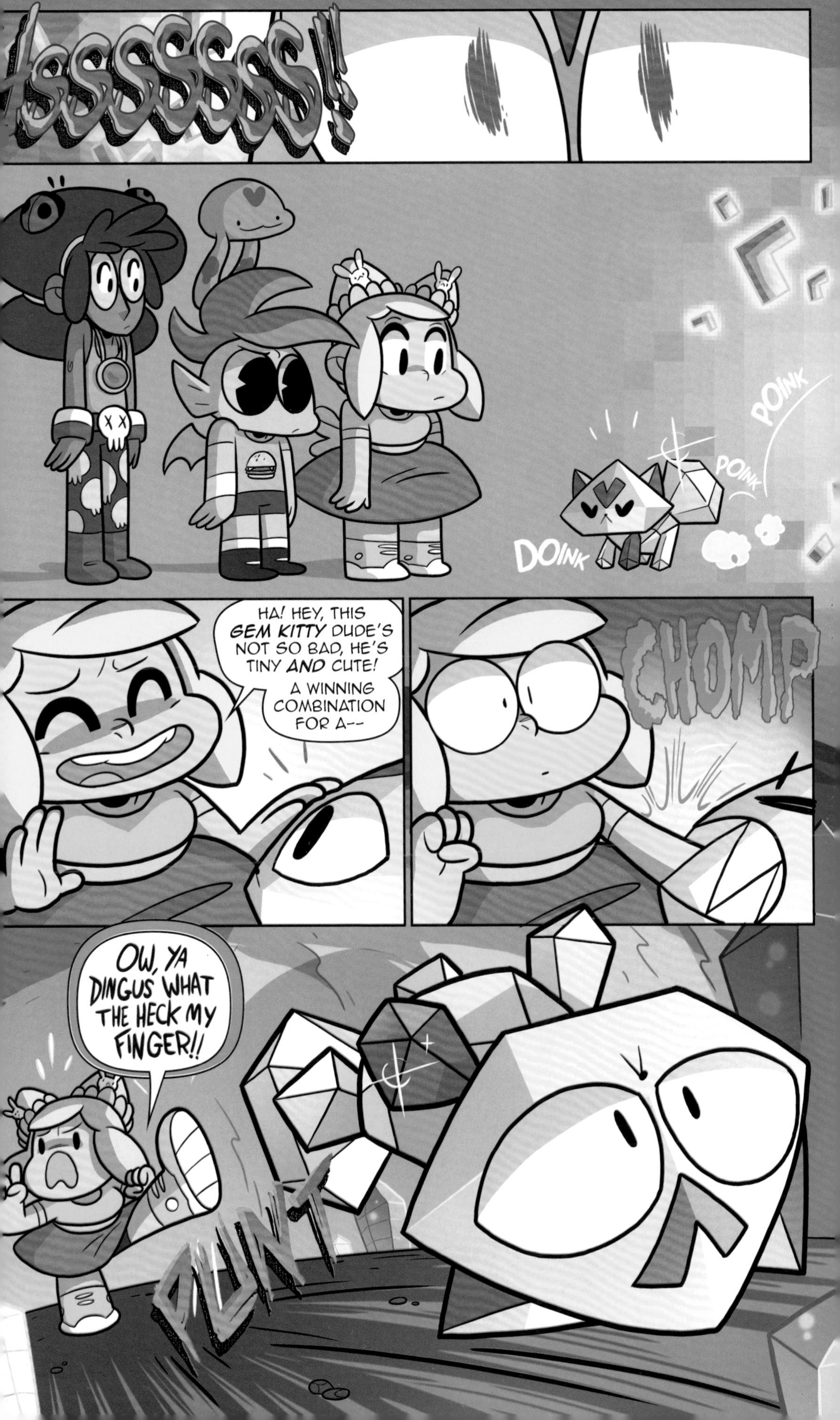
HSSSSSS!!
POINK
POINK
DOINK
HA! HEY, THIS *GEM KITTY* DUDE'S NOT SO BAD, HE'S TINY *AND* CUTE!
A WINNING COMBINATION FOR A--
CHOMP
OW, YA DINGUS WHAT THE HECK MY FINGER!!
PUNT

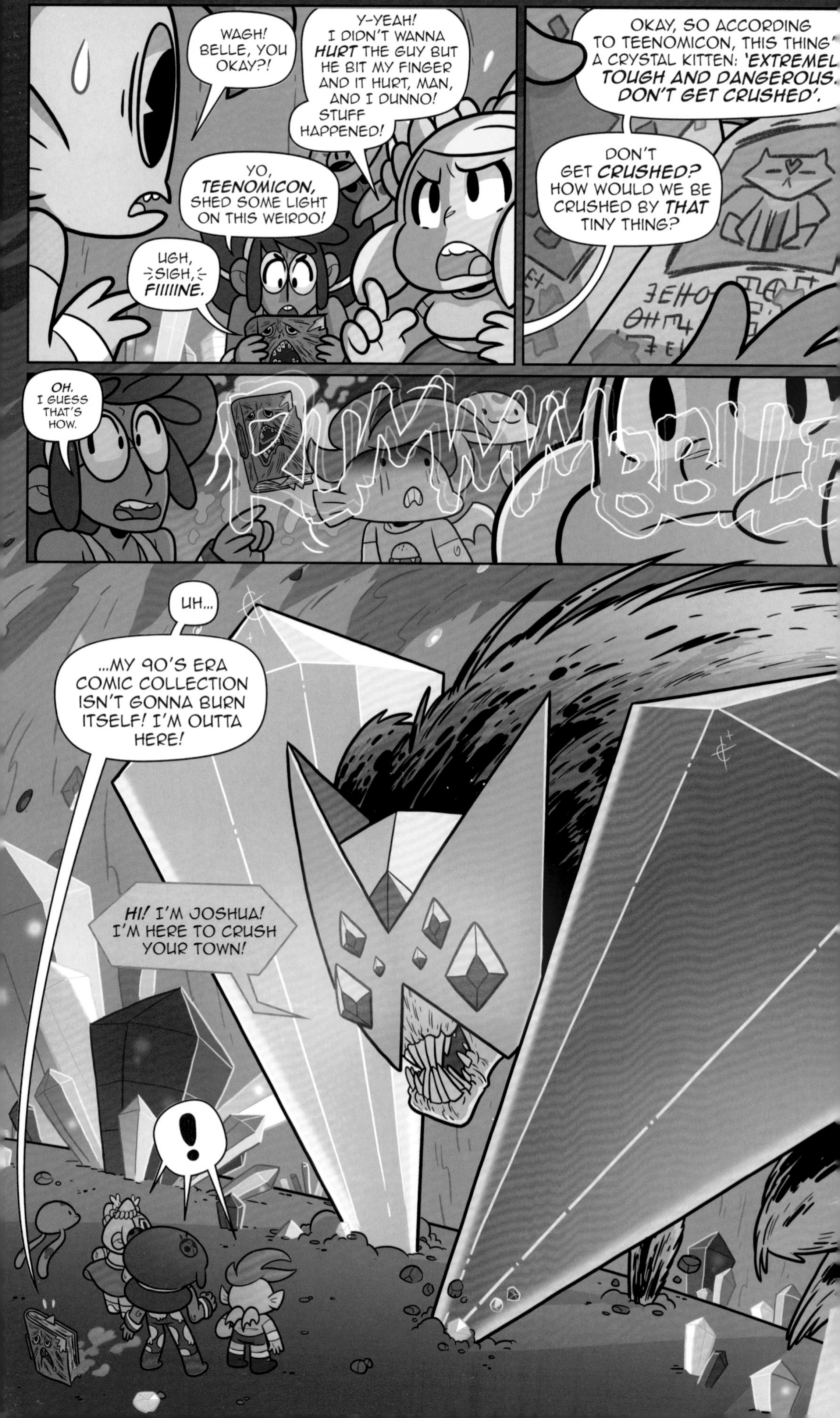
WAGH! BELLE, YOU OKAY?!
Y-YEAH! I DIDN'T WANNA HURT THE GUY BUT HE BIT MY FINGER AND IT HURT, MAN, AND I DUNNO! STUFF HAPPENED!
YO, TEENOMICON, SHED SOME LIGHT ON THIS WEIRDO!
UGH, SIGH, FIIIIINE.
OKAY, SO ACCORDING TO TEENOMICON, THIS THING' A CRYSTAL KITTEN: 'EXTREMEL TOUGH AND DANGEROUS. DON'T GET CRUSHED'.
DON'T GET CRUSHED? HOW WOULD WE BE CRUSHED BY THAT TINY THING?
OH. I GUESS THAT'S HOW.
RUMMMMBBLLE
UH...
...MY 90'S ERA COMIC COLLECTION ISN'T GONNA BURN ITSELF! I'M OUTTA HERE!
HI! I'M JOSHUA! I'M HERE TO CRUSH YOUR TOWN!
!

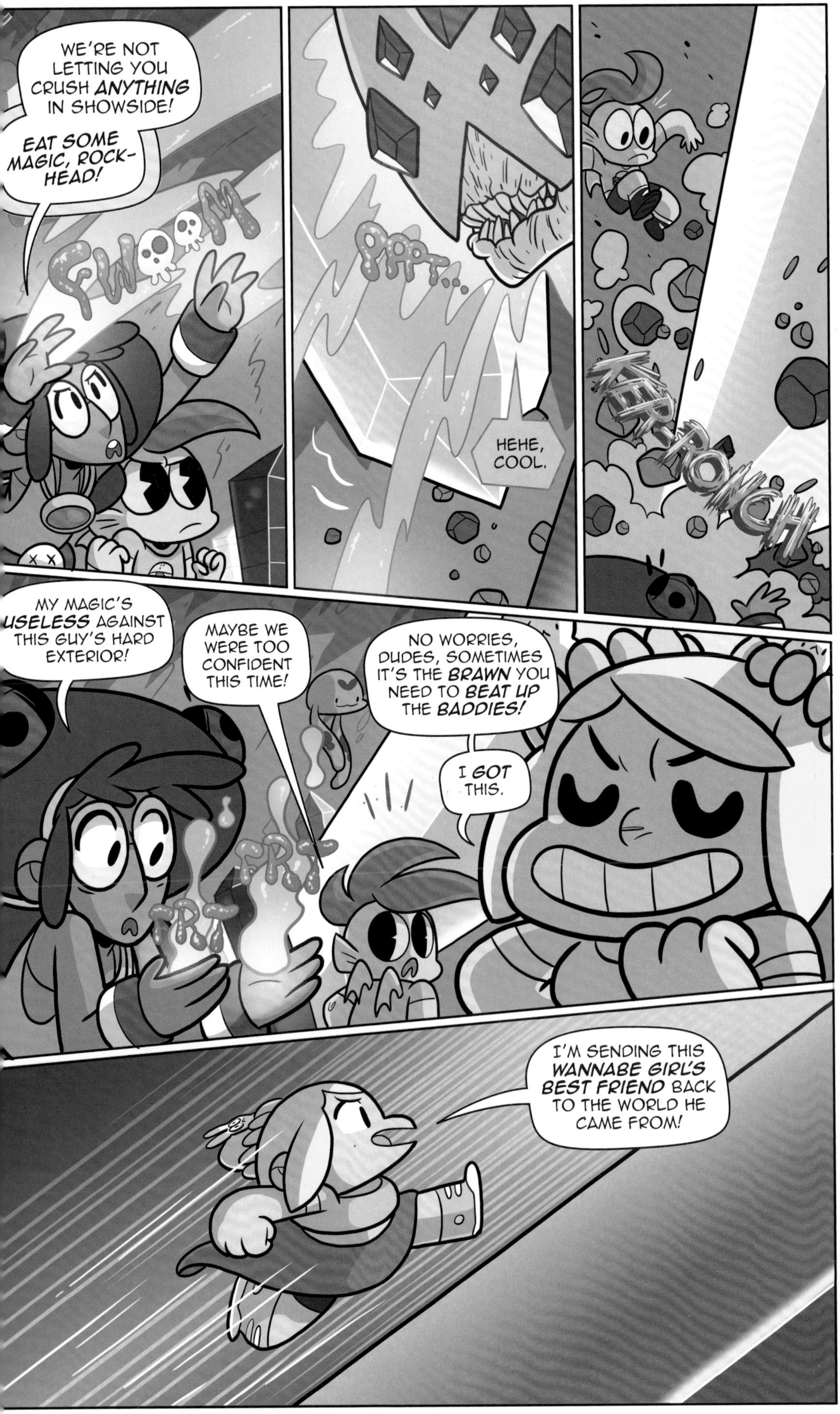
WE'RE NOT LETTING YOU CRUSH ANYTHING IN SHOWSIDE!
EAT SOME MAGIC, ROCK-HEAD!
FWOOM
PPPT...
HEHE, COOL.
KER-ROTCH
MY MAGIC'S USELESS AGAINST THIS GUY'S HARD EXTERIOR!
MAYBE WE WERE TOO CONFIDENT THIS TIME!
NO WORRIES, DUDES, SOMETIMES IT'S THE BRAWN YOU NEED TO BEAT UP THE BADDIES!
I GOT THIS.
FRT- FRT
I'M SENDING THIS WANNABE GIRL'S BEST FRIEND BACK TO THE WORLD HE CAME FROM!

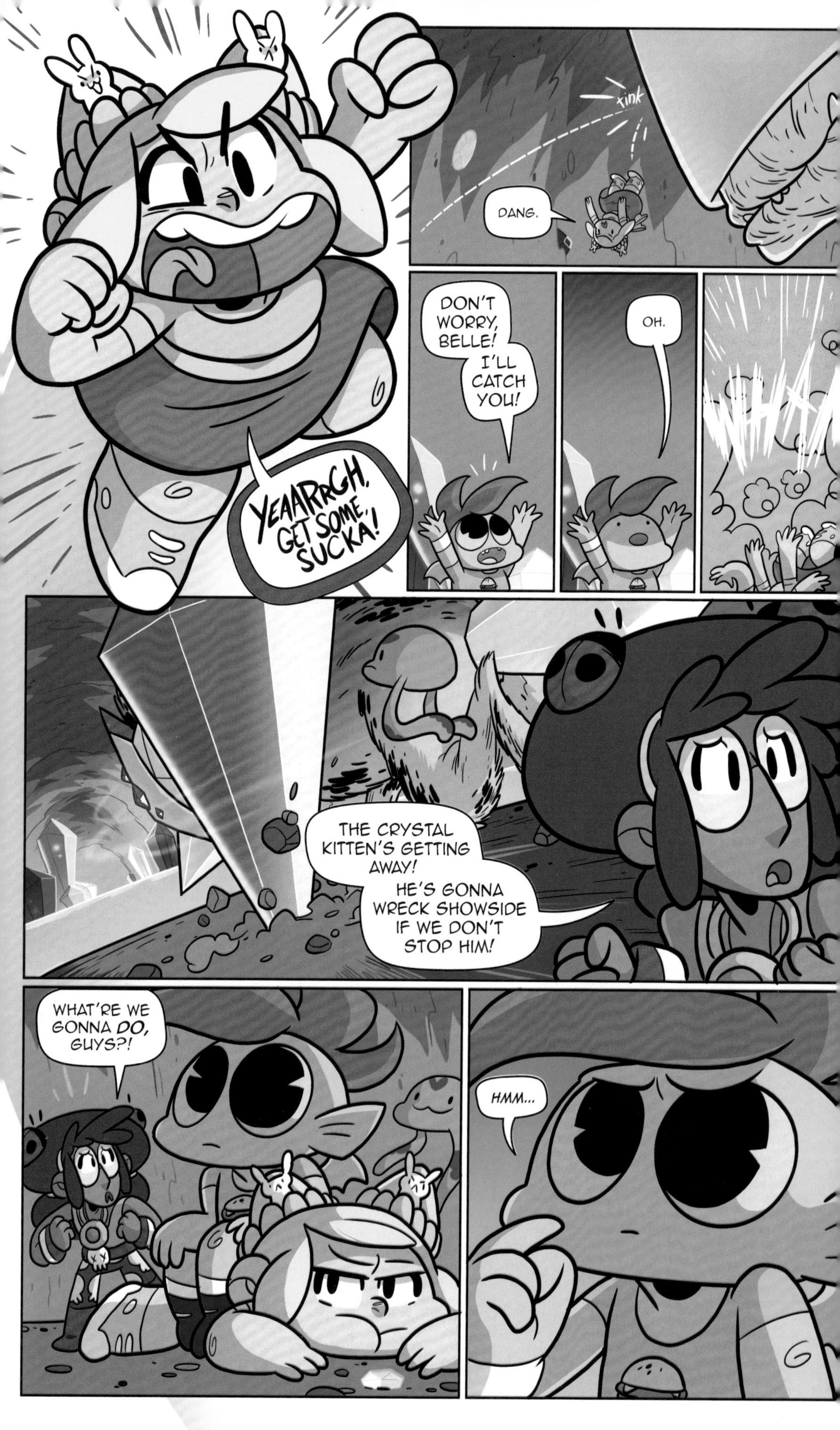
YEAARRGH, GET SOME, SUCKA!
tink
DANG.
DON'T WORRY, BELLE!
I'LL CATCH YOU!
OH.
THE CRYSTAL KITTEN'S GETTING AWAY!
HE'S GONNA WRECK SHOWSIDE IF WE DON'T STOP HIM!
WHAT'RE WE GONNA *DO*, GUYS?!
HMM...

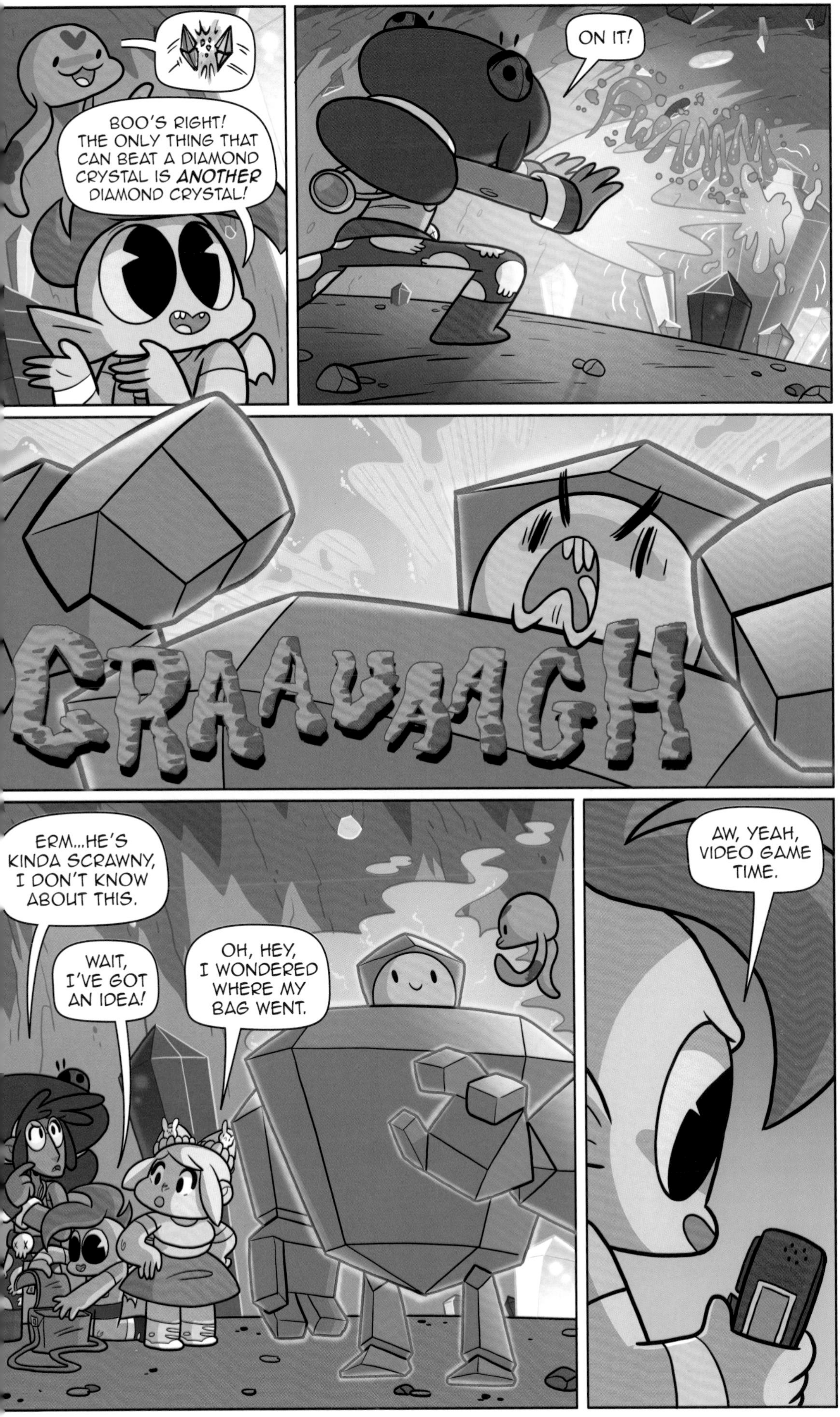
BOO'S RIGHT! THE ONLY THING THAT CAN BEAT A DIAMOND CRYSTAL IS *ANOTHER* DIAMOND CRYSTAL!
ON IT!
FWAMM
GRAUAAGH
ERM...HE'S KINDA SCRAWNY, I DON'T KNOW ABOUT THIS.
WAIT, I'VE GOT AN IDEA!
OH, HEY, I WONDERED WHERE MY BAG WENT.
AW, YEAH, VIDEO GAME TIME.

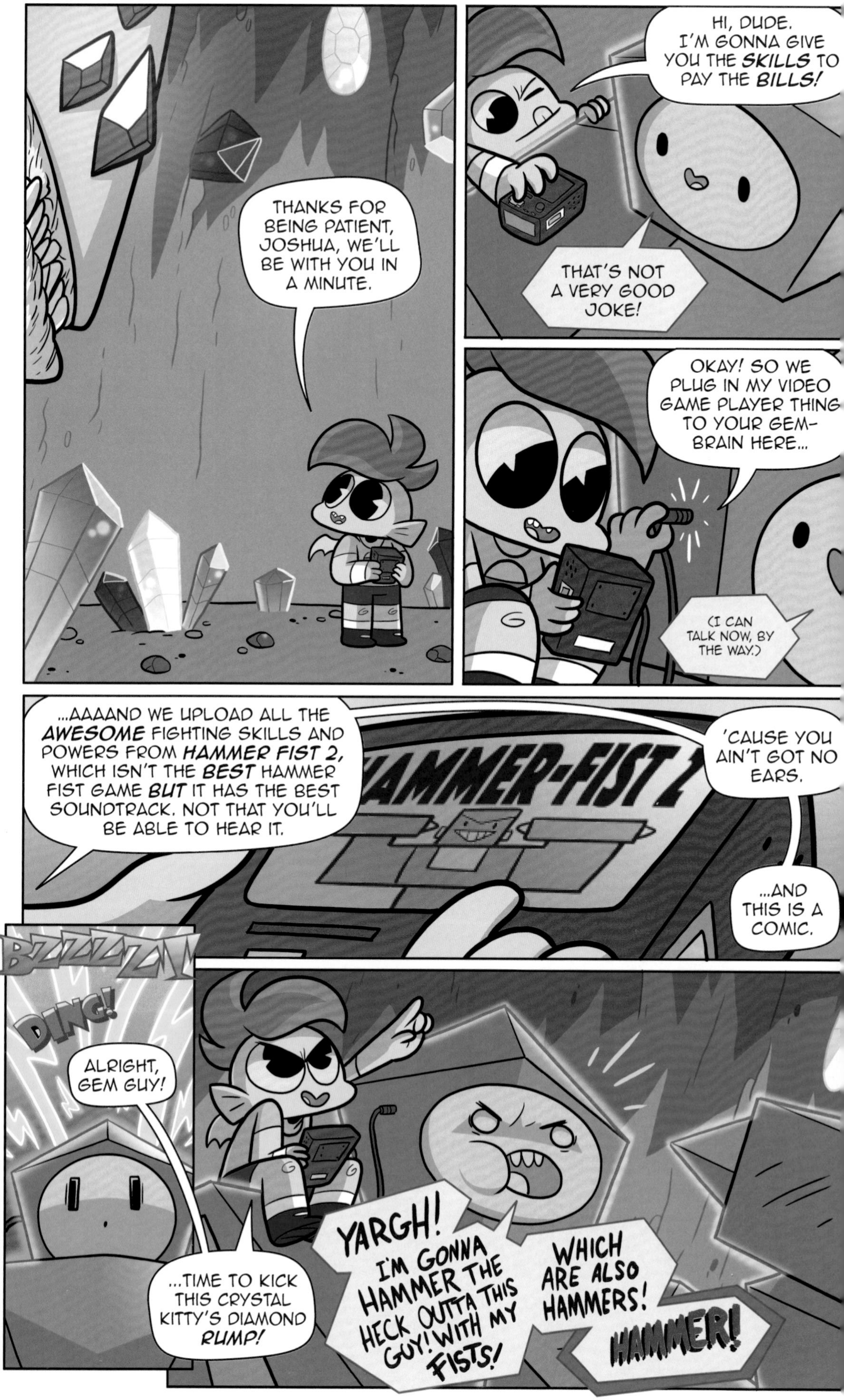
THANKS FOR BEING PATIENT, JOSHUA, WE'LL BE WITH YOU IN A MINUTE.
HI, DUDE. I'M GONNA GIVE YOU THE SKILLS TO PAY THE BILLS!
THAT'S NOT A VERY GOOD JOKE!
OKAY! SO WE PLUG IN MY VIDEO GAME PLAYER THING TO YOUR GEM-BRAIN HERE...
(I CAN TALK NOW, BY THE WAY.)
...AAAAND WE UPLOAD ALL THE AWESOME FIGHTING SKILLS AND POWERS FROM HAMMER FIST 2, WHICH ISN'T THE BEST HAMMER FIST GAME BUT IT HAS THE BEST SOUNDTRACK. NOT THAT YOU'LL BE ABLE TO HEAR IT.
'CAUSE YOU AIN'T GOT NO EARS.
...AND THIS IS A COMIC.
BZZZZZ!!
DING!
ALRIGHT, GEM GUY!
...TIME TO KICK THIS CRYSTAL KITTY'S DIAMOND RUMP!
YARGH! I'M GONNA HAMMER THE HECK OUTTA THIS GUY! WITH MY FISTS!
WHICH ARE ALSO HAMMERS!
HAMMER!

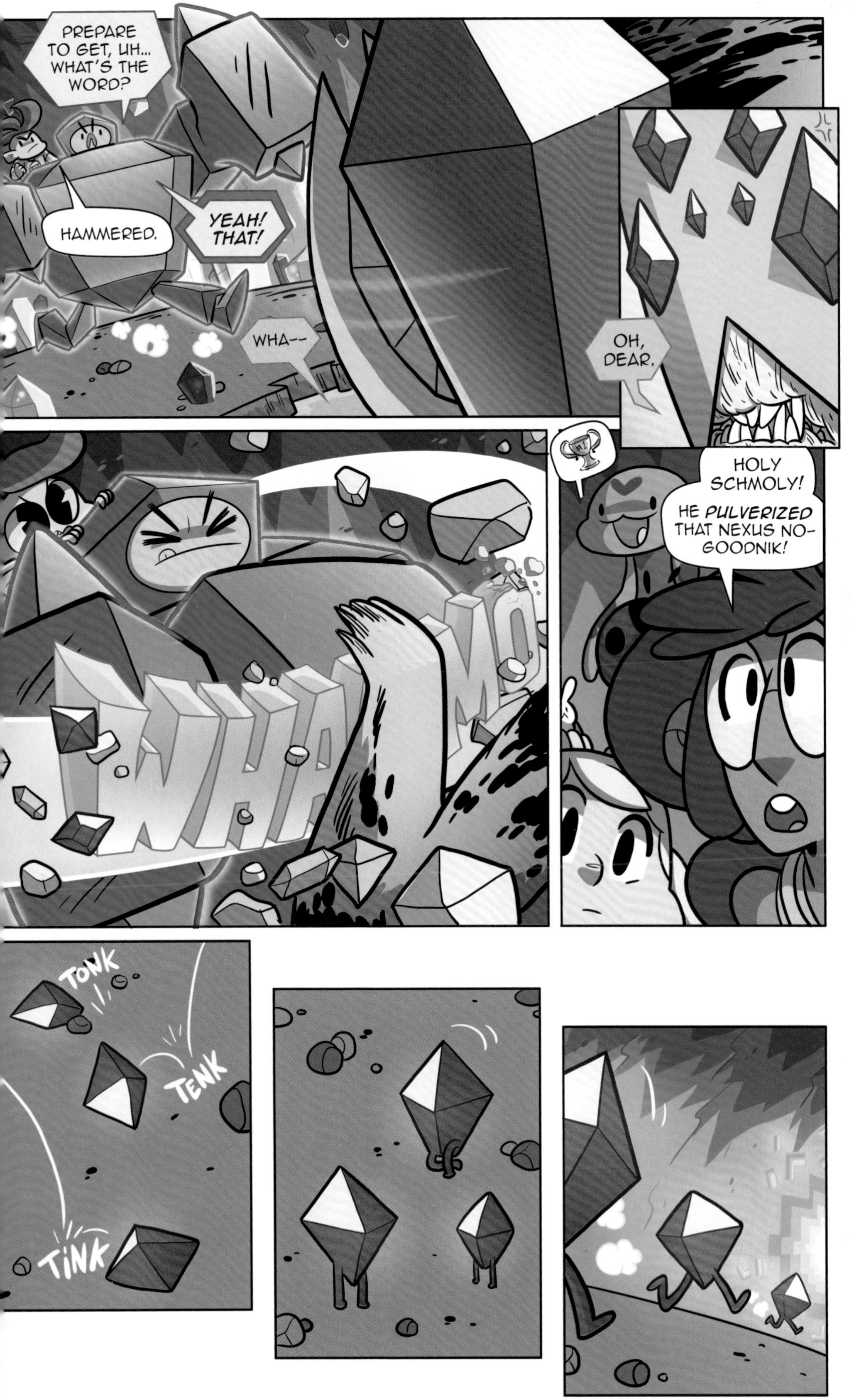
PREPARE TO GET, UH... WHAT'S THE WORD?
HAMMERED.
YEAH! THAT!
WHA--
OH, DEAR.
WHAMMO
HOLY SCHMOLY!
HE PULVERIZED THAT NEXUS NO-GOODNIK!
TONK
TENK
TINK

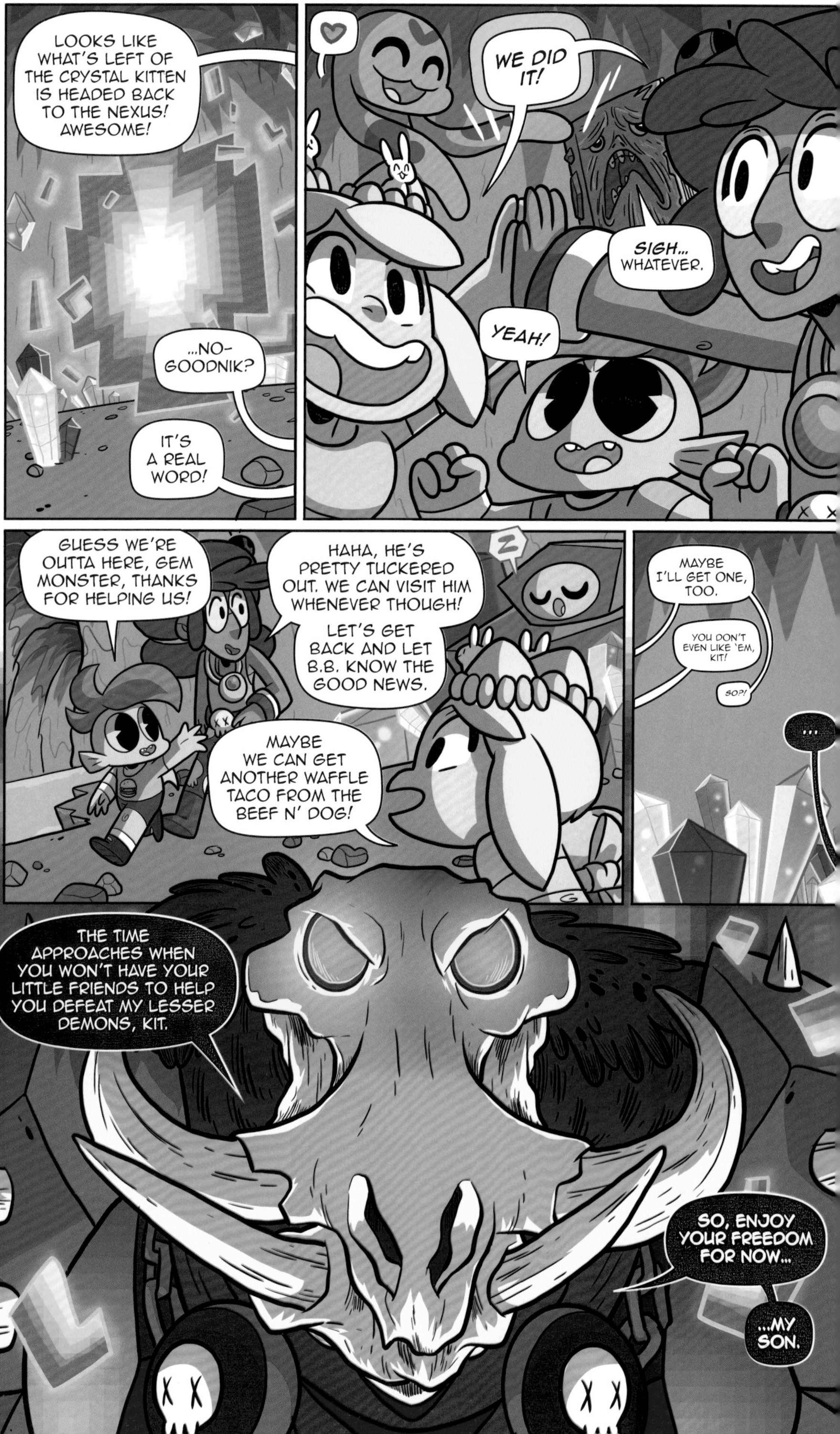
LOOKS LIKE WHAT'S LEFT OF THE CRYSTAL KITTEN IS HEADED BACK TO THE NEXUS! AWESOME!
...NO-GOODNIK?
IT'S A REAL WORD!
WE DID IT!
SIGH... WHATEVER.
YEAH!
GUESS WE'RE OUTTA HERE, GEM MONSTER, THANKS FOR HELPING US!
HAHA, HE'S PRETTY TUCKERED OUT. WE CAN VISIT HIM WHENEVER THOUGH!
LET'S GET BACK AND LET B.B. KNOW THE GOOD NEWS.
MAYBE WE CAN GET ANOTHER WAFFLE TACO FROM THE BEEF N' DOG!
MAYBE I'LL GET ONE, TOO.
YOU DON'T EVEN LIKE 'EM, KIT!
SO?!
...
THE TIME APPROACHES WHEN YOU WON'T HAVE YOUR LITTLE FRIENDS TO HELP YOU DEFEAT MY LESSER DEMONS, KIT.
SO, ENJOY YOUR FREEDOM FOR NOW...
...MY SON.

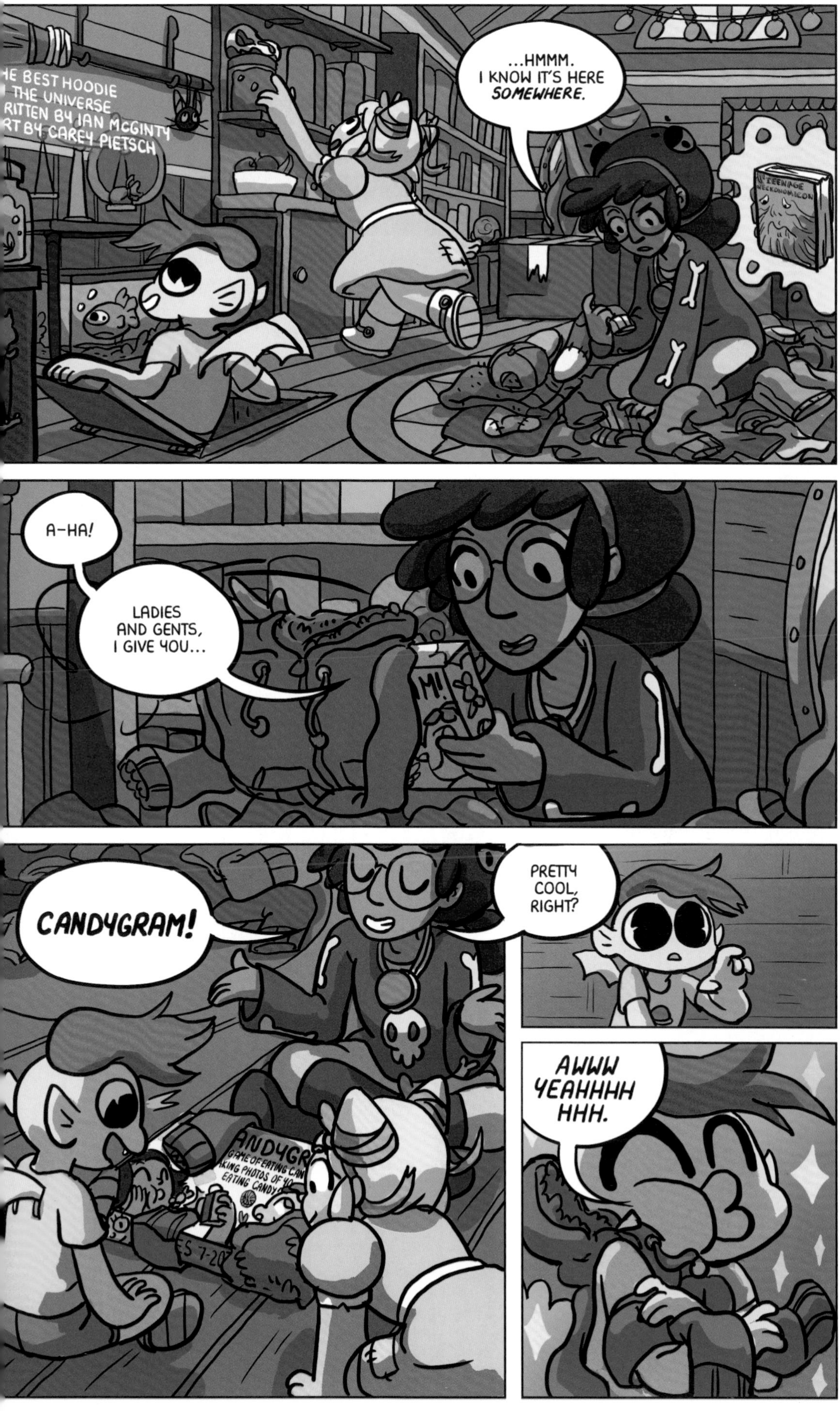
HE BEST HOODIE
THE UNIVERSE
RITTEN BY IAN McGINTY
RT BY CAREY PIETSCH
...HMMM. I KNOW IT'S HERE *SOMEWHERE.*
A-HA!
LADIES AND GENTS, I GIVE YOU...
CANDYGRAM!
PRETTY COOL, RIGHT?
AWWW YEAHHHH HHH.

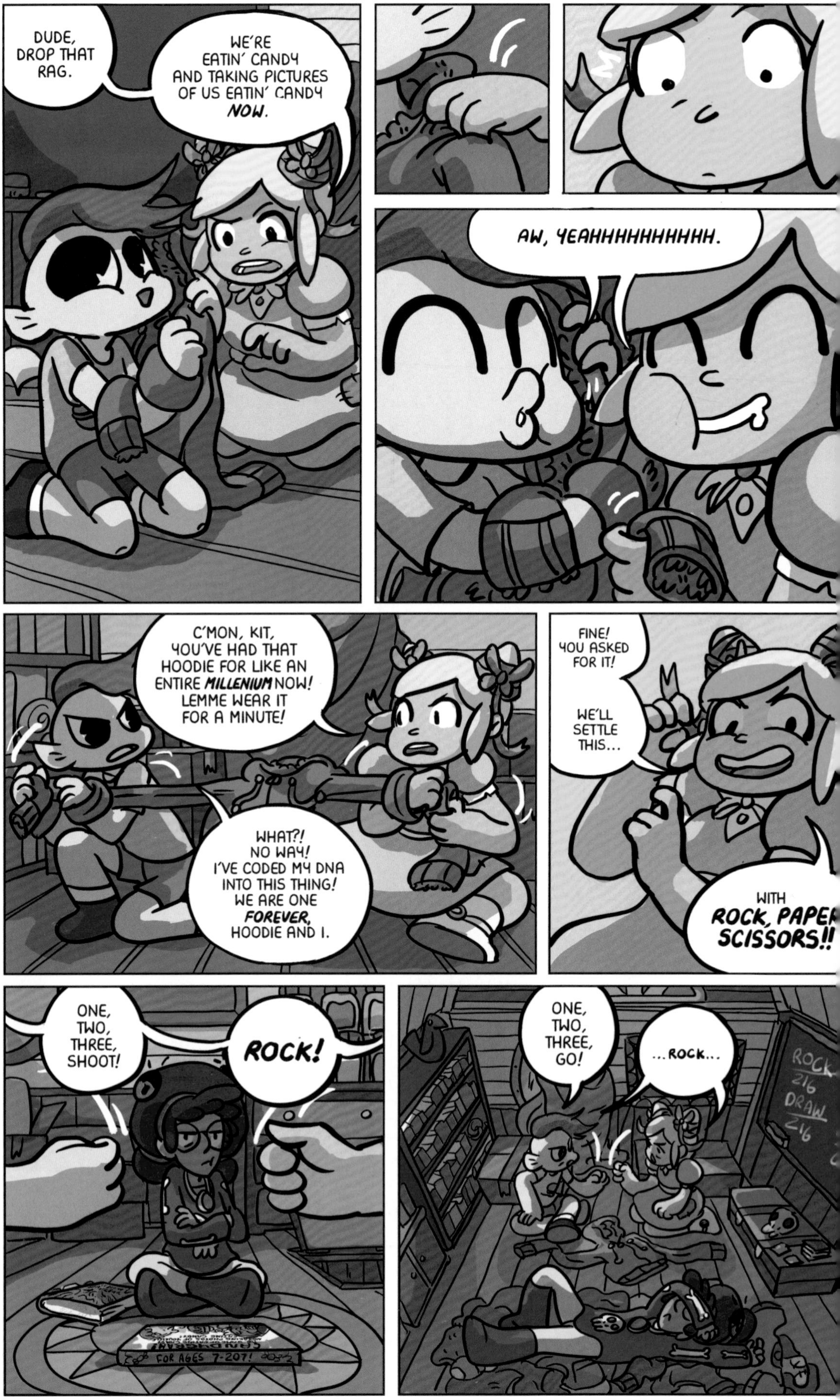
DUDE, DROP THAT RAG.
WE'RE EATIN' CANDY AND TAKING PICTURES OF US EATIN' CANDY NOW.
AW, YEAHHHHHHHHHH.
C'MON, KIT, YOU'VE HAD THAT HOODIE FOR LIKE AN ENTIRE MILLENIUM NOW! LEMME WEAR IT FOR A MINUTE!
WHAT?! NO WAY! I'VE CODED MY DNA INTO THIS THING! WE ARE ONE FOREVER, HOODIE AND I.
FINE! YOU ASKED FOR IT!
WE'LL SETTLE THIS...
WITH ROCK, PAPER SCISSORS!!
ONE, TWO, THREE, SHOOT!
ROCK!
FOR AGES 7-207!
ONE, TWO, THREE, GO!
...ROCK...
ROCK 216
DRAW 216

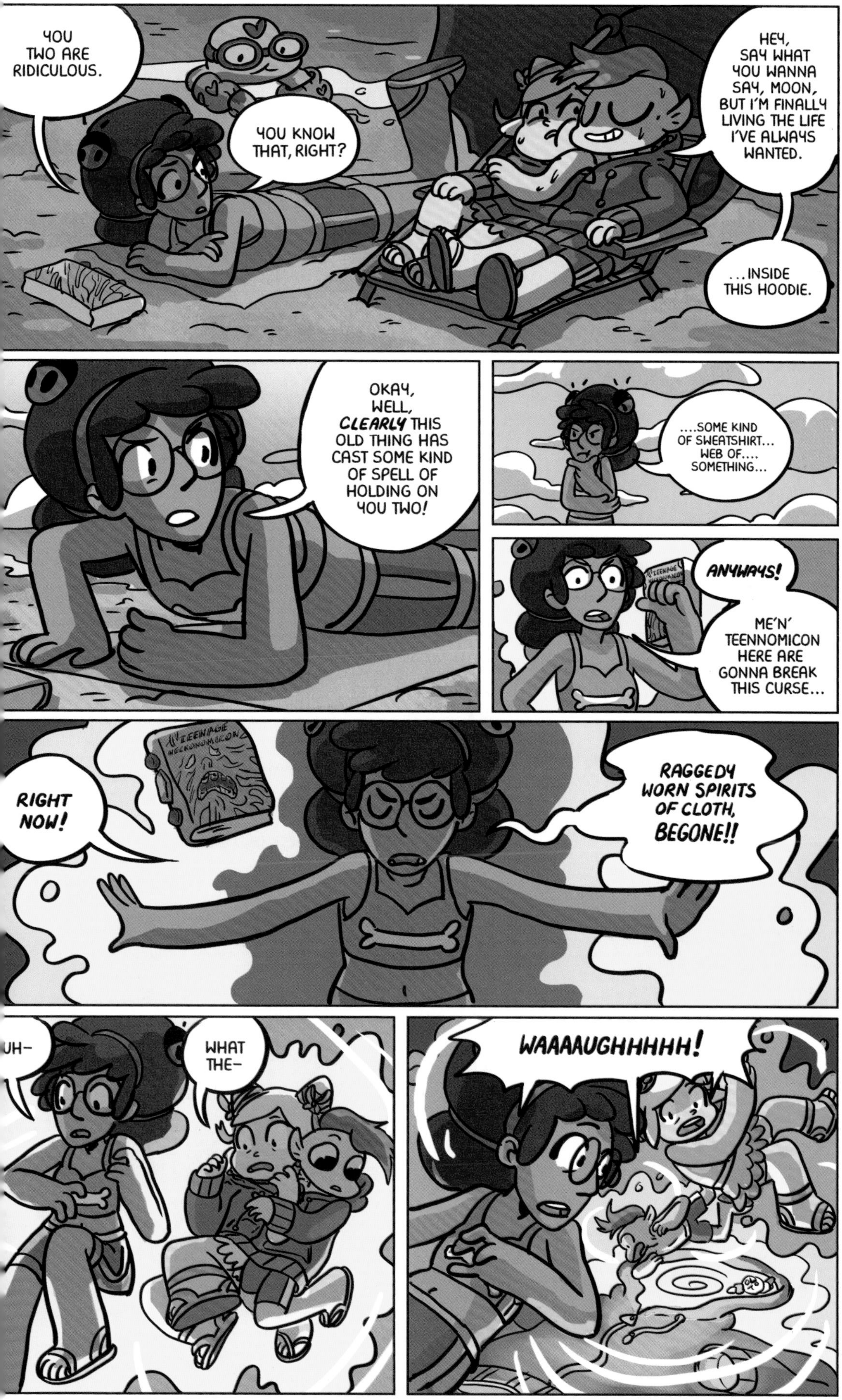

YOU TWO ARE RIDICULOUS.
YOU KNOW THAT, RIGHT?
HEY, SAY WHAT YOU WANNA SAY, MOON, BUT I'M FINALLY LIVING THE LIFE I'VE ALWAYS WANTED.
...INSIDE THIS HOODIE.
OKAY, WELL, CLEARLY THIS OLD THING HAS CAST SOME KIND OF SPELL OF HOLDING ON YOU TWO!
....SOME KIND OF SWEATSHIRT... WEB OF.... SOMETHING...
ANYWAYS!
TEENAGE NECRONOMICON
ME'N' TEENNOMICON HERE ARE GONNA BREAK THIS CURSE...
RIGHT NOW!
TEENAGE NECRONOMICON
RAGGEDY WORN SPIRITS OF CLOTH, BEGONE!!
UH-
WHAT THE-
WAAAAUGHHHHH!

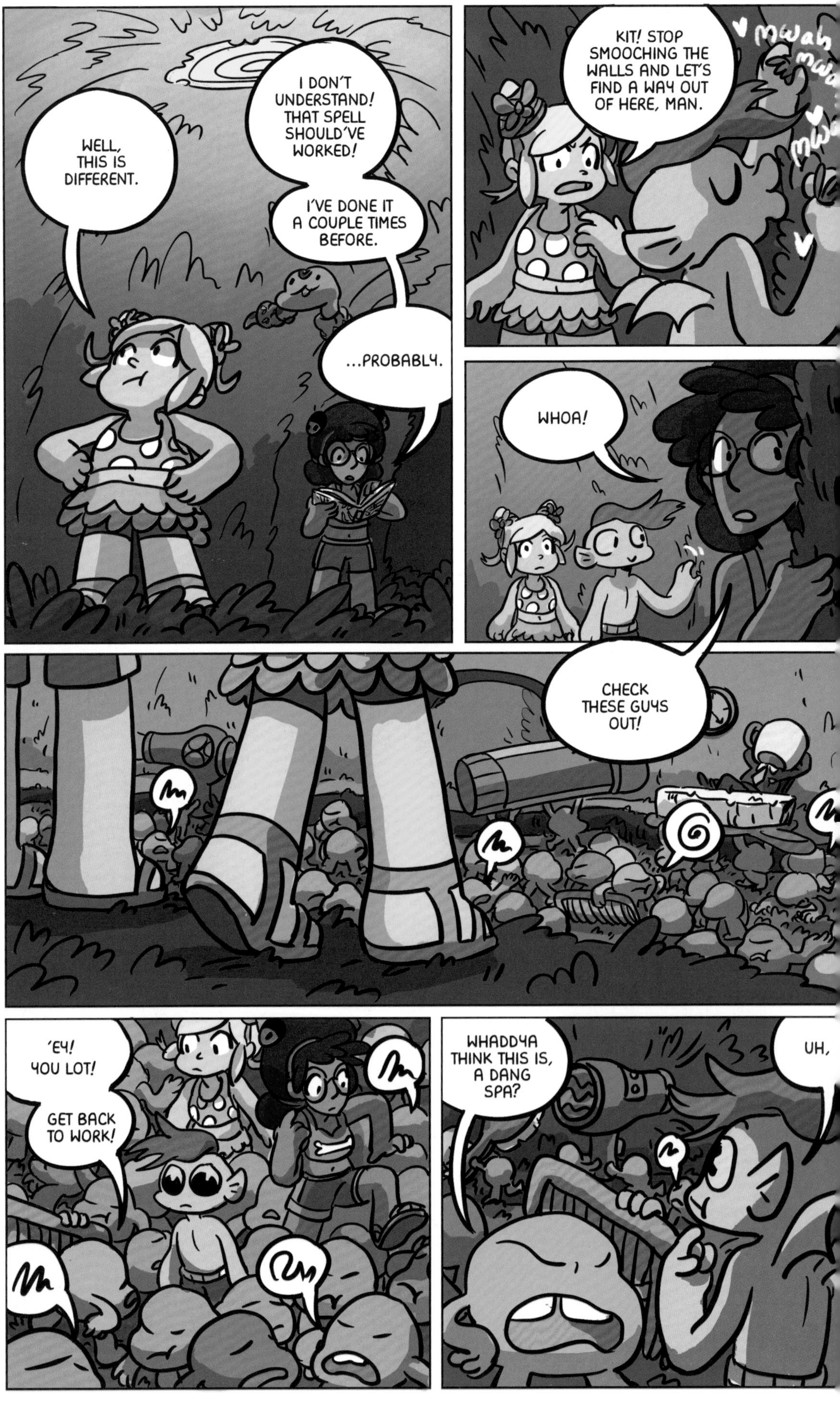
WELL, THIS IS DIFFERENT.
I DON'T UNDERSTAND! THAT SPELL SHOULD'VE WORKED!
I'VE DONE IT A COUPLE TIMES BEFORE.
...PROBABLY.
KIT! STOP SMOOCHING THE WALLS AND LET'S FIND A WAY OUT OF HERE, MAN.
MWAH
WHOA!
CHECK THESE GUYS OUT!
'EY! YOU LOT!
GET BACK TO WORK!
WHADDYA THINK THIS IS, A DANG SPA?
UH,

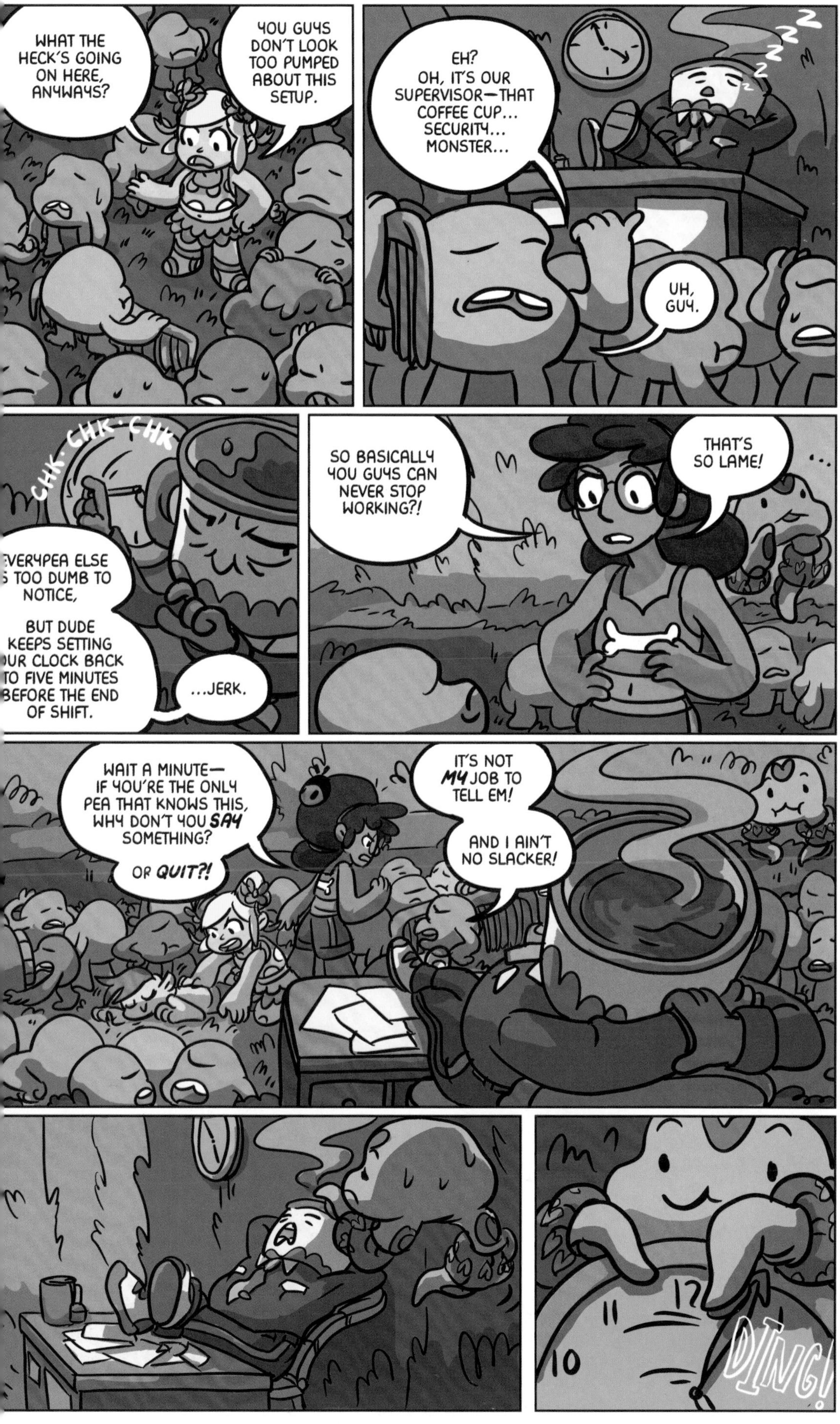
WHAT THE HECK'S GOING ON HERE, ANYWAYS?
YOU GUYS DON'T LOOK TOO PUMPED ABOUT THIS SETUP.
EH? OH, IT'S OUR SUPERVISOR—THAT COFFEE CUP... SECURITY... MONSTER...
UH, GUY.
CHK·CHK·CHK
EVERYPEA ELSE IS TOO DUMB TO NOTICE,
BUT DUDE KEEPS SETTING OUR CLOCK BACK TO FIVE MINUTES BEFORE THE END OF SHIFT.
...JERK.
SO BASICALLY YOU GUYS CAN NEVER STOP WORKING?!
THAT'S SO LAME!
...
WAIT A MINUTE— IF YOU'RE THE ONLY PEA THAT KNOWS THIS, WHY DON'T YOU SAY SOMETHING?
OR QUIT?!
IT'S NOT MY JOB TO TELL EM!
AND I AIN'T NO SLACKER!
DING!

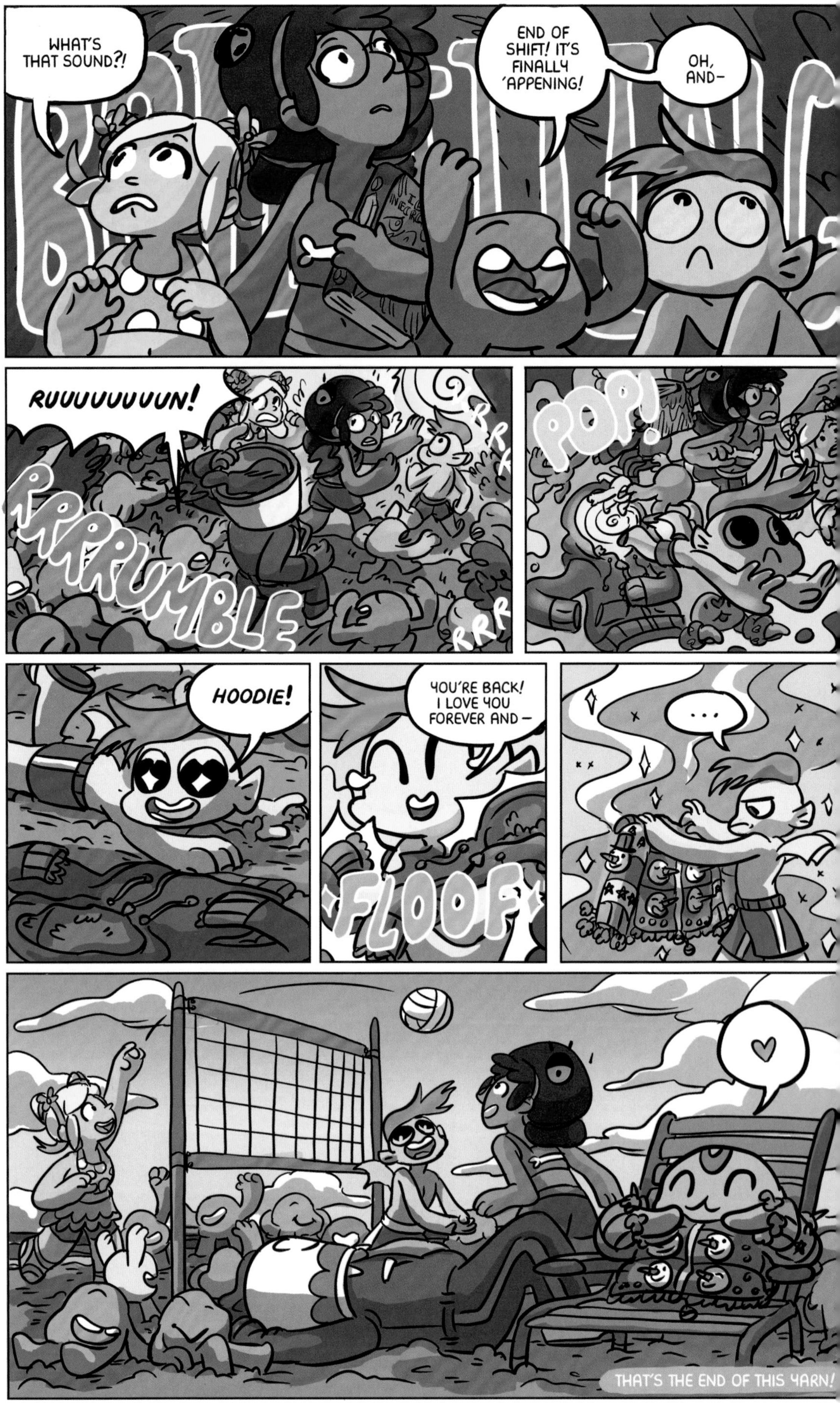
WHAT'S THAT SOUND?!
END OF SHIFT! IT'S FINALLY 'APPENING!
OH, AND—
RUUUUUUUUN!
RRRRUMBLE
RRR
RRR
POP!
HOODIE!
YOU'RE BACK! I LOVE YOU FOREVER AND—
FLOOF
...
♡
THAT'S THE END OF THIS YARN!

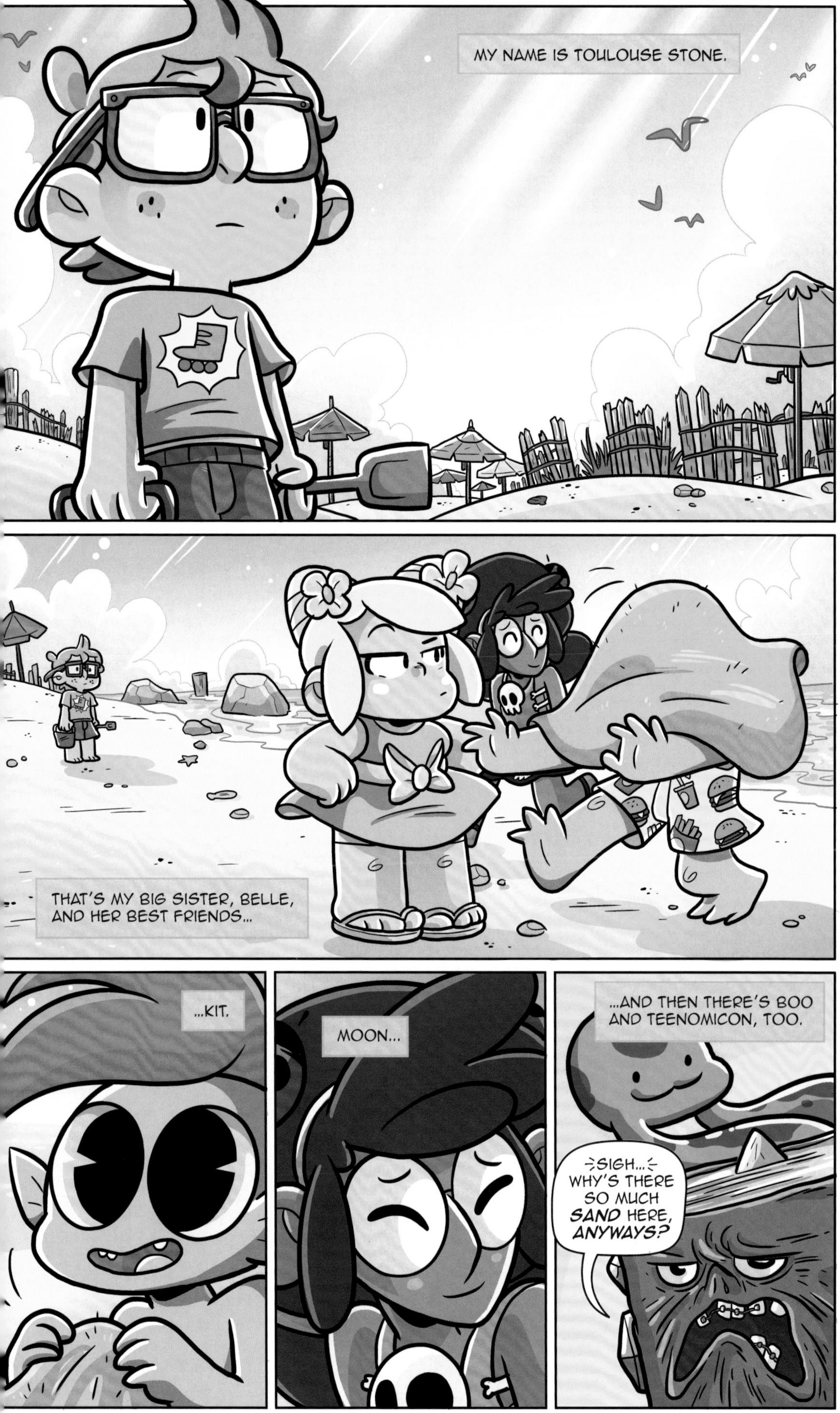
MY NAME IS TOULOUSE STONE.
THAT'S MY BIG SISTER, BELLE, AND HER BEST FRIENDS...
...KIT.
MOON...
...AND THEN THERE'S BOO AND TEENOMICON, TOO.
SIGH... WHY'S THERE SO MUCH SAND HERE, ANYWAYS?

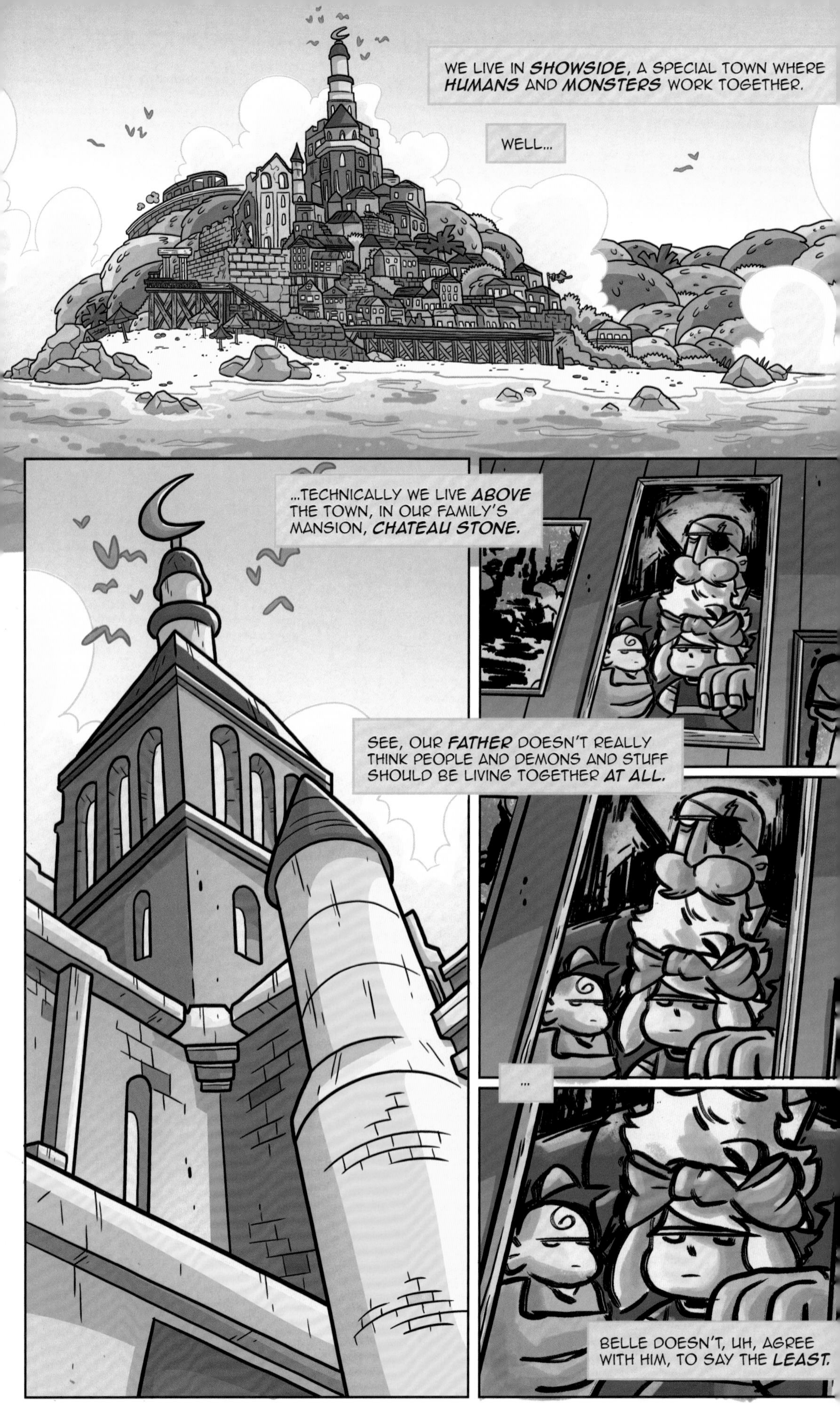
WE LIVE IN SHOWSIDE, A SPECIAL TOWN WHERE HUMANS AND MONSTERS WORK TOGETHER.
WELL...
...TECHNICALLY WE LIVE ABOVE THE TOWN, IN OUR FAMILY'S MANSION, CHATEAU STONE.
SEE, OUR FATHER DOESN'T REALLY THINK PEOPLE AND DEMONS AND STUFF SHOULD BE LIVING TOGETHER AT ALL.
...
BELLE DOESN'T, UH, AGREE WITH HIM, TO SAY THE LEAST.

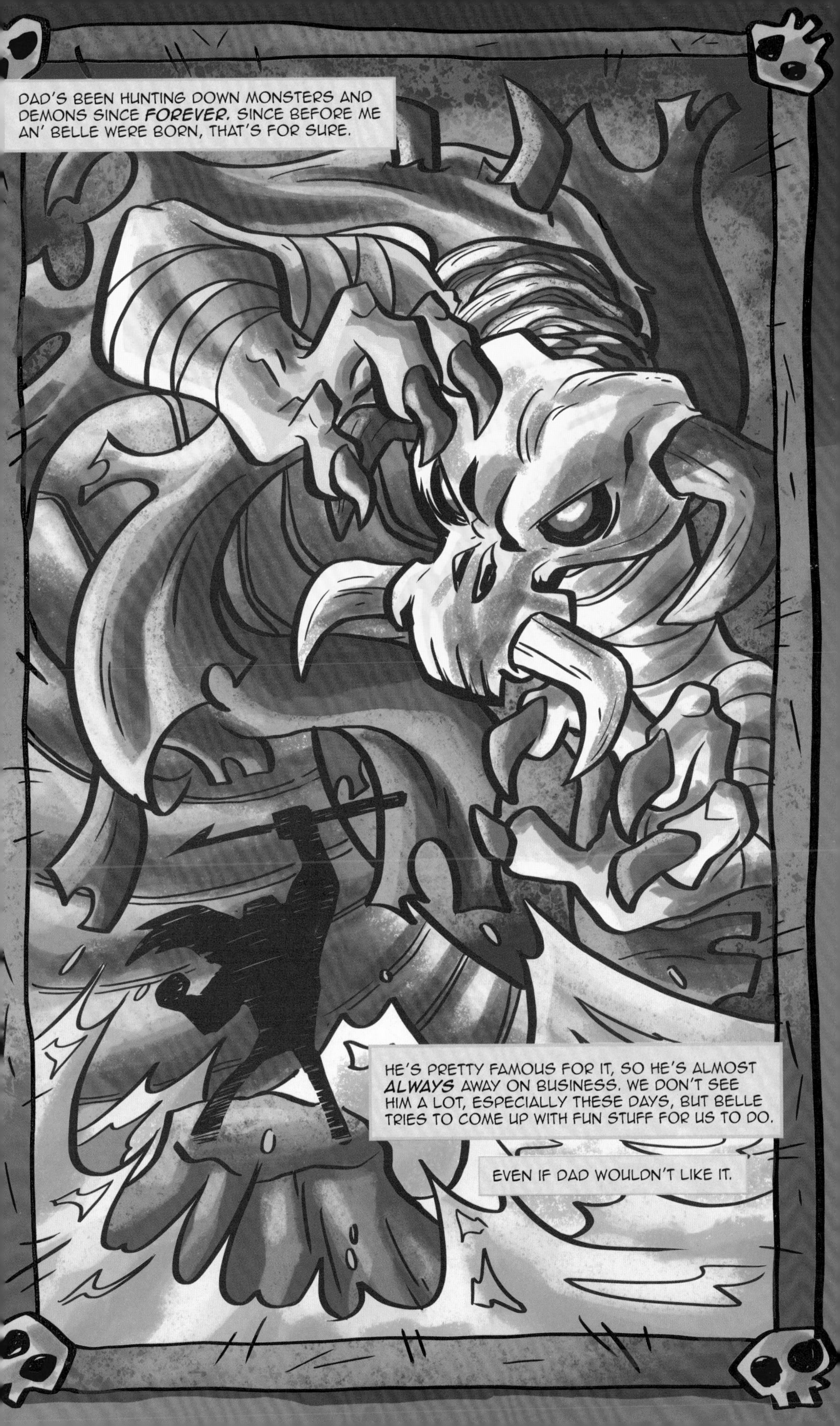
DAD'S BEEN HUNTING DOWN MONSTERS AND DEMONS SINCE *FOREVER.* SINCE BEFORE ME AN' BELLE WERE BORN, THAT'S FOR SURE.
HE'S PRETTY FAMOUS FOR IT, SO HE'S ALMOST *ALWAYS* AWAY ON BUSINESS. WE DON'T SEE HIM A LOT, ESPECIALLY THESE DAYS, BUT BELLE TRIES TO COME UP WITH FUN STUFF FOR US TO DO.
EVEN IF DAD WOULDN'T LIKE IT.

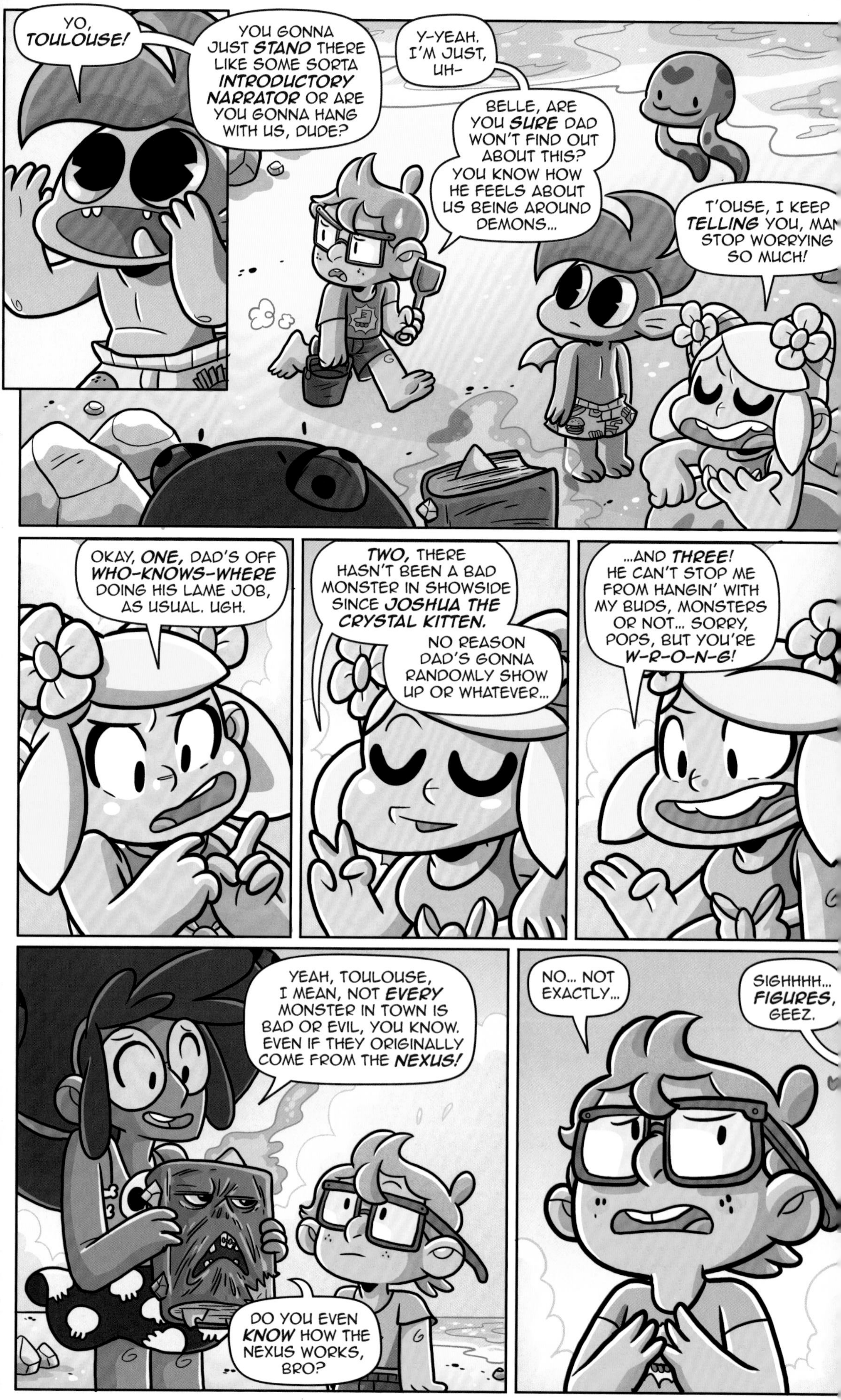
YO, TOULOUSE!
YOU GONNA JUST STAND THERE LIKE SOME SORTA INTRODUCTORY NARRATOR OR ARE YOU GONNA HANG WITH US, DUDE?
Y-YEAH. I'M JUST, UH-
BELLE, ARE YOU SURE DAD WON'T FIND OUT ABOUT THIS? YOU KNOW HOW HE FEELS ABOUT US BEING AROUND DEMONS...
T'OUSE, I KEEP TELLING YOU, MA STOP WORRYING SO MUCH!
OKAY, ONE, DAD'S OFF WHO-KNOWS-WHERE DOING HIS LAME JOB, AS USUAL. UGH.
TWO, THERE HASN'T BEEN A BAD MONSTER IN SHOWSIDE SINCE JOSHUA THE CRYSTAL KITTEN.
NO REASON DAD'S GONNA RANDOMLY SHOW UP OR WHATEVER...
...AND THREE! HE CAN'T STOP ME FROM HANGIN' WITH MY BUDS, MONSTERS OR NOT... SORRY, POPS, BUT YOU'RE W-R-O-N-G!
YEAH, TOULOUSE, I MEAN, NOT EVERY MONSTER IN TOWN IS BAD OR EVIL, YOU KNOW. EVEN IF THEY ORIGINALLY COME FROM THE NEXUS!
DO YOU EVEN KNOW HOW THE NEXUS WORKS, BRO?
NO... NOT EXACTLY...
SIGHHHH... FIGURES, GEEZ.

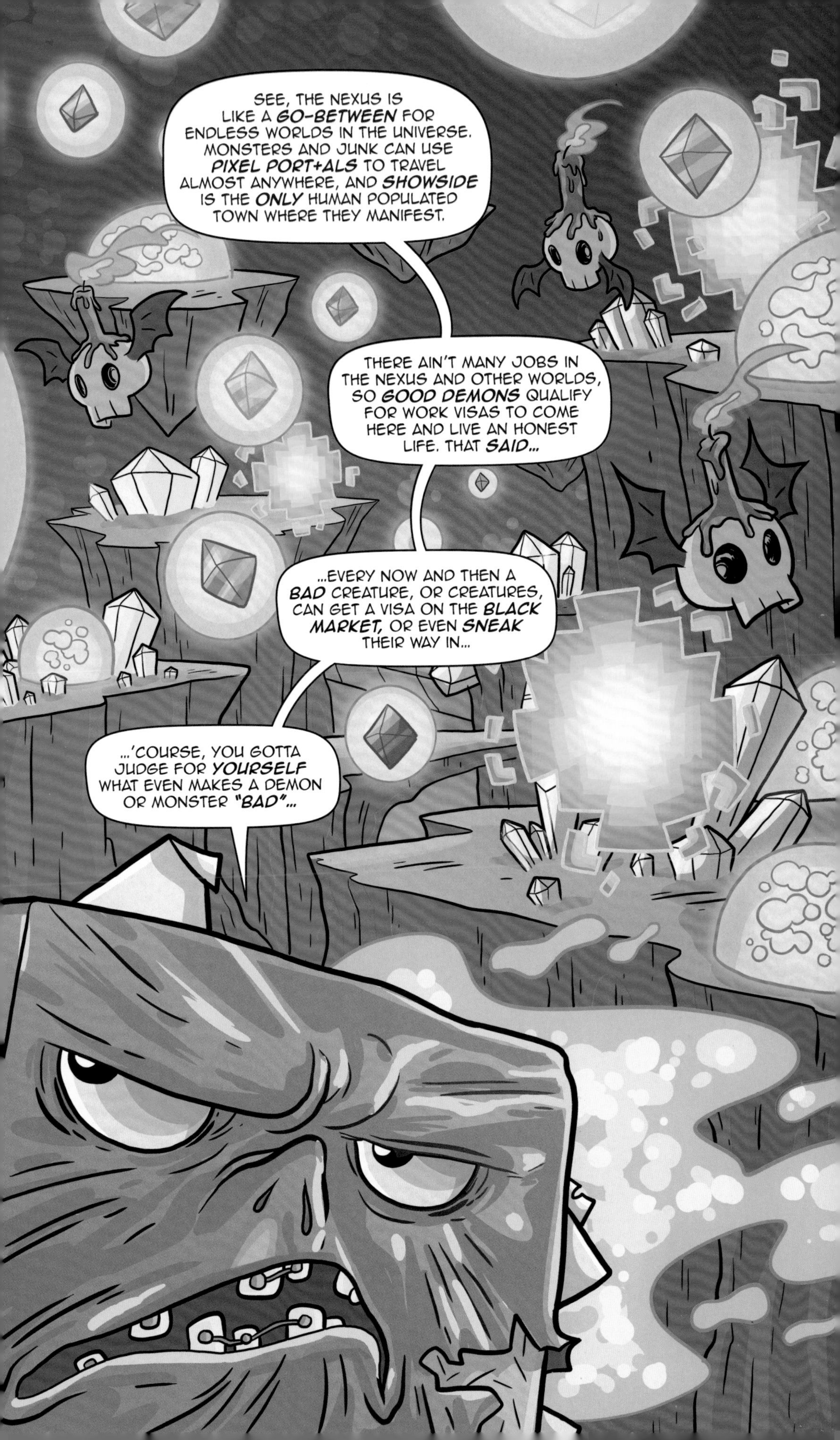
SEE, THE NEXUS IS LIKE A GO-BETWEEN FOR ENDLESS WORLDS IN THE UNIVERSE. MONSTERS AND JUNK CAN USE PIXEL PORT+ALS TO TRAVEL ALMOST ANYWHERE, AND SHOWSIDE IS THE ONLY HUMAN POPULATED TOWN WHERE THEY MANIFEST.
THERE AIN'T MANY JOBS IN THE NEXUS AND OTHER WORLDS, SO GOOD DEMONS QUALIFY FOR WORK VISAS TO COME HERE AND LIVE AN HONEST LIFE. THAT SAID...
...EVERY NOW AND THEN A BAD CREATURE, OR CREATURES, CAN GET A VISA ON THE BLACK MARKET, OR EVEN SNEAK THEIR WAY IN...
...'COURSE, YOU GOTTA JUDGE FOR YOURSELF WHAT EVEN MAKES A DEMON OR MONSTER "BAD"...

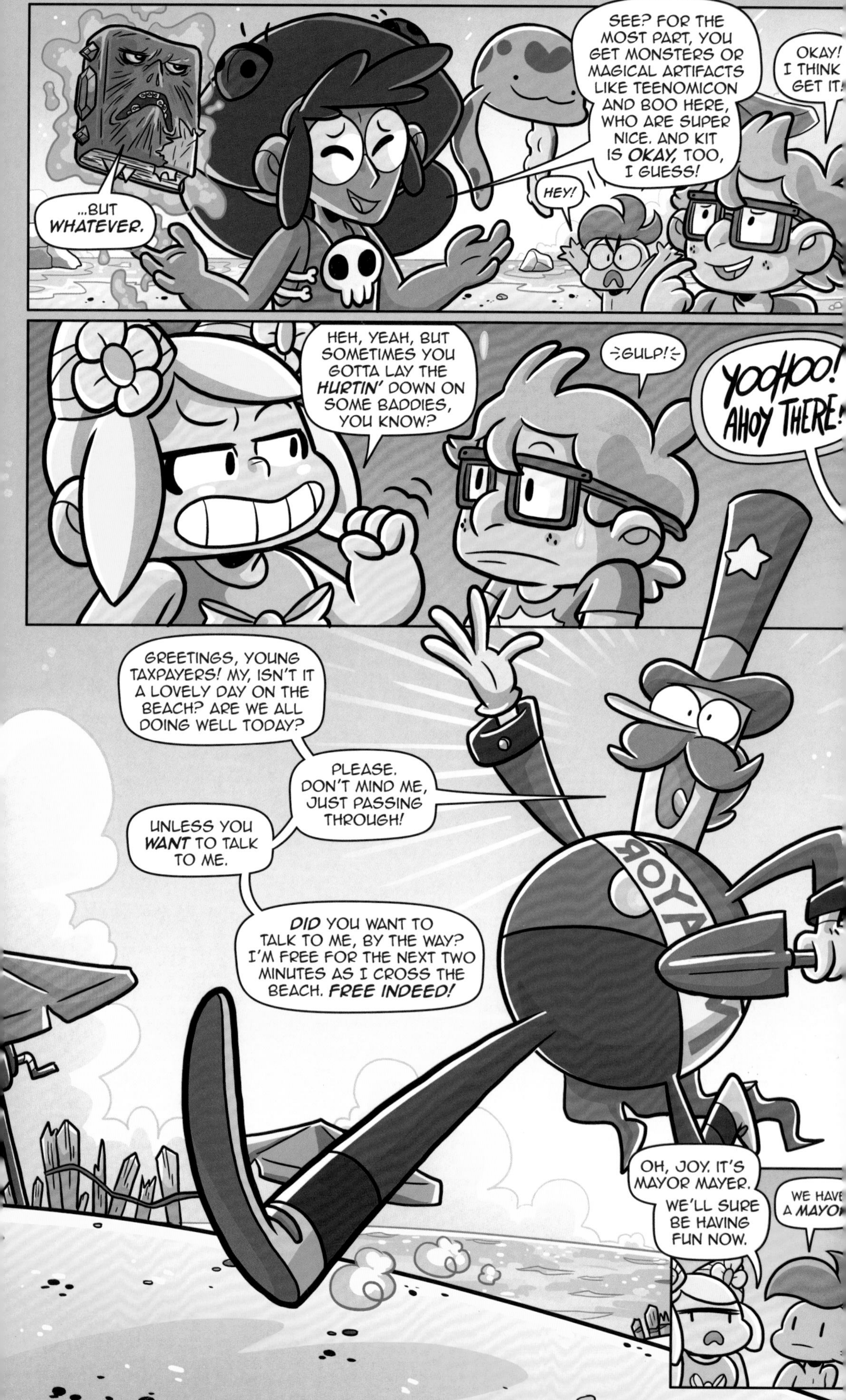

SEE? FOR THE MOST PART, YOU GET MONSTERS OR MAGICAL ARTIFACTS LIKE TEENOMICON AND BOO HERE, WHO ARE SUPER NICE. AND KIT IS *OKAY,* TOO, I GUESS!
HEY!
...BUT *WHATEVER.*
OKAY! I THINK I GET IT!
HEH, YEAH, BUT SOMETIMES YOU GOTTA LAY THE *HURTIN'* DOWN ON SOME BADDIES, YOU KNOW?
GULP!
YOOHOO! AHOY THERE!
GREETINGS, YOUNG TAXPAYERS! MY, ISN'T IT A LOVELY DAY ON THE BEACH? ARE WE ALL DOING WELL TODAY?
PLEASE. DON'T MIND ME, JUST PASSING THROUGH!
UNLESS YOU *WANT* TO TALK TO ME.
DID YOU WANT TO TALK TO ME, BY THE WAY? I'M FREE FOR THE NEXT TWO MINUTES AS I CROSS THE BEACH. *FREE INDEED!*
OH, JOY. IT'S MAYOR MAYER.
WE'LL SURE BE HAVING FUN NOW.
WE HAVE A *MAYOR*

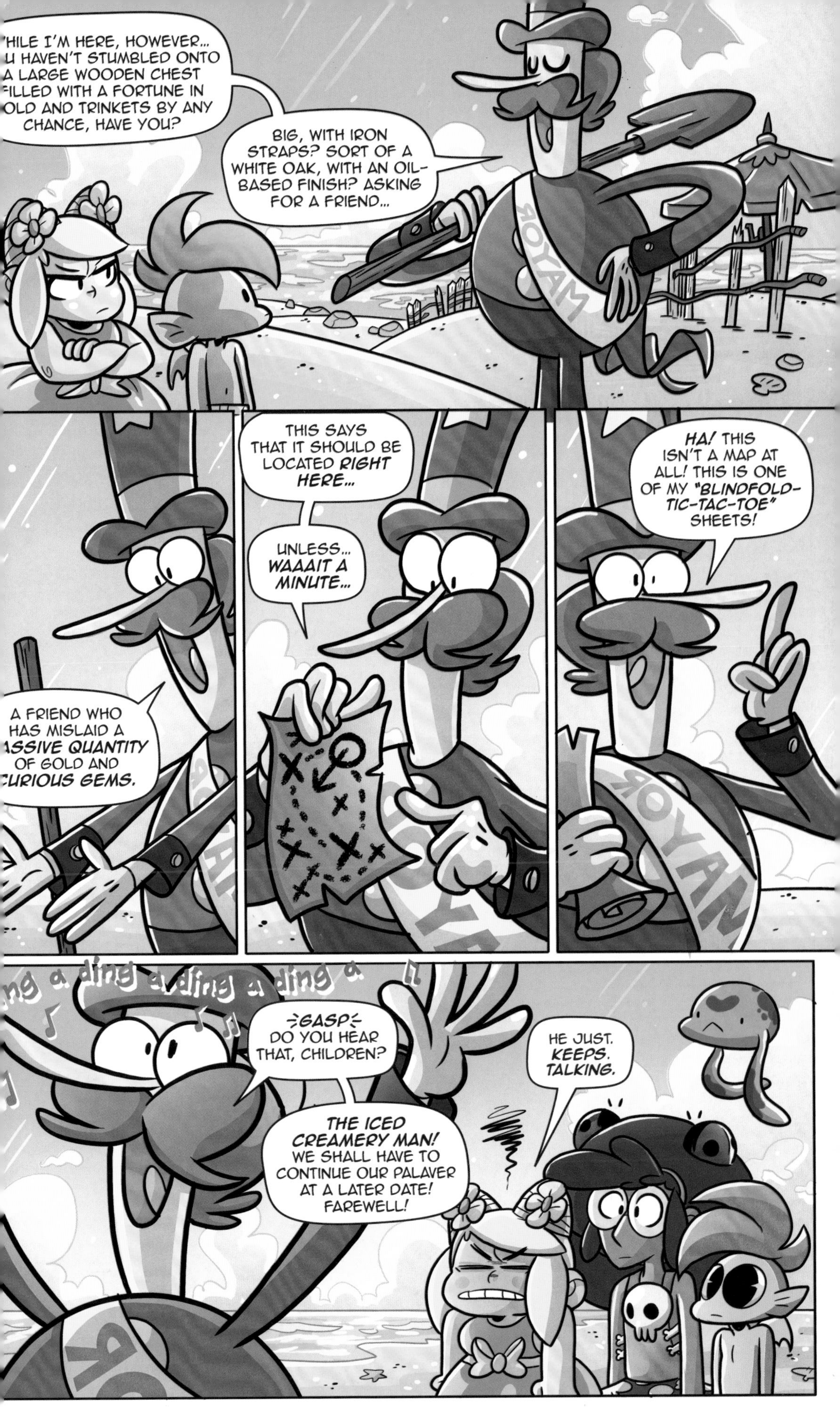

HILE I'M HERE, HOWEVER... U HAVEN'T STUMBLED ONTO A LARGE WOODEN CHEST FILLED WITH A FORTUNE IN OLD AND TRINKETS BY ANY CHANCE, HAVE YOU?
BIG, WITH IRON STRAPS? SORT OF A WHITE OAK, WITH AN OIL-BASED FINISH? ASKING FOR A FRIEND...
MAYOR
A FRIEND WHO HAS MISLAID A ASSIVE QUANTITY OF GOLD AND URIOUS GEMS.
THIS SAYS THAT IT SHOULD BE LOCATED RIGHT HERE...
UNLESS... WAAAIT A MINUTE...
HA! THIS ISN'T A MAP AT ALL! THIS IS ONE OF MY "BLINDFOLD-TIC-TAC-TOE" SHEETS!
MAYOR
ng a ding a ding a ding a
GASP DO YOU HEAR THAT, CHILDREN?
THE ICED CREAMERY MAN! WE SHALL HAVE TO CONTINUE OUR PALAVER AT A LATER DATE! FAREWELL!
HE JUST. KEEPS. TALKING.

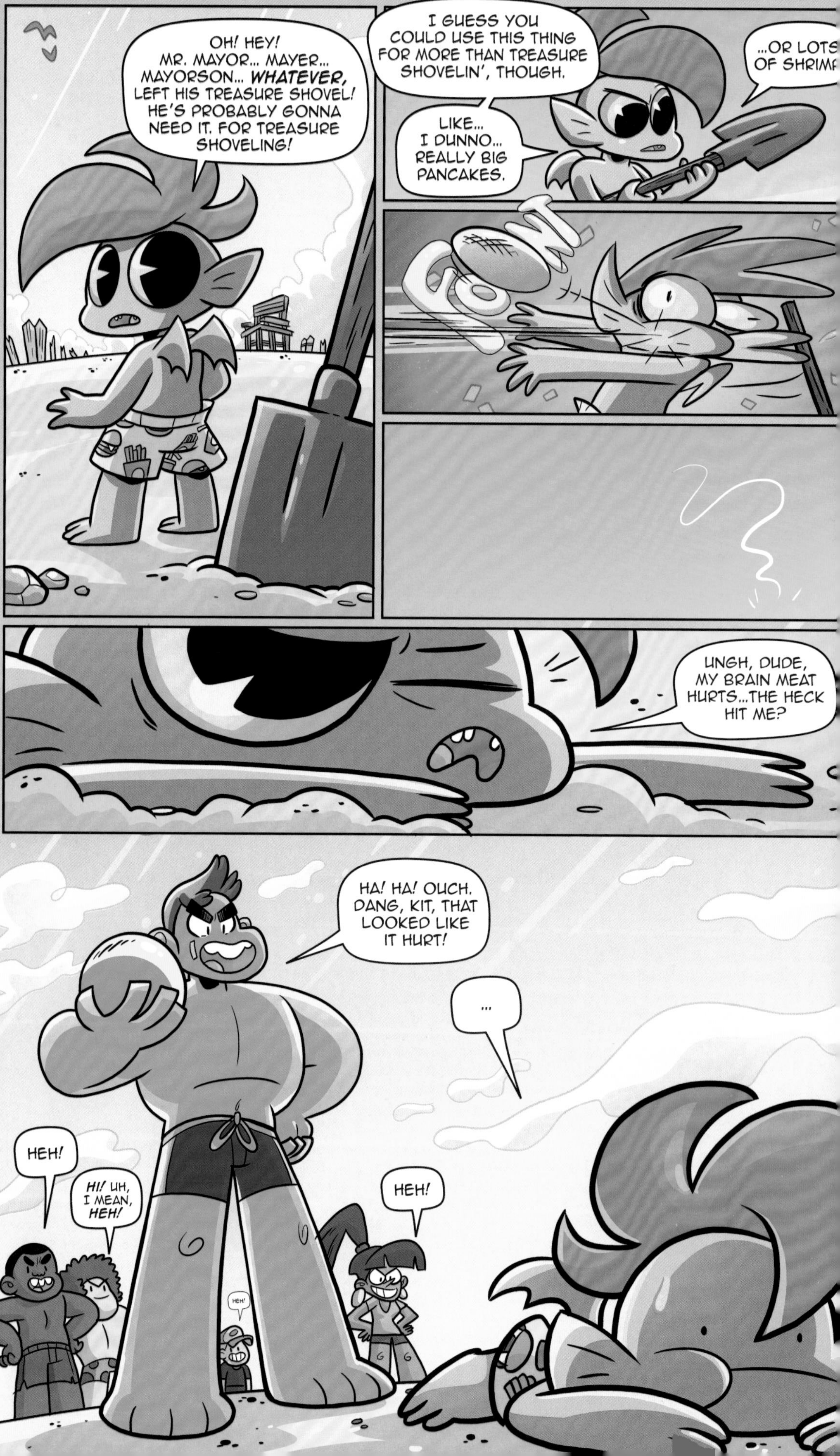
OH! HEY! MR. MAYOR... MAYER... MAYORSON... *WHATEVER,* LEFT HIS TREASURE SHOVEL! HE'S PROBABLY GONNA NEED IT. FOR TREASURE SHOVELING!
I GUESS YOU COULD USE THIS THING FOR MORE THAN TREASURE SHOVELIN', THOUGH.
LIKE... I DUNNO... REALLY BIG PANCAKES.
...OR LOTS OF SHRIMP
TOMP
UNGH, DUDE, MY BRAIN MEAT HURTS...THE HECK HIT ME?
HA! HA! OUCH. DANG, KIT, THAT LOOKED LIKE IT HURT!
...
HEH!
HI! UH, I MEAN, *HEH!*
HEH!
HEH!

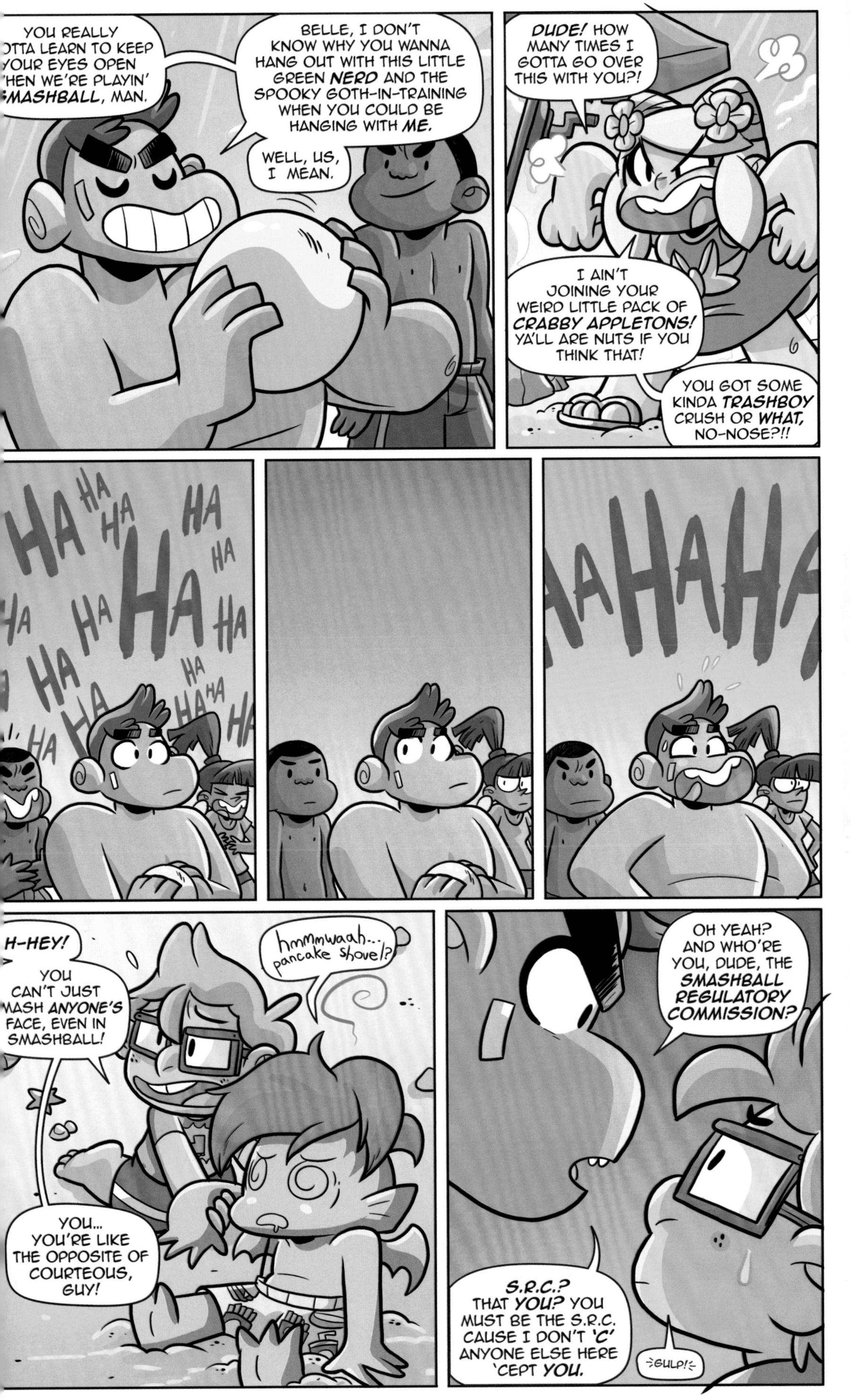
YOU REALLY
OTTA LEARN TO KEEP
YOUR EYES OPEN
HEN WE'RE PLAYIN'
SMASHBALL, MAN.
BELLE, I DON'T KNOW WHY YOU WANNA HANG OUT WITH THIS LITTLE GREEN NERD AND THE SPOOKY GOTH-IN-TRAINING WHEN YOU COULD BE HANGING WITH ME.
WELL, US, I MEAN.
DUDE! HOW MANY TIMES I GOTTA GO OVER THIS WITH YOU?!
I AIN'T JOINING YOUR WEIRD LITTLE PACK OF CRABBY APPLETONS! YA'LL ARE NUTS IF YOU THINK THAT!
YOU GOT SOME KINDA TRASHBOY CRUSH OR WHAT, NO-NOSE?!!
HA HA HA HA HA HA HA HA HA HA HA HA HA HA HA HA HA
AHAHAHAHA
H-HEY!
YOU CAN'T JUST
MASH ANYONE'S
FACE, EVEN IN
SMASHBALL!
hmmmwaah... pancake shovel!?
YOU... YOU'RE LIKE THE OPPOSITE OF COURTEOUS, GUY!
OH YEAH? AND WHO'RE YOU, DUDE, THE SMASHBALL REGULATORY COMMISSION?
S.R.C.? THAT YOU? YOU MUST BE THE S.R.C. CAUSE I DON'T 'C' ANYONE ELSE HERE 'CEPT YOU.
GULP!

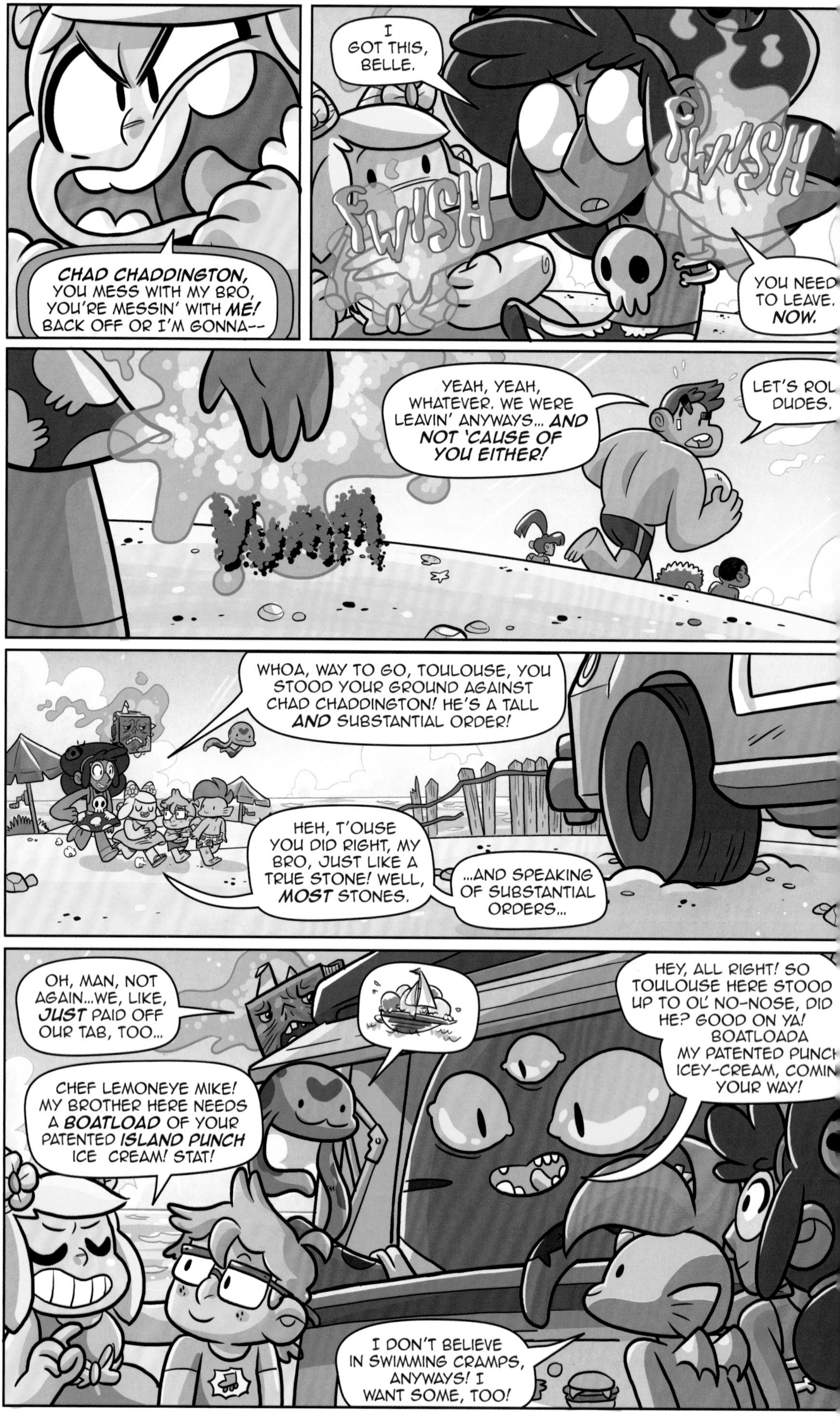
CHAD CHADDINGTON, YOU MESS WITH MY BRO, YOU'RE MESSIN' WITH ME! BACK OFF OR I'M GONNA--
I GOT THIS, BELLE.
FWISH
FWISH
YOU NEED TO LEAVE. NOW.
YEAH, YEAH, WHATEVER. WE WERE LEAVIN' ANYWAYS... AND NOT 'CAUSE OF YOU EITHER!
LET'S ROL DUDES.
VUMM
WHOA, WAY TO GO, TOULOUSE, YOU STOOD YOUR GROUND AGAINST CHAD CHADDINGTON! HE'S A TALL AND SUBSTANTIAL ORDER!
HEH, T'OUSE YOU DID RIGHT, MY BRO, JUST LIKE A TRUE STONE! WELL, MOST STONES.
...AND SPEAKING OF SUBSTANTIAL ORDERS...
OH, MAN, NOT AGAIN...WE, LIKE, JUST PAID OFF OUR TAB, TOO...
CHEF LEMONEYE MIKE! MY BROTHER HERE NEEDS A BOATLOAD OF YOUR PATENTED ISLAND PUNCH ICE CREAM! STAT!
HEY, ALL RIGHT! SO TOULOUSE HERE STOOD UP TO OL' NO-NOSE, DID HE? GOOD ON YA! BOATLOADA MY PATENTED PUNCI ICEY-CREAM, COMIN YOUR WAY!
I DON'T BELIEVE IN SWIMMING CRAMPS, ANYWAYS! I WANT SOME, TOO!

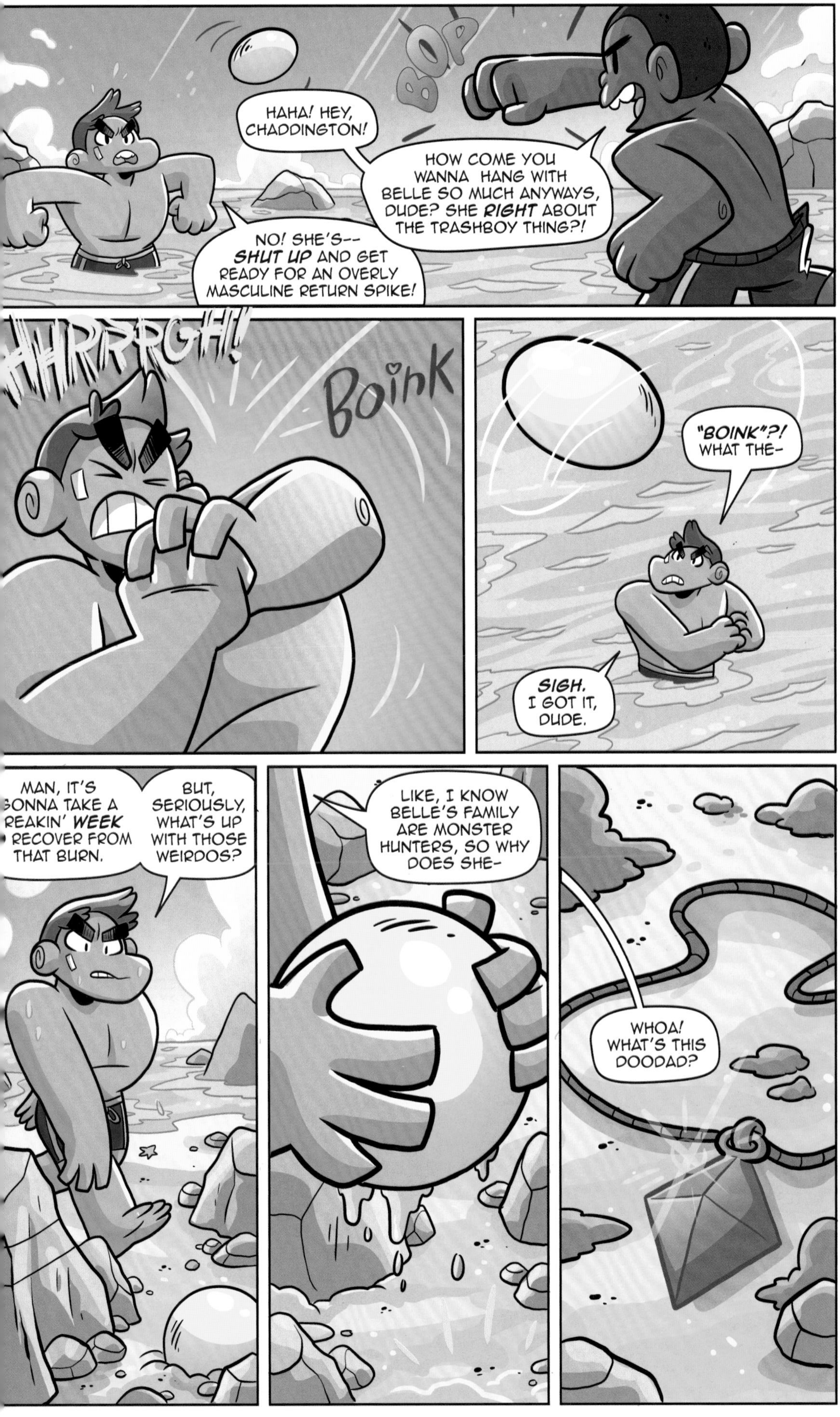
BOP
HAHA! HEY, CHADDINGTON!
HOW COME YOU WANNA HANG WITH BELLE SO MUCH ANYWAYS, DUDE? SHE **RIGHT** ABOUT THE TRASHBOY THING?!
NO! SHE'S-- **SHUT UP** AND GET READY FOR AN OVERLY MASCULINE RETURN SPIKE!
HRRRGH!
Boink
"BOINK"?! WHAT THE-
SIGH. I GOT IT, DUDE.
MAN, IT'S ONNA TAKE A REAKIN' **WEEK** RECOVER FROM THAT BURN.
BUT, SERIOUSLY, WHAT'S UP WITH THOSE WEIRDOS?
LIKE, I KNOW BELLE'S FAMILY ARE MONSTER HUNTERS, SO WHY DOES SHE-
WHOA! WHAT'S THIS DOODAD?

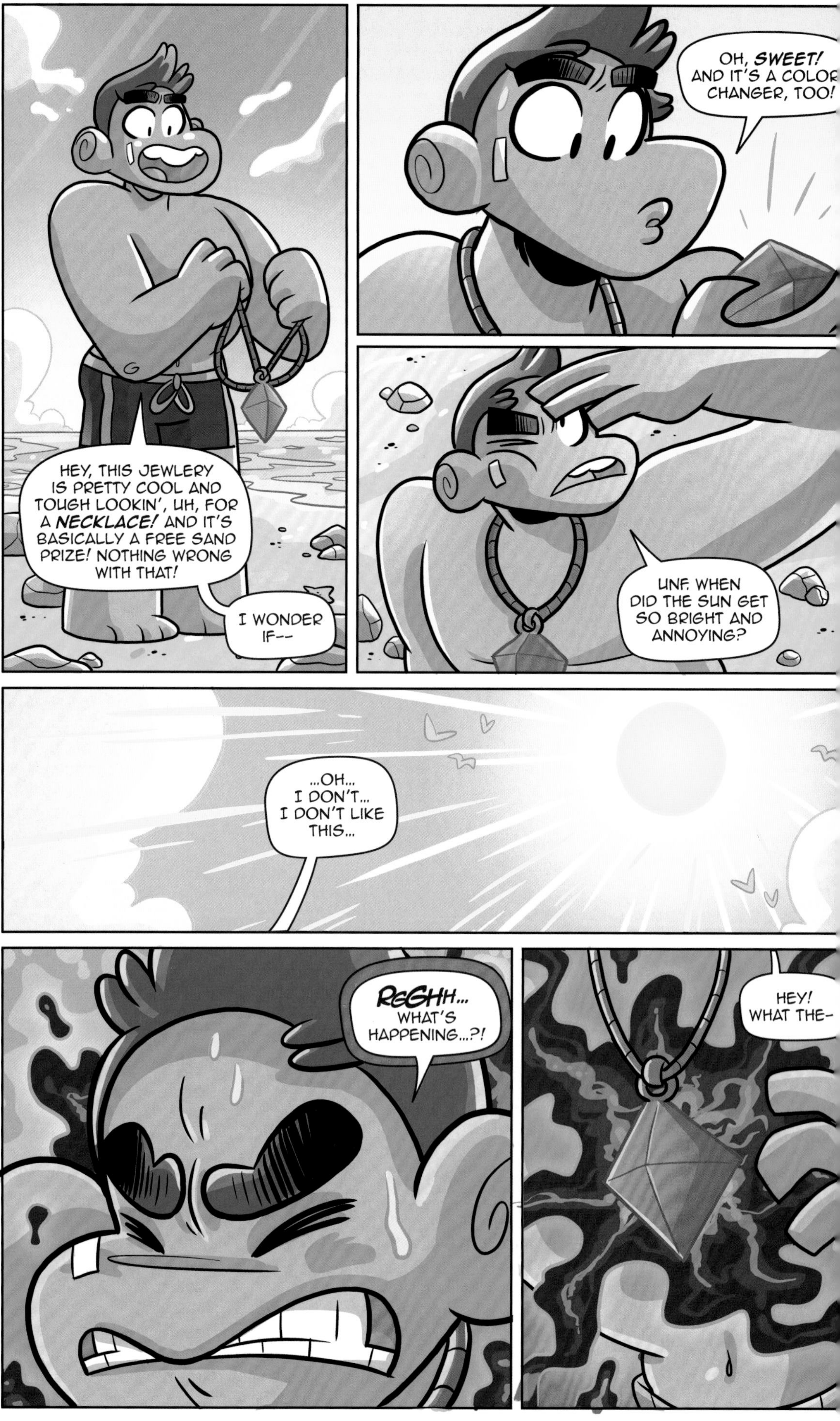
HEY, THIS JEWLERY IS PRETTY COOL AND TOUGH LOOKIN', UH, FOR A ***NECKLACE!*** AND IT'S BASICALLY A FREE SAND PRIZE! NOTHING WRONG WITH THAT!
I WONDER IF--
OH, ***SWEET!*** AND IT'S A COLOR CHANGER, TOO!
UNF. WHEN DID THE SUN GET SO BRIGHT AND ANNOYING?
...OH... I DON'T... I DON'T LIKE THIS...
RGGHH... WHAT'S HAPPENING...?!
HEY! WHAT THE-

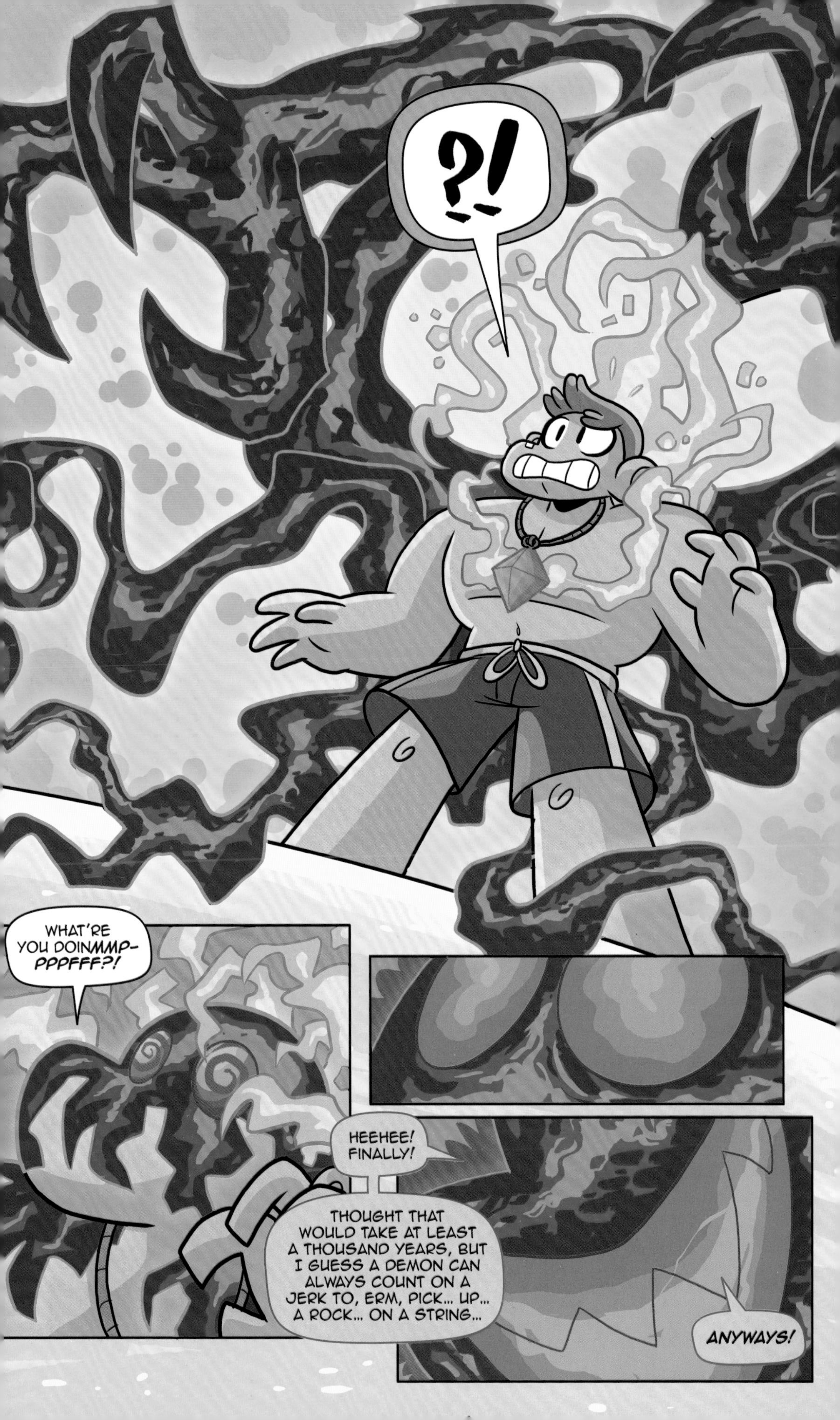
?!
WHAT'RE YOU DOINMMP-PPPFFF?!
HEEHEE! FINALLY!
THOUGHT THAT WOULD TAKE AT LEAST A THOUSAND YEARS, BUT I GUESS A DEMON CAN ALWAYS COUNT ON A JERK TO, ERM, PICK... UP... A ROCK... ON A STRING...
ANYWAYS!

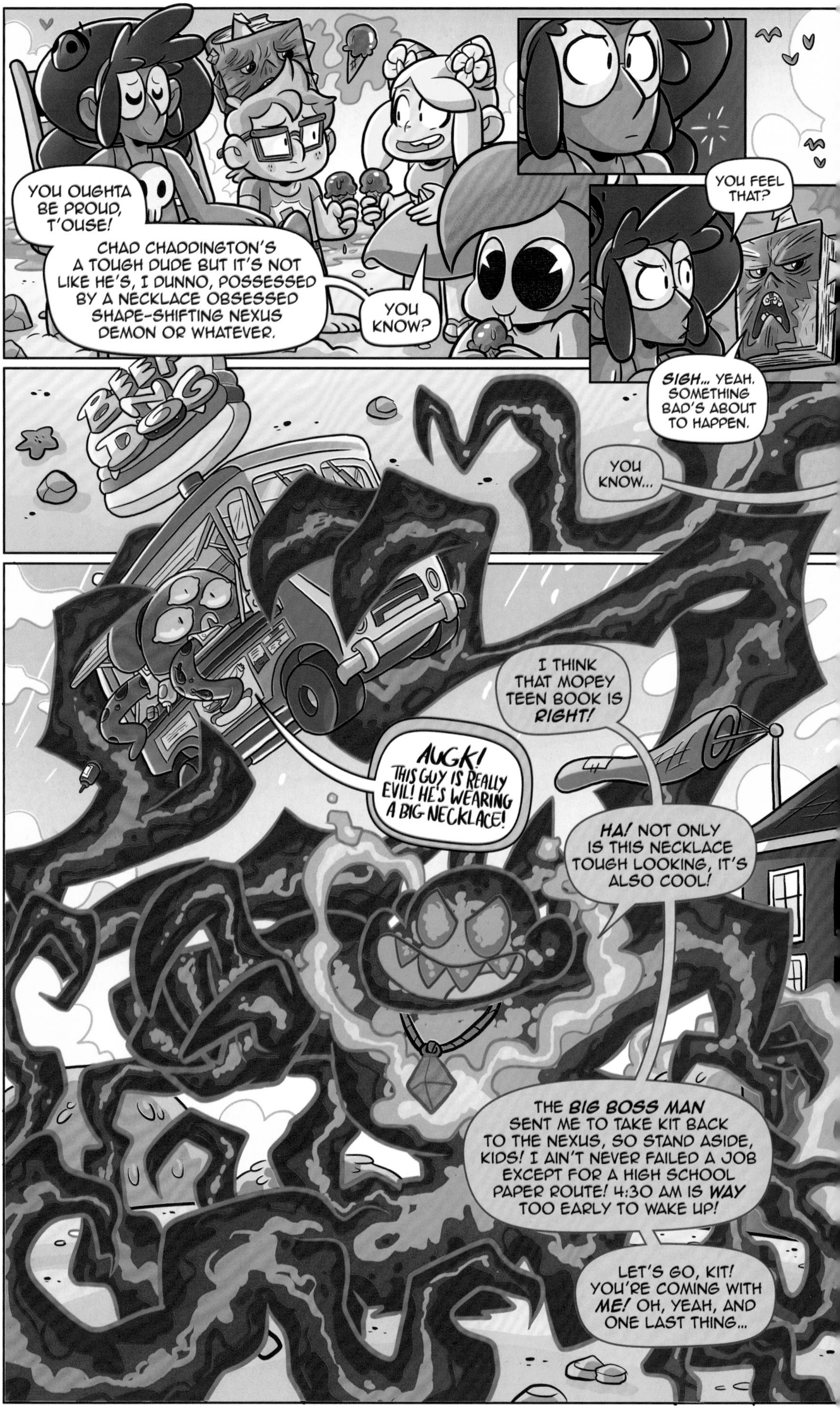
YOU OUGHTA BE PROUD, T'OUSE!
CHAD CHADDINGTON'S A TOUGH DUDE BUT IT'S NOT LIKE HE'S, I DUNNO, POSSESSED BY A NECKLACE OBSESSED SHAPE-SHIFTING NEXUS DEMON OR WHATEVER.
YOU KNOW?
YOU FEEL THAT?
SIGH... YEAH. SOMETHING BAD'S ABOUT TO HAPPEN.
YOU KNOW...
I THINK THAT MOPEY TEEN BOOK IS RIGHT!
AUGK! THIS GUY IS REALLY EVIL! HE'S WEARING A BIG NECKLACE!
HA! NOT ONLY IS THIS NECKLACE TOUGH LOOKING, IT'S ALSO COOL!
THE BIG BOSS MAN SENT ME TO TAKE KIT BACK TO THE NEXUS, SO STAND ASIDE, KIDS! I AIN'T NEVER FAILED A JOB EXCEPT FOR A HIGH SCHOOL PAPER ROUTE! 4:30 AM IS WAY TOO EARLY TO WAKE UP!
LET'S GO, KIT! YOU'RE COMING WITH ME! OH, YEAH, AND ONE LAST THING...

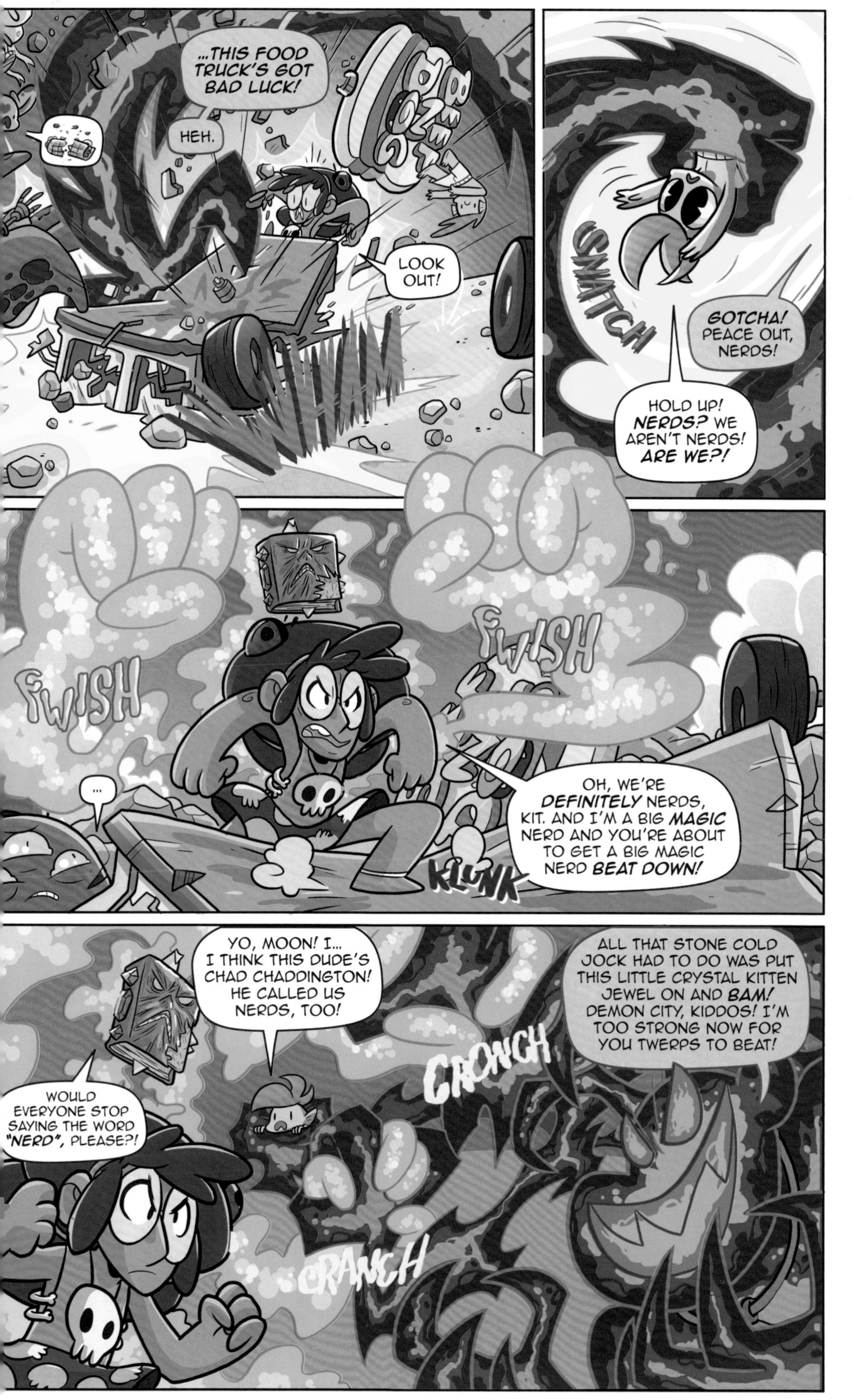
...THIS FOOD TRUCK'S GOT BAD LUCK!
HEH.
LOOK OUT!
WHAM
SNATCH
GOTCHA! PEACE OUT, NERDS!
HOLD UP! NERDS? WE AREN'T NERDS! ARE WE?!
FWISH
FWISH
...
OH, WE'RE DEFINITELY NERDS, KIT. AND I'M A BIG MAGIC NERD AND YOU'RE ABOUT TO GET A BIG MAGIC NERD BEAT DOWN!
KLUNK
YO, MOON! I... I THINK THIS DUDE'S CHAD CHADDINGTON! HE CALLED US NERDS, TOO!
ALL THAT STONE COLD JOCK HAD TO DO WAS PUT THIS LITTLE CRYSTAL KITTEN JEWEL ON AND BAM! DEMON CITY, KIDDOS! I'M TOO STRONG NOW FOR YOU TWERPS TO BEAT!
WOULD EVERYONE STOP SAYING THE WORD "NERD", PLEASE?!
CRONCH
CRANCH

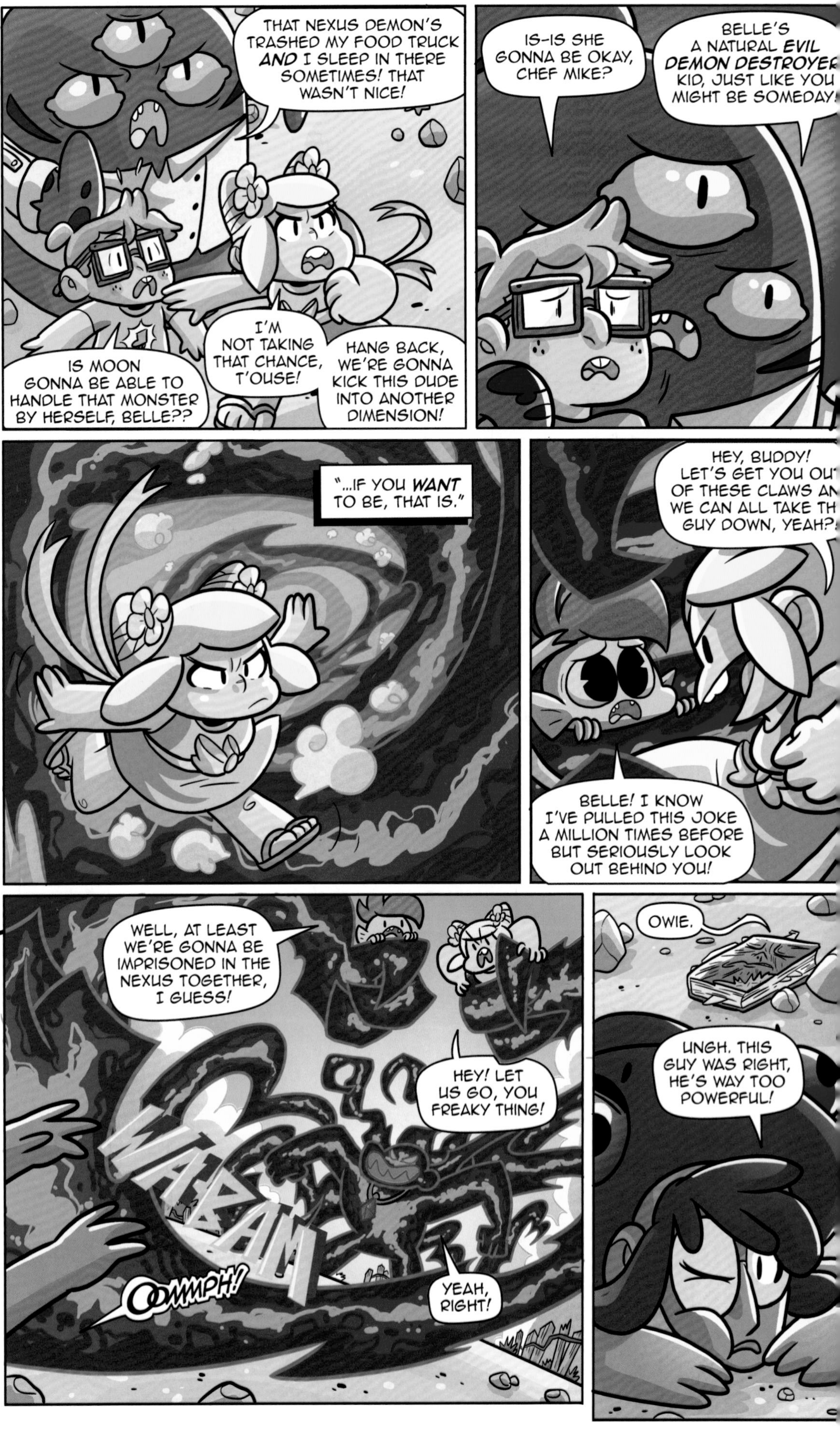

THAT NEXUS DEMON'S TRASHED MY FOOD TRUCK *AND* I SLEEP IN THERE SOMETIMES! THAT WASN'T NICE!
IS MOON GONNA BE ABLE TO HANDLE THAT MONSTER BY HERSELF, BELLE??
I'M NOT TAKING THAT CHANCE, T'OUSE!
HANG BACK, WE'RE GONNA KICK THIS DUDE INTO ANOTHER DIMENSION!
IS-IS SHE GONNA BE OKAY, CHEF MIKE?
BELLE'S A NATURAL ***EVIL DEMON DESTROYER*** KID, JUST LIKE YOU MIGHT BE SOMEDAY!
"...IF YOU ***WANT*** TO BE, THAT IS."
HEY, BUDDY! LET'S GET YOU OUT OF THESE CLAWS AN WE CAN ALL TAKE TH GUY DOWN, YEAH?
BELLE! I KNOW I'VE PULLED THIS JOKE A MILLION TIMES BEFORE BUT SERIOUSLY LOOK OUT BEHIND YOU!
WELL, AT LEAST WE'RE GONNA BE IMPRISONED IN THE NEXUS TOGETHER, I GUESS!
HEY! LET US GO, YOU FREAKY THING!
YEAH, RIGHT!
OOMMPH!
OWIE.
UNGH. THIS GUY WAS RIGHT, HE'S WAY TOO POWERFUL!

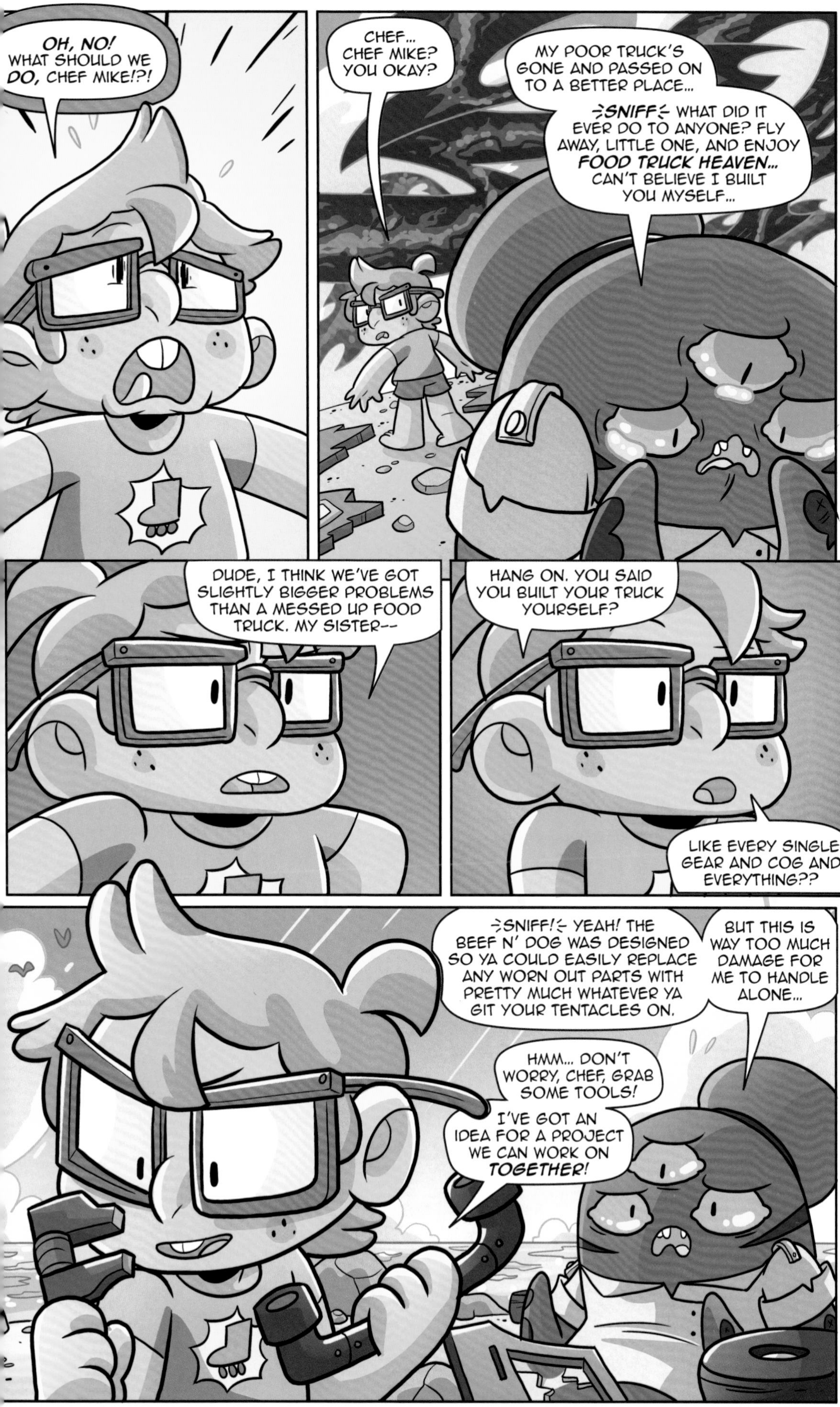

OH, NO! WHAT SHOULD WE DO, CHEF MIKE!?!
CHEF... CHEF MIKE? YOU OKAY?
MY POOR TRUCK'S GONE AND PASSED ON TO A BETTER PLACE...
SNIFF WHAT DID IT EVER DO TO ANYONE? FLY AWAY, LITTLE ONE, AND ENJOY FOOD TRUCK HEAVEN... CAN'T BELIEVE I BUILT YOU MYSELF...
DUDE, I THINK WE'VE GOT SLIGHTLY BIGGER PROBLEMS THAN A MESSED UP FOOD TRUCK. MY SISTER--
HANG ON. YOU SAID YOU BUILT YOUR TRUCK YOURSELF?
LIKE EVERY SINGLE GEAR AND COG AND EVERYTHING??
SNIFF! YEAH! THE BEEF N' DOG WAS DESIGNED SO YA COULD EASILY REPLACE ANY WORN OUT PARTS WITH PRETTY MUCH WHATEVER YA GIT YOUR TENTACLES ON.
BUT THIS IS WAY TOO MUCH DAMAGE FOR ME TO HANDLE ALONE...
HMM... DON'T WORRY, CHEF, GRAB SOME TOOLS!
I'VE GOT AN IDEA FOR A PROJECT WE CAN WORK ON TOGETHER!

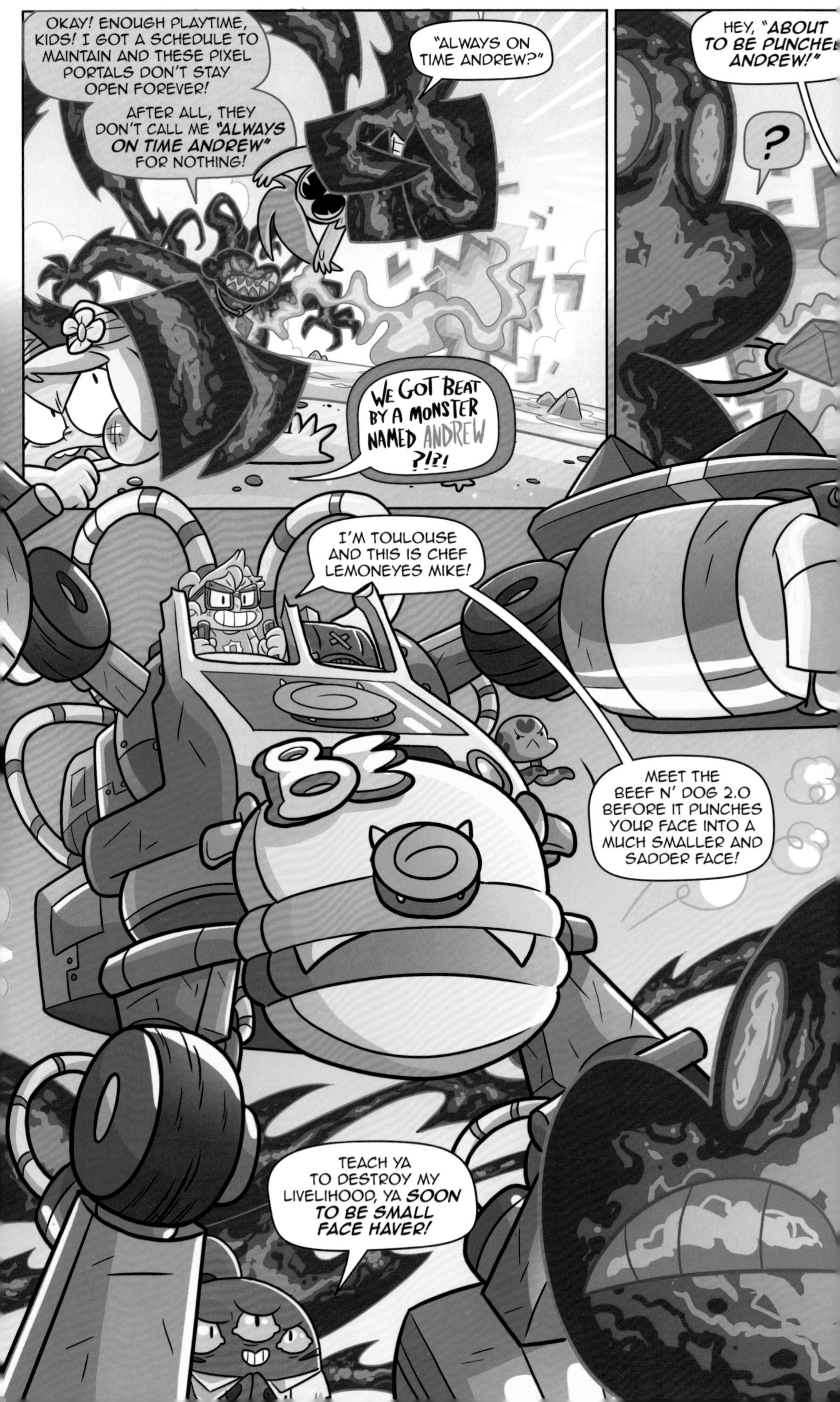
OKAY! ENOUGH PLAYTIME, KIDS! I GOT A SCHEDULE TO MAINTAIN AND THESE PIXEL PORTALS DON'T STAY OPEN FOREVER!
AFTER ALL, THEY DON'T CALL ME *"ALWAYS ON TIME ANDREW"* FOR NOTHING!
"ALWAYS ON TIME ANDREW?"
WE GOT BEAT BY A MONSTER NAMED ANDREW ?!?!
HEY, *"ABOUT TO BE PUNCHE ANDREW!"*
?
I'M TOULOUSE AND THIS IS CHEF LEMONEYES MIKE!
MEET THE BEEF N' DOG 2.0 BEFORE IT PUNCHES YOUR FACE INTO A MUCH SMALLER AND SADDER FACE!
TEACH YA TO DESTROY MY LIVELIHOOD, YA *SOON TO BE SMALL FACE HAVER!*

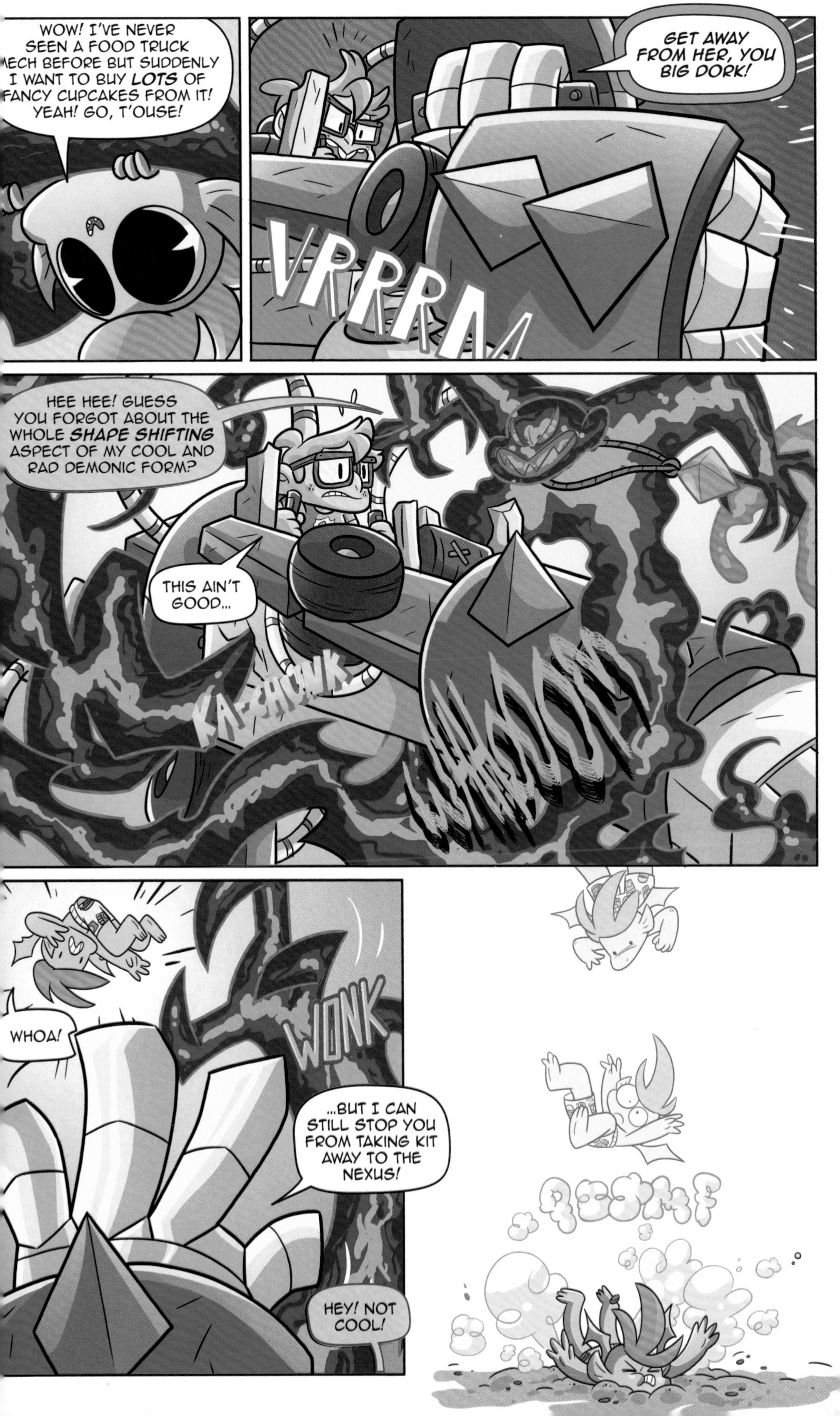
WOW! I'VE NEVER SEEN A FOOD TRUCK MECH BEFORE BUT SUDDENLY I WANT TO BUY *LOTS* OF FANCY CUPCAKES FROM IT! YEAH! GO, T'OUSE!
GET AWAY FROM HER, YOU BIG DORK!
HEE HEE! GUESS YOU FORGOT ABOUT THE WHOLE *SHAPE SHIFTING* ASPECT OF MY COOL AND RAD DEMONIC FORM?
THIS AIN'T GOOD...
KACHUNK
WHOA!
WONK
...BUT I CAN STILL STOP YOU FROM TAKING KIT AWAY TO THE NEXUS!
HEY! NOT COOL!

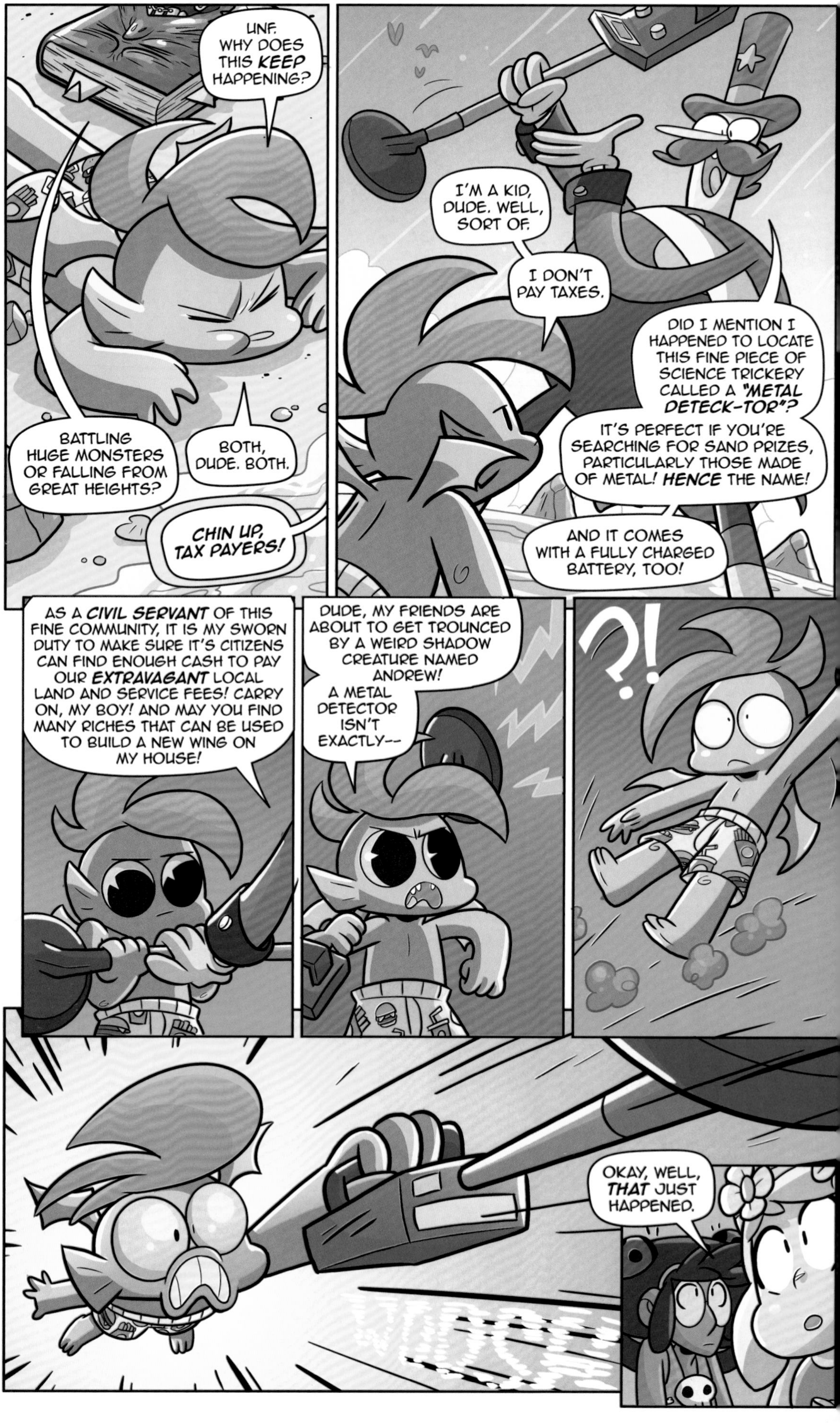
UNF. WHY DOES THIS KEEP HAPPENING?
BATTLING HUGE MONSTERS OR FALLING FROM GREAT HEIGHTS?
BOTH, DUDE. BOTH.
CHIN UP, TAX PAYERS!
I'M A KID, DUDE. WELL, SORT OF.
I DON'T PAY TAXES.
DID I MENTION I HAPPENED TO LOCATE THIS FINE PIECE OF SCIENCE TRICKERY CALLED A "METAL DETECK-TOR"?
IT'S PERFECT IF YOU'RE SEARCHING FOR SAND PRIZES, PARTICULARLY THOSE MADE OF METAL! HENCE THE NAME!
AND IT COMES WITH A FULLY CHARGED BATTERY, TOO!
AS A CIVIL SERVANT OF THIS FINE COMMUNITY, IT IS MY SWORN DUTY TO MAKE SURE IT'S CITIZENS CAN FIND ENOUGH CASH TO PAY OUR EXTRAVAGANT LOCAL LAND AND SERVICE FEES! CARRY ON, MY BOY! AND MAY YOU FIND MANY RICHES THAT CAN BE USED TO BUILD A NEW WING ON MY HOUSE!
DUDE, MY FRIENDS ARE ABOUT TO GET TROUNCED BY A WEIRD SHADOW CREATURE NAMED ANDREW!
A METAL DETECTOR ISN'T EXACTLY--
?!
OKAY, WELL, THAT JUST HAPPENED.

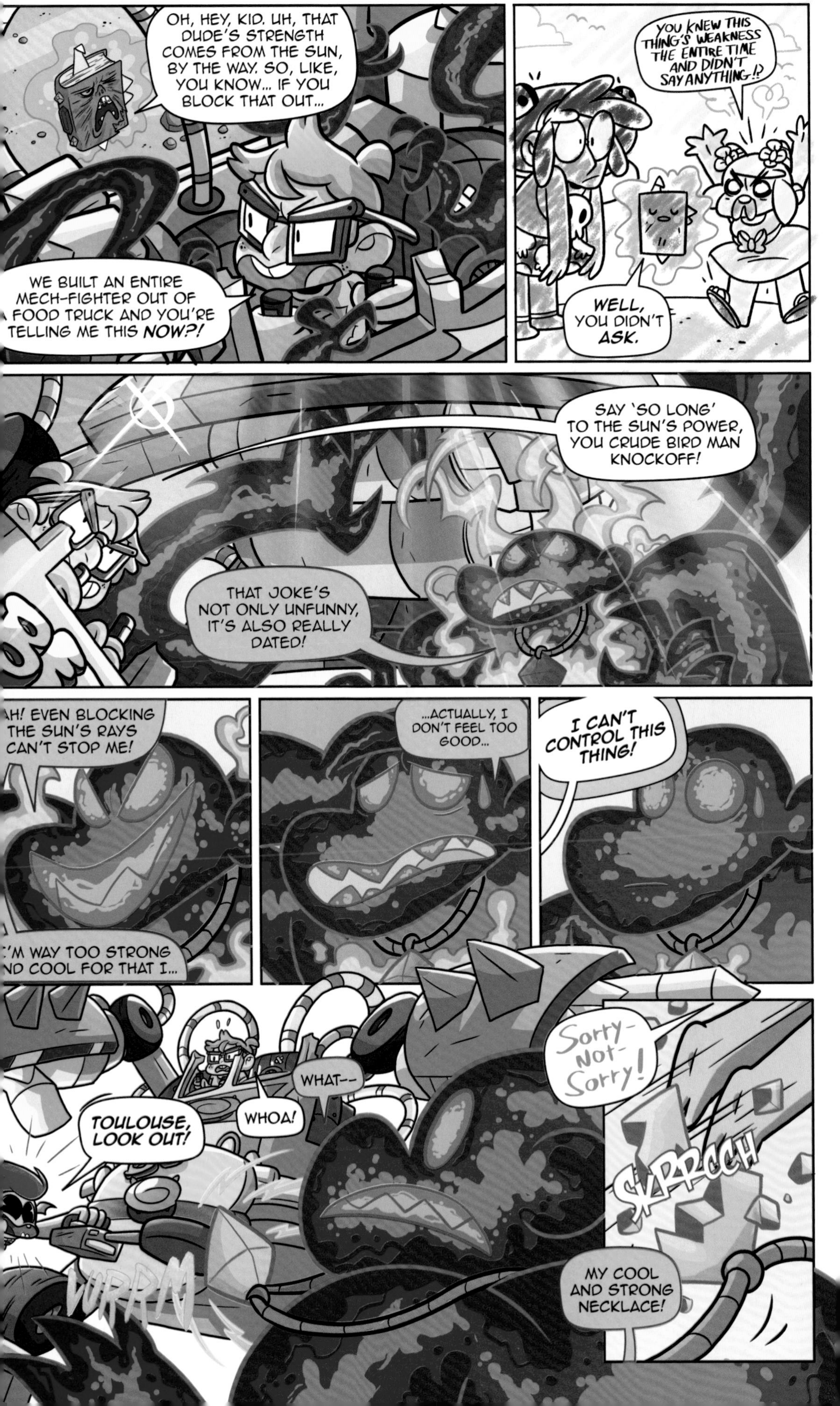
OH, HEY, KID. UH, THAT DUDE'S STRENGTH COMES FROM THE SUN, BY THE WAY. SO, LIKE, YOU KNOW... IF YOU BLOCK THAT OUT...
WE BUILT AN ENTIRE MECH-FIGHTER OUT OF A FOOD TRUCK AND YOU'RE TELLING ME THIS *NOW?!*
YOU KNEW THIS THING'S WEAKNESS THE ENTIRE TIME AND DIDN'T SAY ANYTHING!?
WELL, YOU DIDN'T *ASK.*
SAY 'SO LONG' TO THE SUN'S POWER, YOU CRUDE BIRD MAN KNOCKOFF!
THAT JOKE'S NOT ONLY UNFUNNY, IT'S ALSO REALLY DATED!
AH! EVEN BLOCKING THE SUN'S RAYS CAN'T STOP ME!
I'M WAY TOO STRONG AND COOL FOR THAT I...
...ACTUALLY, I DON'T FEEL TOO GOOD...
I CAN'T CONTROL THIS THING!
TOULOUSE, LOOK OUT!
WHOA!
WHAT--
Sorry-Not-Sorry!
SKRRCCH
MY COOL AND STRONG NECKLACE!
VRRRM

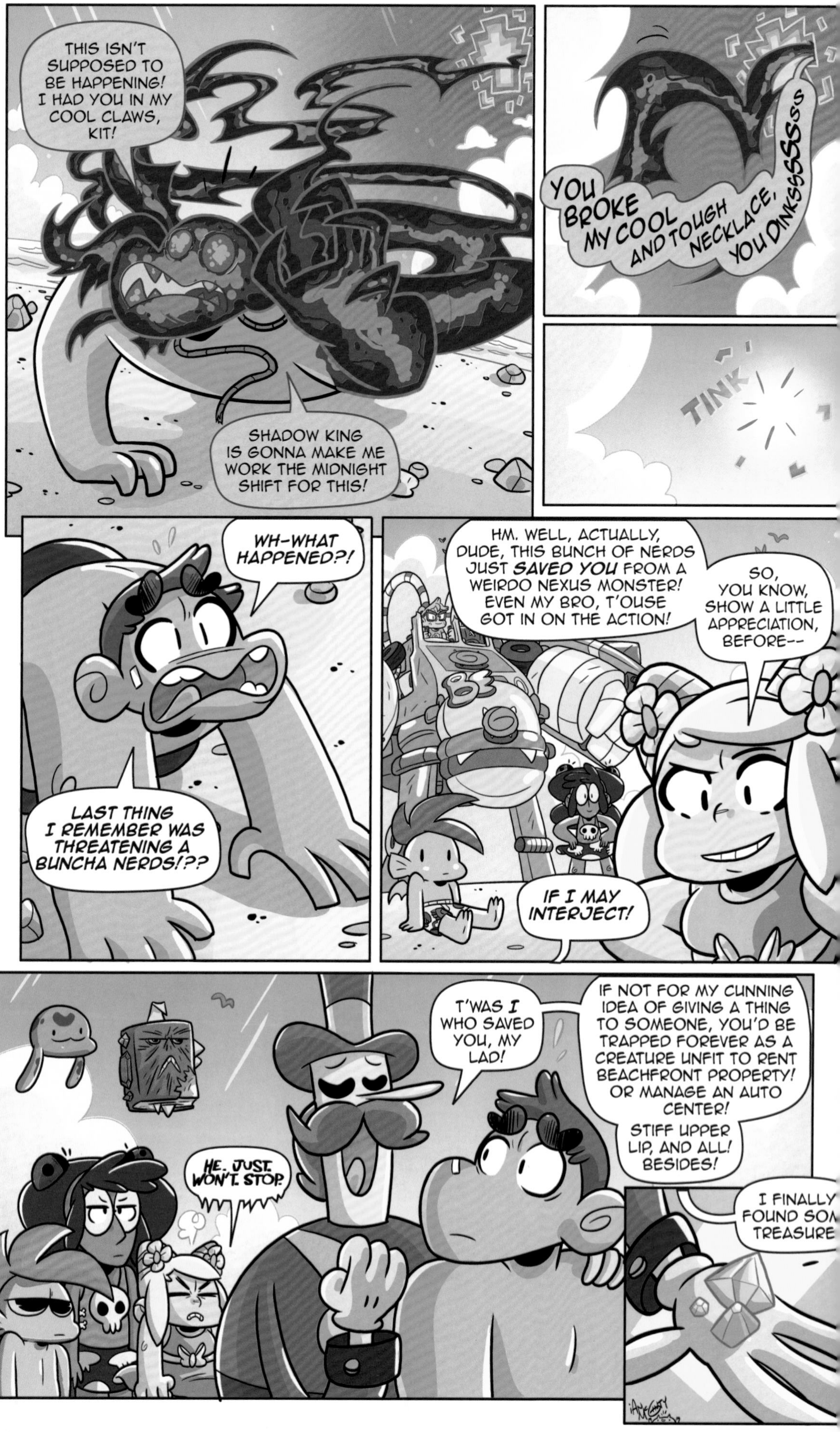
THIS ISN'T SUPPOSED TO BE HAPPENING! I HAD YOU IN MY COOL CLAWS, KIT!
SHADOW KING IS GONNA MAKE ME WORK THE MIDNIGHT SHIFT FOR THIS!
YOU BROKE MY COOL AND TOUGH NECKLACE, YOU DINKSSSSSSSSS
TINK
WH-WHAT HAPPENED?!
LAST THING I REMEMBER WAS THREATENING A BUNCHA NERDS!??
HM. WELL, ACTUALLY, DUDE, THIS BUNCH OF NERDS JUST SAVED YOU FROM A WEIRDO NEXUS MONSTER! EVEN MY BRO, T'OUSE GOT IN ON THE ACTION!
SO, YOU KNOW, SHOW A LITTLE APPRECIATION, BEFORE--
IF I MAY INTERJECT!
T'WAS I WHO SAVED YOU, MY LAD!
IF NOT FOR MY CUNNING IDEA OF GIVING A THING TO SOMEONE, YOU'D BE TRAPPED FOREVER AS A CREATURE UNFIT TO RENT BEACHFRONT PROPERTY! OR MANAGE AN AUTO CENTER!
STIFF UPPER LIP, AND ALL! BESIDES!
HE. JUST. WON'T. STOP.
I FINALLY FOUND SOM TREASURE

HOT CHOCOLATE, COOL GHOST

WRITTEN BY IAN McGINTY
ART BY CAROLYN NOWAK

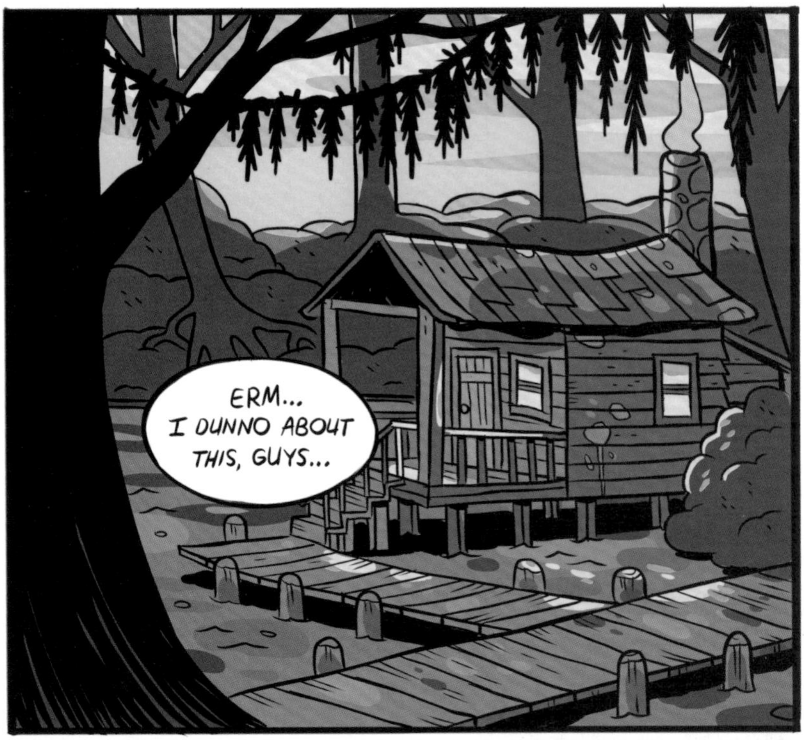
ERM... I DUNNO ABOUT THIS, GUYS...

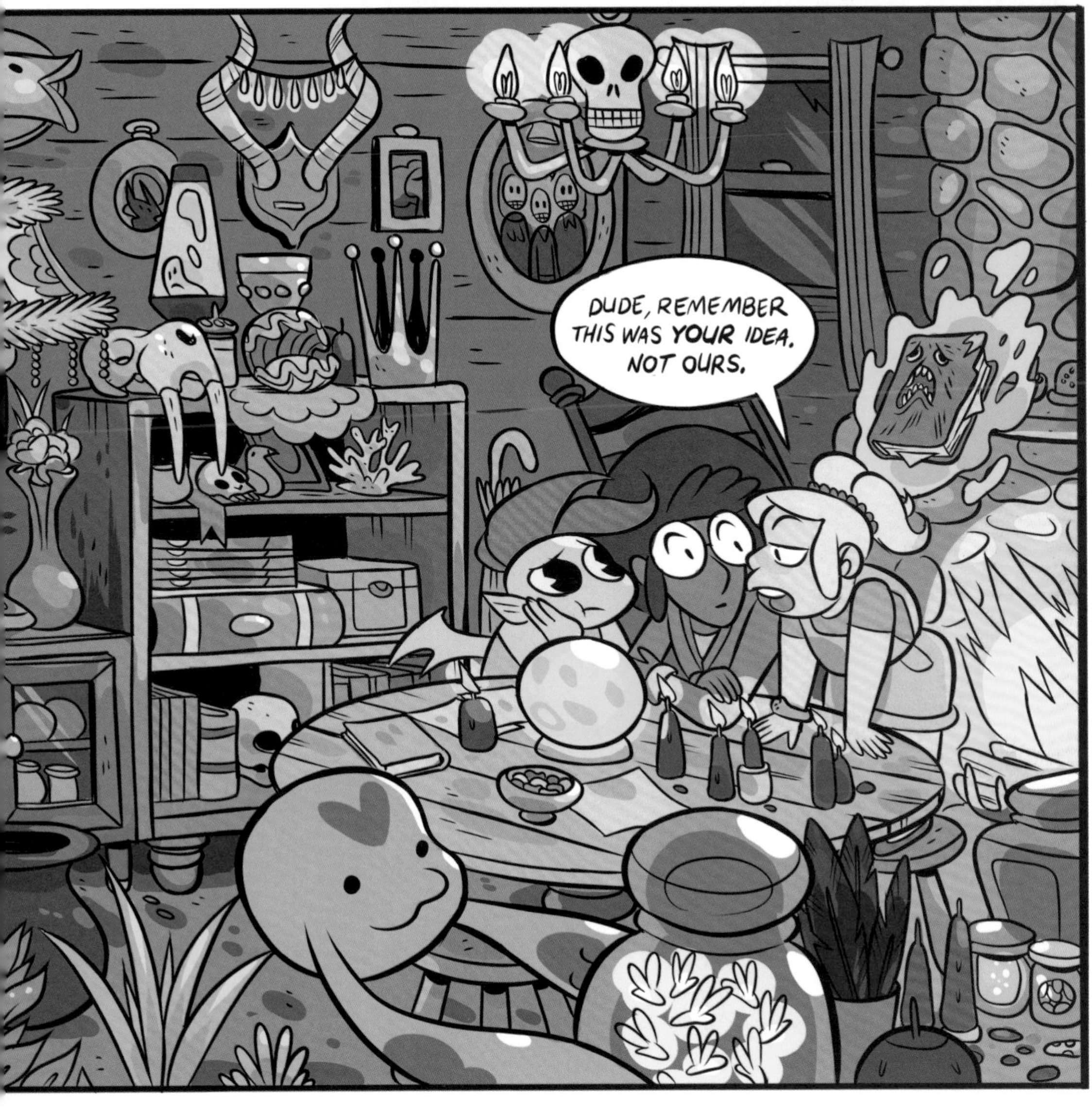
DUDE, REMEMBER THIS WAS YOUR IDEA. NOT OURS.

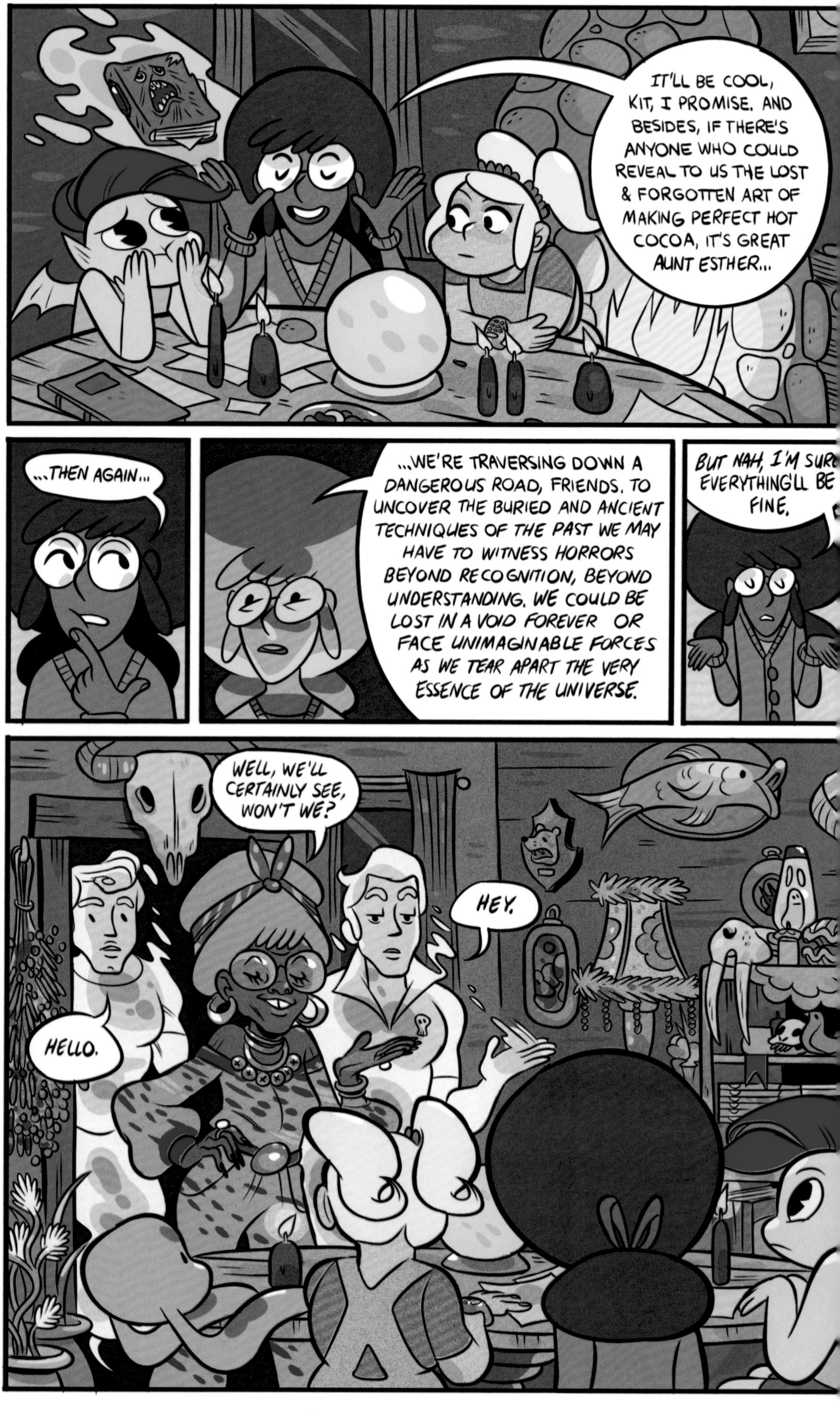
IT'LL BE COOL, KIT, I PROMISE. AND BESIDES, IF THERE'S ANYONE WHO COULD REVEAL TO US THE LOST & FORGOTTEN ART OF MAKING PERFECT HOT COCOA, IT'S GREAT AUNT ESTHER...
...THEN AGAIN...
...WE'RE TRAVERSING DOWN A DANGEROUS ROAD, FRIENDS. TO UNCOVER THE BURIED AND ANCIENT TECHNIQUES OF THE PAST WE MAY HAVE TO WITNESS HORRORS BEYOND RECOGNITION, BEYOND UNDERSTANDING. WE COULD BE LOST IN A VOID FOREVER OR FACE UNIMAGINABLE FORCES AS WE TEAR APART THE VERY ESSENCE OF THE UNIVERSE.
BUT NAH, I'M SURE EVERYTHING'LL BE FINE.
WELL, WE'LL CERTAINLY SEE, WON'T WE?
HEY.
HELLO.

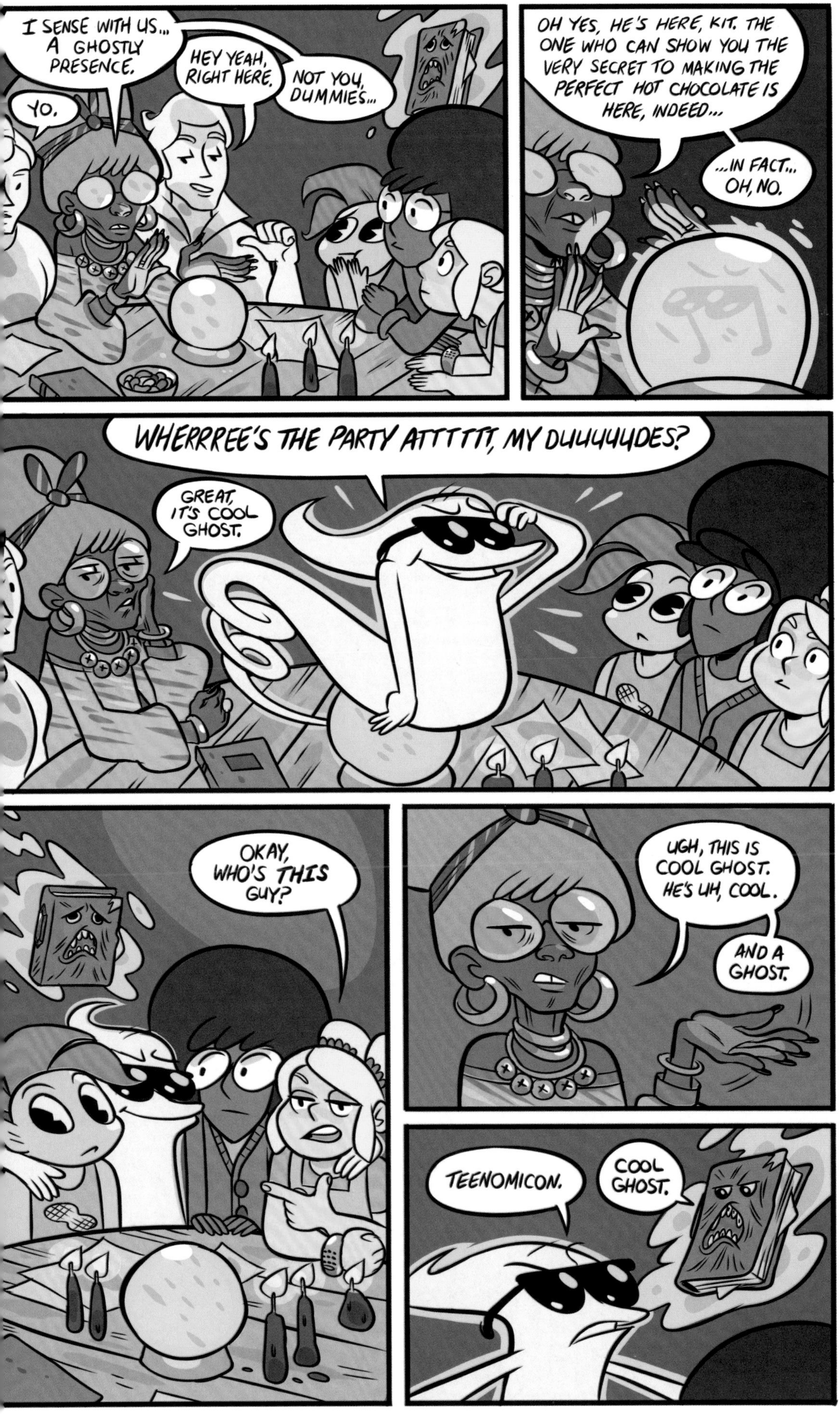
I SENSE WITH US... A GHOSTLY PRESENCE.
YO.
HEY YEAH, RIGHT HERE.
NOT YOU, DUMMIES...
OH YES, HE'S HERE, KIT. THE ONE WHO CAN SHOW YOU THE VERY SECRET TO MAKING THE PERFECT HOT CHOCOLATE IS HERE, INDEED...
...IN FACT... OH, NO.
WHERRREE'S THE PARTY ATTTTT, MY DUUUUUDES?
GREAT, IT'S COOL GHOST.
OKAY, WHO'S THIS GUY?
UGH, THIS IS COOL GHOST. HE'S UH, COOL.
AND A GHOST.
TEENOMICON.
COOL GHOST.

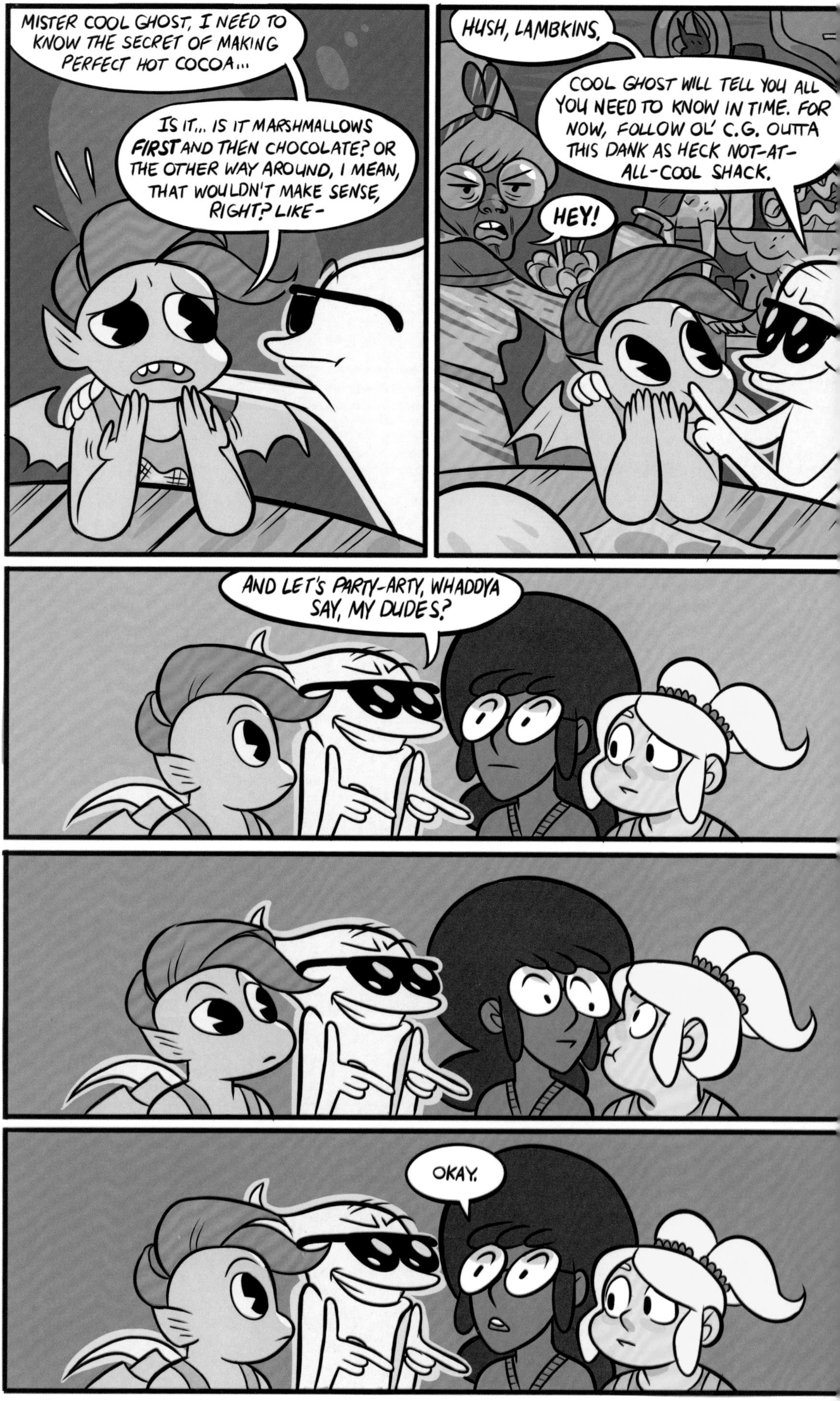
MISTER COOL GHOST, I NEED TO KNOW THE SECRET OF MAKING PERFECT HOT COCOA...
IS IT... IS IT MARSHMALLOWS FIRST AND THEN CHOCOLATE? OR THE OTHER WAY AROUND, I MEAN, THAT WOULDN'T MAKE SENSE, RIGHT? LIKE-
HUSH, LAMBKINS.
COOL GHOST WILL TELL YOU ALL YOU NEED TO KNOW IN TIME. FOR NOW, FOLLOW OL' C.G. OUTTA THIS DANK AS HECK NOT-AT-ALL-COOL SHACK.
HEY!
AND LET'S PARTY-ARTY, WHADDYA SAY, MY DUDES?
OKAY.

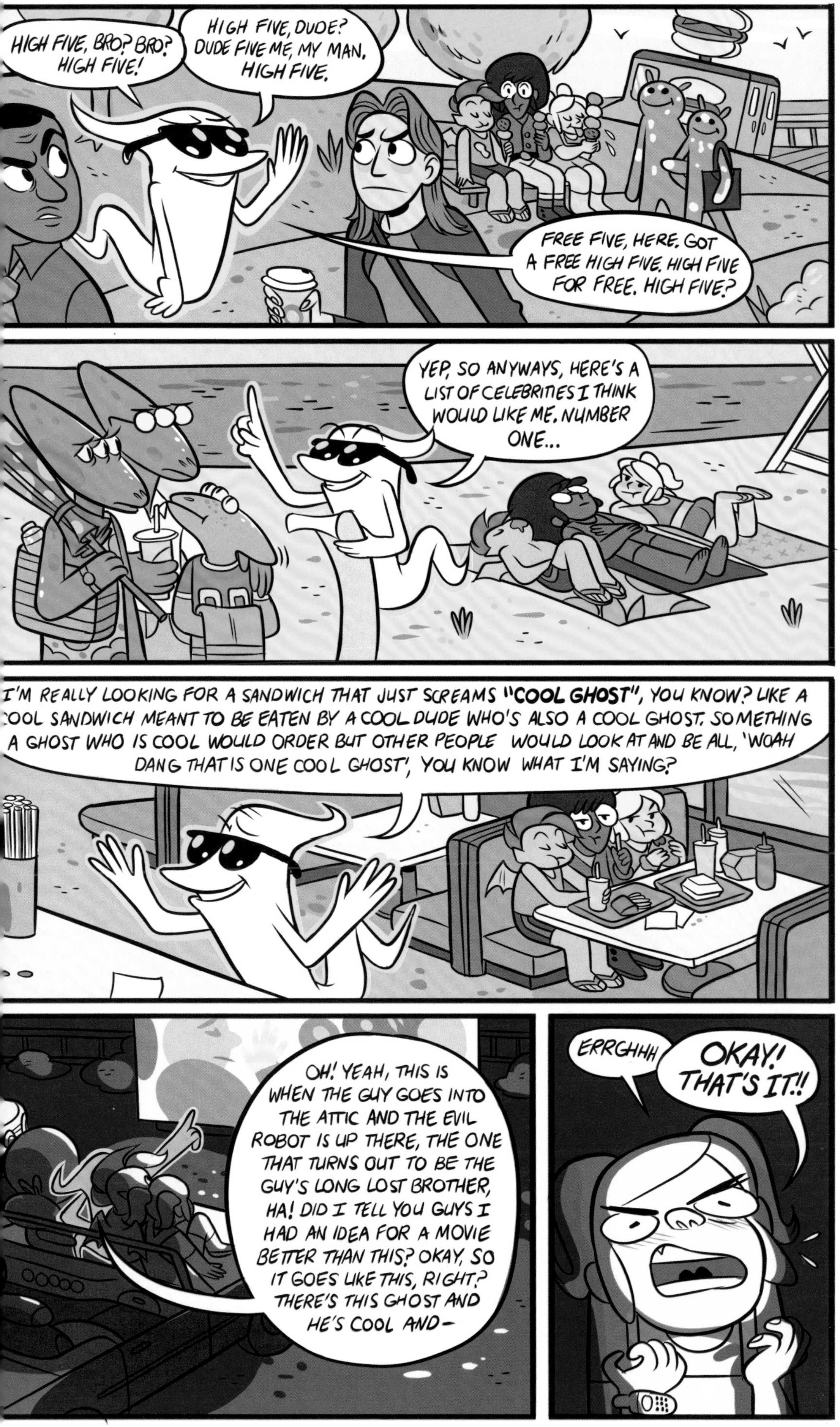
HIGH FIVE, BRO? BRO? HIGH FIVE!
HIGH FIVE, DUDE? DUDE FIVE ME, MY MAN. HIGH FIVE.
FREE FIVE, HERE. GOT A FREE HIGH FIVE. HIGH FIVE FOR FREE. HIGH FIVE?
YEP, SO ANYWAYS, HERE'S A LIST OF CELEBRITIES I THINK WOULD LIKE ME. NUMBER ONE...
I'M REALLY LOOKING FOR A SANDWICH THAT JUST SCREAMS "COOL GHOST", YOU KNOW? LIKE A COOL SANDWICH MEANT TO BE EATEN BY A COOL DUDE WHO'S ALSO A COOL GHOST. SOMETHING A GHOST WHO IS COOL WOULD ORDER BUT OTHER PEOPLE WOULD LOOK AT AND BE ALL, 'WOAH DANG THAT IS ONE COOL GHOST', YOU KNOW WHAT I'M SAYING?
OH! YEAH, THIS IS WHEN THE GUY GOES INTO THE ATTIC AND THE EVIL ROBOT IS UP THERE, THE ONE THAT TURNS OUT TO BE THE GUY'S LONG LOST BROTHER, HA! DID I TELL YOU GUYS I HAD AN IDEA FOR A MOVIE BETTER THAN THIS? OKAY, SO IT GOES LIKE THIS, RIGHT? THERE'S THIS GHOST AND HE'S COOL AND—
ERRGHHH
OKAY! THAT'S IT!!

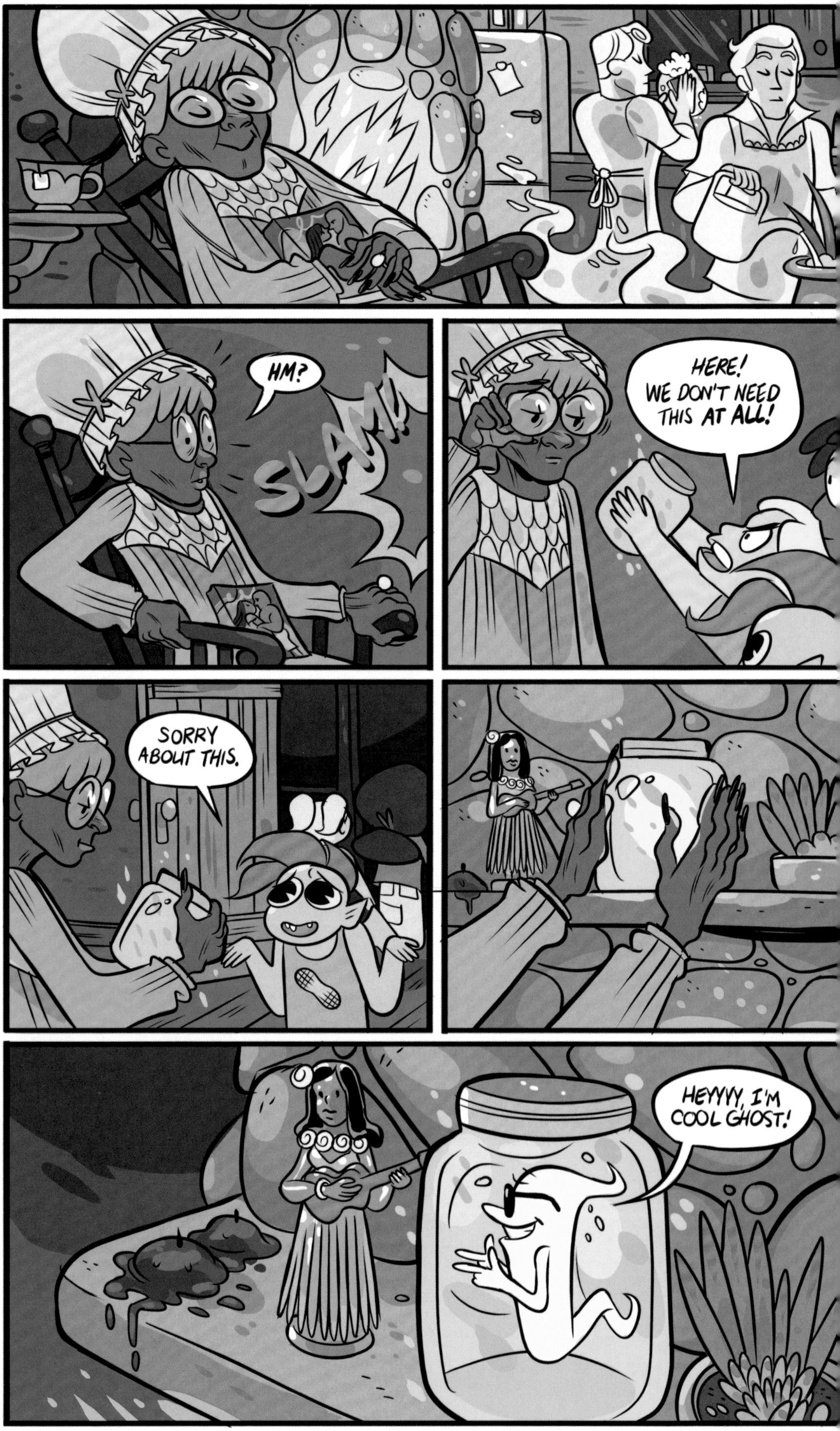
HM?
SLAM!
HERE! WE DON'T NEED THIS AT ALL!
SORRY ABOUT THIS.
HEYYYY, I'M COOL GHOST!

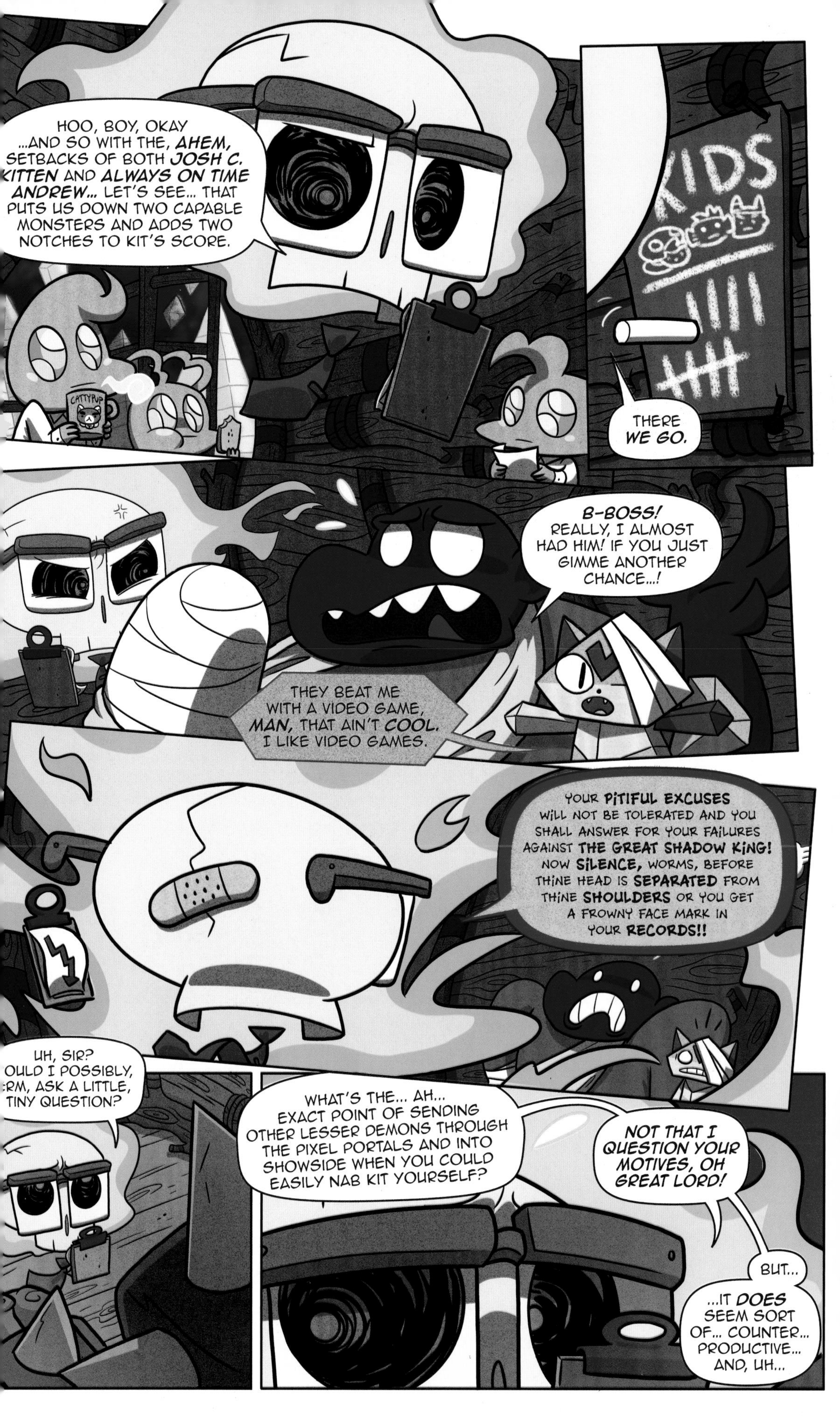
HOO, BOY, OKAY ...AND SO WITH THE, AHEM, SETBACKS OF BOTH JOSH C. KITTEN AND ALWAYS ON TIME ANDREW... LET'S SEE... THAT PUTS US DOWN TWO CAPABLE MONSTERS AND ADDS TWO NOTCHES TO KIT'S SCORE.
CATTYPUP
KIDS
THERE WE GO.
B-BOSS! REALLY, I ALMOST HAD HIM! IF YOU JUST GIMME ANOTHER CHANCE...!
THEY BEAT ME WITH A VIDEO GAME, MAN, THAT AIN'T COOL. I LIKE VIDEO GAMES.
YOUR PITIFUL EXCUSES WILL NOT BE TOLERATED AND YOU SHALL ANSWER FOR YOUR FAILURES AGAINST THE GREAT SHADOW KING! NOW SILENCE, WORMS, BEFORE THINE HEAD IS SEPARATED FROM THINE SHOULDERS OR YOU GET A FROWNY FACE MARK IN YOUR RECORDS!!
UH, SIR? OULD I POSSIBLY, RM, ASK A LITTLE, TINY QUESTION?
WHAT'S THE... AH... EXACT POINT OF SENDING OTHER LESSER DEMONS THROUGH THE PIXEL PORTALS AND INTO SHOWSIDE WHEN YOU COULD EASILY NAB KIT YOURSELF?
NOT THAT I QUESTION YOUR MOTIVES, OH GREAT LORD!
BUT...
...IT DOES SEEM SORT OF... COUNTER... PRODUCTIVE... AND, UH...

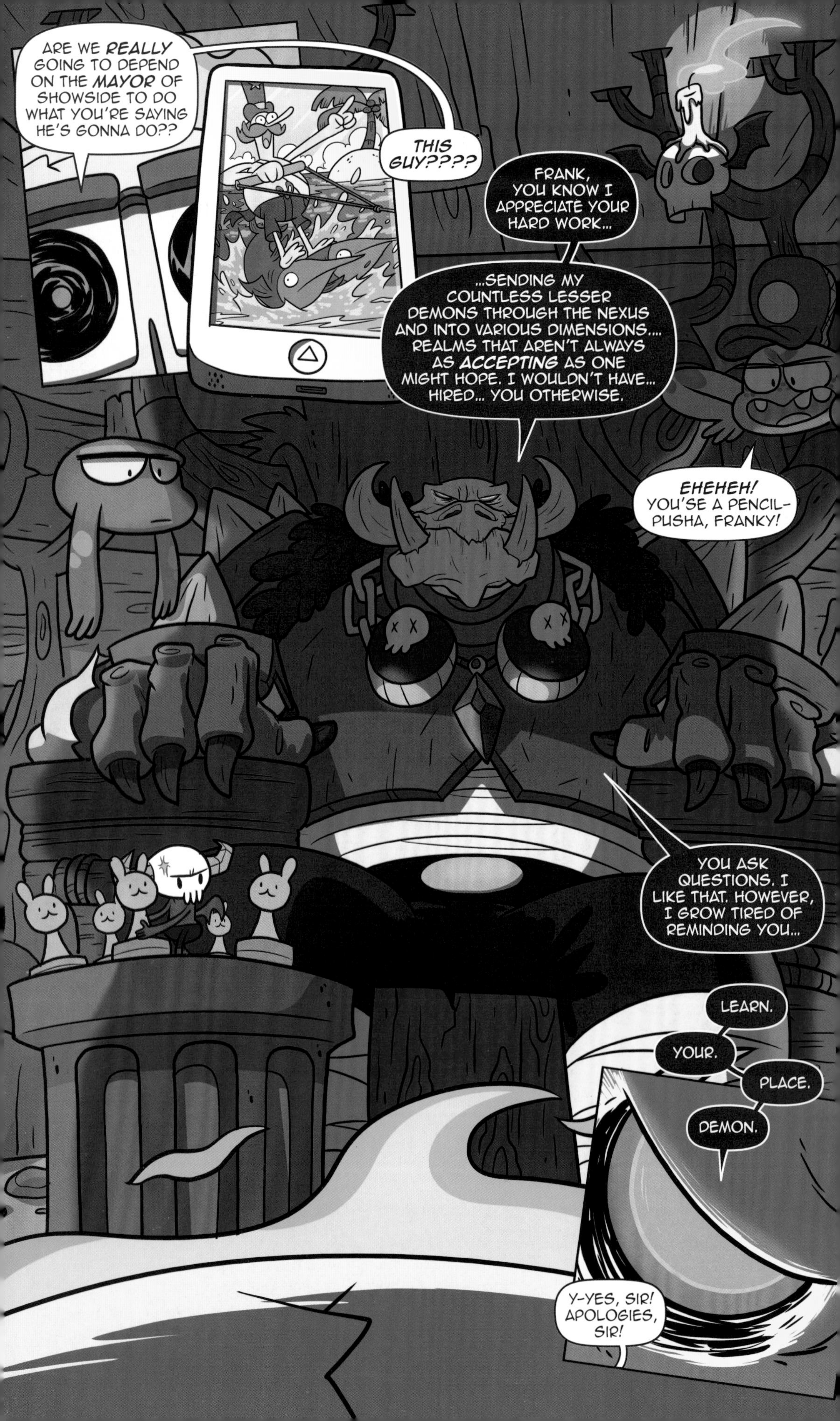
ARE WE REALLY GOING TO DEPEND ON THE MAYOR OF SHOWSIDE TO DO WHAT YOU'RE SAYING HE'S GONNA DO??
THIS GUY????
FRANK, YOU KNOW I APPRECIATE YOUR HARD WORK...
...SENDING MY COUNTLESS LESSER DEMONS THROUGH THE NEXUS AND INTO VARIOUS DIMENSIONS.... REALMS THAT AREN'T ALWAYS AS ACCEPTING AS ONE MIGHT HOPE. I WOULDN'T HAVE... HIRED... YOU OTHERWISE.
EHEHEH! YOU'SE A PENCIL-PUSHA, FRANKY!
YOU ASK QUESTIONS. I LIKE THAT. HOWEVER, I GROW TIRED OF REMINDING YOU...
LEARN.
YOUR.
PLACE.
DEMON.
Y-YES, SIR! APOLOGIES, SIR!

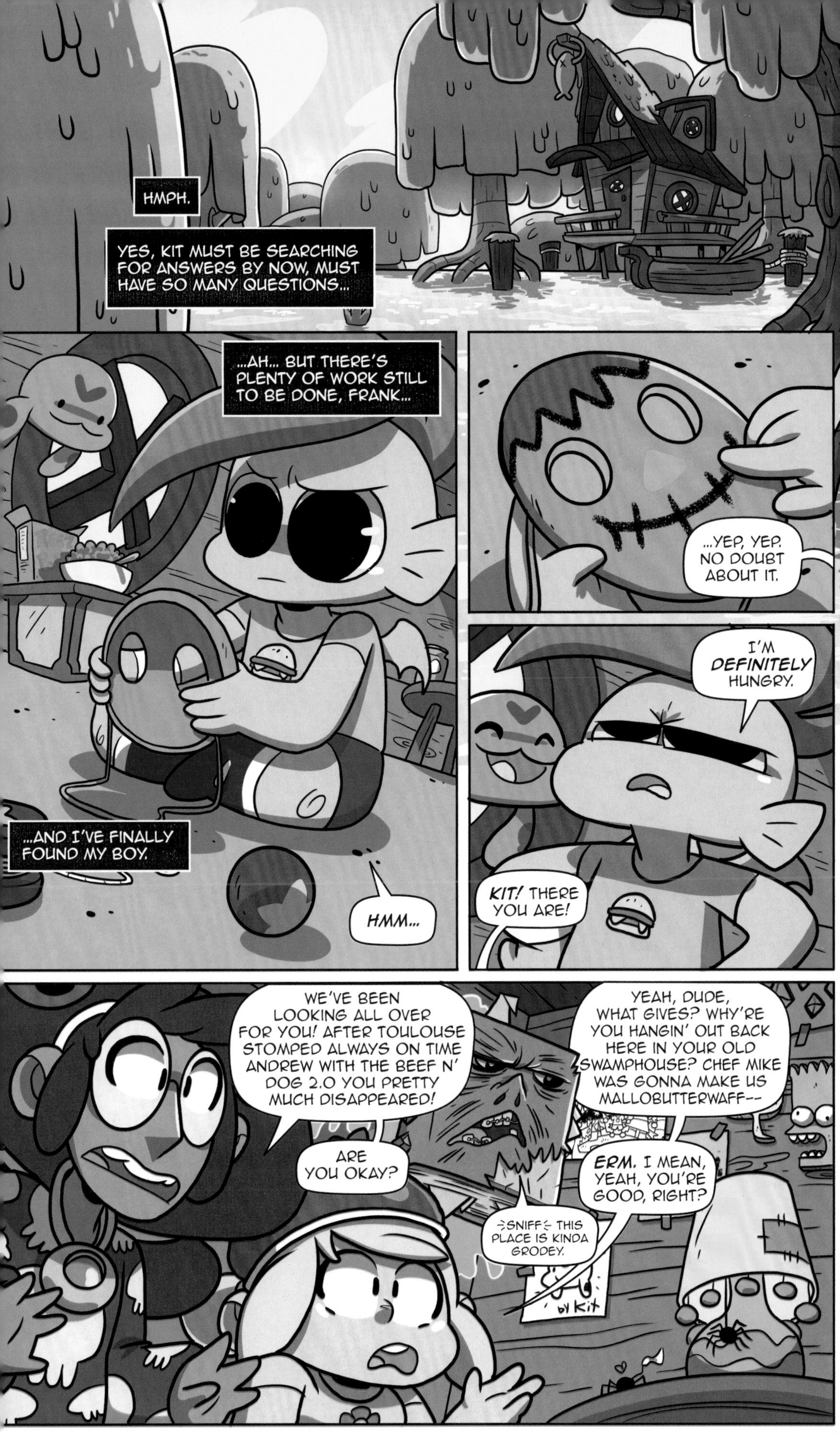
HMPH.
YES, KIT MUST BE SEARCHING FOR ANSWERS BY NOW, MUST HAVE SO MANY QUESTIONS...
...AH... BUT THERE'S PLENTY OF WORK STILL TO BE DONE, FRANK...
...AND I'VE FINALLY FOUND MY BOY.
HMM...
...YEP, YEP. NO DOUBT ABOUT IT.
I'M DEFINITELY HUNGRY.
KIT! THERE YOU ARE!
WE'VE BEEN LOOKING ALL OVER FOR YOU! AFTER TOULOUSE STOMPED ALWAYS ON TIME ANDREW WITH THE BEEF N' DOG 2.0 YOU PRETTY MUCH DISAPPEARED!
ARE YOU OKAY?
YEAH, DUDE, WHAT GIVES? WHY'RE YOU HANGIN' OUT BACK HERE IN YOUR OLD SWAMPHOUSE? CHEF MIKE WAS GONNA MAKE US MALLOBUTTERWAFF--
ERM. I MEAN, YEAH, YOU'RE GOOD, RIGHT?
≈SNIFF≈ THIS PLACE IS KINDA GRODEY.
by Kit

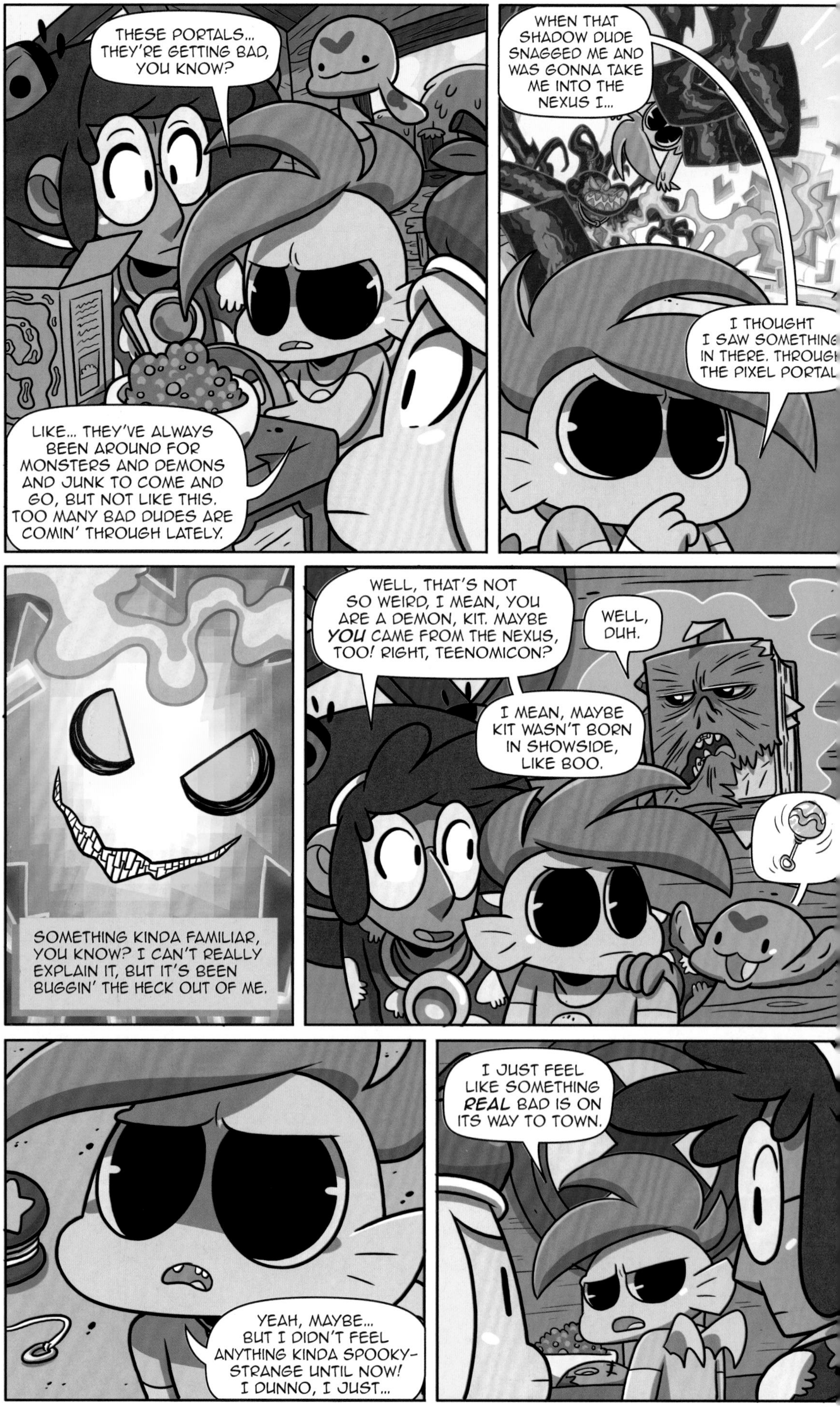
THESE PORTALS... THEY'RE GETTING BAD, YOU KNOW?
LIKE... THEY'VE ALWAYS BEEN AROUND FOR MONSTERS AND DEMONS AND JUNK TO COME AND GO, BUT NOT LIKE THIS. TOO MANY BAD DUDES ARE COMIN' THROUGH LATELY.
WHEN THAT SHADOW DUDE SNAGGED ME AND WAS GONNA TAKE ME INTO THE NEXUS I...
I THOUGHT I SAW SOMETHING IN THERE. THROUGH THE PIXEL PORTAL
SOMETHING KINDA FAMILIAR, YOU KNOW? I CAN'T REALLY EXPLAIN IT, BUT IT'S BEEN BUGGIN' THE HECK OUT OF ME.
WELL, THAT'S NOT SO WEIRD, I MEAN, YOU ARE A DEMON, KIT. MAYBE *YOU* CAME FROM THE NEXUS, TOO! RIGHT, TEENOMICON?
WELL, DUH.
I MEAN, MAYBE KIT WASN'T BORN IN SHOWSIDE, LIKE BOO.
YEAH, MAYBE... BUT I DIDN'T FEEL ANYTHING KINDA SPOOKY-STRANGE UNTIL NOW! I DUNNO, I JUST...
I JUST FEEL LIKE SOMETHING *REAL* BAD IS ON ITS WAY TO TOWN.

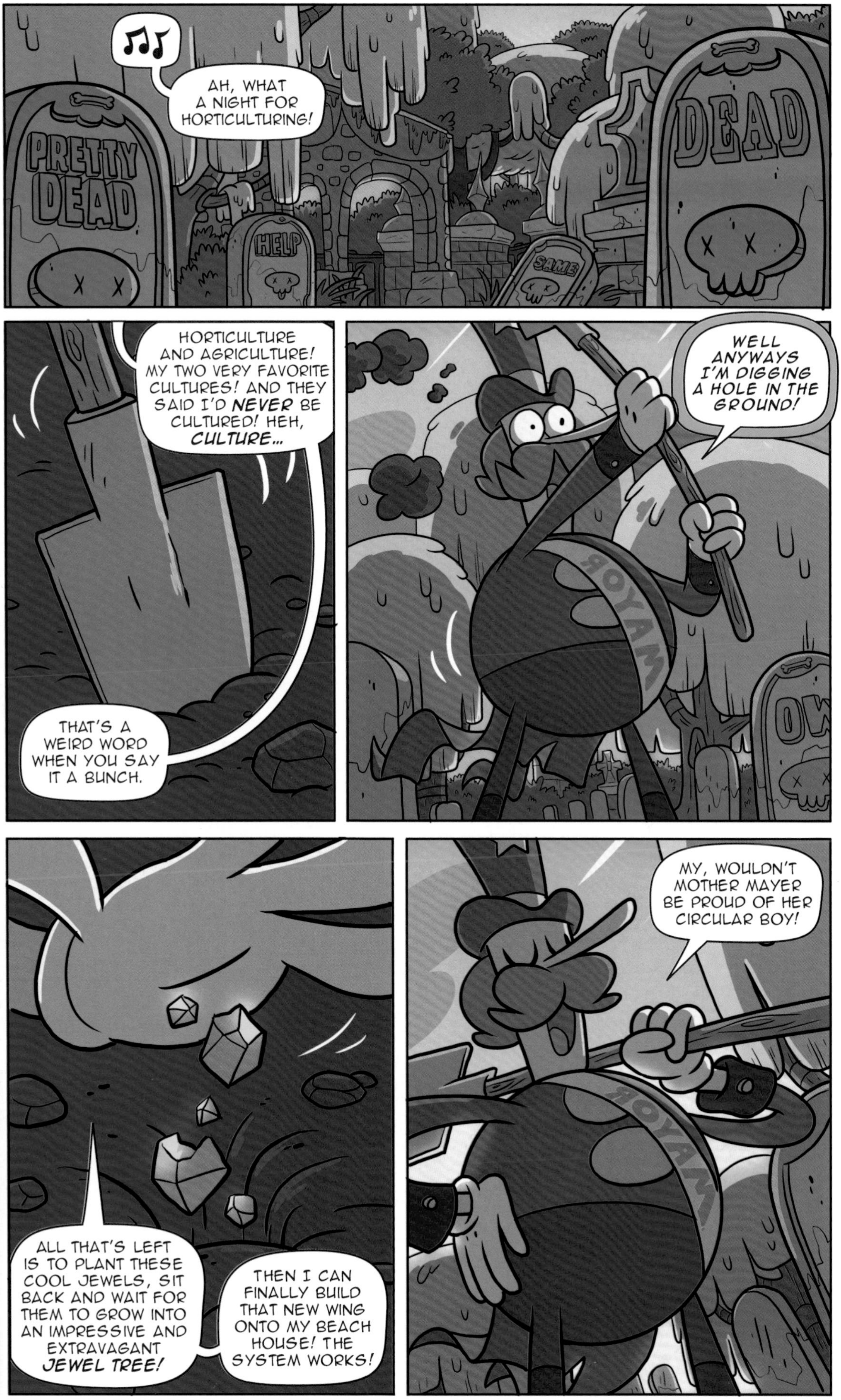
♫♪
AH, WHAT A NIGHT FOR HORTICULTURING!
PRETTY DEAD
HELP
SAME
DEAD
HORTICULTURE AND AGRICULTURE! MY TWO VERY FAVORITE CULTURES! AND THEY SAID I'D **NEVER** BE CULTURED! HEH, ***CULTURE...***
THAT'S A WEIRD WORD WHEN YOU SAY IT A BUNCH.
WELL ANYWAYS I'M DIGGING A HOLE IN THE GROUND!
MAYOR
OW
ALL THAT'S LEFT IS TO PLANT THESE COOL JEWELS, SIT BACK AND WAIT FOR THEM TO GROW INTO AN IMPRESSIVE AND EXTRAVAGANT ***JEWEL TREE!***
THEN I CAN FINALLY BUILD THAT NEW WING ONTO MY BEACH HOUSE! THE SYSTEM WORKS!
MY, WOULDN'T MOTHER MAYER BE PROUD OF HER CIRCULAR BOY!
MAYOR

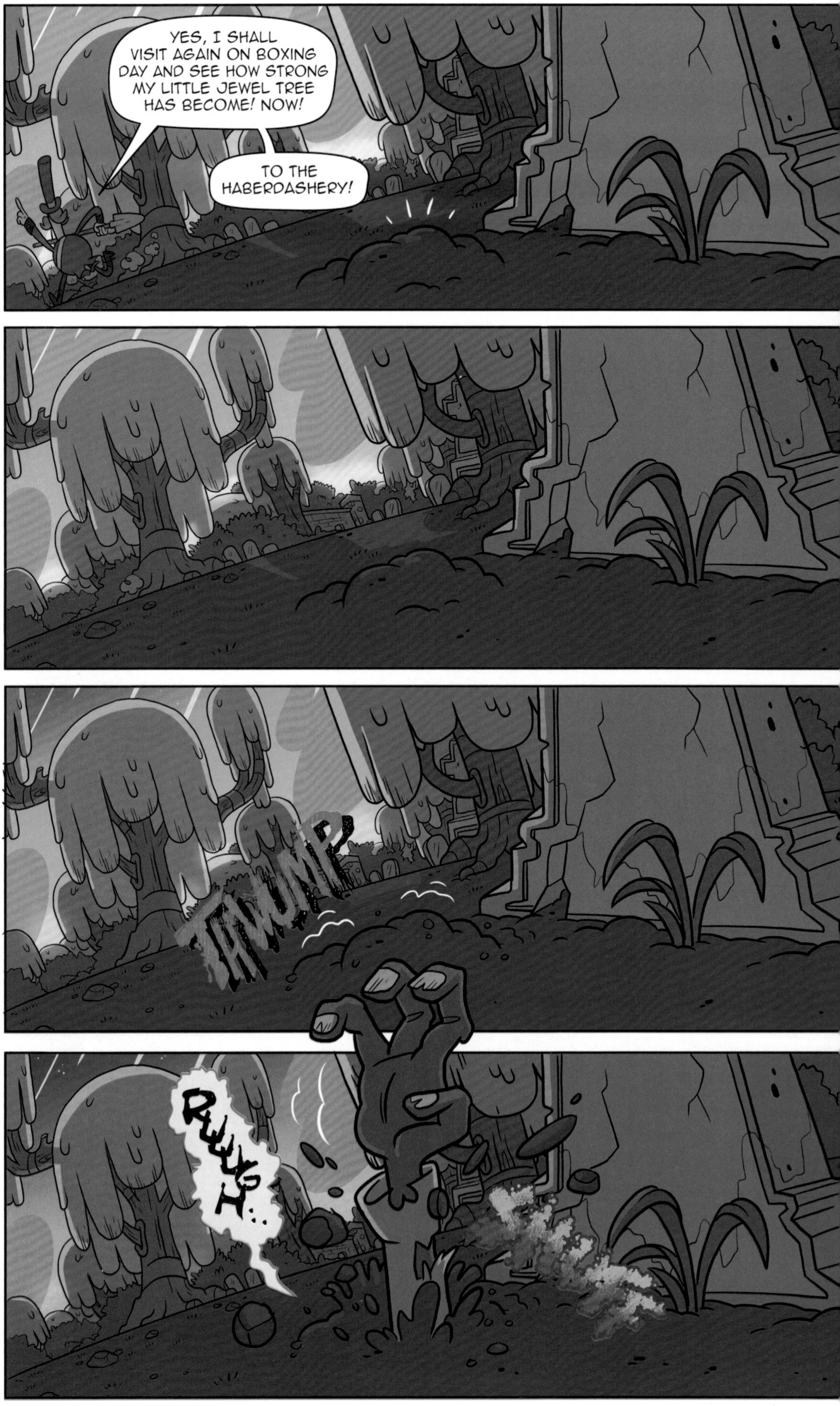
YES, I SHALL VISIT AGAIN ON BOXING DAY AND SEE HOW STRONG MY LITTLE JEWEL TREE HAS BECOME! NOW!
TO THE HABERDASHERY!
THUMP
RUUUGH...

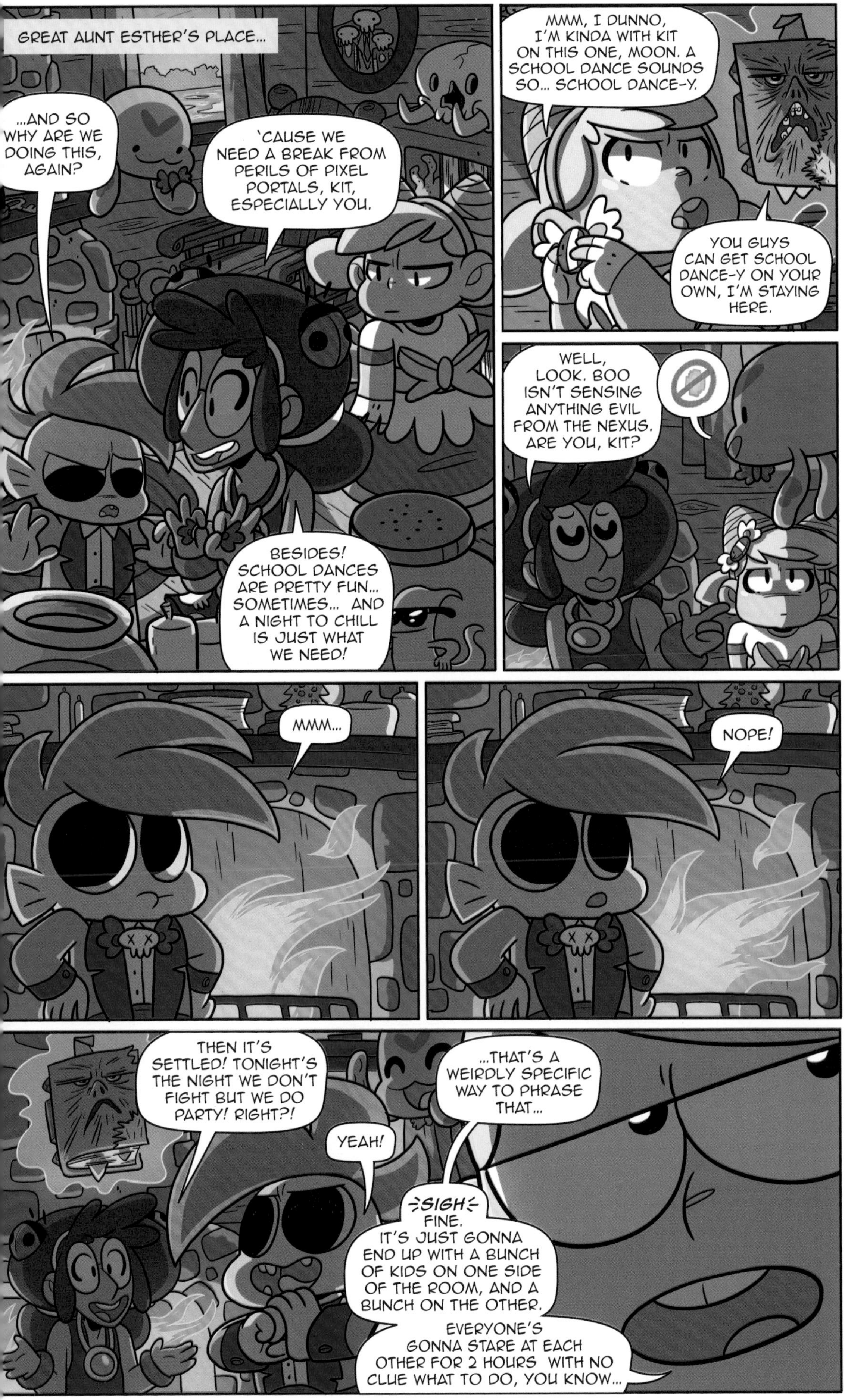
GREAT AUNT ESTHER'S PLACE...
...AND SO WHY ARE WE DOING THIS, AGAIN?
'CAUSE WE NEED A BREAK FROM PERILS OF PIXEL PORTALS, KIT, ESPECIALLY YOU.
BESIDES! SCHOOL DANCES ARE PRETTY FUN... SOMETIMES... AND A NIGHT TO CHILL IS JUST WHAT WE NEED!
MMM, I DUNNO, I'M KINDA WITH KIT ON THIS ONE, MOON. A SCHOOL DANCE SOUNDS SO... SCHOOL DANCE-Y.
YOU GUYS CAN GET SCHOOL DANCE-Y ON YOUR OWN, I'M STAYING HERE.
WELL, LOOK. BOO ISN'T SENSING ANYTHING EVIL FROM THE NEXUS. ARE YOU, KIT?
MMM...
NOPE!
THEN IT'S SETTLED! TONIGHT'S THE NIGHT WE DON'T FIGHT BUT WE DO PARTY! RIGHT?!
YEAH!
...THAT'S A WEIRDLY SPECIFIC WAY TO PHRASE THAT...
SIGH
FINE. IT'S JUST GONNA END UP WITH A BUNCH OF KIDS ON ONE SIDE OF THE ROOM, AND A BUNCH ON THE OTHER.
EVERYONE'S GONNA STARE AT EACH OTHER FOR 2 HOURS WITH NO CLUE WHAT TO DO, YOU KNOW...

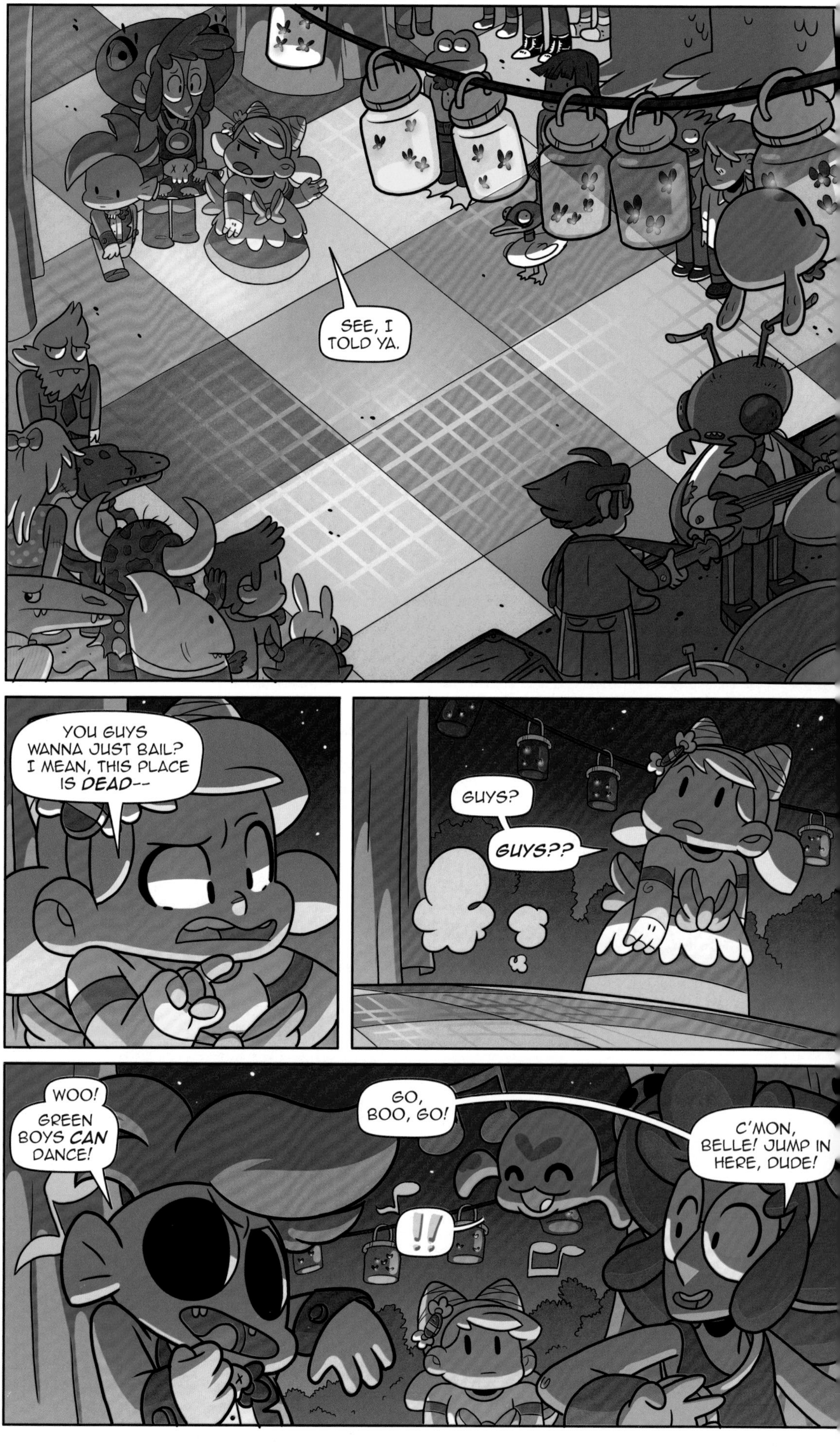
SEE, I TOLD YA.
YOU GUYS WANNA JUST BAIL? I MEAN, THIS PLACE IS *DEAD*--
GUYS?
GUYS??
WOO!
GREEN BOYS *CAN* DANCE!
GO, BOO, GO!
C'MON, BELLE! JUMP IN HERE, DUDE!
!!

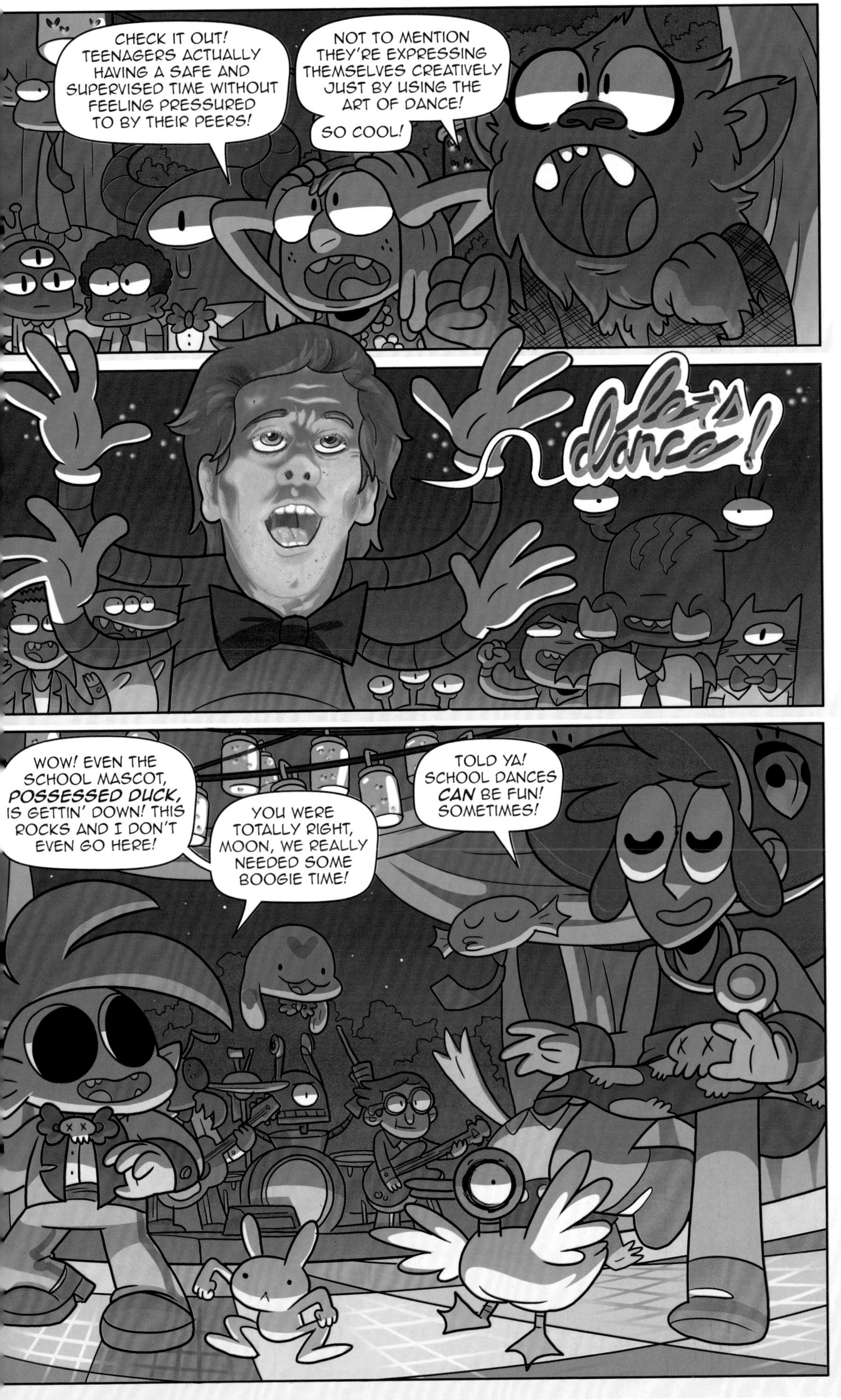
CHECK IT OUT! TEENAGERS ACTUALLY HAVING A SAFE AND SUPERVISED TIME WITHOUT FEELING PRESSURED TO BY THEIR PEERS!
NOT TO MENTION THEY'RE EXPRESSING THEMSELVES CREATIVELY JUST BY USING THE ART OF DANCE!
SO COOL!
let's dance!
WOW! EVEN THE SCHOOL MASCOT, POSSESSED DUCK, IS GETTIN' DOWN! THIS ROCKS AND I DON'T EVEN GO HERE!
YOU WERE TOTALLY RIGHT, MOON, WE REALLY NEEDED SOME BOOGIE TIME!
TOLD YA! SCHOOL DANCES CAN BE FUN! SOMETIMES!

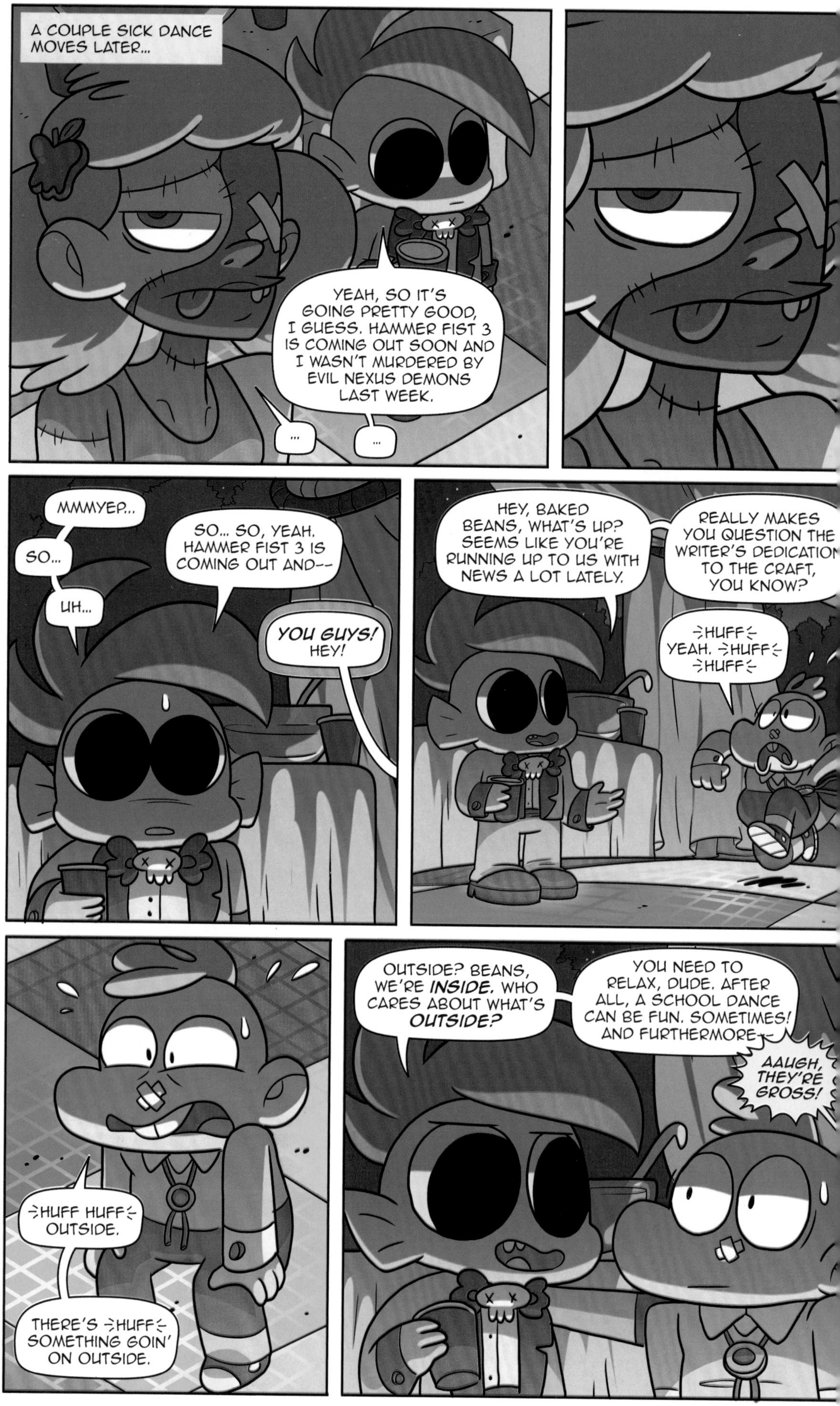
A COUPLE SICK DANCE MOVES LATER...
YEAH, SO IT'S GOING PRETTY GOOD, I GUESS. HAMMER FIST 3 IS COMING OUT SOON AND I WASN'T MURDERED BY EVIL NEXUS DEMONS LAST WEEK.
...
...
MMMYEP...
SO...
UH...
SO... SO, YEAH. HAMMER FIST 3 IS COMING OUT AND--
YOU GUYS! HEY!
HEY, BAKED BEANS, WHAT'S UP? SEEMS LIKE YOU'RE RUNNING UP TO US WITH NEWS A LOT LATELY.
REALLY MAKES YOU QUESTION THE WRITER'S DEDICATION TO THE CRAFT, YOU KNOW?
HUFF YEAH. HUFF HUFF
HUFF HUFF OUTSIDE.
THERE'S HUFF SOMETHING GOIN' ON OUTSIDE.
OUTSIDE? BEANS, WE'RE *INSIDE.* WHO CARES ABOUT WHAT'S *OUTSIDE?*
YOU NEED TO RELAX, DUDE. AFTER ALL, A SCHOOL DANCE CAN BE FUN. SOMETIMES! AND FURTHERMORE--
AAUGH, THEY'RE GROSS!

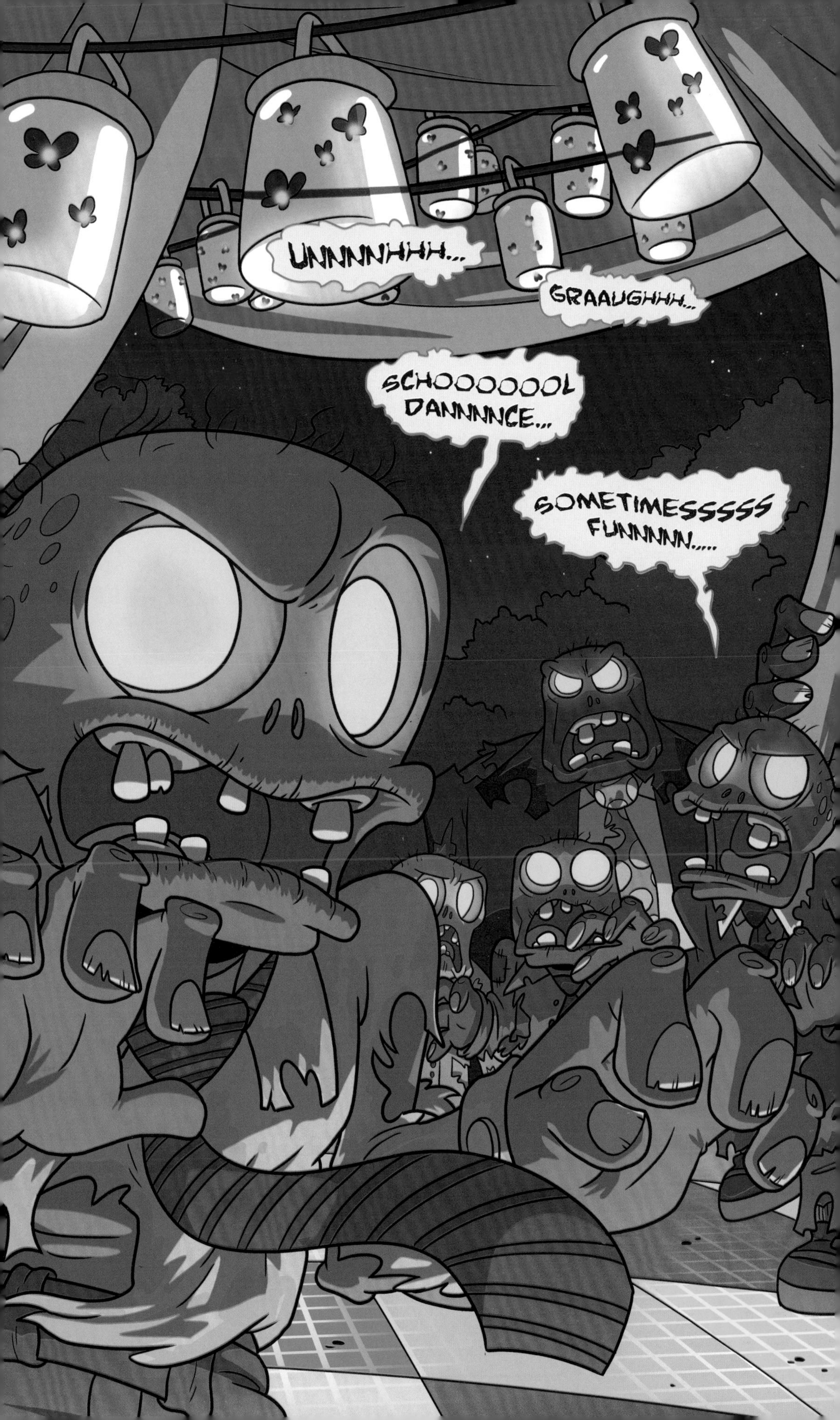
UNNNNHHH...
GRAAUGHHH...
SCHOOOOOOL DANNNNCE...
SOMETIMESSSSS FUNNNNN.....

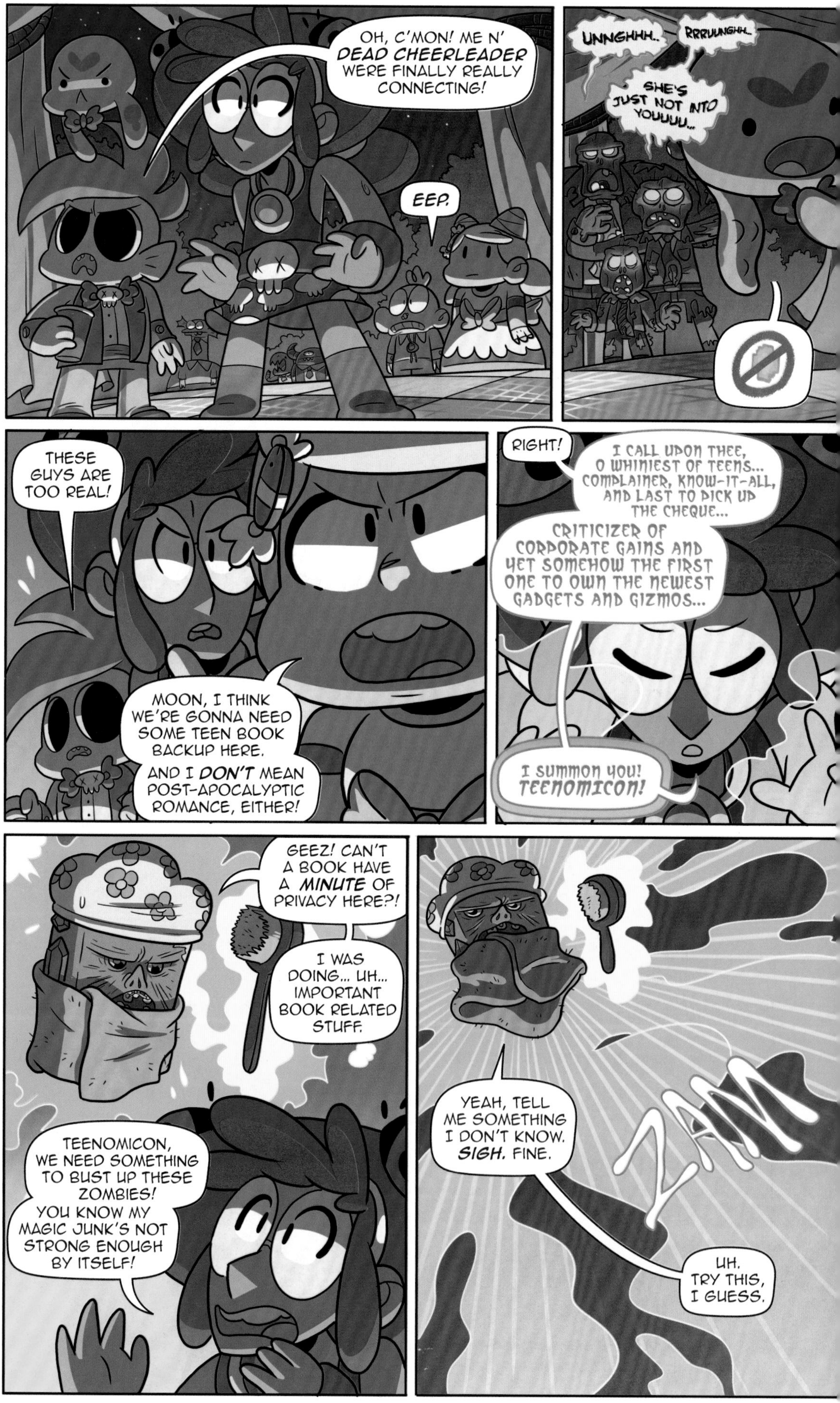
OH, C'MON! ME N' DEAD CHEERLEADER WERE FINALLY REALLY CONNECTING!
EEP.
UNNGHHH..
RRRUUNGHH..
SHE'S JUST NOT INTO YOUUUU...
THESE GUYS ARE TOO REAL!
MOON, I THINK WE'RE GONNA NEED SOME TEEN BOOK BACKUP HERE.
AND I DON'T MEAN POST-APOCALYPTIC ROMANCE, EITHER!
RIGHT!
I CALL UPON THEE, O WHINIEST OF TEENS... COMPLAINER, KNOW-IT-ALL, AND LAST TO PICK UP THE CHEQUE...
CRITICIZER OF CORPORATE GAINS AND YET SOMEHOW THE FIRST ONE TO OWN THE NEWEST GADGETS AND GIZMOS...
I SUMMON YOU! TEENOMICON!
GEEZ! CAN'T A BOOK HAVE A MINUTE OF PRIVACY HERE?!
I WAS DOING... UH... IMPORTANT BOOK RELATED STUFF.
TEENOMICON, WE NEED SOMETHING TO BUST UP THESE ZOMBIES!
YOU KNOW MY MAGIC JUNK'S NOT STRONG ENOUGH BY ITSELF!
YEAH, TELL ME SOMETHING I DON'T KNOW. SIGH. FINE.
ZAM
UH. TRY THIS, I GUESS.

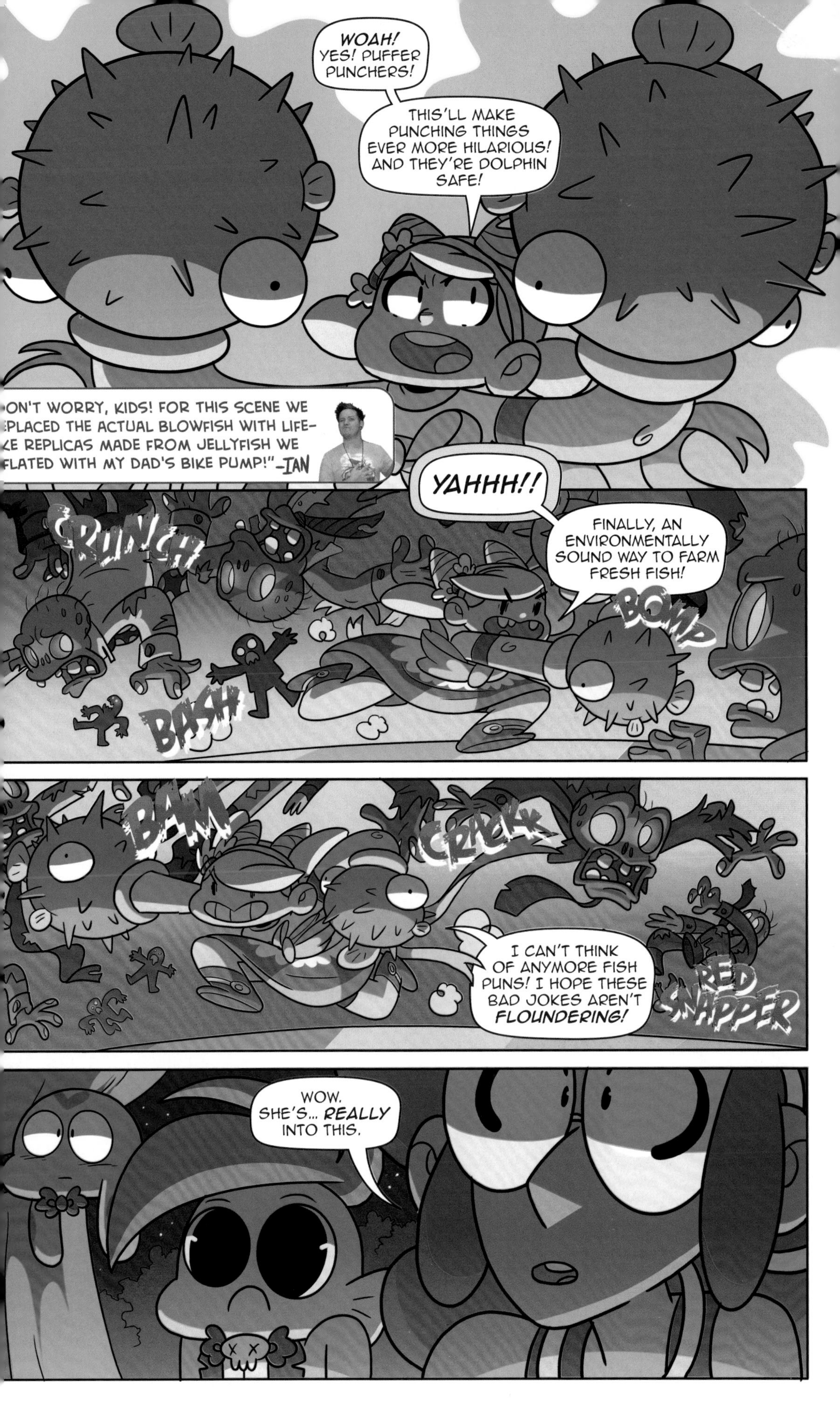
WOAH! YES! PUFFER PUNCHERS!
THIS'LL MAKE PUNCHING THINGS EVER MORE HILARIOUS! AND THEY'RE DOLPHIN SAFE!
ON'T WORRY, KIDS! FOR THIS SCENE WE EPLACED THE ACTUAL BLOWFISH WITH LIFE-KE REPLICAS MADE FROM JELLYFISH WE FLATED WITH MY DAD'S BIKE PUMP!" –IAN
YAHHH!!
FINALLY, AN ENVIRONMENTALLY SOUND WAY TO FARM FRESH FISH!
CRUNCH
BASH
BOMP
BAM
CRACKK
I CAN'T THINK OF ANYMORE FISH PUNS! I HOPE THESE BAD JOKES AREN'T FLOUNDERING!
RED SNAPPER
WOW. SHE'S... REALLY INTO THIS.

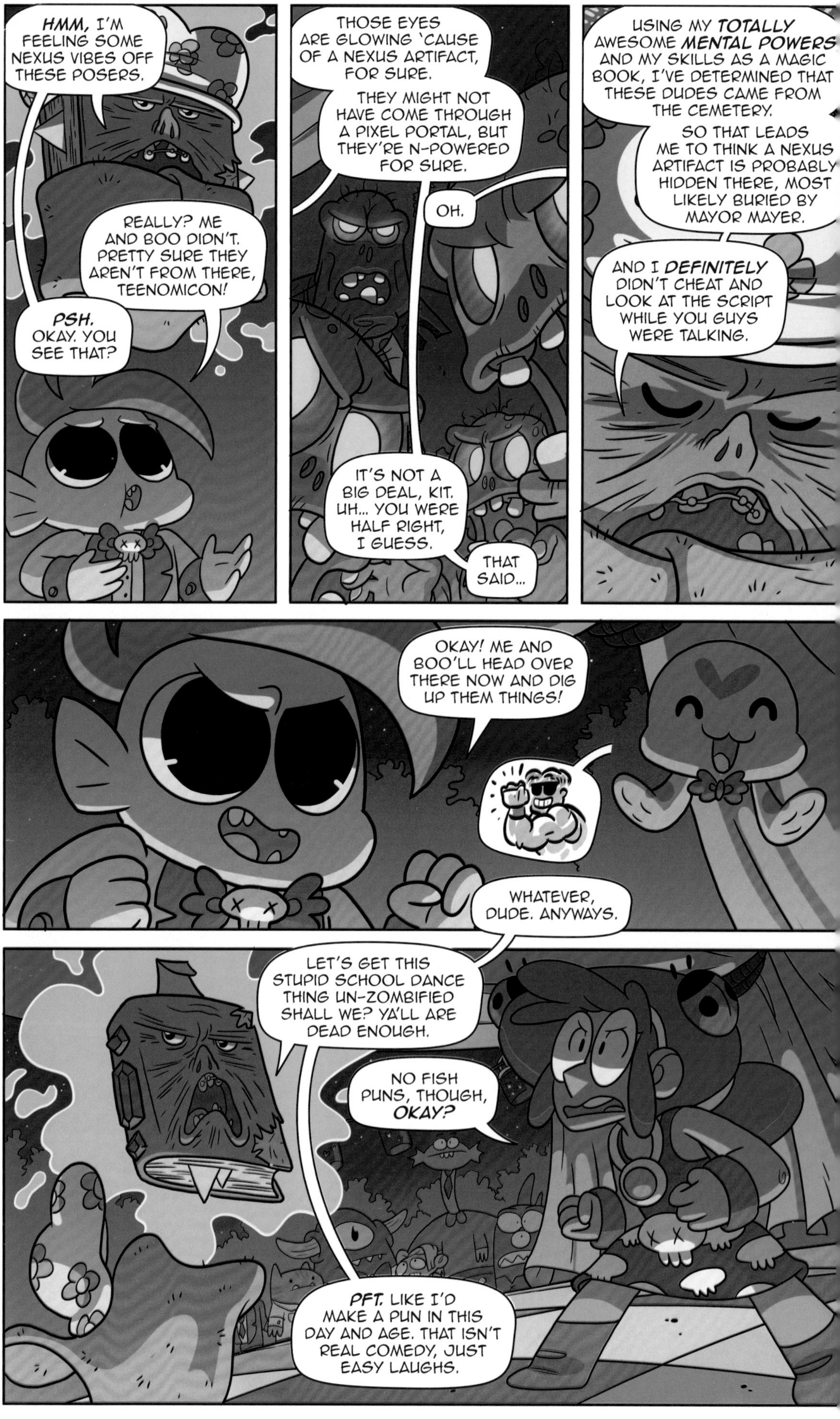
HMM, I'M FEELING SOME NEXUS VIBES OFF THESE POSERS.
REALLY? ME AND BOO DIDN'T. PRETTY SURE THEY AREN'T FROM THERE, TEENOMICON!
PSH. OKAY. YOU SEE THAT?
THOSE EYES ARE GLOWING 'CAUSE OF A NEXUS ARTIFACT, FOR SURE.
THEY MIGHT NOT HAVE COME THROUGH A PIXEL PORTAL, BUT THEY'RE N-POWERED FOR SURE.
OH.
IT'S NOT A BIG DEAL, KIT. UH... YOU WERE HALF RIGHT, I GUESS.
THAT SAID...
USING MY TOTALLY AWESOME MENTAL POWERS AND MY SKILLS AS A MAGIC BOOK, I'VE DETERMINED THAT THESE DUDES CAME FROM THE CEMETERY.
SO THAT LEADS ME TO THINK A NEXUS ARTIFACT IS PROBABLY HIDDEN THERE, MOST LIKELY BURIED BY MAYOR MAYER.
AND I DEFINITELY DIDN'T CHEAT AND LOOK AT THE SCRIPT WHILE YOU GUYS WERE TALKING.
OKAY! ME AND BOO'LL HEAD OVER THERE NOW AND DIG UP THEM THINGS!
WHATEVER, DUDE. ANYWAYS.
LET'S GET THIS STUPID SCHOOL DANCE THING UN-ZOMBIFIED SHALL WE? YA'LL ARE DEAD ENOUGH.
NO FISH PUNS, THOUGH, OKAY?
PFT. LIKE I'D MAKE A PUN IN THIS DAY AND AGE. THAT ISN'T REAL COMEDY, JUST EASY LAUGHS.

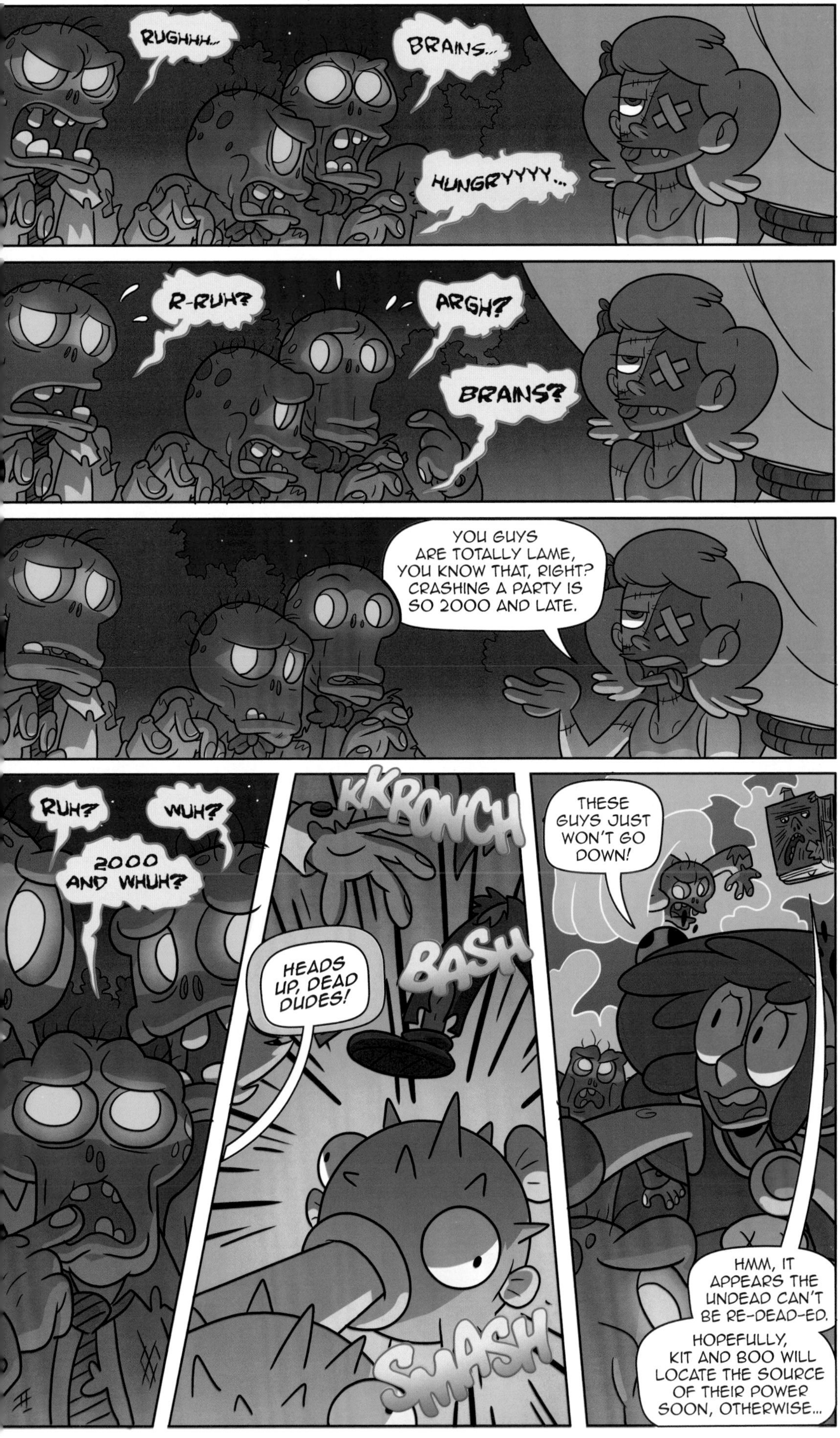
RUGHHH...
BRAINS...
HUNGRYYYY...
R-RUH?
ARGH?
BRAINS?
YOU GUYS ARE TOTALLY LAME, YOU KNOW THAT, RIGHT? CRASHING A PARTY IS SO 2000 AND LATE.
RUH?
WUH?
2000 AND WHUH?
KKRONCH
BASH
HEADS UP, DEAD DUDES!
SMASH
THESE GUYS JUST WON'T GO DOWN!
HMM, IT APPEARS THE UNDEAD CAN'T BE RE-DEAD-ED.
HOPEFULLY, KIT AND BOO WILL LOCATE THE SOURCE OF THEIR POWER SOON, OTHERWISE...

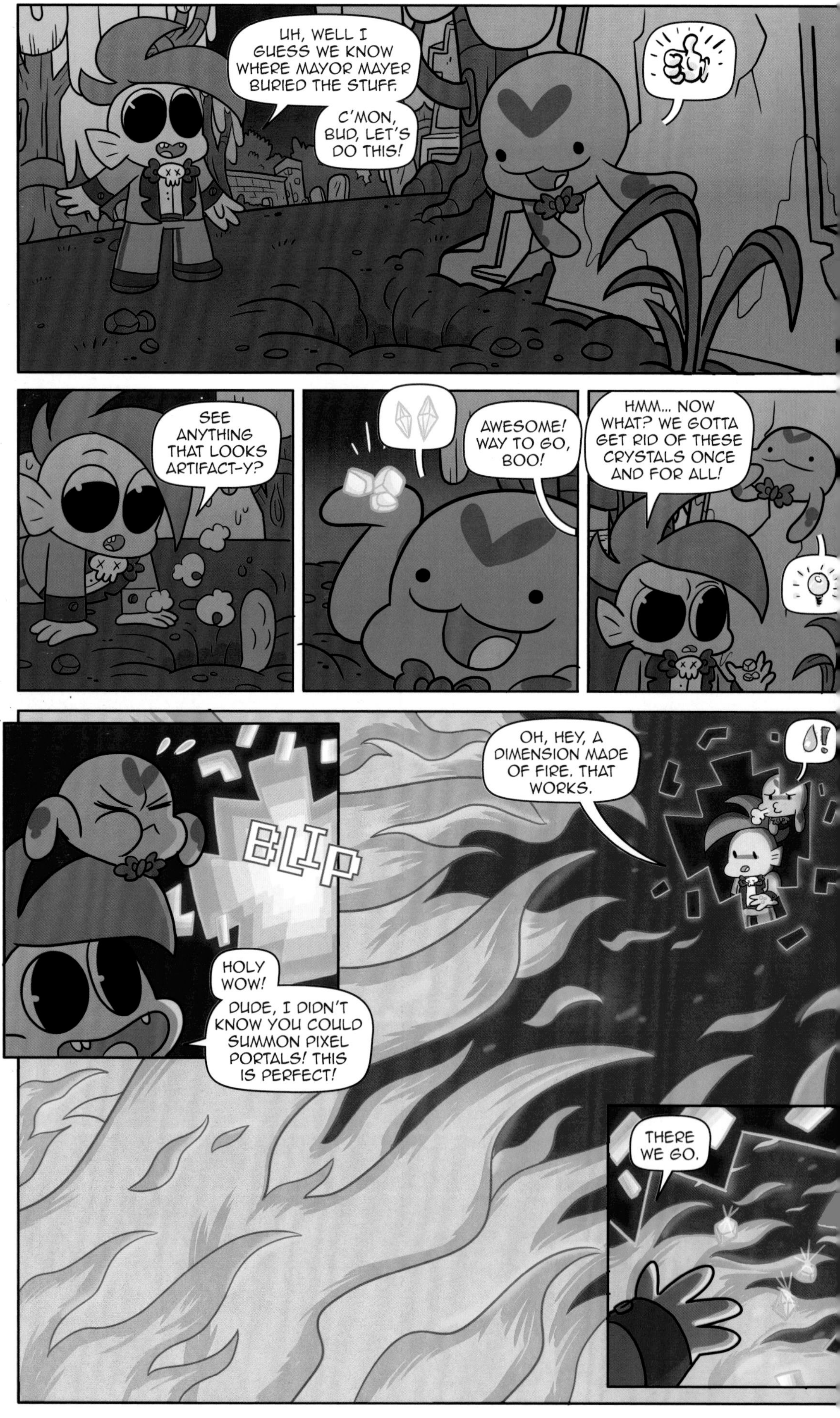
UH, WELL I GUESS WE KNOW WHERE MAYOR MAYER BURIED THE STUFF.
C'MON, BUD, LET'S DO THIS!
SEE ANYTHING THAT LOOKS ARTIFACT-Y?
AWESOME! WAY TO GO, BOO!
HMM... NOW WHAT? WE GOTTA GET RID OF THESE CRYSTALS ONCE AND FOR ALL!
BLIP
HOLY WOW!
DUDE, I DIDN'T KNOW YOU COULD SUMMON PIXEL PORTALS! THIS IS PERFECT!
OH, HEY, A DIMENSION MADE OF FIRE. THAT WORKS.
!
THERE WE GO.

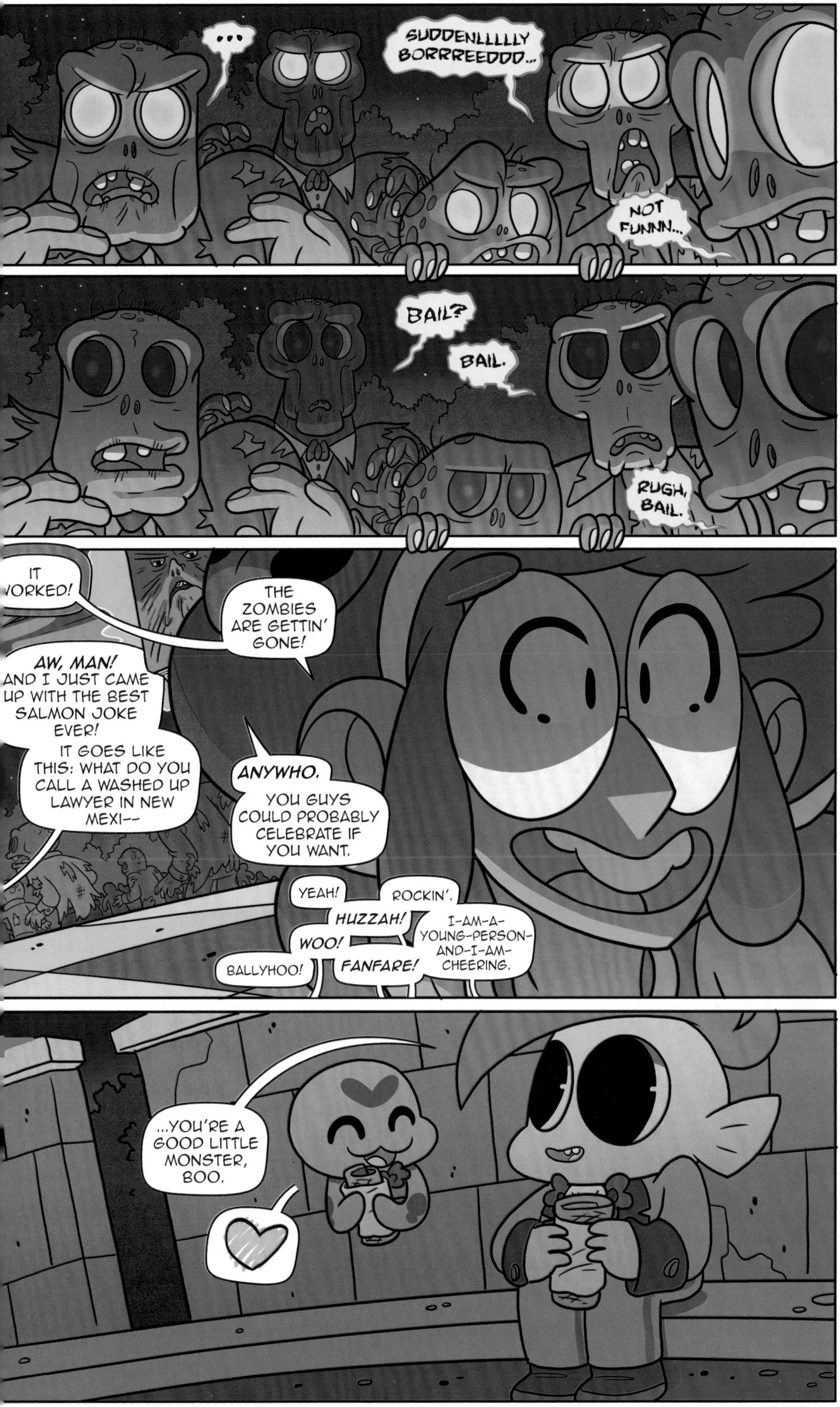
...
SUDDENLLLLLY BORRREEDDD...
NOT FUNNN...
BAIL?
BAIL.
RUGH, BAIL.
IT WORKED!
THE ZOMBIES ARE GETTIN' GONE!
AW, MAN! AND I JUST CAME UP WITH THE BEST SALMON JOKE EVER!
IT GOES LIKE THIS: WHAT DO YOU CALL A WASHED UP LAWYER IN NEW MEXI--
ANYWHO.
YOU GUYS COULD PROBABLY CELEBRATE IF YOU WANT.
YEAH!
ROCKIN'.
HUZZAH!
I-AM-A-YOUNG-PERSON-AND-I-AM-CHEERING.
WOO!
FANFARE!
BALLYHOO!
...YOU'RE A GOOD LITTLE MONSTER, BOO.

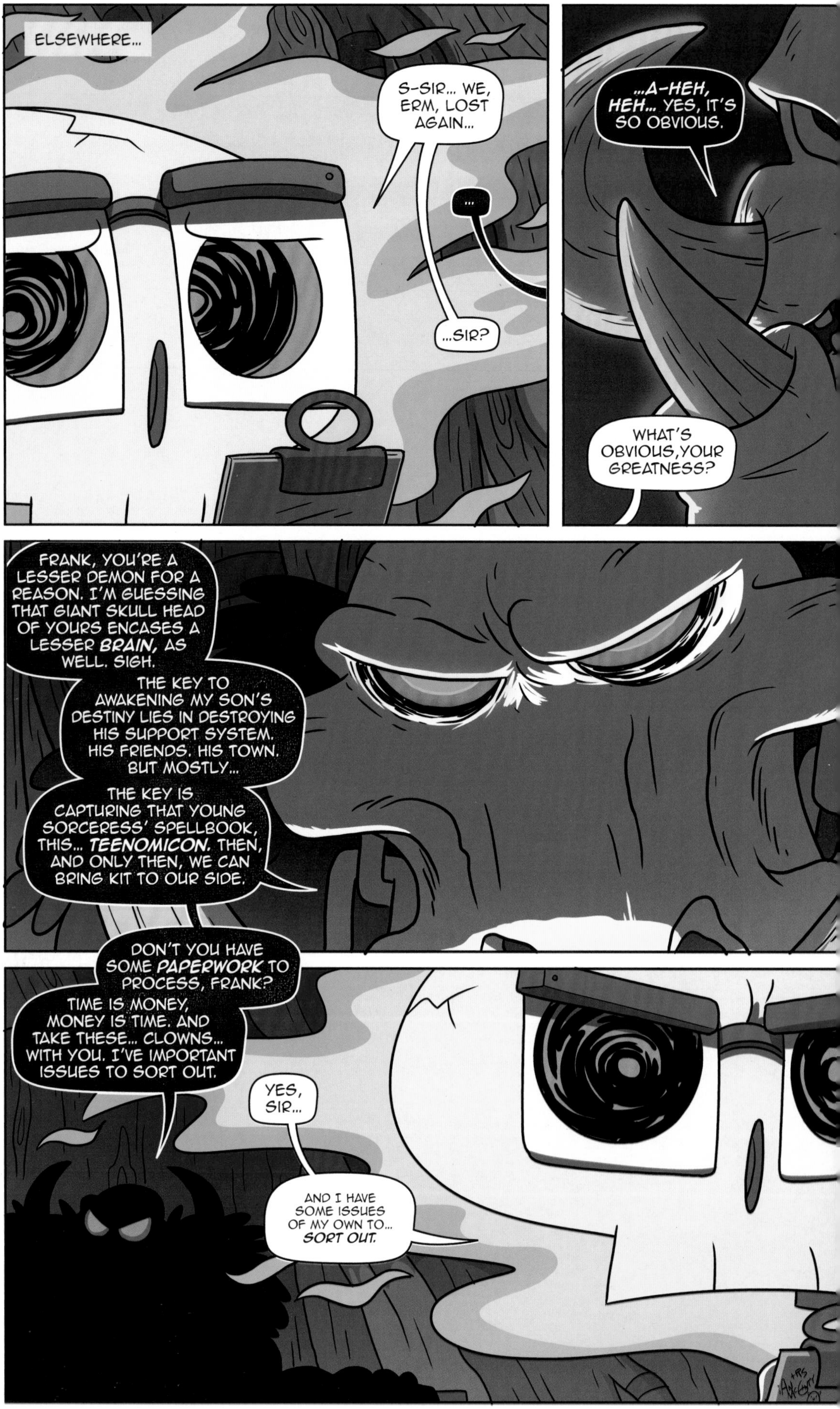
ELSEWHERE...
S-SIR... WE, ERM, LOST AGAIN...
...
...SIR?
...A-HEH, HEH... YES, IT'S SO OBVIOUS.
WHAT'S OBVIOUS,YOUR GREATNESS?
FRANK, YOU'RE A LESSER DEMON FOR A REASON. I'M GUESSING THAT GIANT SKULL HEAD OF YOURS ENCASES A LESSER BRAIN, AS WELL. SIGH.
THE KEY TO AWAKENING MY SON'S DESTINY LIES IN DESTROYING HIS SUPPORT SYSTEM. HIS FRIENDS. HIS TOWN. BUT MOSTLY...
THE KEY IS CAPTURING THAT YOUNG SORCERESS' SPELLBOOK, THIS... TEENOMICON. THEN, AND ONLY THEN, WE CAN BRING KIT TO OUR SIDE.
DON'T YOU HAVE SOME PAPERWORK TO PROCESS, FRANK?
TIME IS MONEY, MONEY IS TIME. AND TAKE THESE... CLOWNS... WITH YOU. I'VE IMPORTANT ISSUES TO SORT OUT.
YES, SIR...
AND I HAVE SOME ISSUES OF MY OWN TO... SORT OUT.

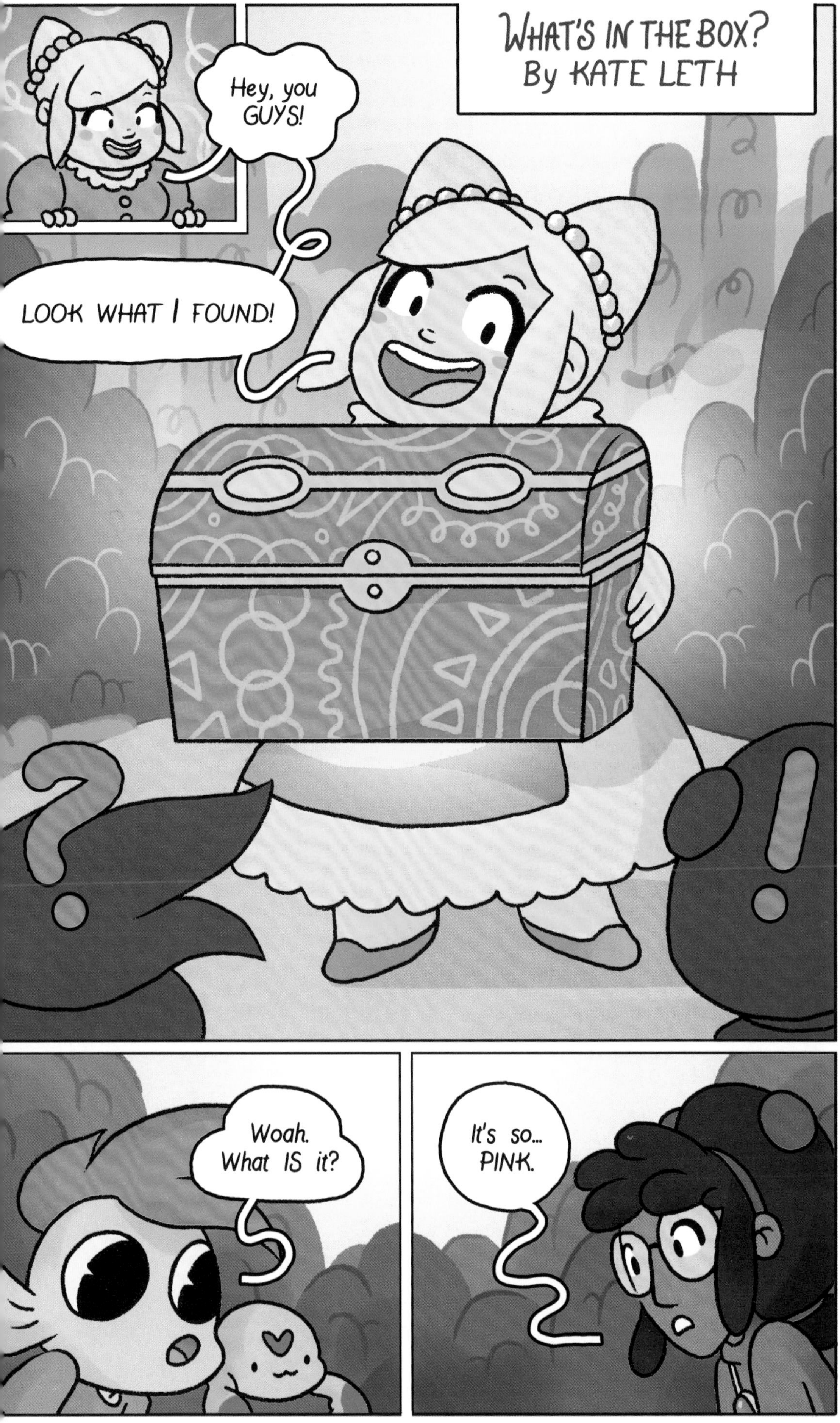
WHAT'S IN THE BOX?
By KATE LETH
Hey, you GUYS!
LOOK WHAT I FOUND!
Woah. What IS it?
It's so... PINK.

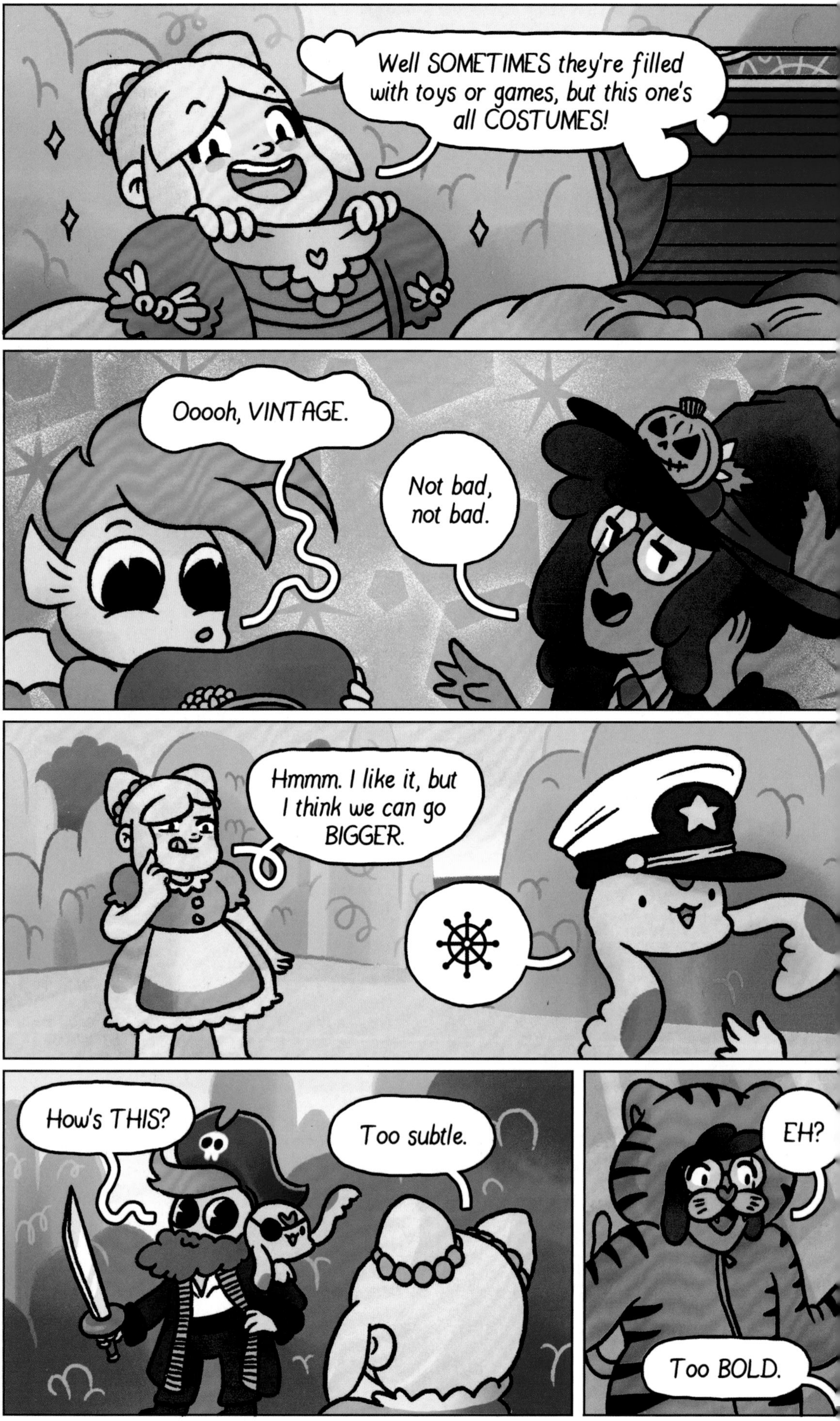

Well SOMETIMES they're filled with toys or games, but this one's all COSTUMES!
Ooooh, VINTAGE.
Not bad, not bad.
Hmmm. I like it, but I think we can go BIGGER.
How's THIS?
Too subtle.
EH?
Too BOLD.

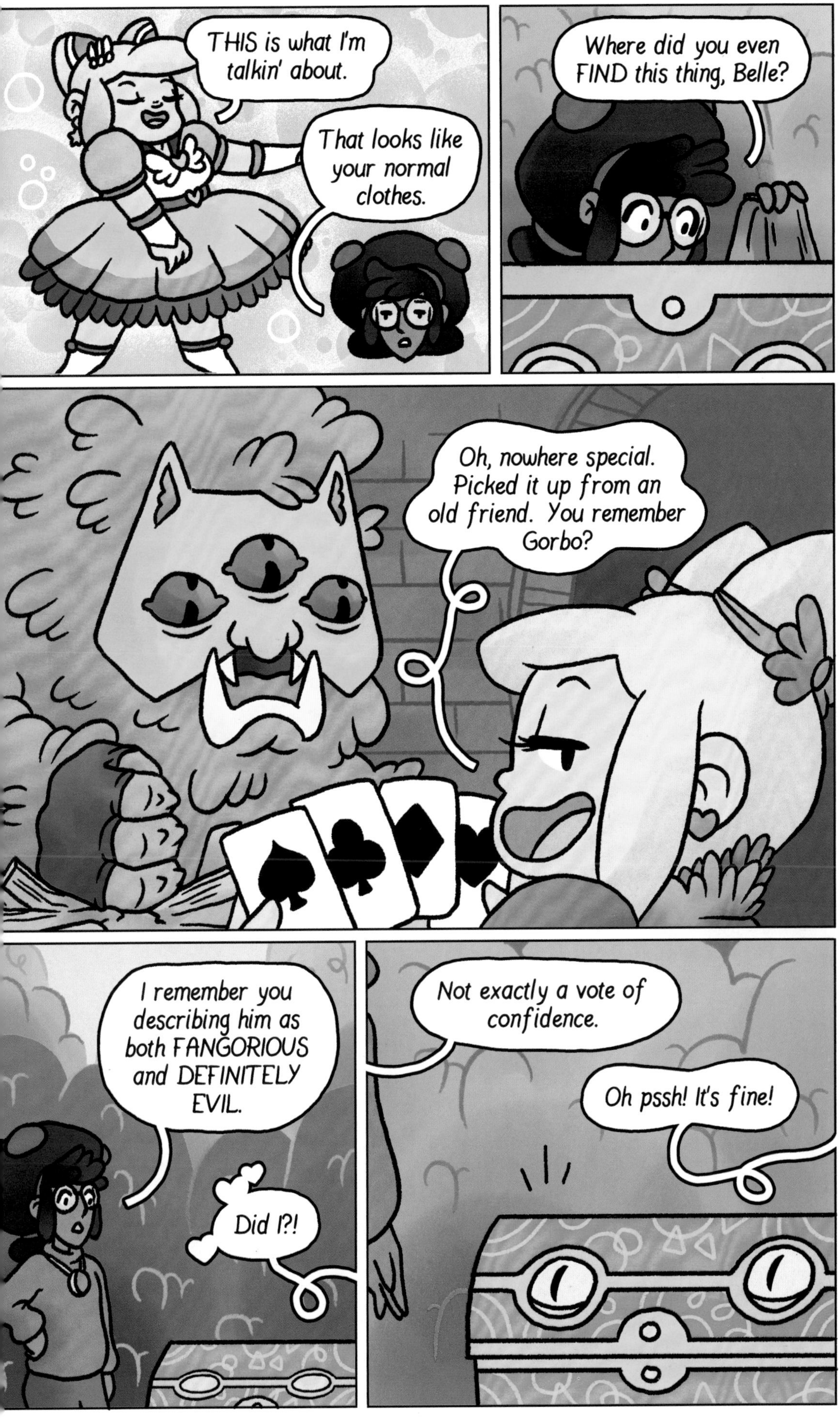
THIS is what I'm talkin' about.
That looks like your normal clothes.
Where did you even FIND this thing, Belle?
Oh, nowhere special. Picked it up from an old friend. You remember Gorbo?
I remember you describing him as both FANGORIOUS and DEFINITELY EVIL.
Did I?!
Not exactly a vote of confidence.
Oh pssh! It's fine!

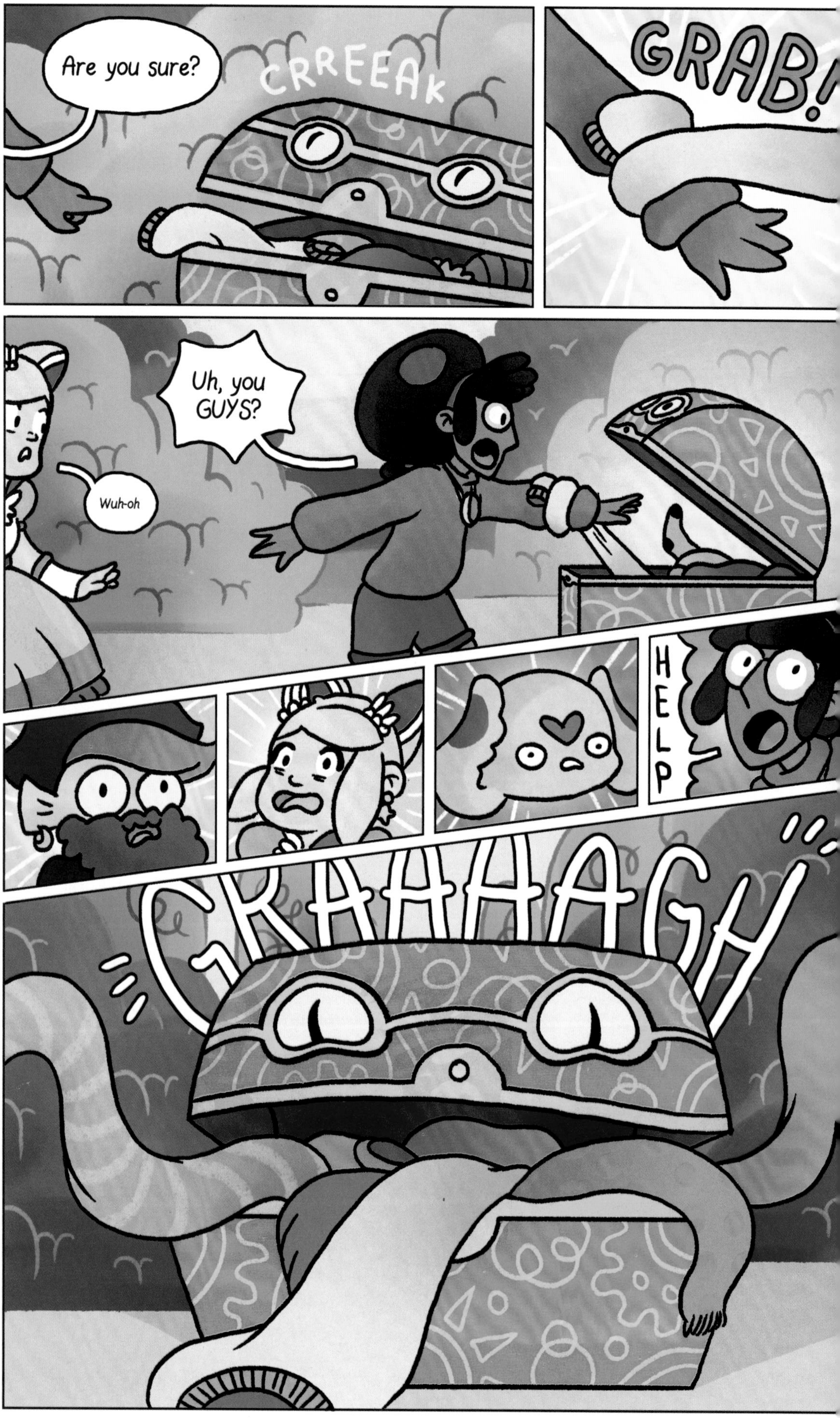
Are you sure?
CRREEAK
GRAB!
Uh, you GUYS?
Wuh-oh
HELP
GRAAHAGH

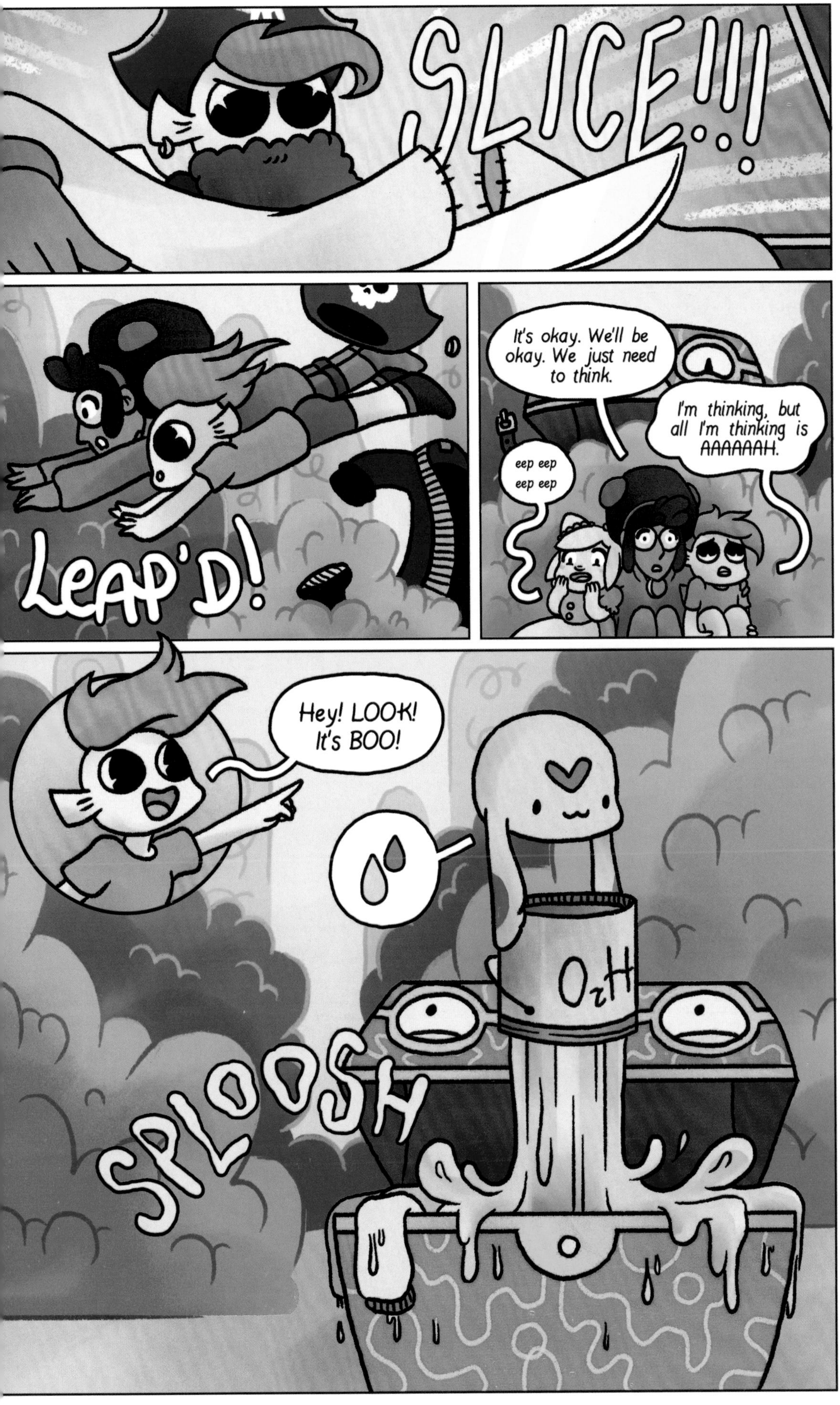
SLICE!!!
LEAP'D!
It's okay. We'll be okay. We just need to think.
I'm thinking, but all I'm thinking is AAAAAAH.
eep eep eep eep
Hey! LOOK! It's BOO!
SPLOOSH

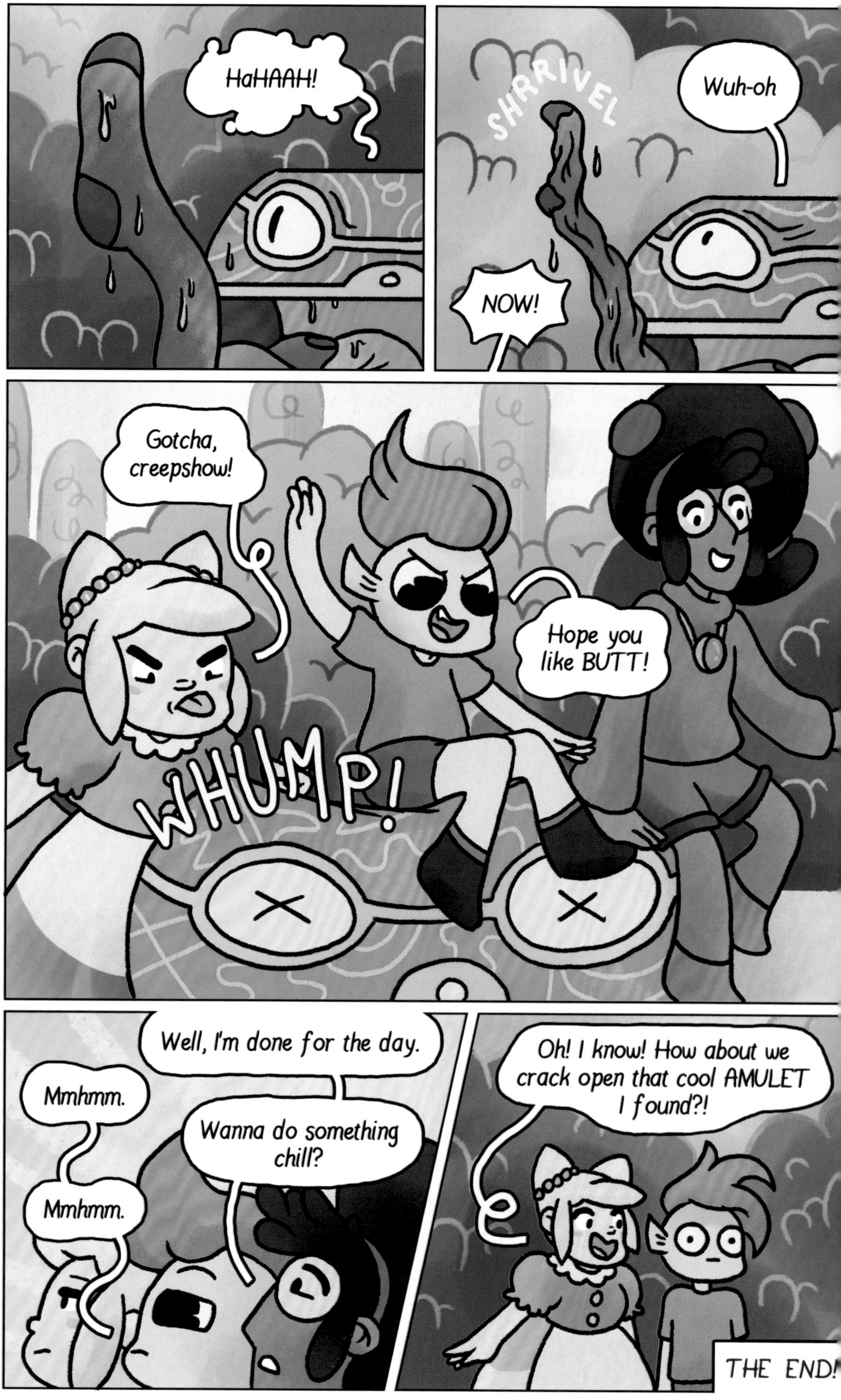
HaHAAH!
SHRRIVEL
Wuh-oh
NOW!
Gotcha, creepshow!
Hope you like BUTT!
WHUMP!
Well, I'm done for the day.
Mmhmm.
Wanna do something chill?
Mmhmm.
Oh! I know! How about we crack open that cool AMULET I found?!
THE END!

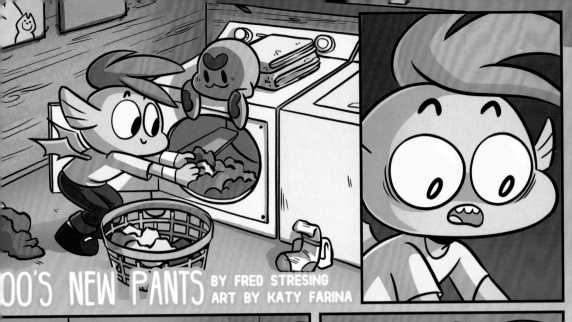

OO'S NEW PANTS BY FRED STRESING
ART BY KATY FARINA

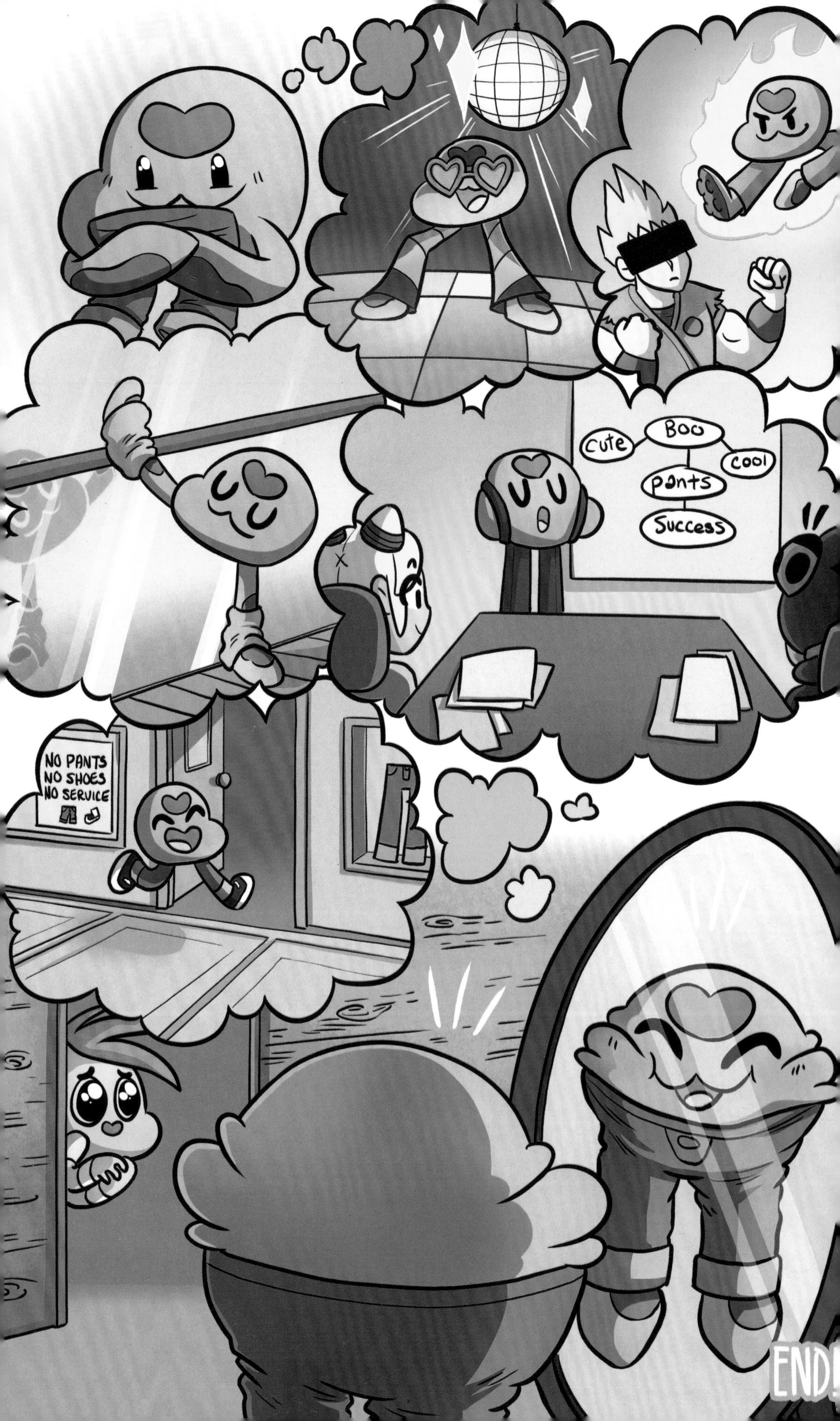
Cute
Boo
cool
pants
Success
NO PANTS
NO SHOES
NO SERVICE
END!

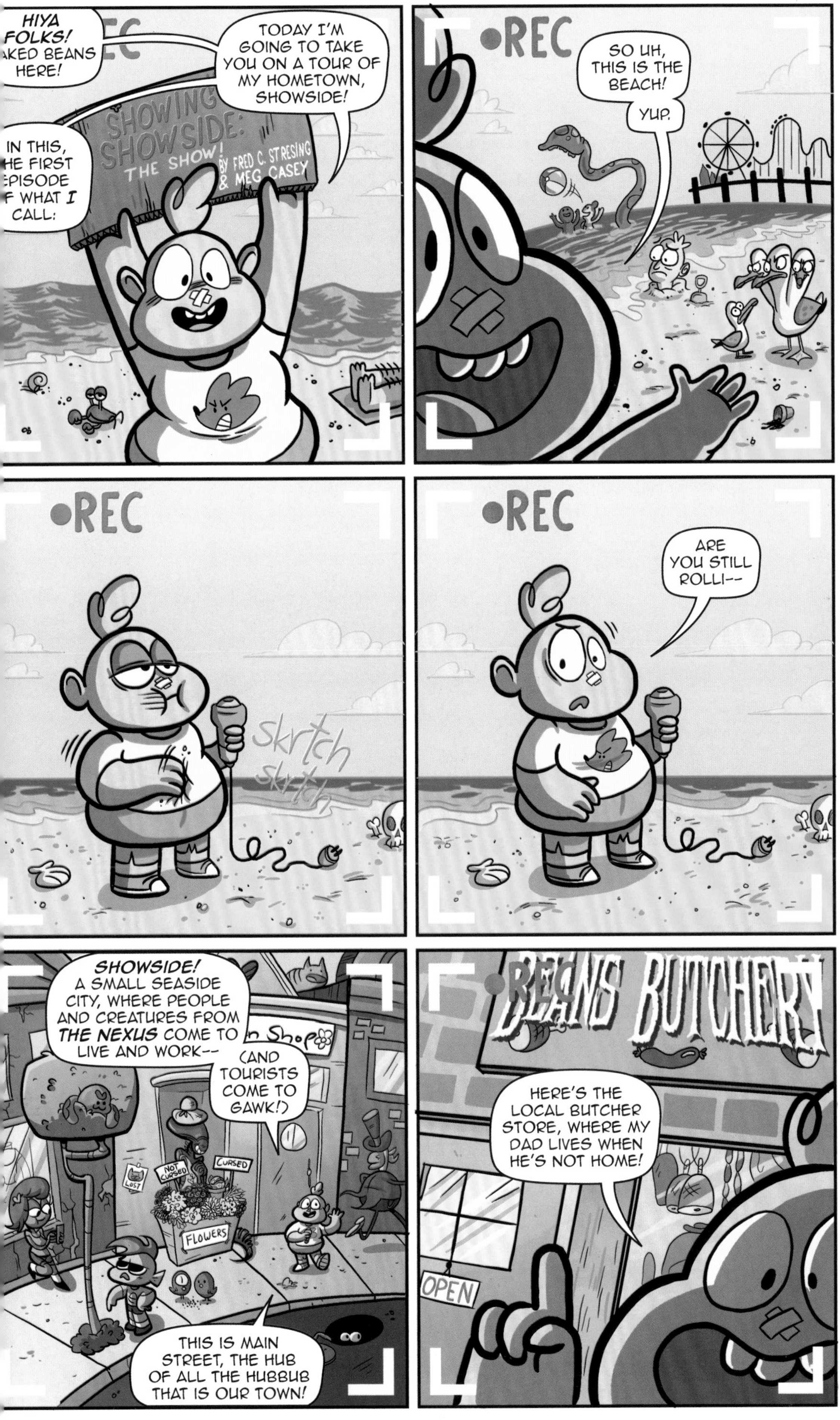

REC
HIYA FOLKS! AKED BEANS HERE!
TODAY I'M GOING TO TAKE YOU ON A TOUR OF MY HOMETOWN, SHOWSIDE!
IN THIS, HE FIRST EPISODE F WHAT I CALL:
SHOWING SHOWSIDE: THE SHOW! BY FRED C. STRESING & MEG CASEY
REC
SO UH, THIS IS THE BEACH!
YUP.
REC
SKRTCH SKRTCH
REC
ARE YOU STILL ROLLI--
SHOWSIDE! A SMALL SEASIDE CITY, WHERE PEOPLE AND CREATURES FROM THE NEXUS COME TO LIVE AND WORK--
(AND TOURISTS COME TO GAWK!)
n Shop
LOST
NOT CURSED
CURSED
FLOWERS
THIS IS MAIN STREET, THE HUB OF ALL THE HUBBUB THAT IS OUR TOWN!
BEANS BUTCHERY
REC
HERE'S THE LOCAL BUTCHER STORE, WHERE MY DAD LIVES WHEN HE'S NOT HOME!
OPEN

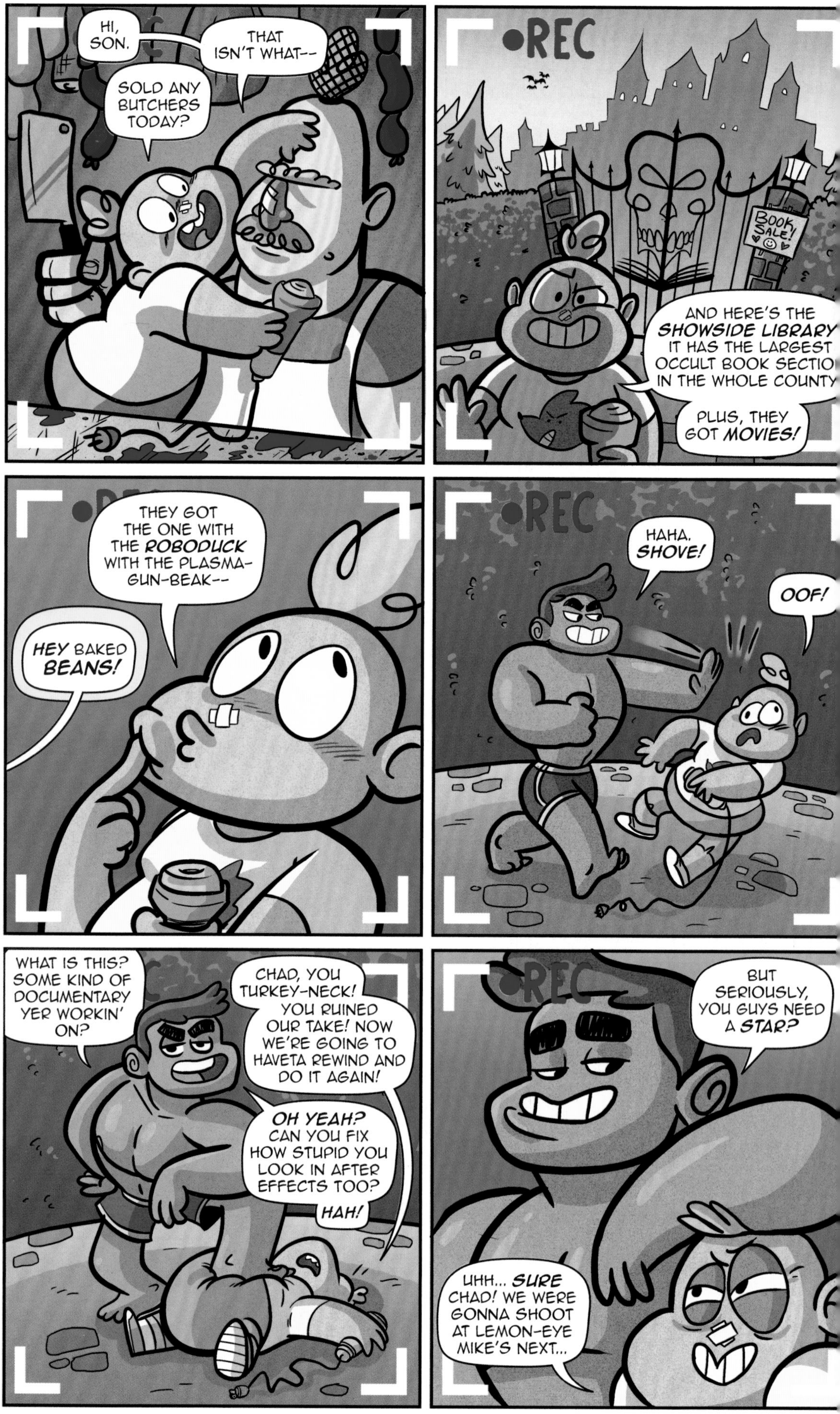
HI, SON.
THAT ISN'T WHAT--
SOLD ANY BUTCHERS TODAY?
•REC
BOOK SALE!
AND HERE'S THE SHOWSIDE LIBRARY IT HAS THE LARGEST OCCULT BOOK SECTIO IN THE WHOLE COUNTY
PLUS, THEY GOT MOVIES!
THEY GOT THE ONE WITH THE ROBODUCK WITH THE PLASMA-GUN-BEAK--
HEY BAKED BEANS!
•REC
HAHA. SHOVE!
OOF!
WHAT IS THIS? SOME KIND OF DOCUMENTARY YER WORKIN' ON?
CHAD, YOU TURKEY-NECK! YOU RUINED OUR TAKE! NOW WE'RE GOING TO HAVETA REWIND AND DO IT AGAIN!
OH YEAH? CAN YOU FIX HOW STUPID YOU LOOK IN AFTER EFFECTS TOO?
HAH!
•REC
BUT SERIOUSLY, YOU GUYS NEED A STAR?
UHH... SURE CHAD! WE WERE GONNA SHOOT AT LEMON-EYE MIKE'S NEXT...

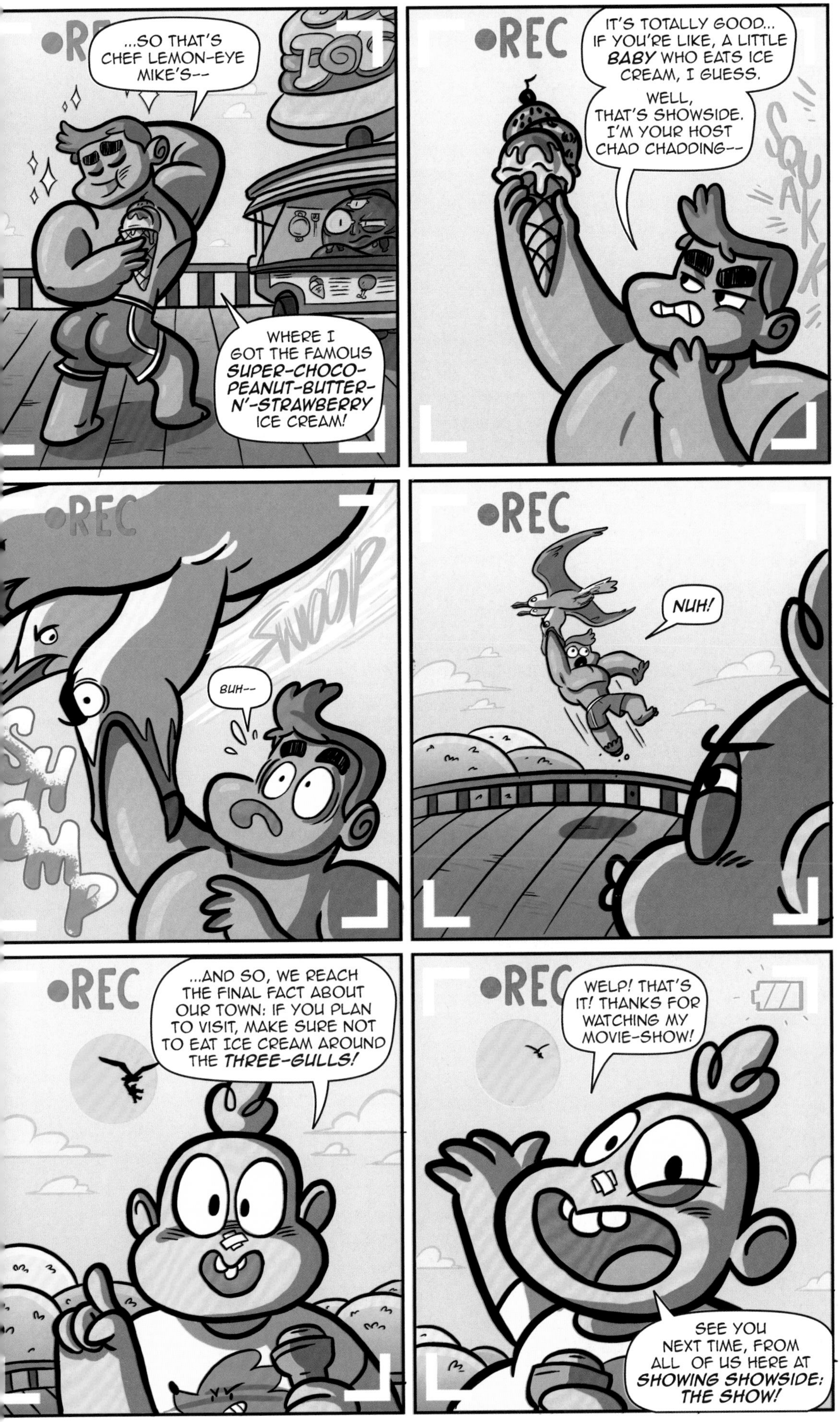

REC
...SO THAT'S CHEF LEMON-EYE MIKE'S--
WHERE I GOT THE FAMOUS SUPER-CHOCO-PEANUT-BUTTER-N'-STRAWBERRY ICE CREAM!
REC
IT'S TOTALLY GOOD... IF YOU'RE LIKE, A LITTLE BABY WHO EATS ICE CREAM, I GUESS.
WELL, THAT'S SHOWSIDE. I'M YOUR HOST CHAD CHADDING--
SQUAK
REC
SWOOP
BUH--
REC
NUH!
REC
...AND SO, WE REACH THE FINAL FACT ABOUT OUR TOWN: IF YOU PLAN TO VISIT, MAKE SURE NOT TO EAT ICE CREAM AROUND THE THREE-GULLS!
REC
WELP! THAT'S IT! THANKS FOR WATCHING MY MOVIE-SHOW!
SEE YOU NEXT TIME, FROM ALL OF US HERE AT SHOWING SHOWSIDE: THE SHOW!

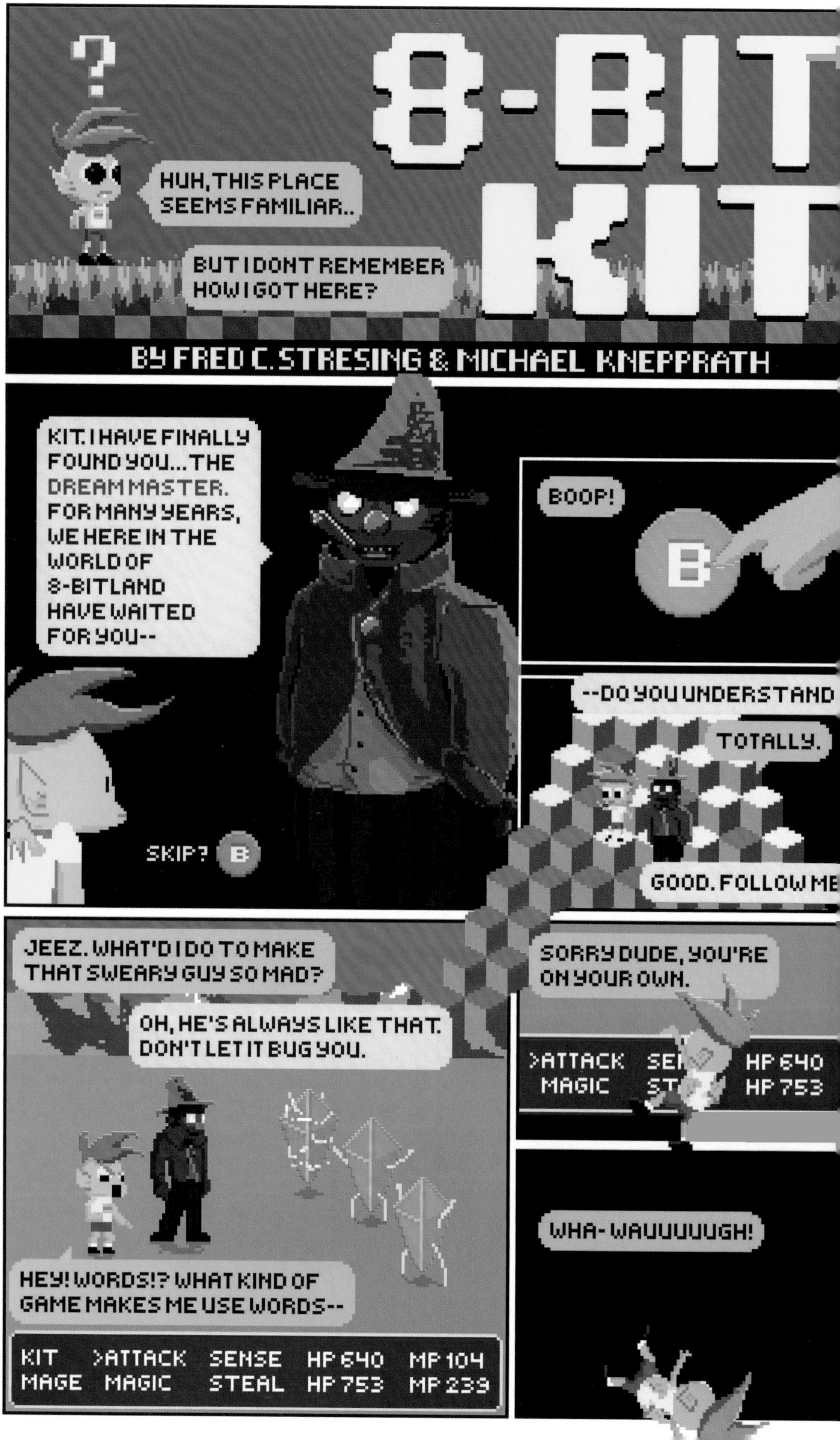

8-BIT KIT

HUH, THIS PLACE SEEMS FAMILIAR..

BUT I DONT REMEMBER HOW I GOT HERE?

BY FRED C. STRESING & MICHAEL KNEPPRATH

KIT. I HAVE FINALLY FOUND YOU... THE DREAM MASTER. FOR MANY YEARS, WE HERE IN THE WORLD OF 8-BITLAND HAVE WAITED FOR YOU--

SKIP? B

BOOP!

B

--DO YOU UNDERSTAND

TOTALLY.

GOOD. FOLLOW ME

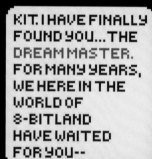

JEEZ. WHAT'D I DO TO MAKE THAT SWEARY GUY SO MAD?

OH, HE'S ALWAYS LIKE THAT. DON'T LET IT BUG YOU.

HEY! WORDS!? WHAT KIND OF GAME MAKES ME USE WORDS--

SORRY DUDE, YOU'RE ON YOUR OWN.

| >ATTACK | SE... | HP 640 |
| MAGIC | ST... | HP 753 |

WHA- WAUUUUUGH!

| KIT | >ATTACK | SENSE | HP 640 | MP 104 |
| MAGE | MAGIC | STEAL | HP 753 | MP 239 |

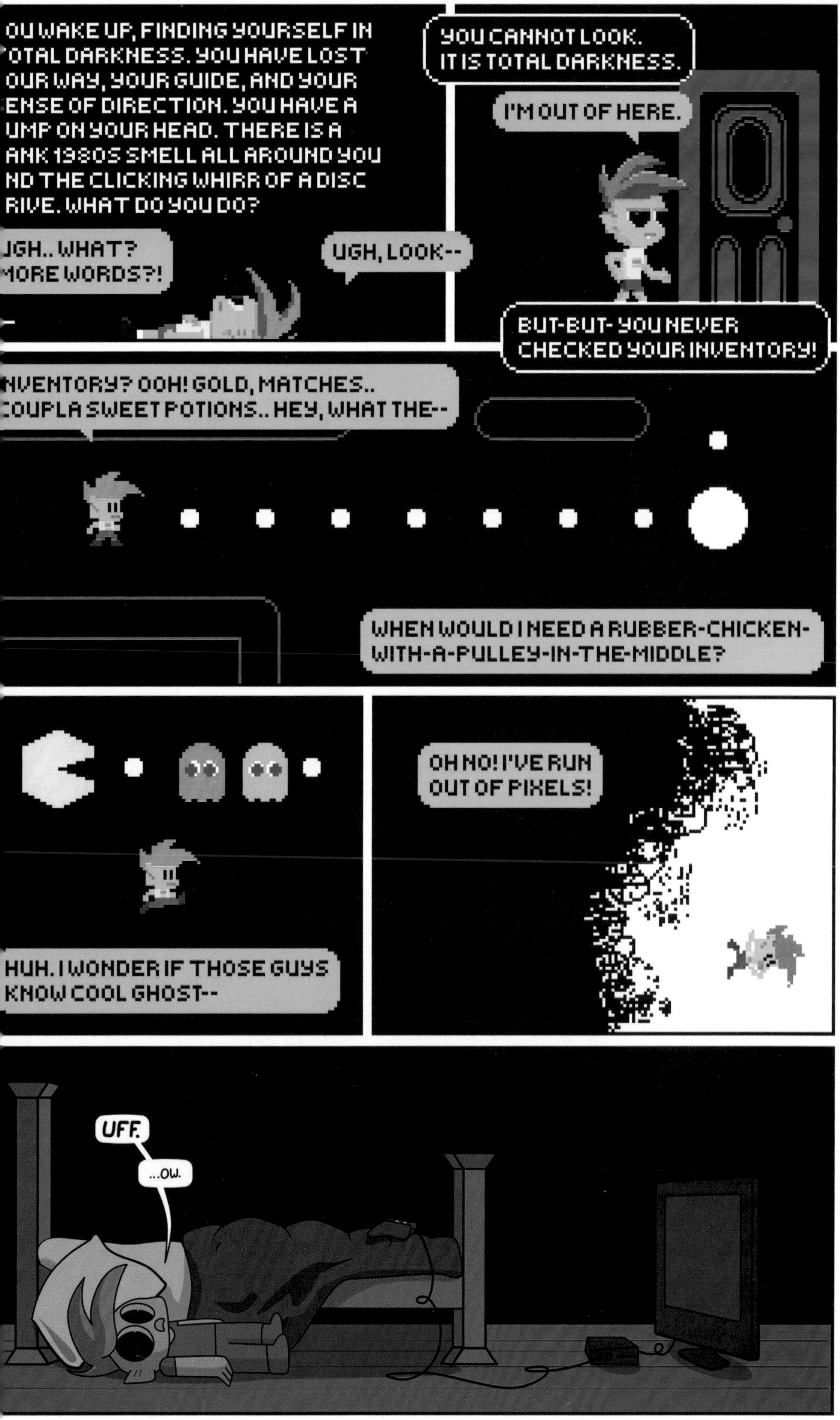

OU WAKE UP, FINDING YOURSELF IN OTAL DARKNESS. YOU HAVE LOST OUR WAY, YOUR GUIDE, AND YOUR ENSE OF DIRECTION. YOU HAVE A UMP ON YOUR HEAD. THERE IS A ANK 1980S SMELL ALL AROUND YOU ND THE CLICKING WHIRR OF A DISC RIVE. WHAT DO YOU DO?
JGH.. WHAT? MORE WORDS?!
UGH, LOOK--
YOU CANNOT LOOK. IT IS TOTAL DARKNESS.
I'M OUT OF HERE.
BUT-BUT- YOU NEVER CHECKED YOUR INVENTORY!
NVENTORY? OOH! GOLD, MATCHES.. COUPLA SWEET POTIONS.. HEY, WHAT THE--
WHEN WOULD I NEED A RUBBER-CHICKEN-WITH-A-PULLEY-IN-THE-MIDDLE?
HUH. I WONDER IF THOSE GUYS KNOW COOL GHOST--
OH NO! I'VE RUN OUT OF PIXELS!
UFF.
...OW.

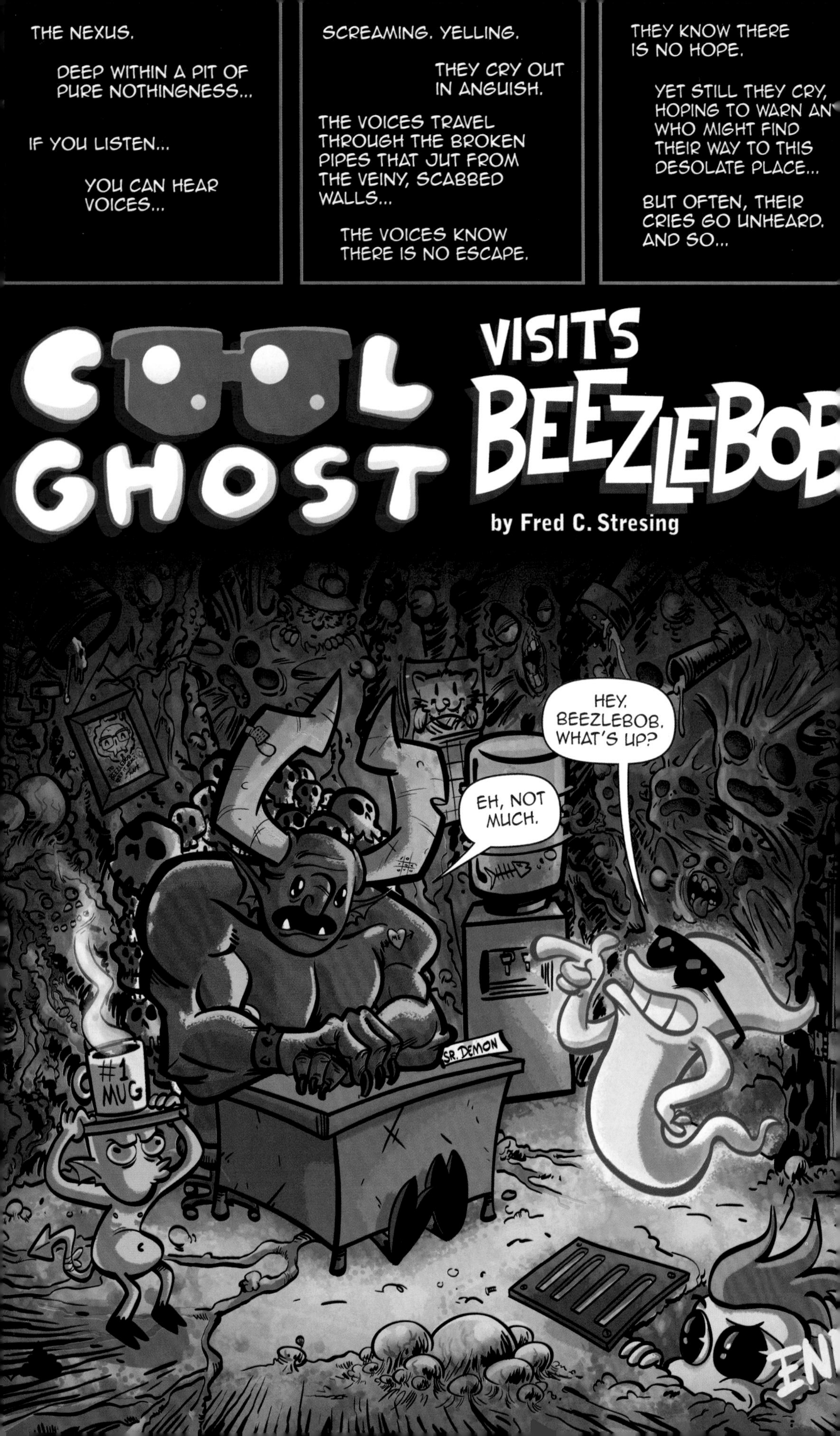
THE NEXUS.
DEEP WITHIN A PIT OF PURE NOTHINGNESS...
IF YOU LISTEN...
YOU CAN HEAR VOICES...
SCREAMING. YELLING.
THEY CRY OUT IN ANGUISH.
THE VOICES TRAVEL THROUGH THE BROKEN PIPES THAT JUT FROM THE VEINY, SCABBED WALLS...
THE VOICES KNOW THERE IS NO ESCAPE.
THEY KNOW THERE IS NO HOPE.
YET STILL THEY CRY, HOPING TO WARN AN WHO MIGHT FIND THEIR WAY TO THIS DESOLATE PLACE...
BUT OFTEN, THEIR CRIES GO UNHEARD. AND SO...
COOL GHOST VISITS BEEZLEBOB
by Fred C. Stresing
HEY. BEEZLEBOB. WHAT'S UP?
EH, NOT MUCH.
SR. DEMON
#1 MUG
EN

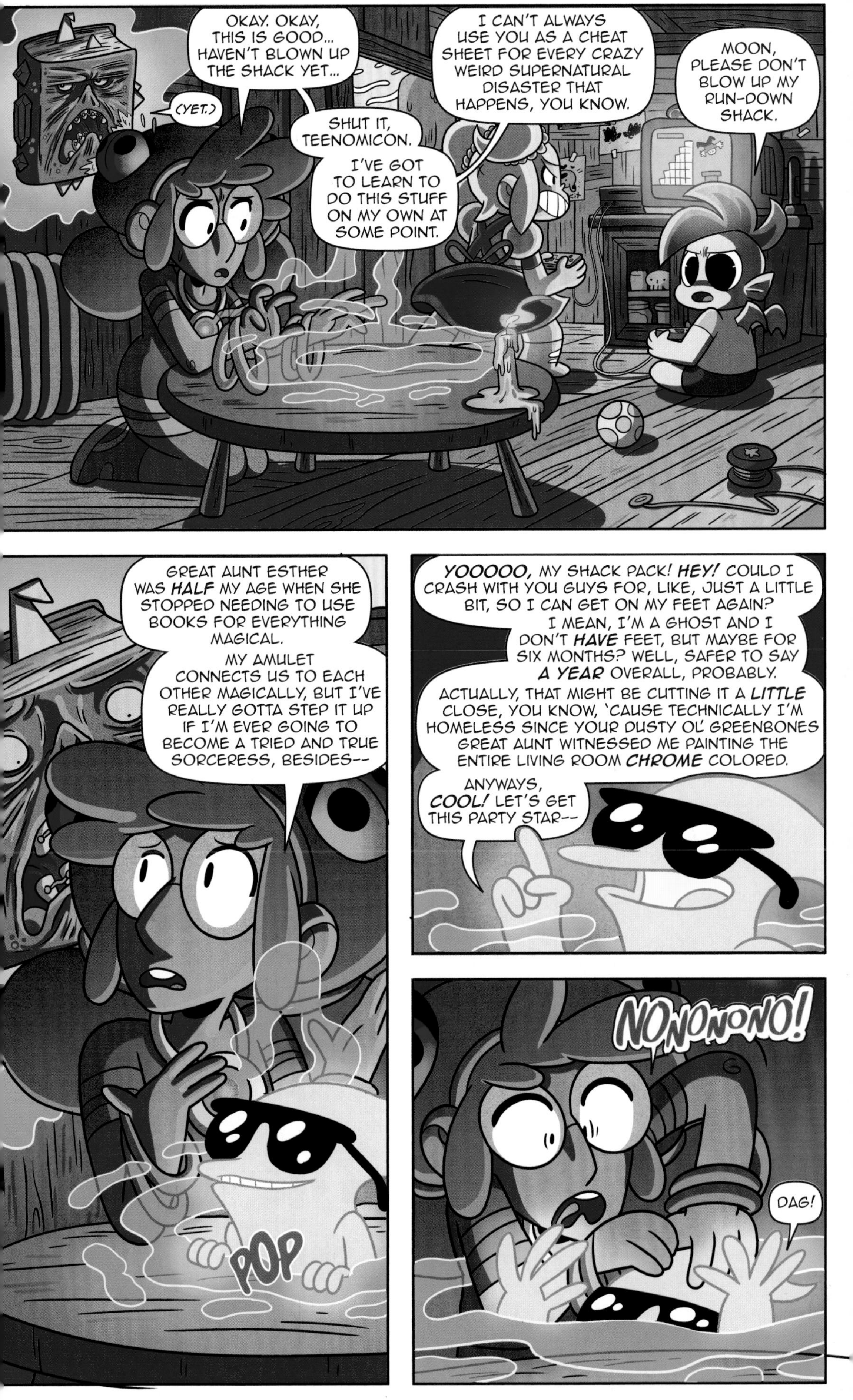

OKAY. OKAY, THIS IS GOOD... HAVEN'T BLOWN UP THE SHACK YET...
(YET.)
SHUT IT, TEENOMICON.
I'VE GOT TO LEARN TO DO THIS STUFF ON MY OWN AT SOME POINT.
I CAN'T ALWAYS USE YOU AS A CHEAT SHEET FOR EVERY CRAZY WEIRD SUPERNATURAL DISASTER THAT HAPPENS, YOU KNOW.
MOON, PLEASE DON'T BLOW UP MY RUN-DOWN SHACK.
GREAT AUNT ESTHER WAS HALF MY AGE WHEN SHE STOPPED NEEDING TO USE BOOKS FOR EVERYTHING MAGICAL.
MY AMULET CONNECTS US TO EACH OTHER MAGICALLY, BUT I'VE REALLY GOTTA STEP IT UP IF I'M EVER GOING TO BECOME A TRIED AND TRUE SORCERESS, BESIDES--
POP
YOOOOO, MY SHACK PACK! HEY! COULD I CRASH WITH YOU GUYS FOR, LIKE, JUST A LITTLE BIT, SO I CAN GET ON MY FEET AGAIN?
I MEAN, I'M A GHOST AND I DON'T HAVE FEET, BUT MAYBE FOR SIX MONTHS? WELL, SAFER TO SAY A YEAR OVERALL, PROBABLY.
ACTUALLY, THAT MIGHT BE CUTTING IT A LITTLE CLOSE, YOU KNOW, 'CAUSE TECHNICALLY I'M HOMELESS SINCE YOUR DUSTY OL' GREENBONES GREAT AUNT WITNESSED ME PAINTING THE ENTIRE LIVING ROOM CHROME COLORED.
ANYWAYS, COOL! LET'S GET THIS PARTY STAR--
NONONONO!
DAG!

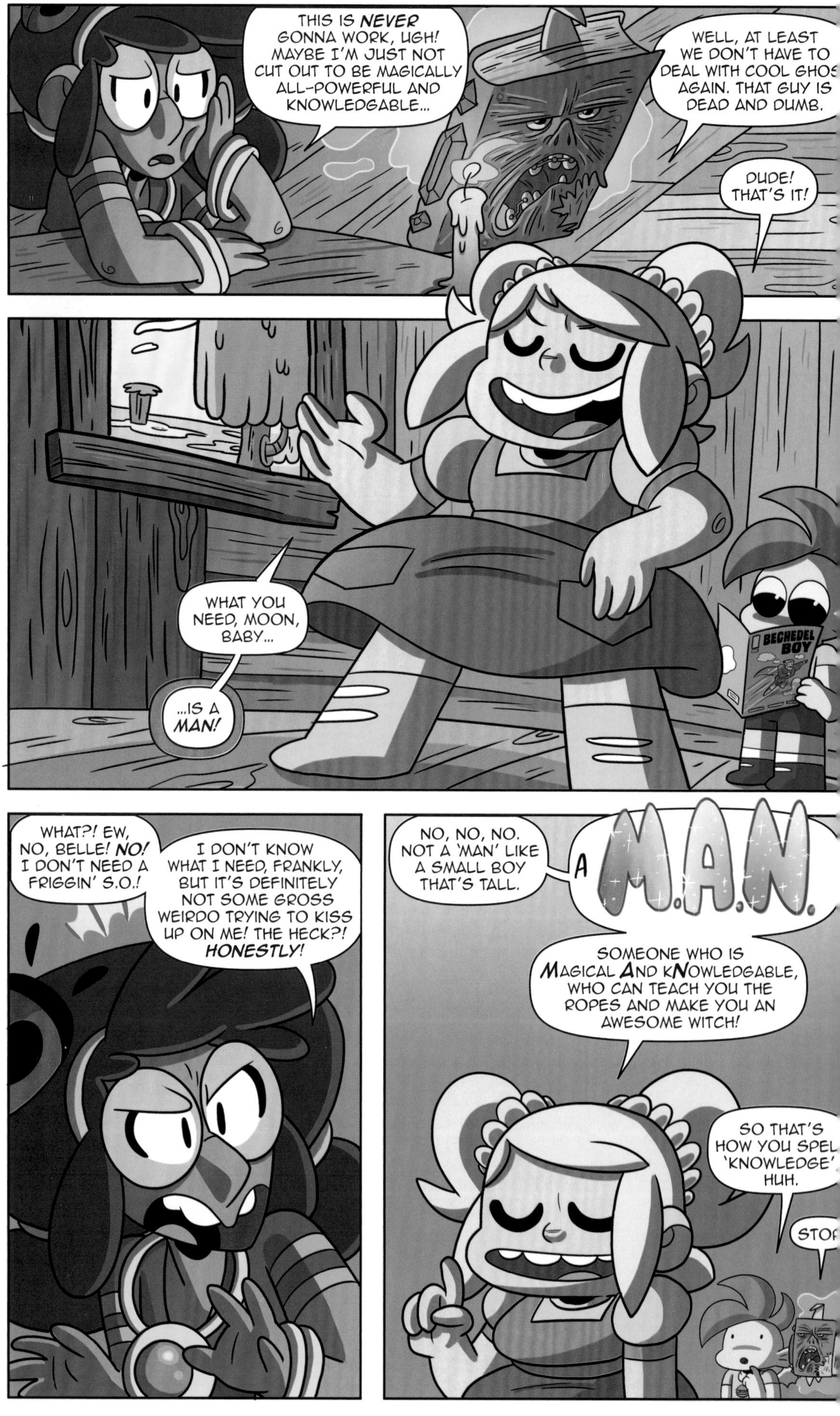
THIS IS NEVER GONNA WORK, UGH! MAYBE I'M JUST NOT CUT OUT TO BE MAGICALLY ALL-POWERFUL AND KNOWLEDGABLE...
WELL, AT LEAST WE DON'T HAVE TO DEAL WITH COOL GHOS AGAIN. THAT GUY IS DEAD AND DUMB.
DUDE! THAT'S IT!
WHAT YOU NEED, MOON, BABY...
...IS A MAN!
BECHEDEL BOY
WHAT?! EW, NO, BELLE! NO! I DON'T NEED A FRIGGIN' S.O.!
I DON'T KNOW WHAT I NEED, FRANKLY, BUT IT'S DEFINITELY NOT SOME GROSS WEIRDO TRYING TO KISS UP ON ME! THE HECK?! HONESTLY!
NO, NO, NO. NOT A 'MAN' LIKE A SMALL BOY THAT'S TALL.
A M.A.N.
SOMEONE WHO IS MAGICAL AND KNOWLEDGABLE, WHO CAN TEACH YOU THE ROPES AND MAKE YOU AN AWESOME WITCH!
SO THAT'S HOW YOU SPEL 'KNOWLEDGE' HUH.
STOP

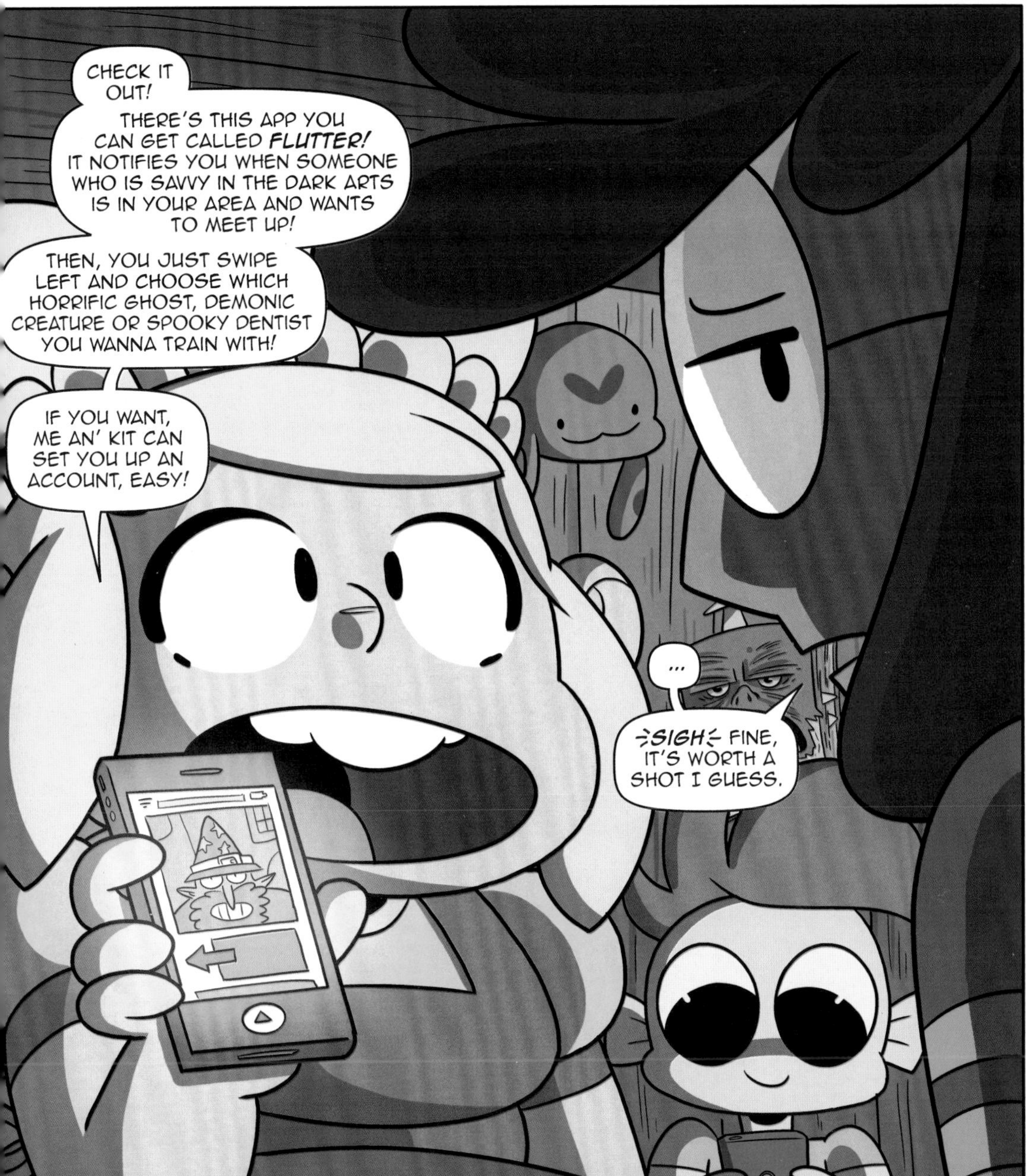
CHECK IT OUT!
THERE'S THIS APP YOU CAN GET CALLED FLUTTER! IT NOTIFIES YOU WHEN SOMEONE WHO IS SAVVY IN THE DARK ARTS IS IN YOUR AREA AND WANTS TO MEET UP!
THEN, YOU JUST SWIPE LEFT AND CHOOSE WHICH HORRIFIC GHOST, DEMONIC CREATURE OR SPOOKY DENTIST YOU WANNA TRAIN WITH!
IF YOU WANT, ME AN' KIT CAN SET YOU UP AN ACCOUNT, EASY!
...
SIGH FINE, IT'S WORTH A SHOT I GUESS.

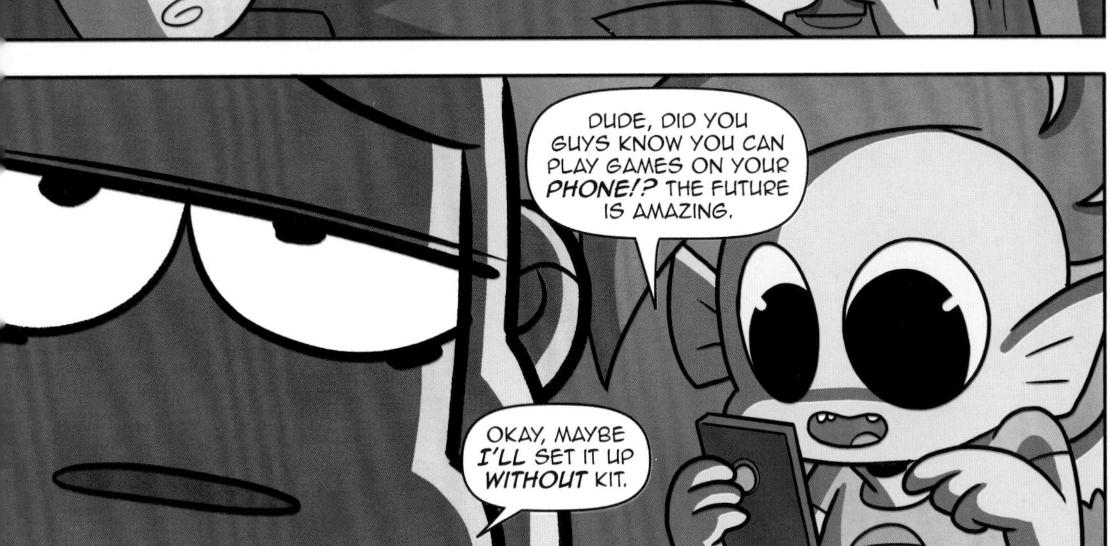
DUDE, DID YOU GUYS KNOW YOU CAN PLAY GAMES ON YOUR PHONE!? THE FUTURE IS AMAZING.
OKAY, MAYBE I'LL SET IT UP WITHOUT KIT.

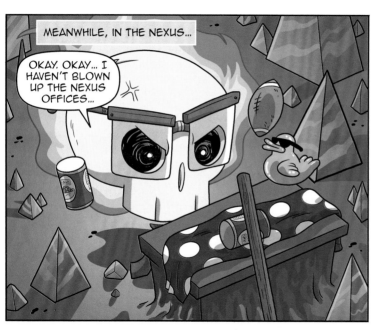

MEANWHILE, IN THE NEXUS...

OKAY. OKAY... I HAVEN'T BLOWN UP THE NEXUS OFFICES...

YET.

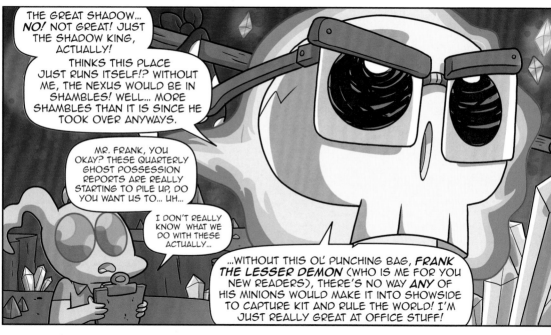

THE GREAT SHADOW... *NO!* NOT GREAT! JUST THE SHADOW KING, ACTUALLY!

THINKS THIS PLACE JUST RUNS ITSELF!? WITHOUT ME, THE NEXUS WOULD BE IN SHAMBLES! WELL... MORE SHAMBLES THAN IT IS SINCE HE TOOK OVER ANYWAYS.

MR. FRANK, YOU OKAY? THESE QUARTERLY GHOST POSSESSION REPORTS ARE REALLY STARTING TO PILE UP, DO YOU WANT US TO... UH...

I DON'T REALLY KNOW WHAT WE DO WITH THESE ACTUALLY...

...WITHOUT THIS OL' PUNCHING BAG, *FRANK THE LESSER DEMON* (WHO IS ME FOR YOU NEW READERS), THERE'S NO WAY *ANY* OF HIS MINIONS WOULD MAKE IT INTO SHOWSIDE TO CAPTURE KIT AND RULE THE WORLD! I'M JUST REALLY GREAT AT OFFICE STUFF!

...BUT I BET I CAN BE AN EVEN BETTER WORLD RULER.

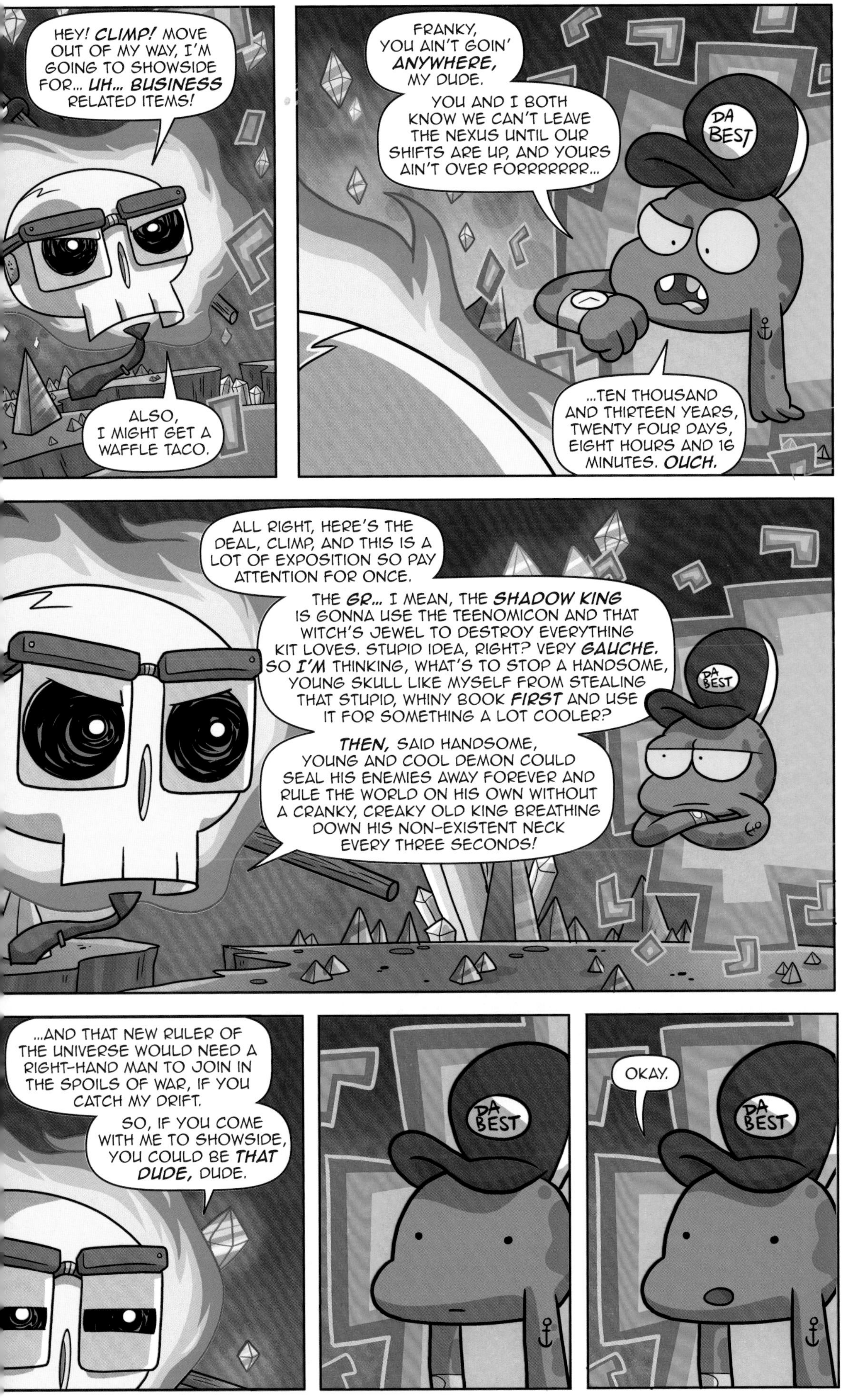
HEY! CLIMP! MOVE OUT OF MY WAY, I'M GOING TO SHOWSIDE FOR... UH... BUSINESS RELATED ITEMS!
ALSO, I MIGHT GET A WAFFLE TACO.
FRANKY, YOU AIN'T GOIN' ANYWHERE, MY DUDE.
YOU AND I BOTH KNOW WE CAN'T LEAVE THE NEXUS UNTIL OUR SHIFTS ARE UP, AND YOURS AIN'T OVER FORRRRRR...
...TEN THOUSAND AND THIRTEEN YEARS, TWENTY FOUR DAYS, EIGHT HOURS AND 16 MINUTES. OUCH.
DA BEST
ALL RIGHT, HERE'S THE DEAL, CLIMP, AND THIS IS A LOT OF EXPOSITION SO PAY ATTENTION FOR ONCE.
THE GR... I MEAN, THE SHADOW KING IS GONNA USE THE TEENOMICON AND THAT WITCH'S JEWEL TO DESTROY EVERYTHING KIT LOVES. STUPID IDEA, RIGHT? VERY GAUCHE. SO I'M THINKING, WHAT'S TO STOP A HANDSOME, YOUNG SKULL LIKE MYSELF FROM STEALING THAT STUPID, WHINY BOOK FIRST AND USE IT FOR SOMETHING A LOT COOLER?
THEN, SAID HANDSOME, YOUNG AND COOL DEMON COULD SEAL HIS ENEMIES AWAY FOREVER AND RULE THE WORLD ON HIS OWN WITHOUT A CRANKY, CREAKY OLD KING BREATHING DOWN HIS NON-EXISTENT NECK EVERY THREE SECONDS!
DA BEST
...AND THAT NEW RULER OF THE UNIVERSE WOULD NEED A RIGHT-HAND MAN TO JOIN IN THE SPOILS OF WAR, IF YOU CATCH MY DRIFT.
SO, IF YOU COME WITH ME TO SHOWSIDE, YOU COULD BE THAT DUDE, DUDE.
DA BEST
OKAY.
DA BEST

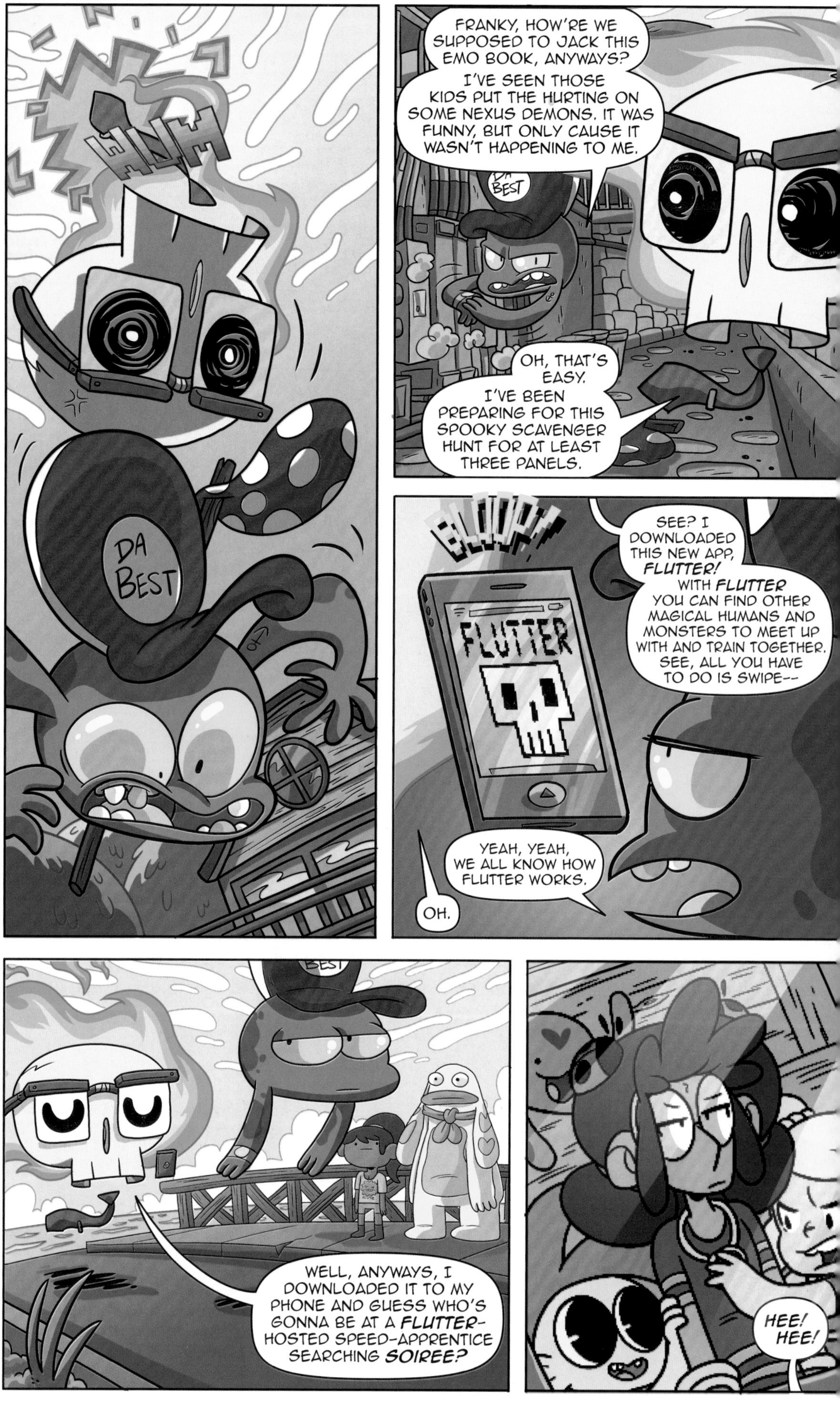
HUH
DA BEST
FRANKY, HOW'RE WE SUPPOSED TO JACK THIS EMO BOOK, ANYWAYS?
I'VE SEEN THOSE KIDS PUT THE HURTING ON SOME NEXUS DEMONS. IT WAS FUNNY, BUT ONLY CAUSE IT WASN'T HAPPENING TO ME.
DA BEST
OH, THAT'S EASY.
I'VE BEEN PREPARING FOR THIS SPOOKY SCAVENGER HUNT FOR AT LEAST THREE PANELS.
BLOOP!
FLUTTER
SEE? I DOWNLOADED THIS NEW APP, FLUTTER!
WITH FLUTTER YOU CAN FIND OTHER MAGICAL HUMANS AND MONSTERS TO MEET UP WITH AND TRAIN TOGETHER. SEE, ALL YOU HAVE TO DO IS SWIPE--
YEAH, YEAH, WE ALL KNOW HOW FLUTTER WORKS.
OH.
BEST
WELL, ANYWAYS, I DOWNLOADED IT TO MY PHONE AND GUESS WHO'S GONNA BE AT A FLUTTER-HOSTED SPEED-APPRENTICE SEARCHING SOIREE?
HEE! HEE!

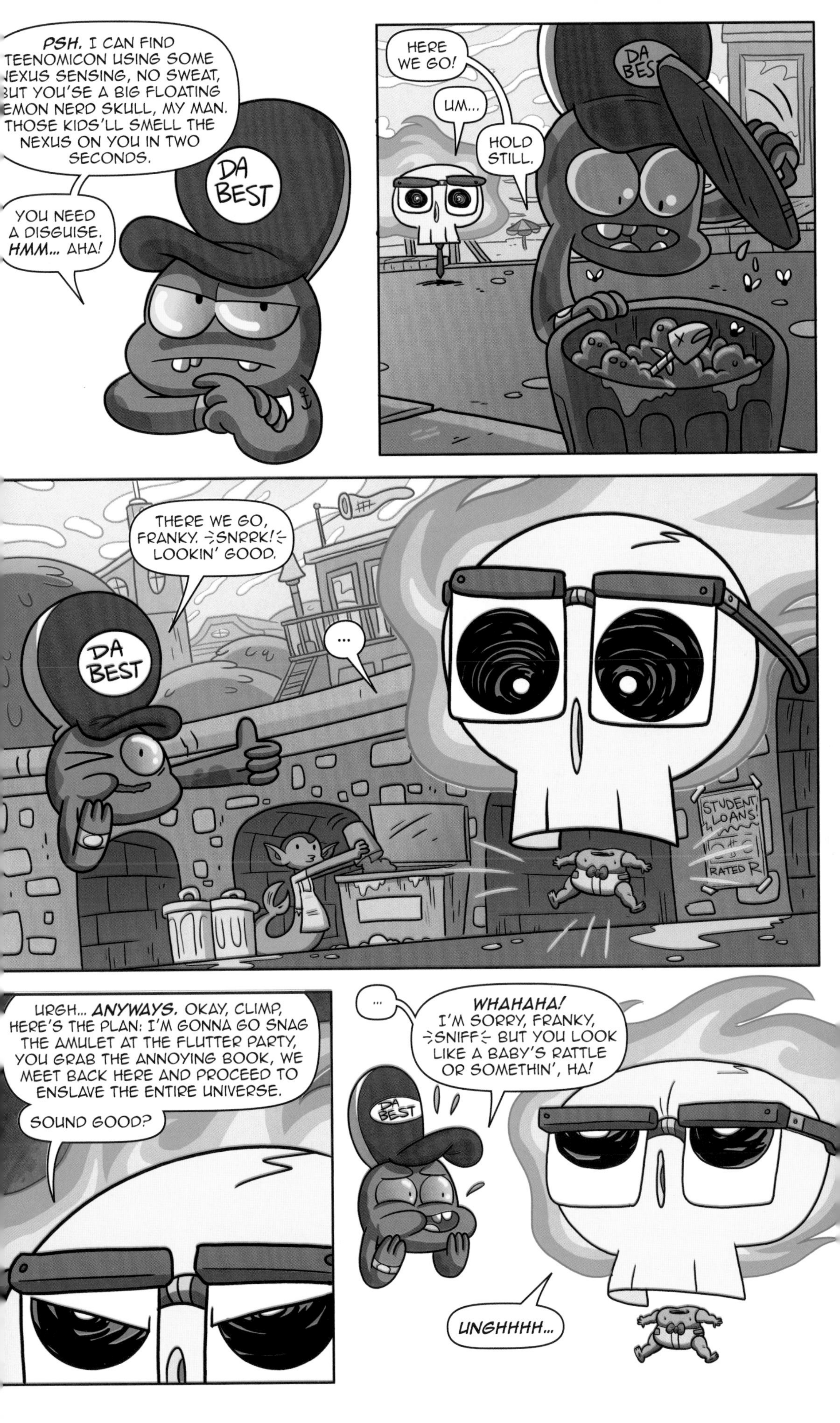
PSH. I CAN FIND TEENOMICON USING SOME NEXUS SENSING, NO SWEAT, BUT YOU'SE A BIG FLOATING DEMON NERD SKULL, MY MAN. THOSE KIDS'LL SMELL THE NEXUS ON YOU IN TWO SECONDS.
YOU NEED A DISGUISE. HMM... AHA!
DA BEST
HERE WE GO!
UM...
HOLD STILL.
THERE WE GO, FRANKY. SNRRK! LOOKIN' GOOD.
...
STUDENT LOANS!
RATED R
URGH... ANYWAYS. OKAY, CLIMP, HERE'S THE PLAN: I'M GONNA GO SNAG THE AMULET AT THE FLUTTER PARTY, YOU GRAB THE ANNOYING BOOK, WE MEET BACK HERE AND PROCEED TO ENSLAVE THE ENTIRE UNIVERSE.
SOUND GOOD?
...
WHAHAHA! I'M SORRY, FRANKY, SNIFF BUT YOU LOOK LIKE A BABY'S RATTLE OR SOMETHIN', HA!
UNGHHHH...

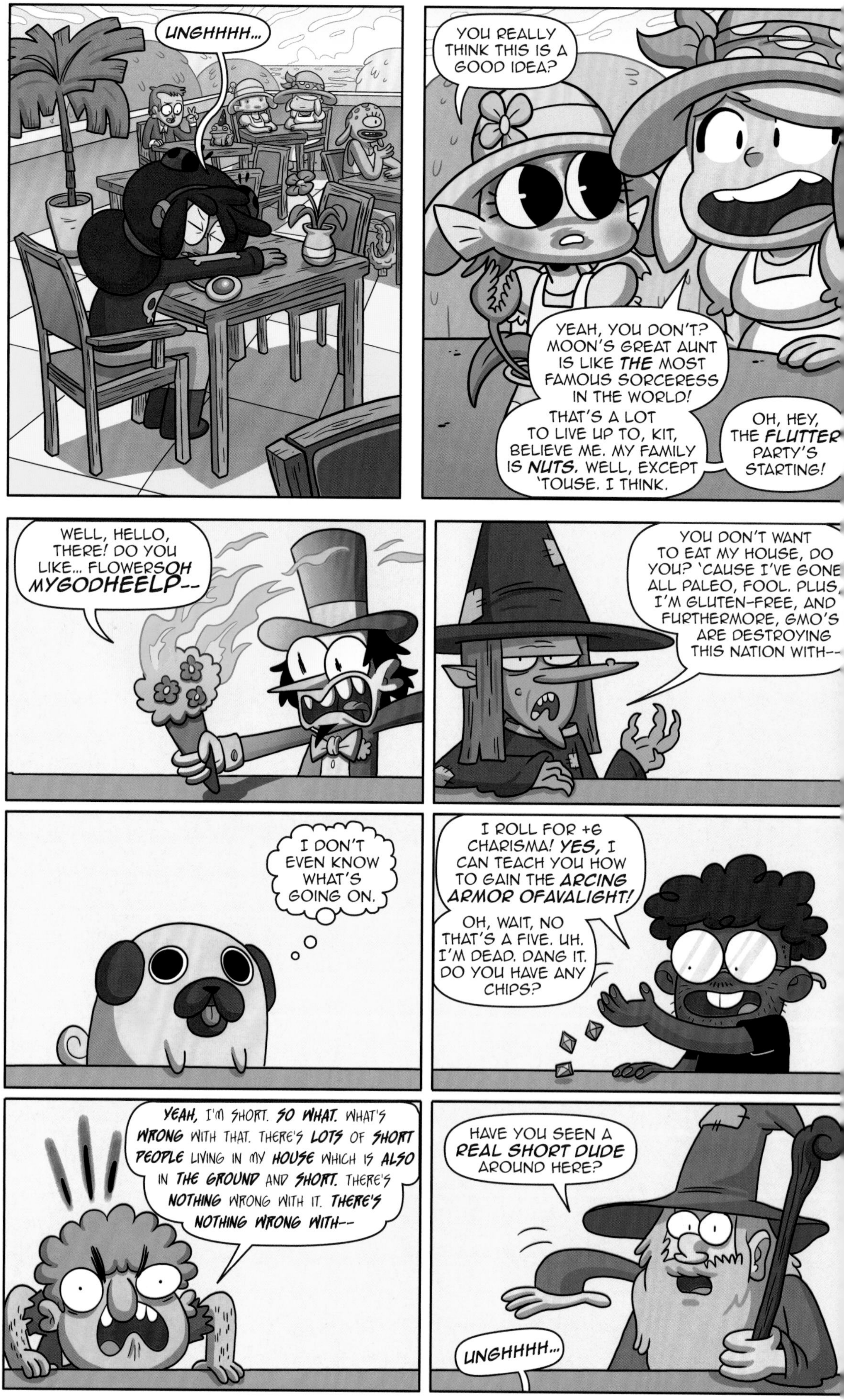
UNGHHHH...
YOU REALLY THINK THIS IS A GOOD IDEA?
YEAH, YOU DON'T? MOON'S GREAT AUNT IS LIKE THE MOST FAMOUS SORCERESS IN THE WORLD!
THAT'S A LOT TO LIVE UP TO, KIT, BELIEVE ME. MY FAMILY IS NUTS. WELL, EXCEPT 'TOUSE. I THINK.
OH, HEY, THE FLUTTER PARTY'S STARTING!
WELL, HELLO, THERE! DO YOU LIKE... FLOWERSOH MYGODHEELP--
YOU DON'T WANT TO EAT MY HOUSE, DO YOU? 'CAUSE I'VE GONE ALL PALEO, FOOL. PLUS, I'M GLUTEN-FREE, AND FURTHERMORE, GMO'S ARE DESTROYING THIS NATION WITH--
I DON'T EVEN KNOW WHAT'S GOING ON.
I ROLL FOR +6 CHARISMA! YES, I CAN TEACH YOU HOW TO GAIN THE ARCING ARMOR OFAVALIGHT!
OH, WAIT, NO THAT'S A FIVE. UH. I'M DEAD. DANG IT. DO YOU HAVE ANY CHIPS?
YEAH, I'M SHORT. SO WHAT. WHAT'S WRONG WITH THAT. THERE'S LOTS OF SHORT PEOPLE LIVING IN MY HOUSE WHICH IS ALSO IN THE GROUND AND SHORT. THERE'S NOTHING WRONG WITH IT. THERE'S NOTHING WRONG WITH--
HAVE YOU SEEN A REAL SHORT DUDE AROUND HERE?
UNGHHHH...

≒SIGH.≒ *FINALLY* A MINUTE ALONE WITH MY VINTAGE VINYL ALBUM COLLECTION, JUST FILLED WITH THE NAMES OF *NON-LIBELOUS COMPLETELY LEGALLY SAFE* BANDS.

MY BREADICAL ROMANCE

DAD SAYS NO WAY

TAKING BACK SUNDAY BRUNCH

the NOVEMBERISTS

...OKAY, THAT ONE COULD BE LIBELOUS.

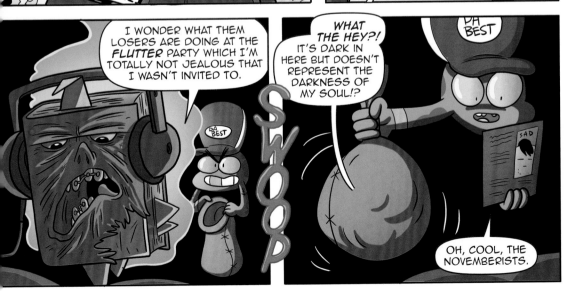

I WONDER WHAT THEM LOSERS ARE DOING AT THE *FLUTTER* PARTY WHICH I'M TOTALLY NOT JEALOUS THAT I WASN'T INVITED TO.

DA BEST

WHAT THE HEY?! IT'S DARK IN HERE BUT DOESN'T REPRESENT THE DARKNESS OF MY SOUL!?

SWOOP

SAD

OH, COOL, THE NOVEMBERISTS.

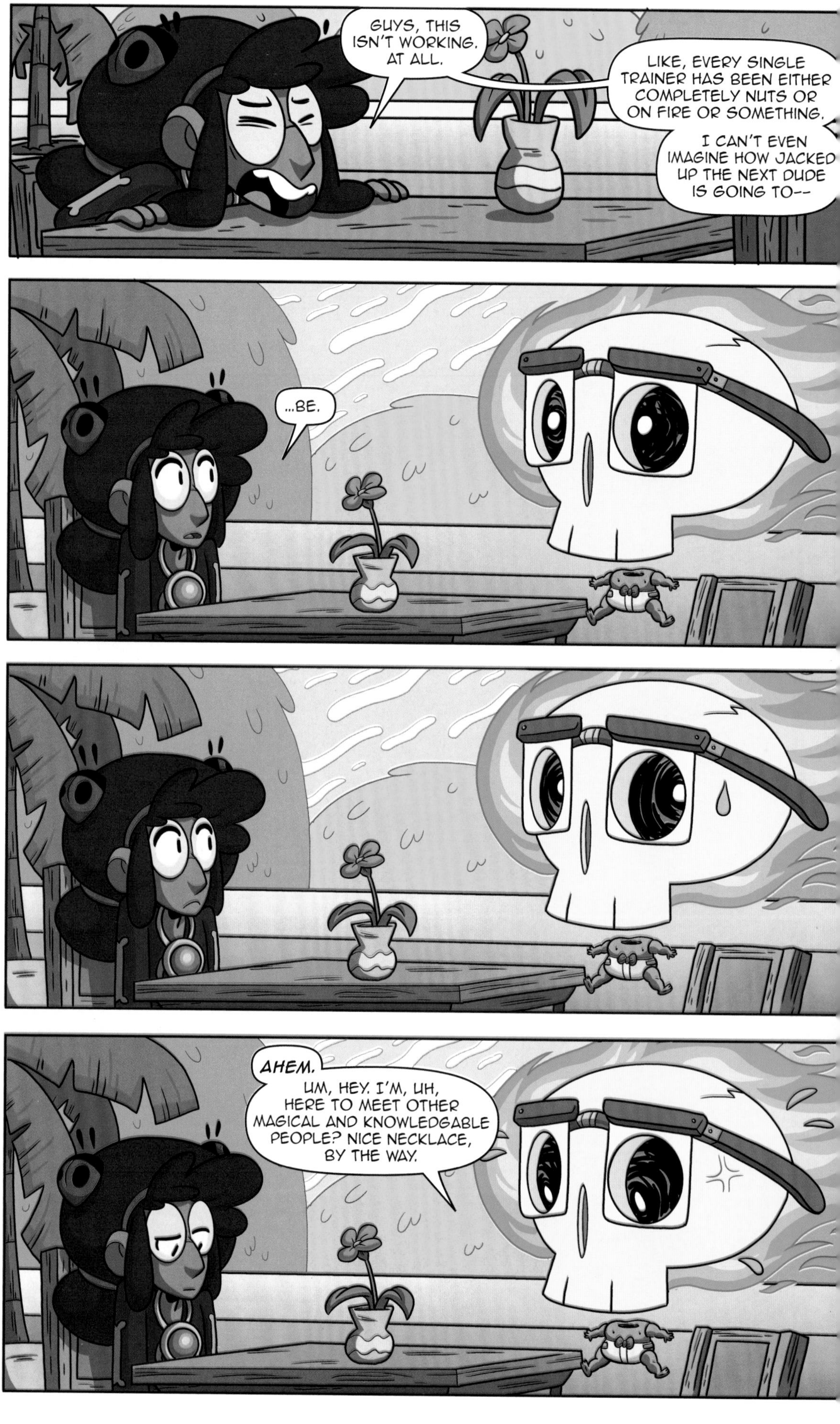
GUYS, THIS ISN'T WORKING. AT ALL.
LIKE, EVERY SINGLE TRAINER HAS BEEN EITHER COMPLETELY NUTS OR ON FIRE OR SOMETHING.
I CAN'T EVEN IMAGINE HOW JACKED UP THE NEXT DUDE IS GOING TO--
...BE.
AHEM.
UM, HEY. I'M, UH, HERE TO MEET OTHER MAGICAL AND KNOWLEDGABLE PEOPLE? NICE NECKLACE, BY THE WAY.

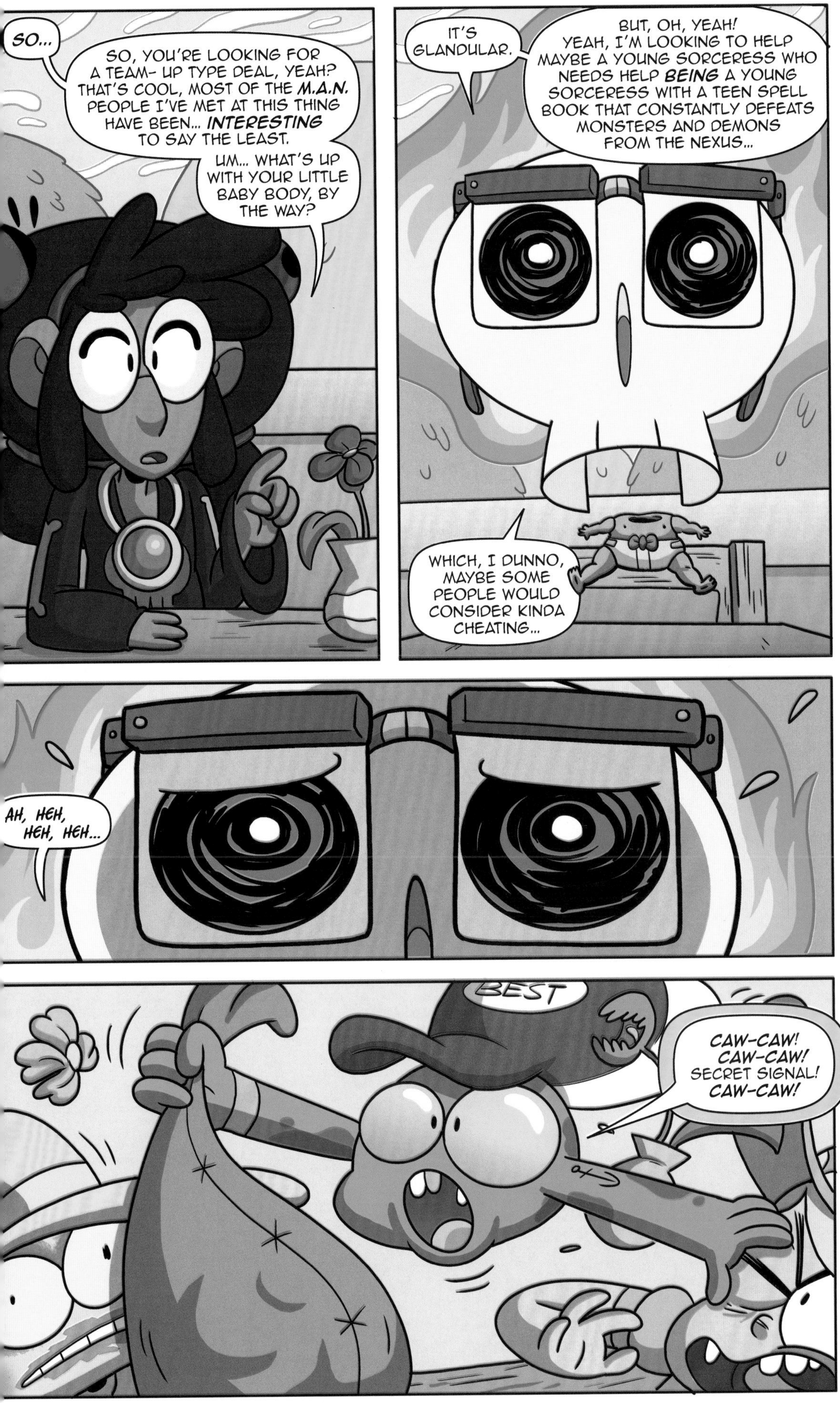

SO...
SO, YOU'RE LOOKING FOR A TEAM- UP TYPE DEAL, YEAH? THAT'S COOL, MOST OF THE *M.A.N.* PEOPLE I'VE MET AT THIS THING HAVE BEEN... *INTERESTING* TO SAY THE LEAST.
UM... WHAT'S UP WITH YOUR LITTLE BABY BODY, BY THE WAY?
IT'S GLANDULAR.
BUT, OH, YEAH! YEAH, I'M LOOKING TO HELP MAYBE A YOUNG SORCERESS WHO NEEDS HELP *BEING* A YOUNG SORCERESS WITH A TEEN SPELL BOOK THAT CONSTANTLY DEFEATS MONSTERS AND DEMONS FROM THE NEXUS...
WHICH, I DUNNO, MAYBE SOME PEOPLE WOULD CONSIDER KINDA CHEATING...
AH, HEH, HEH, HEH...
BEST
CAW-CAW! CAW-CAW! SECRET SIGNAL! *CAW-CAW!*

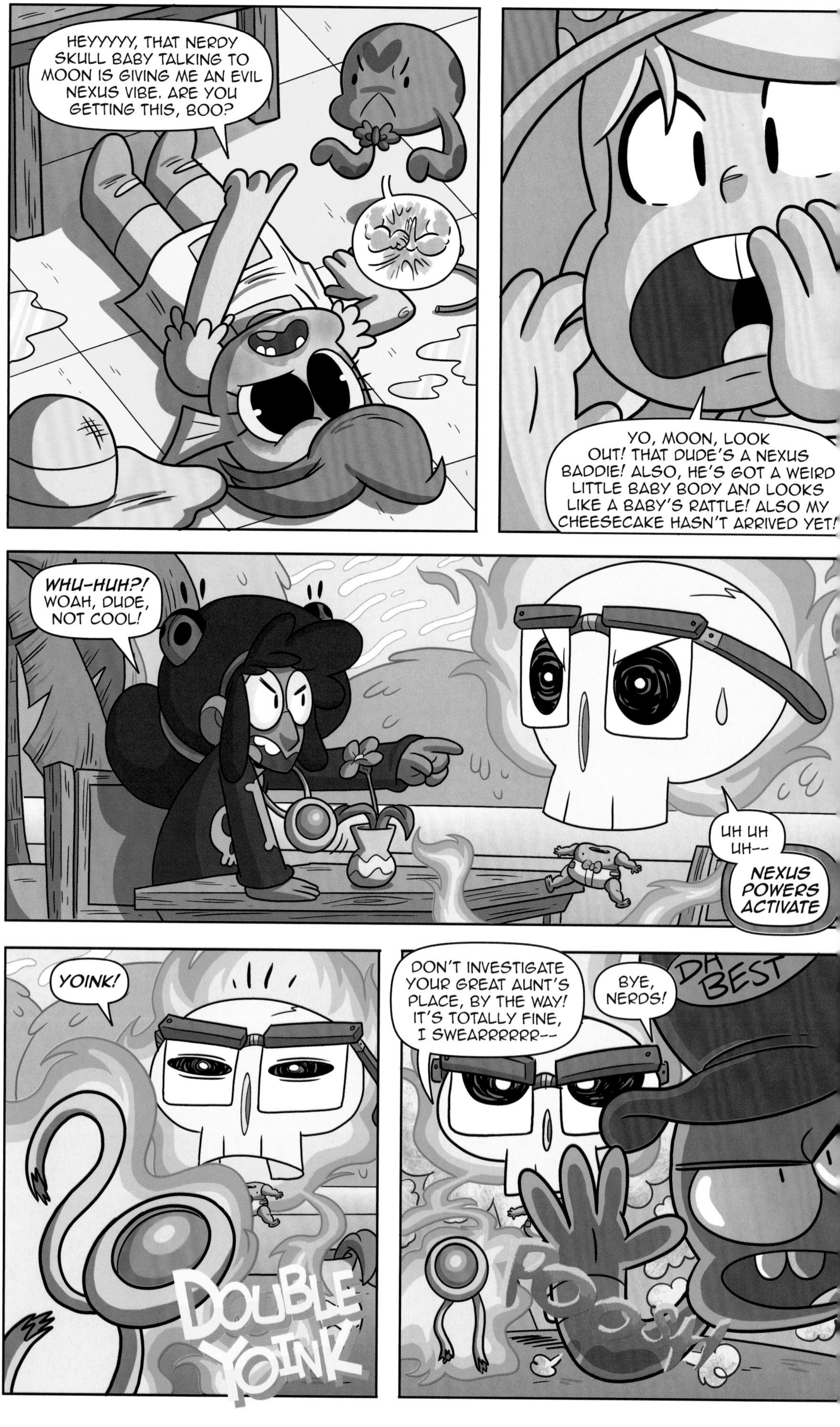
HEYYYYY, THAT NERDY SKULL BABY TALKING TO MOON IS GIVING ME AN EVIL NEXUS VIBE. ARE YOU GETTING THIS, BOO?
YO, MOON, LOOK OUT! THAT DUDE'S A NEXUS BADDIE! ALSO, HE'S GOT A WEIRD LITTLE BABY BODY AND LOOKS LIKE A BABY'S RATTLE! ALSO MY CHEESECAKE HASN'T ARRIVED YET!
WHU-HUH?! WOAH, DUDE, NOT COOL!
UH UH UH--
NEXUS POWERS ACTIVATE
YOINK!
DOUBLE YOINK
DON'T INVESTIGATE YOUR GREAT AUNT'S PLACE, BY THE WAY! IT'S TOTALLY FINE, I SWEARRRRRR--
BYE, NERDS!
DA BEST

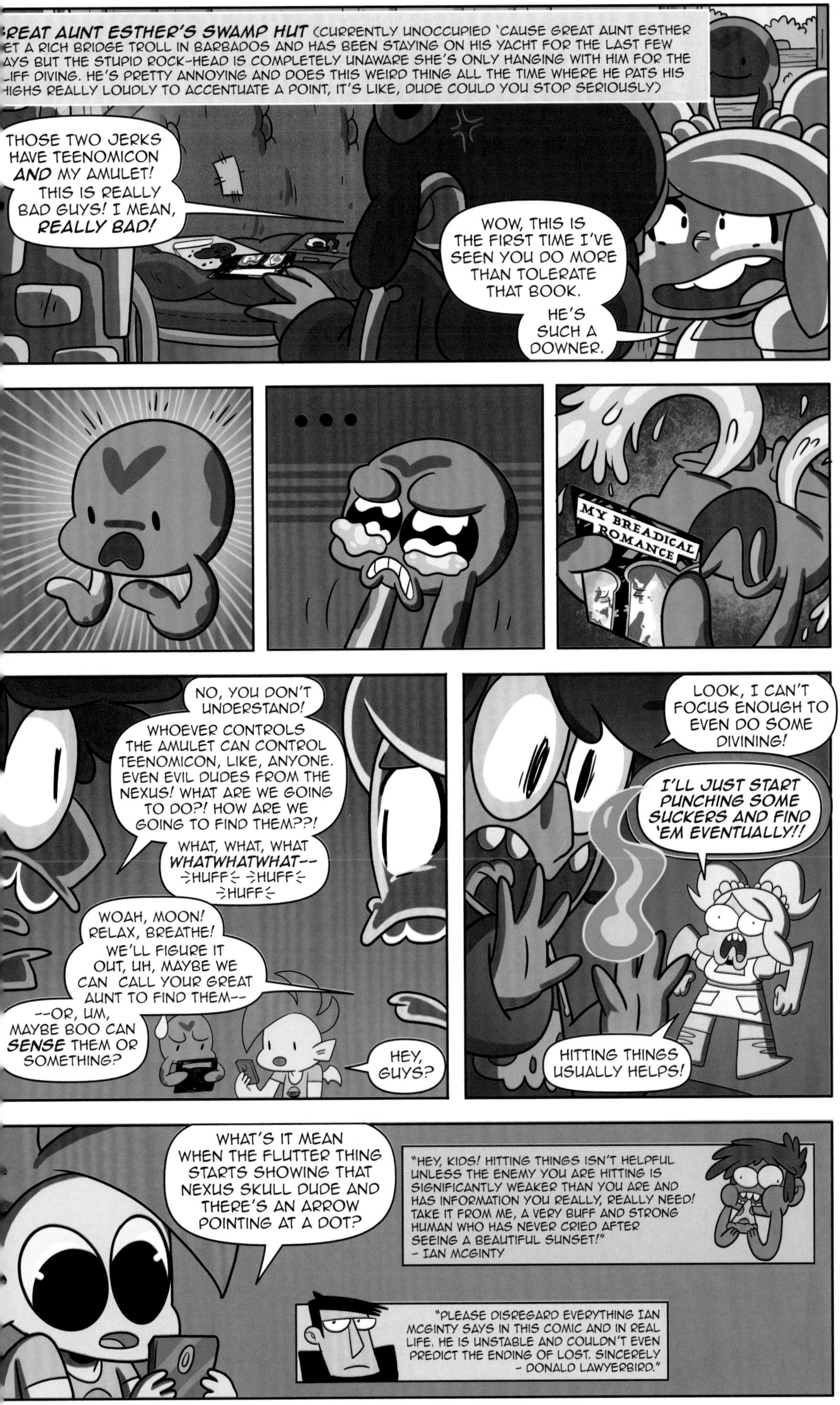

REAT AUNT ESTHER'S SWAMP HUT (CURRENTLY UNOCCUPIED 'CAUSE GREAT AUNT ESTHER
ET A RICH BRIDGE TROLL IN BARBADOS AND HAS BEEN STAYING ON HIS YACHT FOR THE LAST FEW
AYS BUT THE STUPID ROCK-HEAD IS COMPLETELY UNAWARE SHE'S ONLY HANGING WITH HIM FOR THE
LIFF DIVING. HE'S PRETTY ANNOYING AND DOES THIS WEIRD THING ALL THE TIME WHERE HE PATS HIS
HIGHS REALLY LOUDLY TO ACCENTUATE A POINT, IT'S LIKE, DUDE COULD YOU STOP SERIOUSLY)
THOSE TWO JERKS HAVE TEENOMICON ***AND*** MY AMULET! THIS IS REALLY BAD GUYS! I MEAN, ***REALLY BAD!***
WOW, THIS IS THE FIRST TIME I'VE SEEN YOU DO MORE THAN TOLERATE THAT BOOK.
HE'S SUCH A DOWNER.
...
MY BREADICAL ROMANCE
NO, YOU DON'T UNDERSTAND!
WHOEVER CONTROLS THE AMULET CAN CONTROL TEENOMICON, LIKE, ANYONE. EVEN EVIL DUDES FROM THE NEXUS! WHAT ARE WE GOING TO DO?! HOW ARE WE GOING TO FIND THEM??!
WHAT, WHAT, WHAT ***WHATWHATWHAT--*** HUFF HUFF HUFF
WOAH, MOON! RELAX, BREATHE!
WE'LL FIGURE IT OUT, UH, MAYBE WE CAN CALL YOUR GREAT AUNT TO FIND THEM--
--OR, UM, MAYBE BOO CAN ***SENSE*** THEM OR SOMETHING?
HEY, GUYS?
LOOK, I CAN'T FOCUS ENOUGH TO EVEN DO SOME DIVINING!
I'LL JUST START PUNCHING SOME SUCKERS AND FIND 'EM EVENTUALLY!!
HITTING THINGS USUALLY HELPS!
WHAT'S IT MEAN WHEN THE FLUTTER THING STARTS SHOWING THAT NEXUS SKULL DUDE AND THERE'S AN ARROW POINTING AT A DOT?
"HEY, KIDS! HITTING THINGS ISN'T HELPFUL UNLESS THE ENEMY YOU ARE HITTING IS SIGNIFICANTLY WEAKER THAN YOU ARE AND HAS INFORMATION YOU REALLY, REALLY NEED! TAKE IT FROM ME, A VERY BUFF AND STRONG HUMAN WHO HAS NEVER CRIED AFTER SEEING A BEAUTIFUL SUNSET!" - IAN MCGINTY
"PLEASE DISREGARD EVERYTHING IAN MCGINTY SAYS IN THIS COMIC AND IN REAL LIFE. HE IS UNSTABLE AND COULDN'T EVEN PREDICT THE ENDING OF LOST. SINCERELY - DONALD LAWYERBIRD."

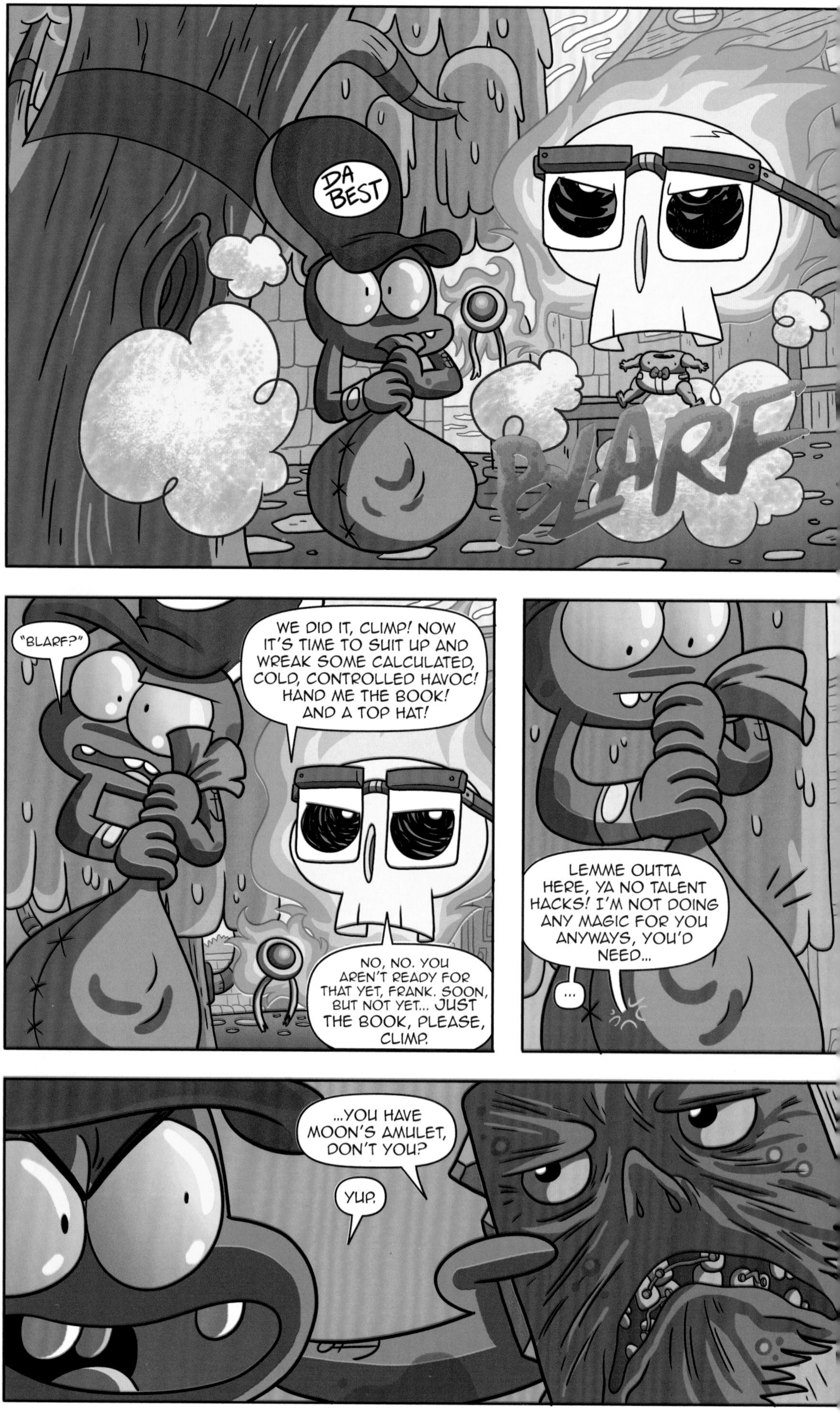
DA BEST
BLARF
"BLARF?"
WE DID IT, CLIMP! NOW IT'S TIME TO SUIT UP AND WREAK SOME CALCULATED, COLD, CONTROLLED HAVOC! HAND ME THE BOOK! AND A TOP HAT!
NO, NO. YOU AREN'T READY FOR THAT YET, FRANK. SOON, BUT NOT YET... JUST THE BOOK, PLEASE, CLIMP.
LEMME OUTTA HERE, YA NO TALENT HACKS! I'M NOT DOING ANY MAGIC FOR YOU ANYWAYS, YOU'D NEED...
...
...YOU HAVE MOON'S AMULET, DON'T YOU?
YUP.

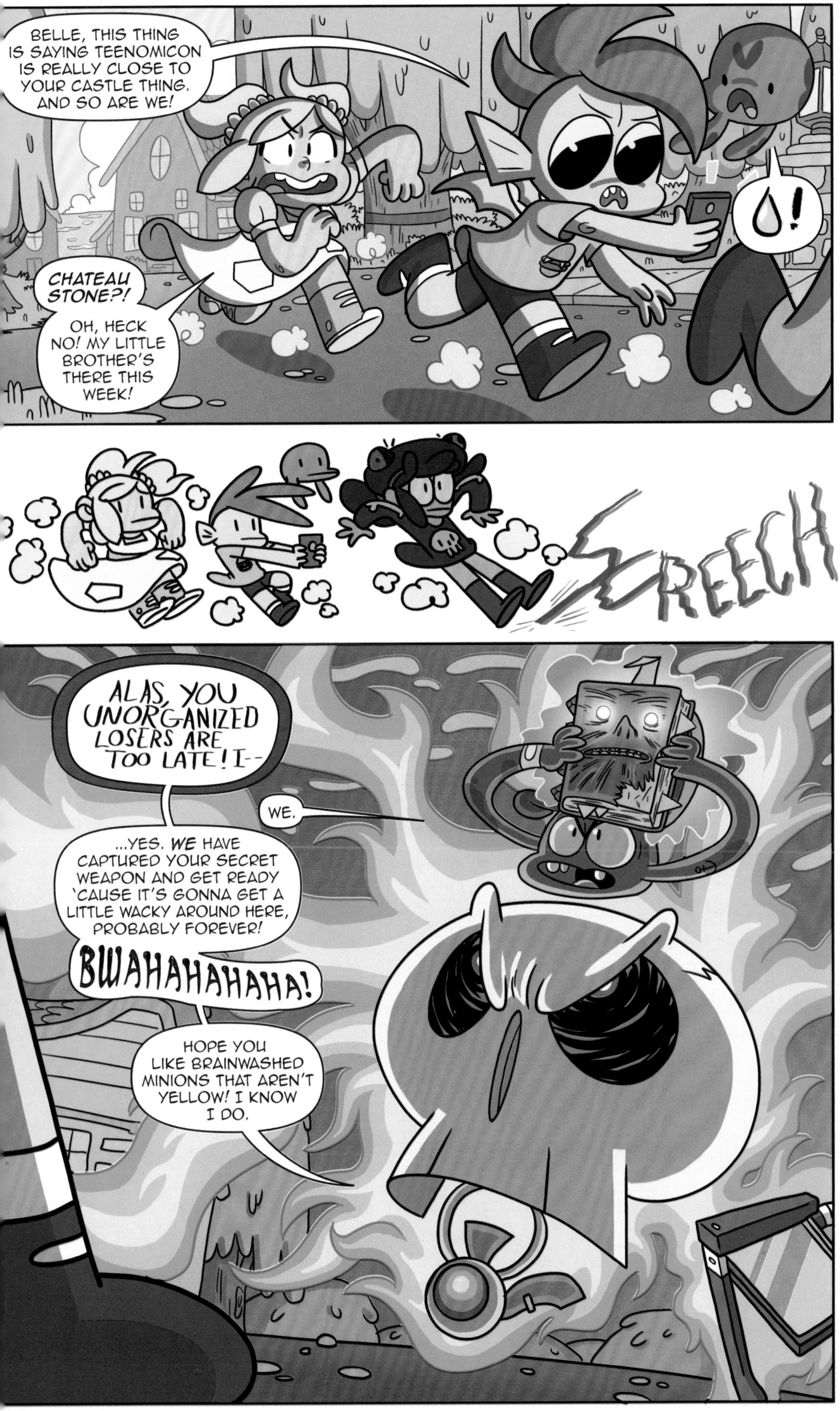
BELLE, THIS THING IS SAYING TEENOMICON IS REALLY CLOSE TO YOUR CASTLE THING. AND SO ARE WE!
CHATEAU STONE?!
OH, HECK NO! MY LITTLE BROTHER'S THERE THIS WEEK!
!
SCREECH
ALAS, YOU UNORGANIZED LOSERS ARE TOO LATE! I--
WE.
...YES. WE HAVE CAPTURED YOUR SECRET WEAPON AND GET READY 'CAUSE IT'S GONNA GET A LITTLE WACKY AROUND HERE, PROBABLY FOREVER!
BWAHAHAHAHA!
HOPE YOU LIKE BRAINWASHED MINIONS THAT AREN'T YELLOW! I KNOW I DO.

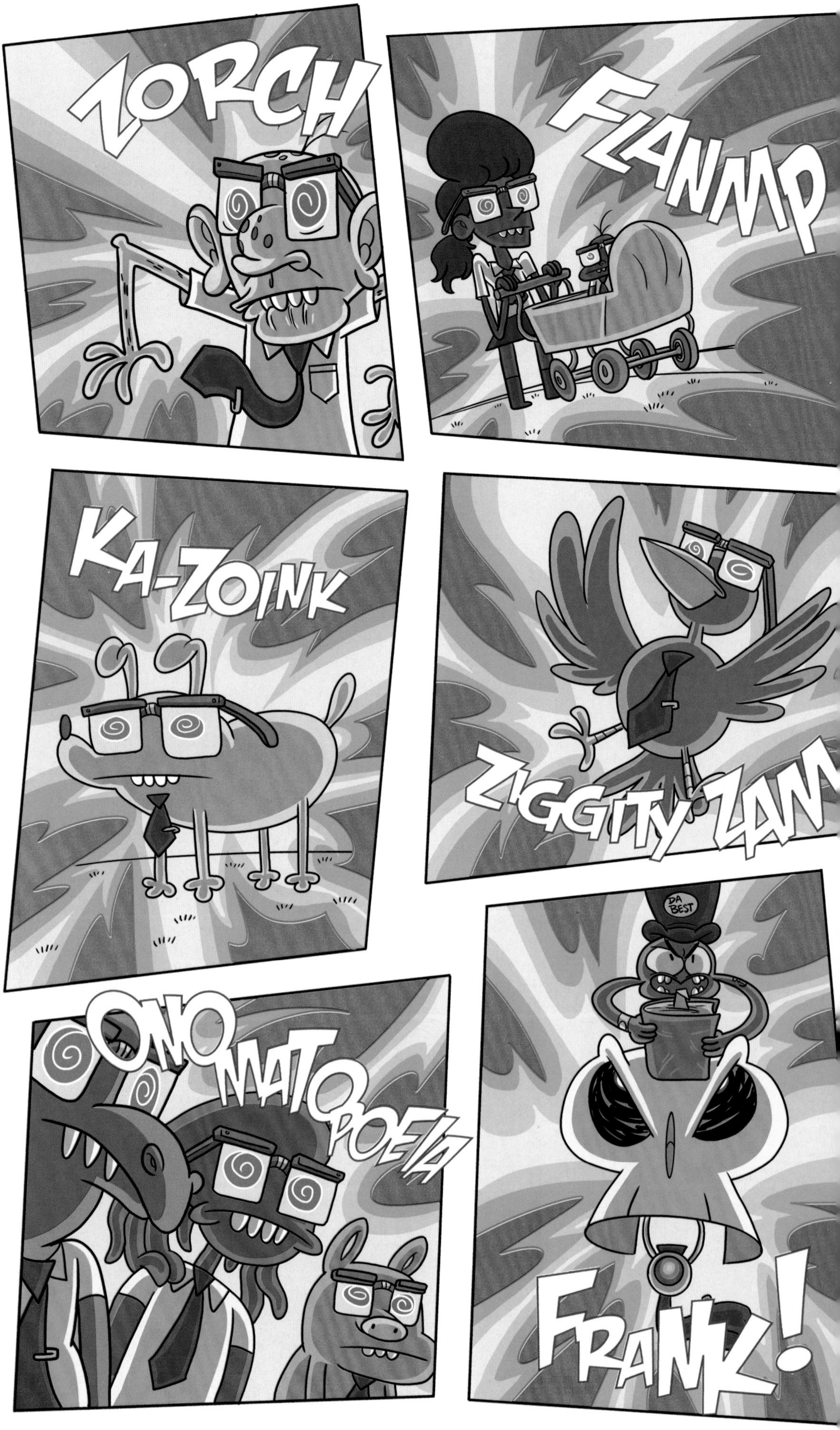
ZORCH
FLAMMP
KA-ZOINK
ZIGGITY ZAM
DA BEST
ONOMATOPOEIA
FRANK!

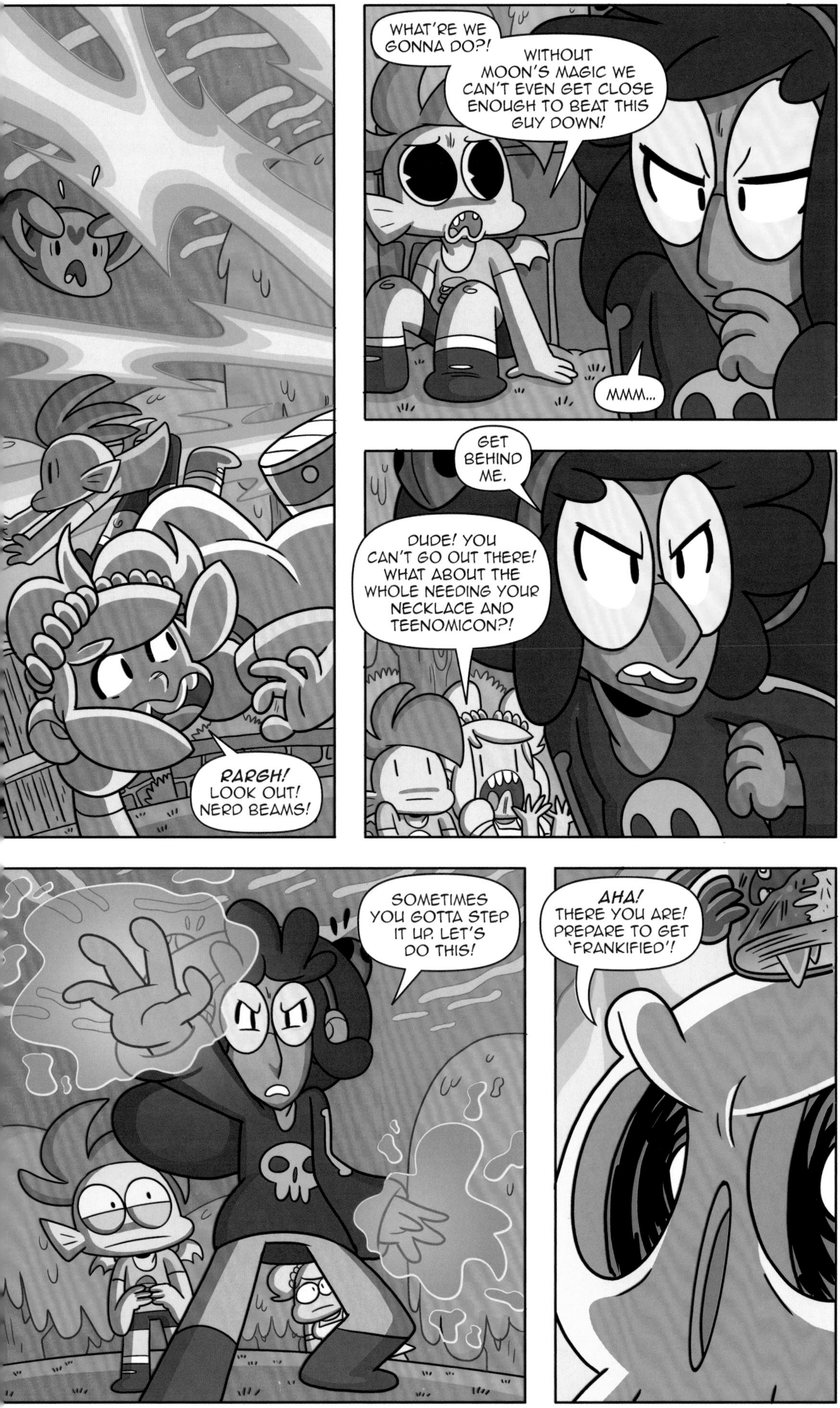
RARGH! LOOK OUT! NERD BEAMS!
WHAT'RE WE GONNA DO?!
WITHOUT MOON'S MAGIC WE CAN'T EVEN GET CLOSE ENOUGH TO BEAT THIS GUY DOWN!
MMM...
GET BEHIND ME.
DUDE! YOU CAN'T GO OUT THERE! WHAT ABOUT THE WHOLE NEEDING YOUR NECKLACE AND TEENOMICON?!
SOMETIMES YOU GOTTA STEP IT UP. LET'S DO THIS!
AHA! THERE YOU ARE! PREPARE TO GET 'FRANKIFIED'!

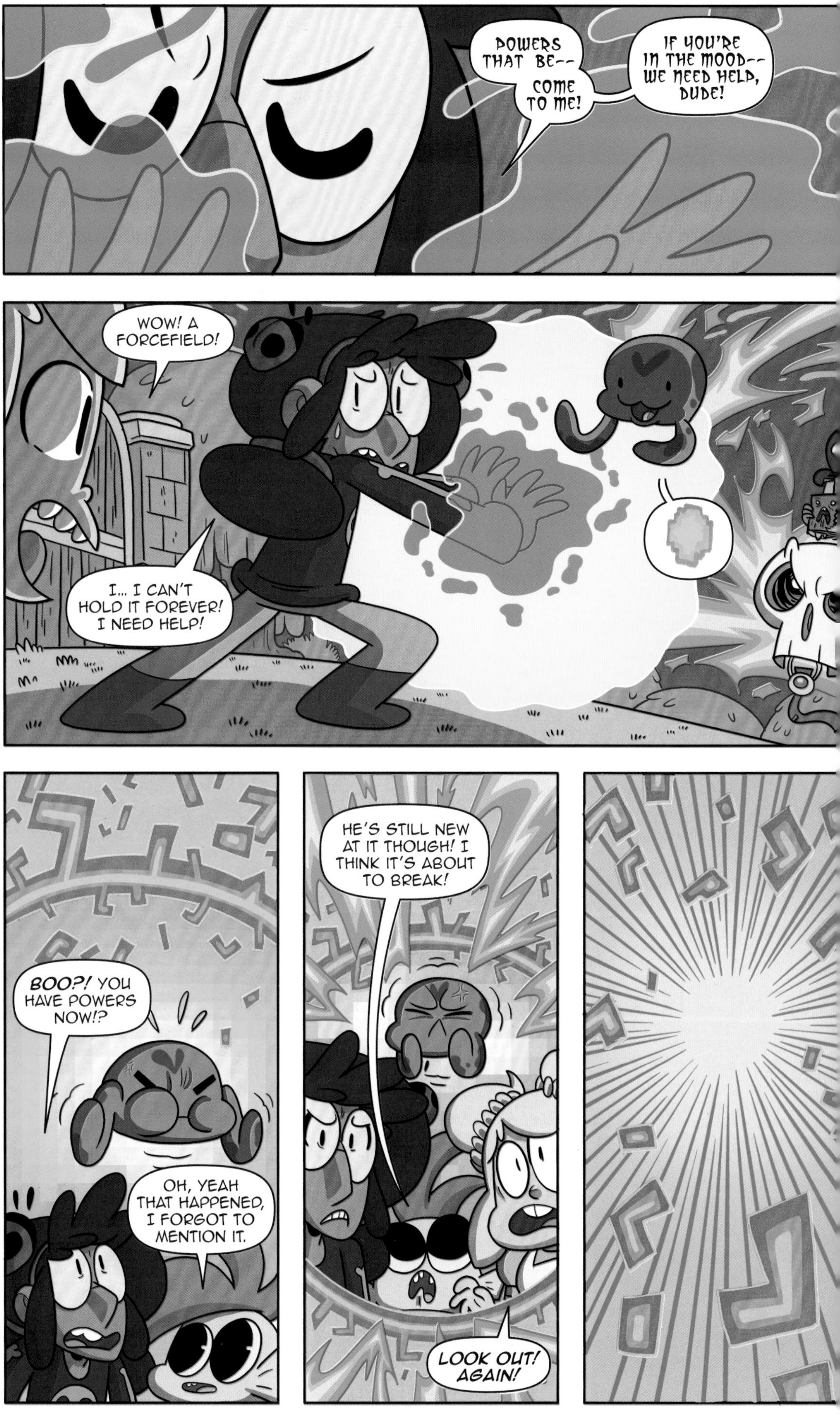
POWERS THAT BE-- COME TO ME!
IF YOU'RE IN THE MOOD-- WE NEED HELP, DUDE!
WOW! A FORCEFIELD!
I... I CAN'T HOLD IT FOREVER! I NEED HELP!
BOO?! YOU HAVE POWERS NOW!?
OH, YEAH THAT HAPPENED, I FORGOT TO MENTION IT.
HE'S STILL NEW AT IT THOUGH! I THINK IT'S ABOUT TO BREAK!
LOOK OUT! AGAIN!

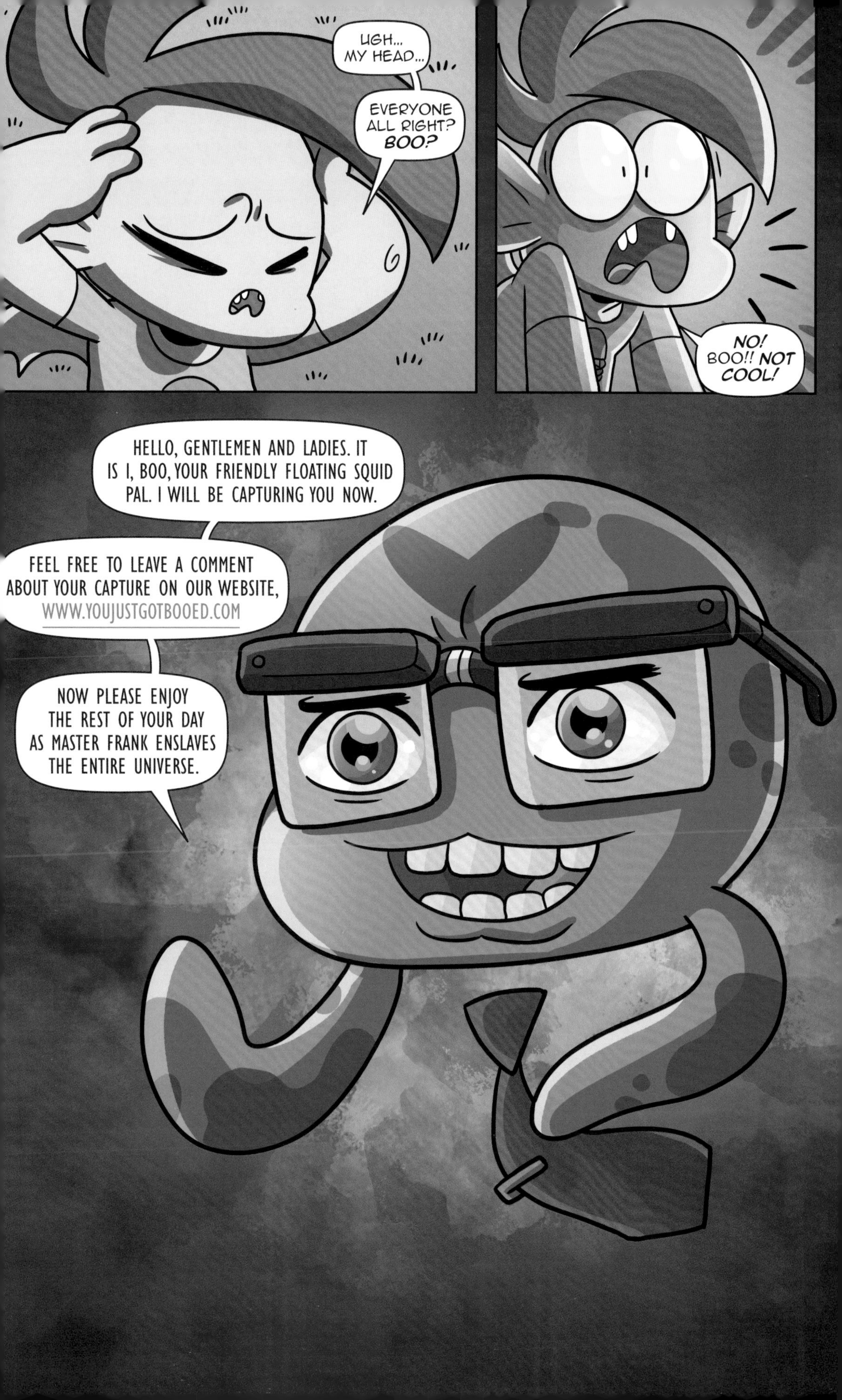
UGH...
MY HEAD...
EVERYONE ALL RIGHT? BOO?
NO! BOO!! NOT COOL!
HELLO, GENTLEMEN AND LADIES. IT IS I, BOO, YOUR FRIENDLY FLOATING SQUID PAL. I WILL BE CAPTURING YOU NOW.
FEEL FREE TO LEAVE A COMMENT ABOUT YOUR CAPTURE ON OUR WEBSITE, WWW.YOUJUSTGOTBOOED.COM
NOW PLEASE ENJOY THE REST OF YOUR DAY AS MASTER FRANK ENSLAVES THE ENTIRE UNIVERSE.

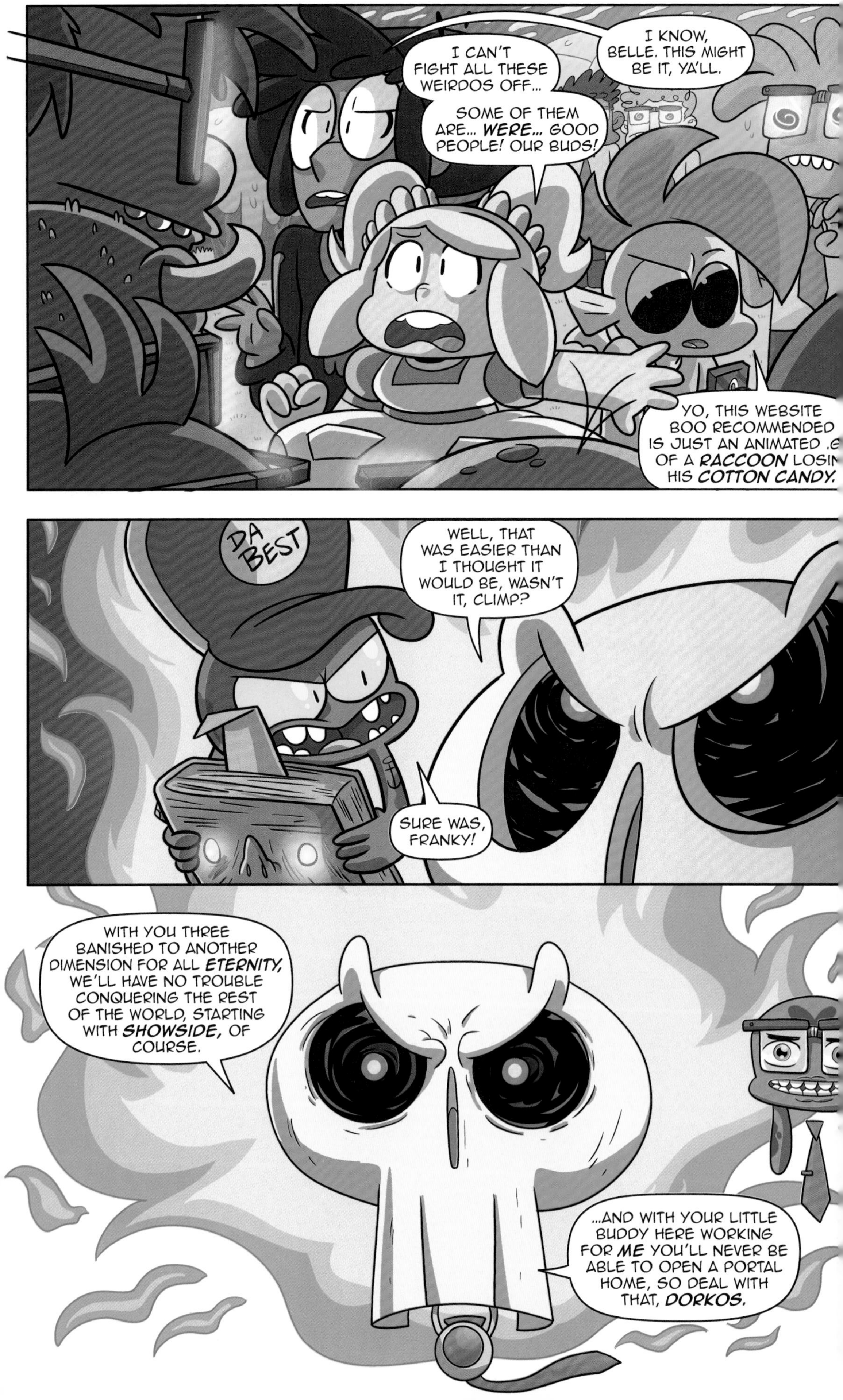
I CAN'T FIGHT ALL THESE WEIRDOS OFF...
I KNOW, BELLE. THIS MIGHT BE IT, YA'LL.
SOME OF THEM ARE... *WERE...* GOOD PEOPLE! OUR BUDS!
YO, THIS WEBSITE BOO RECOMMENDED IS JUST AN ANIMATED . OF A *RACCOON* LOSI HIS *COTTON CANDY.*
DA BEST
WELL, THAT WAS EASIER THAN I THOUGHT IT WOULD BE, WASN'T IT, CLIMP?
SURE WAS, FRANKY!
WITH YOU THREE BANISHED TO ANOTHER DIMENSION FOR ALL *ETERNITY,* WE'LL HAVE NO TROUBLE CONQUERING THE REST OF THE WORLD, STARTING WITH *SHOWSIDE,* OF COURSE.
...AND WITH YOUR LITTLE BUDDY HERE WORKING FOR *ME* YOU'LL NEVER BE ABLE TO OPEN A PORTAL HOME, SO DEAL WITH THAT, *DORKOS.*

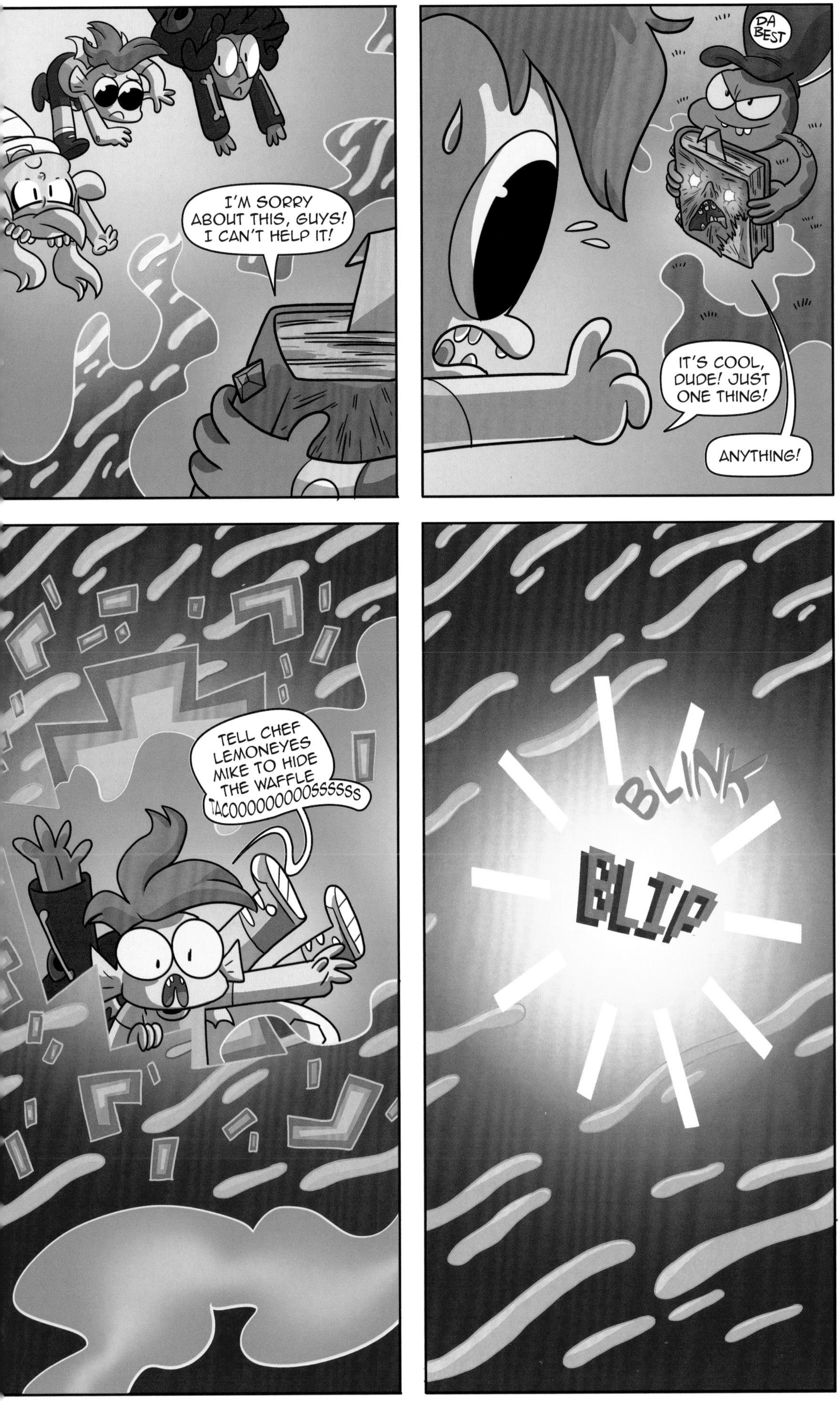
I'M SORRY ABOUT THIS, GUYS! I CAN'T HELP IT!
DA BEST
IT'S COOL, DUDE! JUST ONE THING!
ANYTHING!
TELL CHEF LEMONEYES MIKE TO HIDE THE WAFFLE TACOOOOOOOOOOSSSSSS
BLINK
BLIP

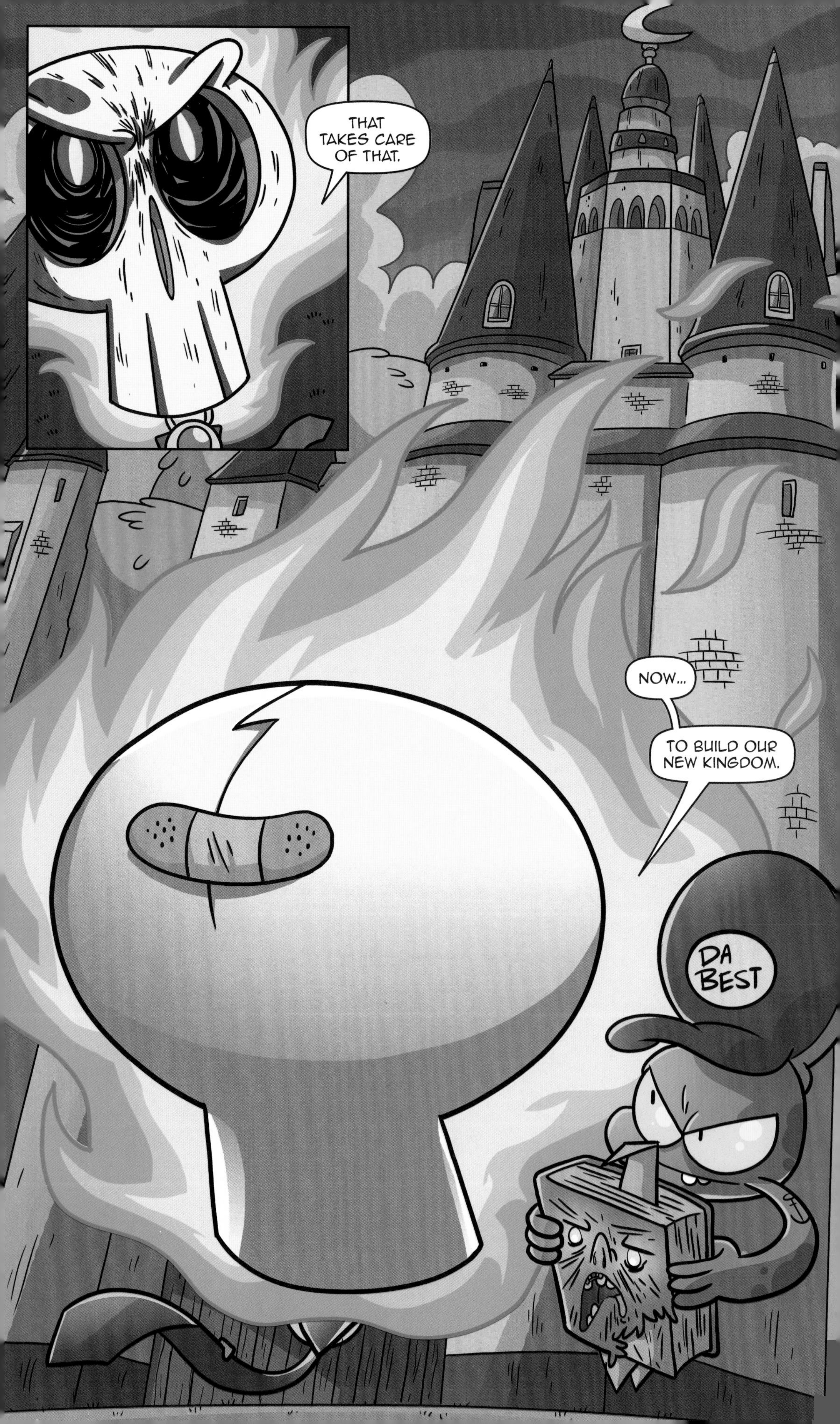
THAT TAKES CARE OF THAT.
NOW...
TO BUILD OUR NEW KINGDOM.
DA BEST

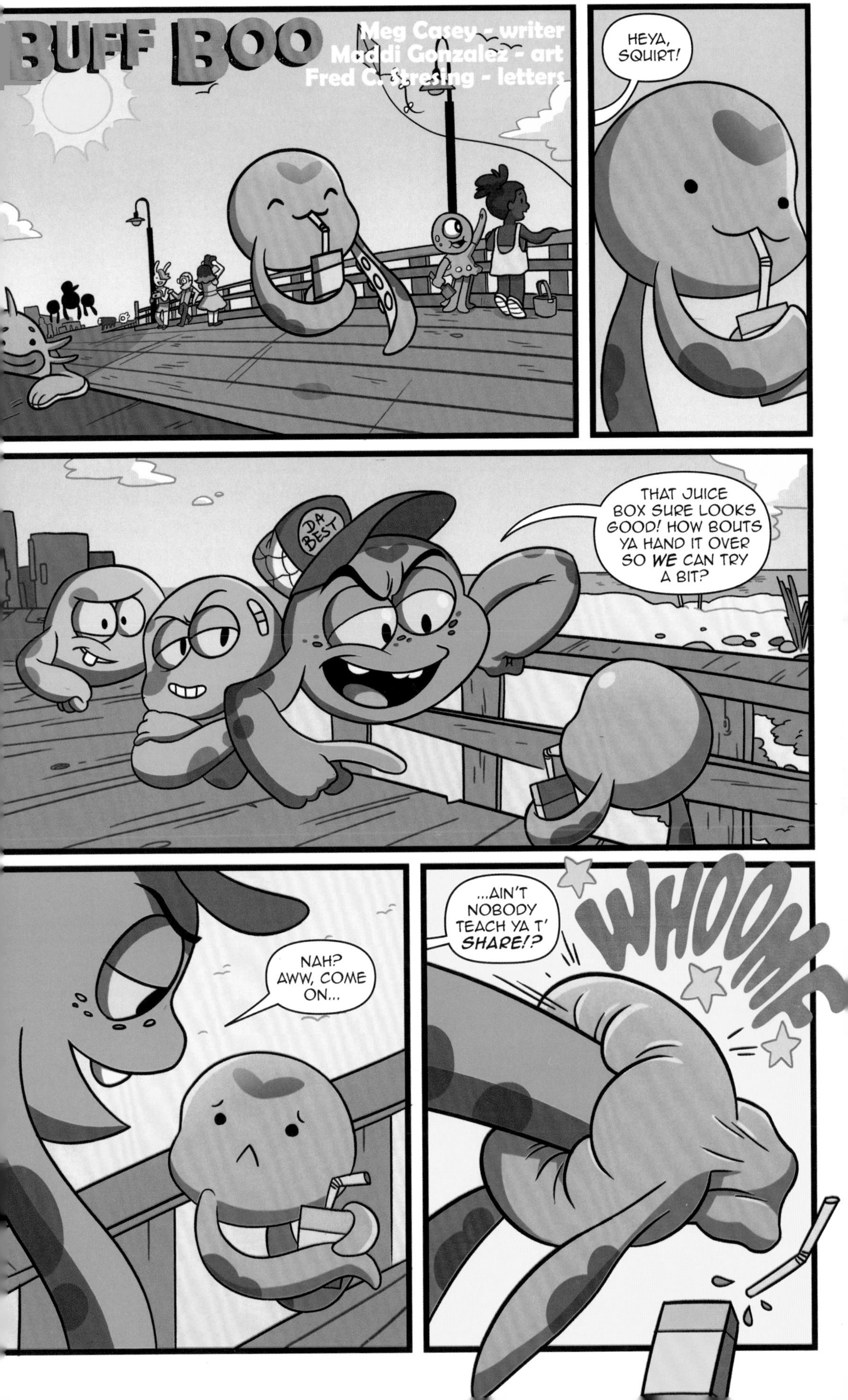
BUFF BOO
Meg Casey - writer
Maddi Gonzalez - art
Fred C. Stresing - letters
HEYA, SQUIRT!
THAT JUICE BOX SURE LOOKS GOOD! HOW BOUTS YA HAND IT OVER SO WE CAN TRY A BIT?
DA BEST
NAH? AWW, COME ON...
...AIN'T NOBODY TEACH YA T' SHARE!?
WHOOMF

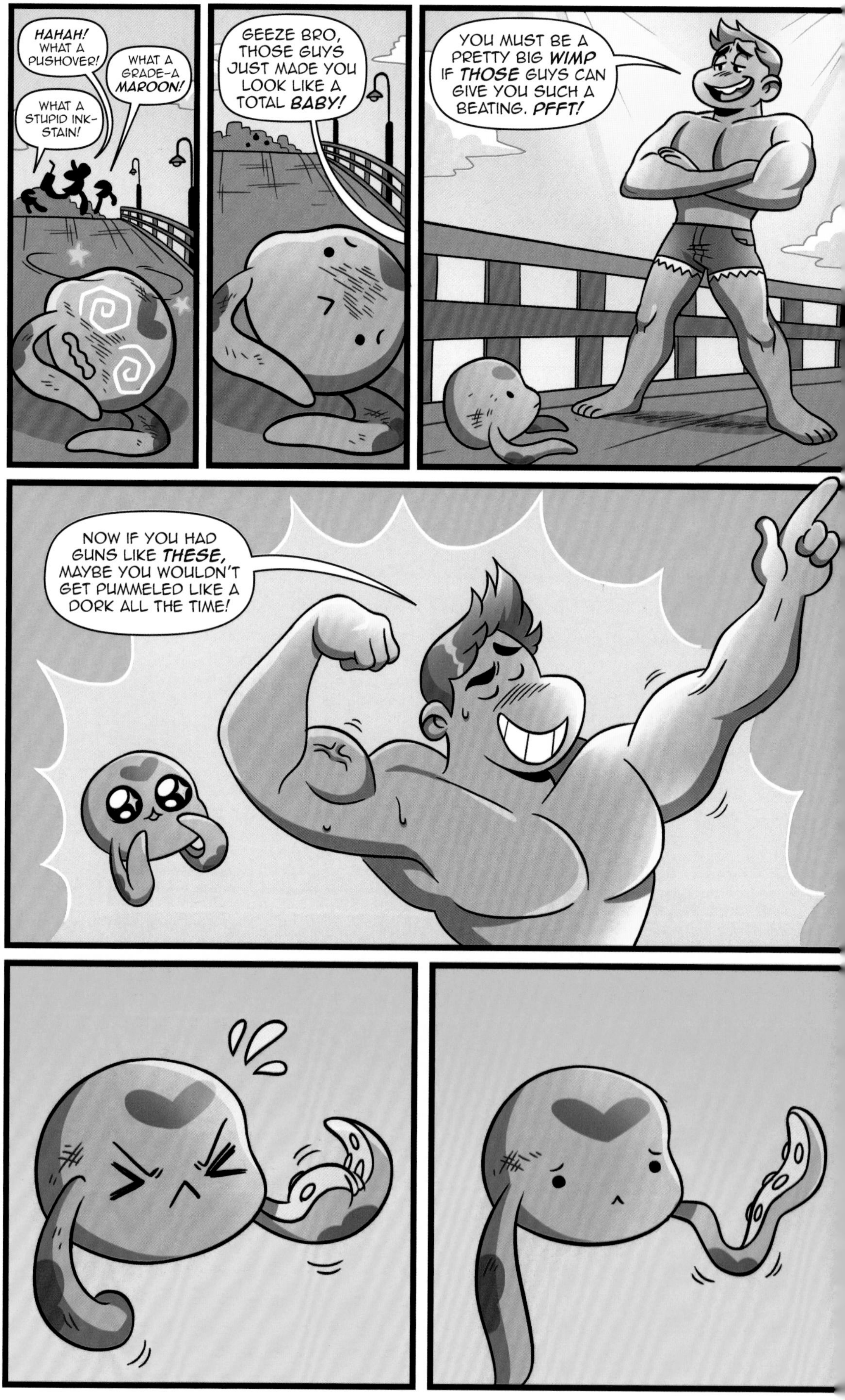
HAHAH! WHAT A PUSHOVER!
WHAT A STUPID INK-STAIN!
WHAT A GRADE-A MAROON!
GEEZE BRO, THOSE GUYS JUST MADE YOU LOOK LIKE A TOTAL BABY!
YOU MUST BE A PRETTY BIG WIMP IF THOSE GUYS CAN GIVE YOU SUCH A BEATING. PFFT!
NOW IF YOU HAD GUNS LIKE THESE, MAYBE YOU WOULDN'T GET PUMMELED LIKE A DORK ALL THE TIME!

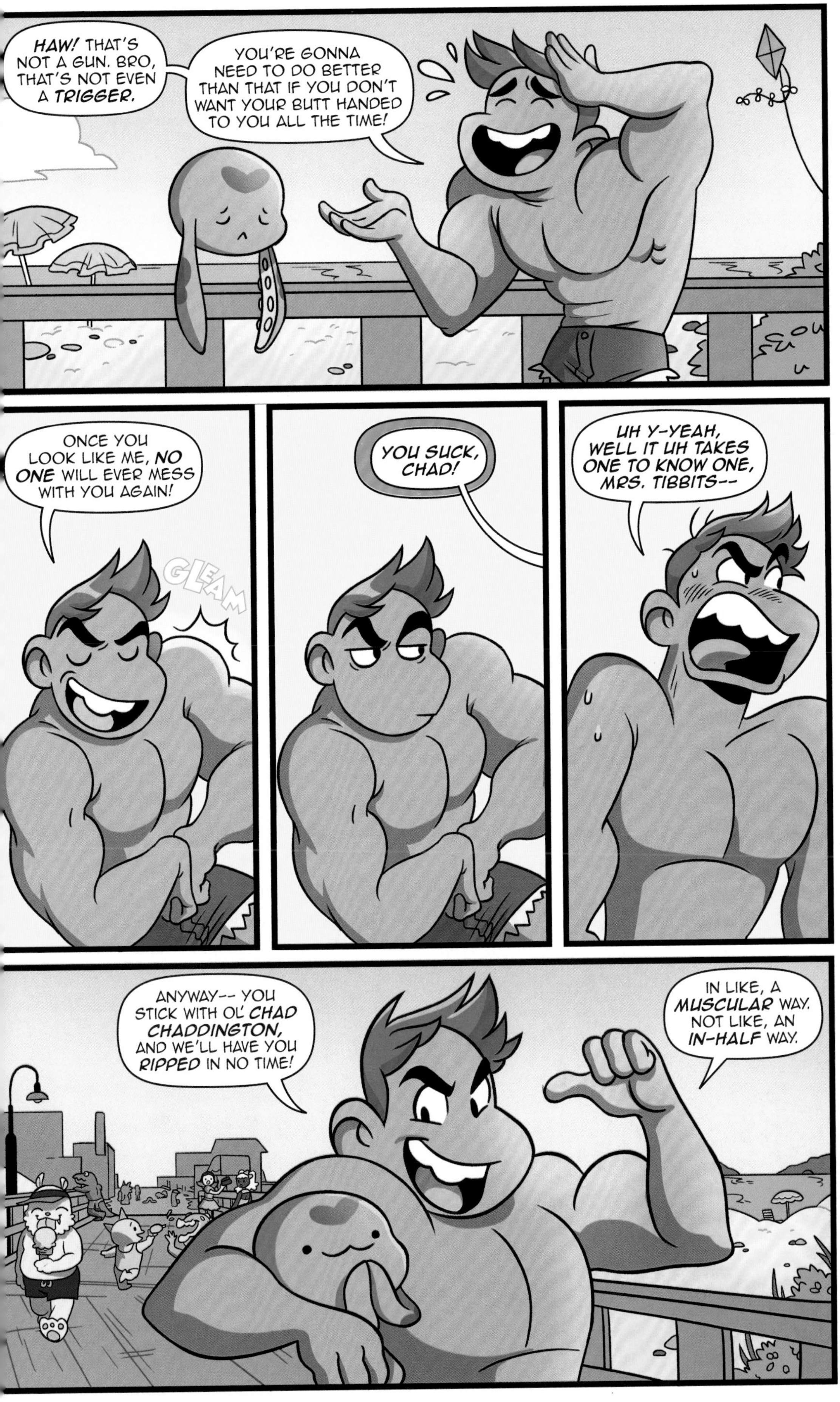

HAW! THAT'S NOT A GUN. BRO, THAT'S NOT EVEN A TRIGGER.
YOU'RE GONNA NEED TO DO BETTER THAN THAT IF YOU DON'T WANT YOUR BUTT HANDED TO YOU ALL THE TIME!
ONCE YOU LOOK LIKE ME, NO ONE WILL EVER MESS WITH YOU AGAIN!
GLEAM
YOU SUCK, CHAD!
UH Y-YEAH, WELL IT UH TAKES ONE TO KNOW ONE, MRS. TIBBITS--
ANYWAY-- YOU STICK WITH OL' CHAD CHADDINGTON, AND WE'LL HAVE YOU RIPPED IN NO TIME!
IN LIKE, A MUSCULAR WAY. NOT LIKE, AN IN-HALF WAY.

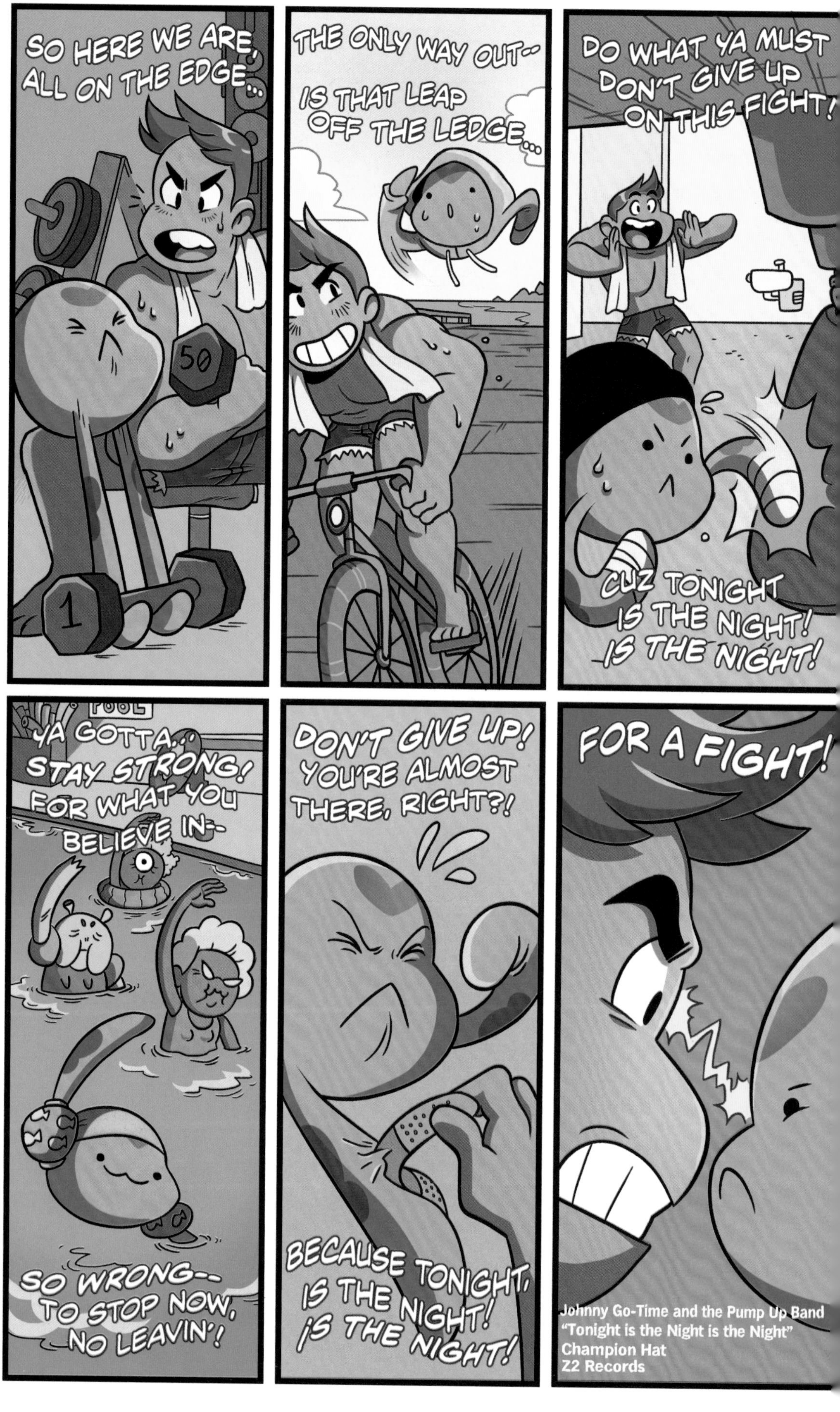
SO HERE WE ARE, ALL ON THE EDGE...
50
1
THE ONLY WAY OUT--
IS THAT LEAP OFF THE LEDGE...
DO WHAT YA MUST DON'T GIVE UP ON THIS FIGHT!
CUZ TONIGHT IS THE NIGHT! IS THE NIGHT!
POOL
YA GOTTA... STAY STRONG! FOR WHAT YOU BELIEVE IN--
SO WRONG-- TO STOP NOW, NO LEAVIN'!
DON'T GIVE UP! YOU'RE ALMOST THERE, RIGHT?!
BECAUSE TONIGHT, IS THE NIGHT! IS THE NIGHT!
FOR A FIGHT!
Johnny Go-Time and the Pump Up Band
"Tonight is the Night is the Night"
Champion Hat
Z2 Records

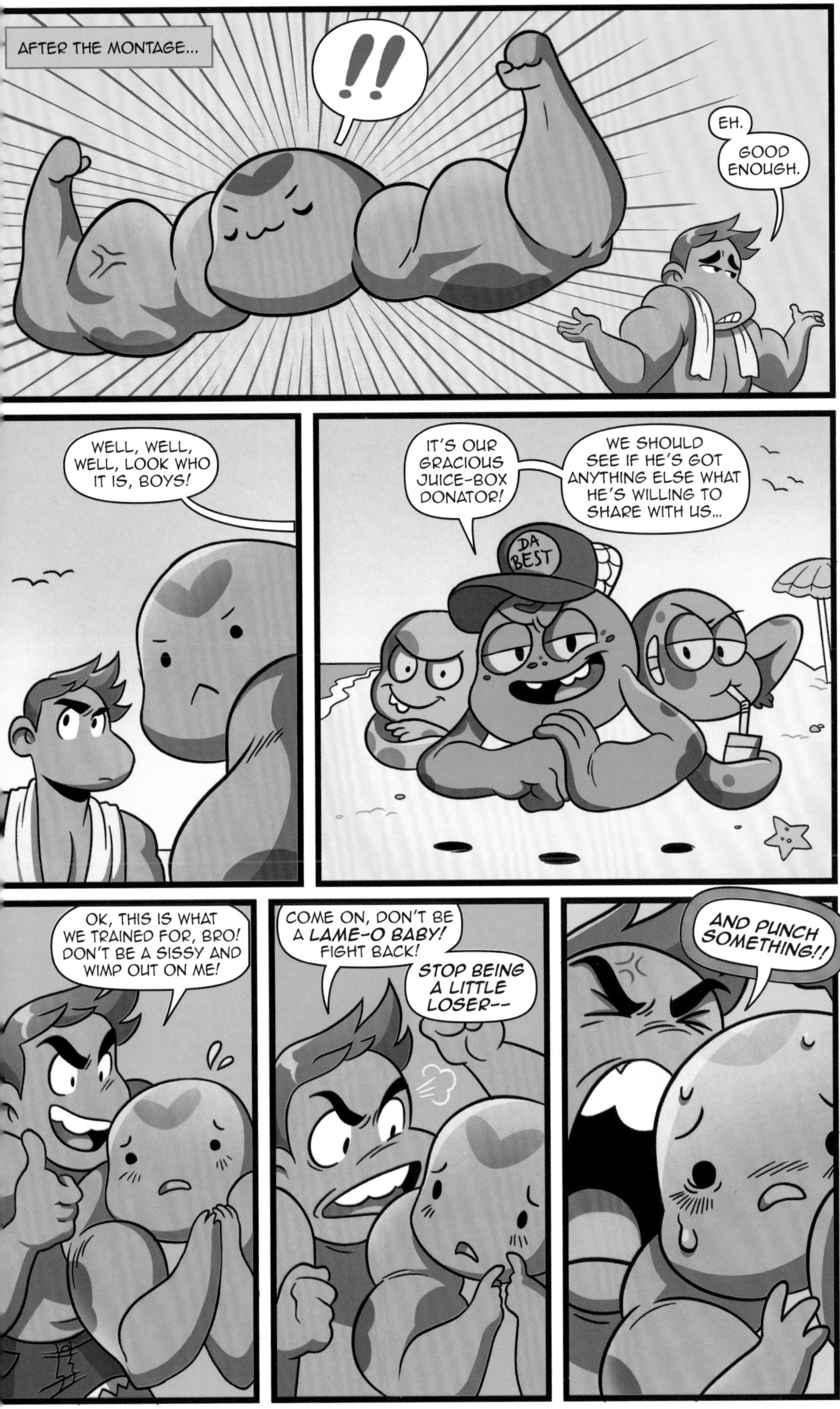
AFTER THE MONTAGE...
!!
EH.
GOOD ENOUGH.
WELL, WELL, WELL, LOOK WHO IT IS, BOYS!
IT'S OUR GRACIOUS JUICE-BOX DONATOR!
WE SHOULD SEE IF HE'S GOT ANYTHING ELSE WHAT HE'S WILLING TO SHARE WITH US...
DA BEST
OK, THIS IS WHAT WE TRAINED FOR, BRO! DON'T BE A SISSY AND WIMP OUT ON ME!
COME ON, DON'T BE A *LAME-O BABY!* FIGHT BACK!
STOP BEING A LITTLE LOSER--
AND PUNCH SOMETHING!!

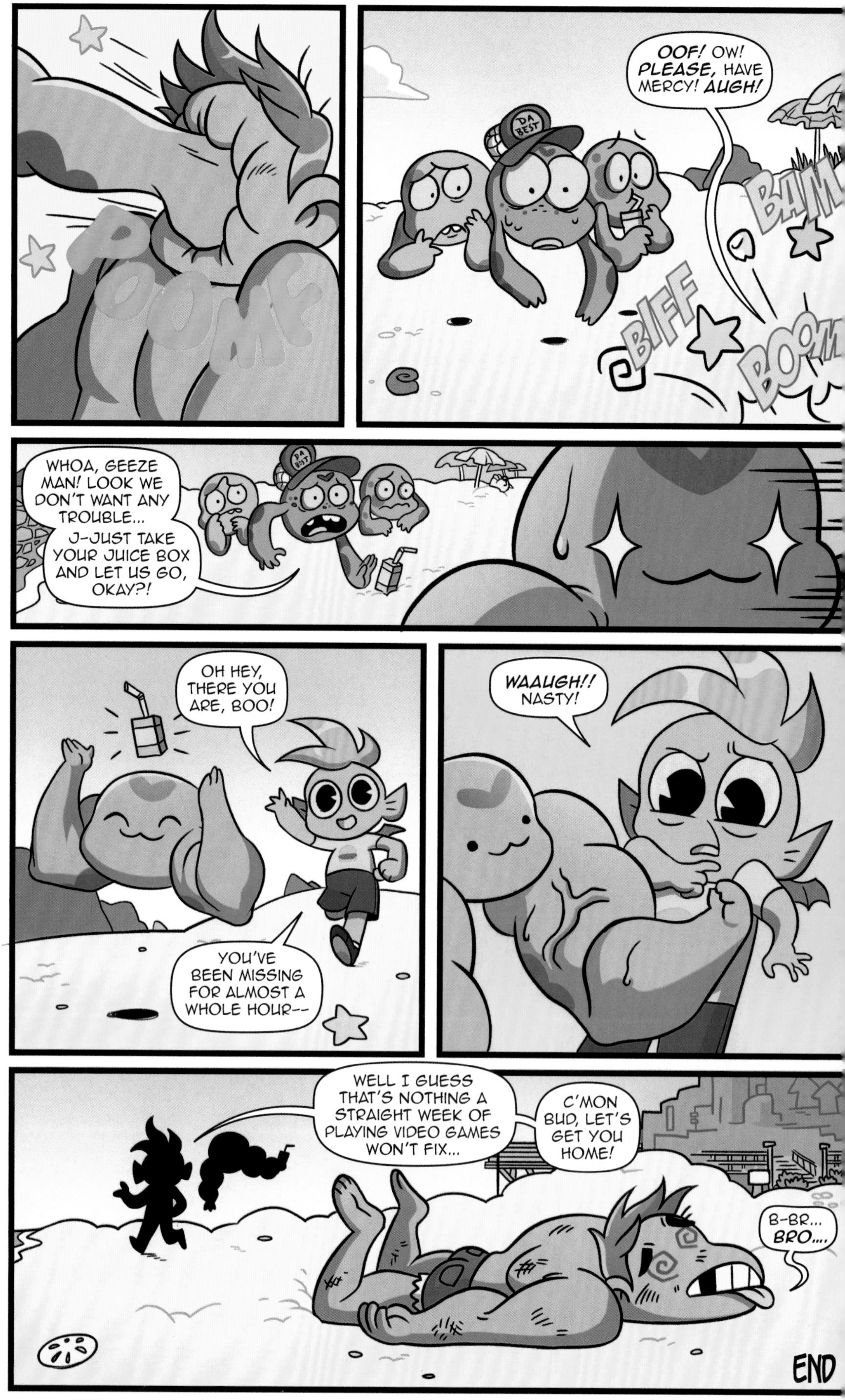
POOMF
OOF! OW! PLEASE, HAVE MERCY! AUGH!
DA BEST
BAM
BIFF
BOOM
WHOA, GEEZE MAN! LOOK WE DON'T WANT ANY TROUBLE...
J-JUST TAKE YOUR JUICE BOX AND LET US GO, OKAY?!
OH HEY, THERE YOU ARE, BOO!
YOU'VE BEEN MISSING FOR ALMOST A WHOLE HOUR--
WAAUGH!! NASTY!
WELL I GUESS THAT'S NOTHING A STRAIGHT WEEK OF PLAYING VIDEO GAMES WON'T FIX...
C'MON BUD, LET'S GET YOU HOME!
B-BR... BRO....
END

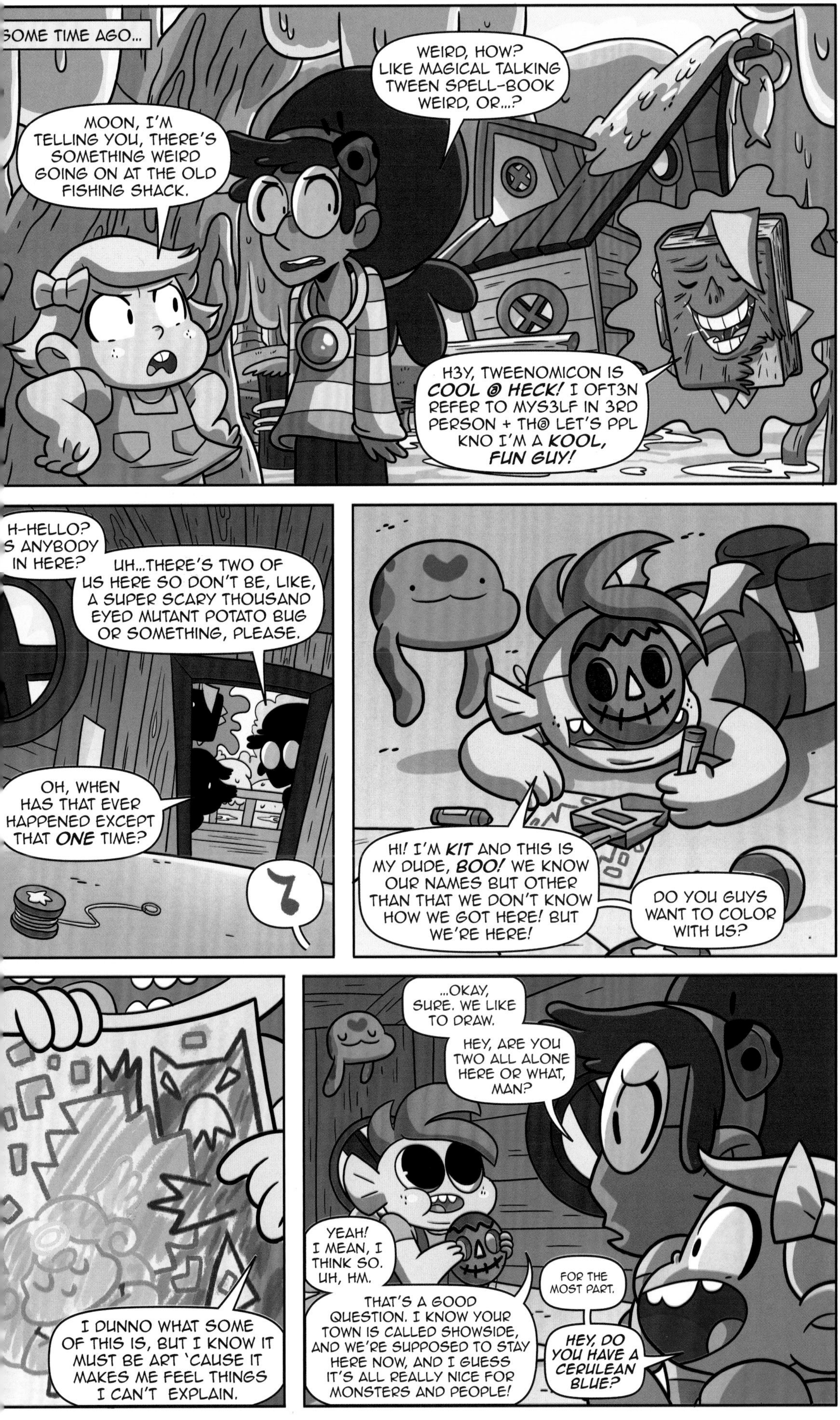
SOME TIME AGO...
MOON, I'M TELLING YOU, THERE'S SOMETHING WEIRD GOING ON AT THE OLD FISHING SHACK.
WEIRD, HOW? LIKE MAGICAL TALKING TWEEN SPELL-BOOK WEIRD, OR...?
H3Y, TWEENOMICON IS COOL @ HECK! I OFT3N REFER TO MYS3LF IN 3RD PERSON + TH@ LET'S PPL KNO I'M A KOOL, FUN GUY!
H-HELLO? IS ANYBODY IN HERE?
UH...THERE'S TWO OF US HERE SO DON'T BE, LIKE, A SUPER SCARY THOUSAND EYED MUTANT POTATO BUG OR SOMETHING, PLEASE.
OH, WHEN HAS THAT EVER HAPPENED EXCEPT THAT ONE TIME?
HI! I'M KIT AND THIS IS MY DUDE, BOO! WE KNOW OUR NAMES BUT OTHER THAN THAT WE DON'T KNOW HOW WE GOT HERE! BUT WE'RE HERE!
DO YOU GUYS WANT TO COLOR WITH US?
I DUNNO WHAT SOME OF THIS IS, BUT I KNOW IT MUST BE ART 'CAUSE IT MAKES ME FEEL THINGS I CAN'T EXPLAIN.
...OKAY, SURE. WE LIKE TO DRAW.
HEY, ARE YOU TWO ALL ALONE HERE OR WHAT, MAN?
YEAH! I MEAN, I THINK SO. UH, HM.
THAT'S A GOOD QUESTION. I KNOW YOUR TOWN IS CALLED SHOWSIDE, AND WE'RE SUPPOSED TO STAY HERE NOW, AND I GUESS IT'S ALL REALLY NICE FOR MONSTERS AND PEOPLE!
FOR THE MOST PART.
HEY, DO YOU HAVE A CERULEAN BLUE?

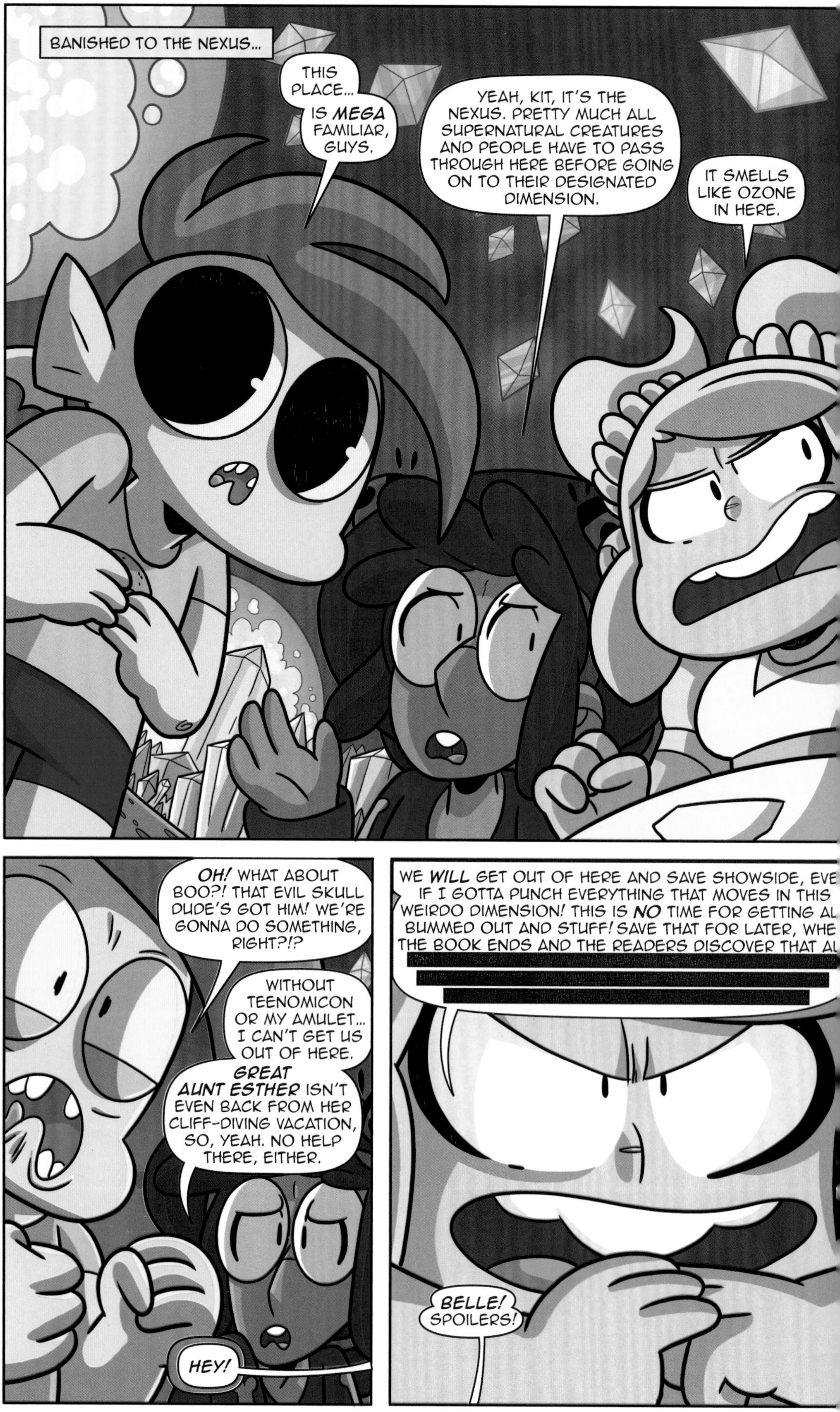
BANISHED TO THE NEXUS...
THIS PLACE...
IS *MEGA* FAMILIAR, GUYS.
YEAH, KIT, IT'S THE NEXUS. PRETTY MUCH ALL SUPERNATURAL CREATURES AND PEOPLE HAVE TO PASS THROUGH HERE BEFORE GOING ON TO THEIR DESIGNATED DIMENSION.
IT SMELLS LIKE OZONE IN HERE.
OH! WHAT ABOUT BOO?! THAT EVIL SKULL DUDE'S GOT HIM! WE'RE GONNA DO SOMETHING, RIGHT?!?
WITHOUT TEENOMICON OR MY AMULET... I CAN'T GET US OUT OF HERE.
GREAT AUNT ESTHER ISN'T EVEN BACK FROM HER CLIFF-DIVING VACATION, SO, YEAH. NO HELP THERE, EITHER.
HEY!
WE *WILL* GET OUT OF HERE AND SAVE SHOWSIDE, EVE IF I GOTTA PUNCH EVERYTHING THAT MOVES IN THIS WEIRDO DIMENSION! THIS IS *NO* TIME FOR GETTING AL BUMMED OUT AND STUFF! SAVE THAT FOR LATER, WHE THE BOOK ENDS AND THE READERS DISCOVER THAT AL [redacted]
BELLE! SPOILERS!

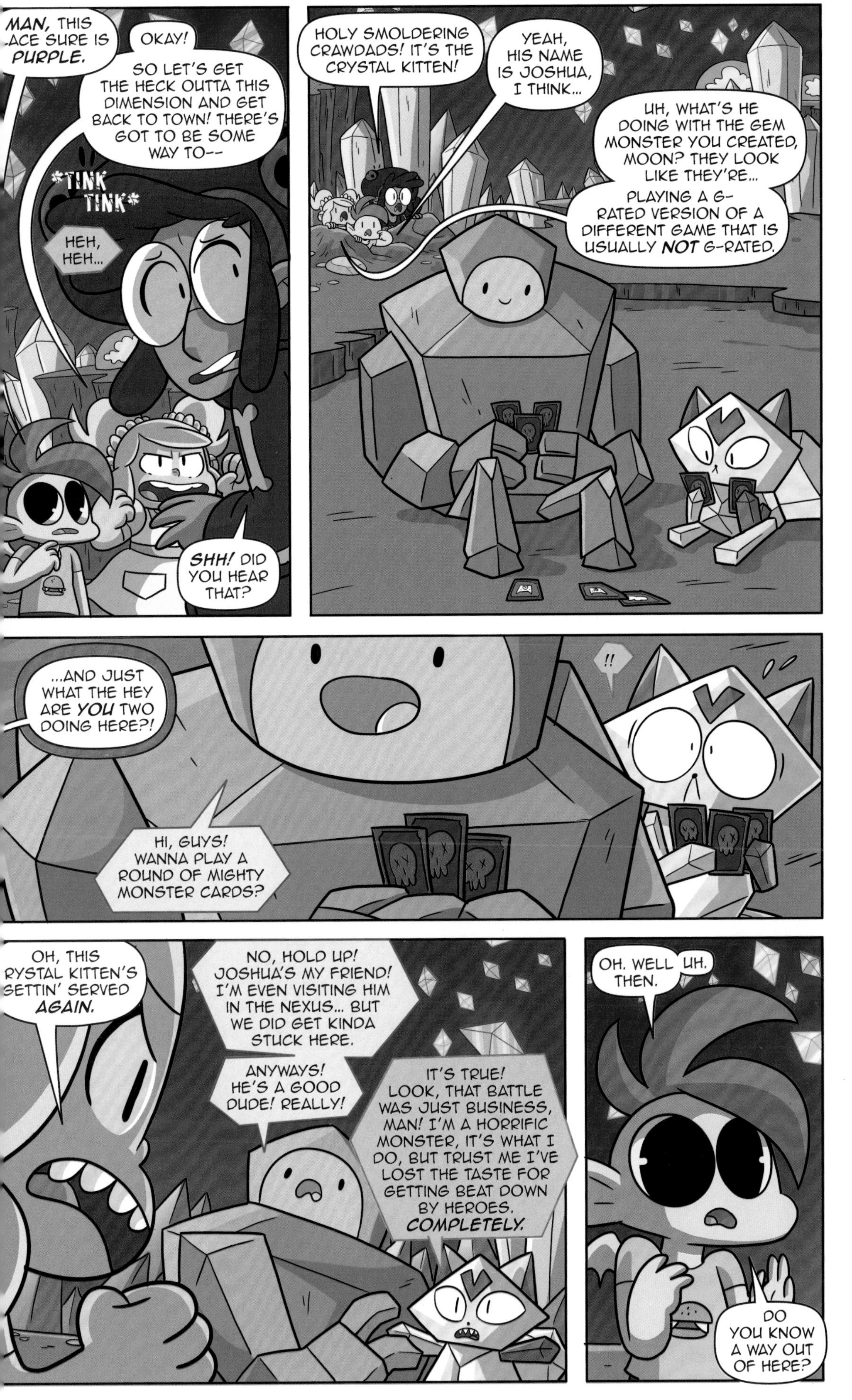

MAN, THIS
-ACE SURE IS
PURPLE.
OKAY!
SO LET'S GET THE HECK OUTTA THIS DIMENSION AND GET BACK TO TOWN! THERE'S GOT TO BE SOME WAY TO--
TINK TINK
HEH, HEH...
SHH! DID YOU HEAR THAT?
HOLY SMOLDERING CRAWDADS! IT'S THE CRYSTAL KITTEN!
YEAH, HIS NAME IS JOSHUA, I THINK...
UH, WHAT'S HE DOING WITH THE GEM MONSTER YOU CREATED, MOON? THEY LOOK LIKE THEY'RE...
PLAYING A G-RATED VERSION OF A DIFFERENT GAME THAT IS USUALLY NOT G-RATED.
...AND JUST WHAT THE HEY ARE YOU TWO DOING HERE?!
!!
HI, GUYS! WANNA PLAY A ROUND OF MIGHTY MONSTER CARDS?
OH, THIS
RYSTAL KITTEN'S
SETTIN' SERVED
AGAIN.
NO, HOLD UP! JOSHUA'S MY FRIEND! I'M EVEN VISITING HIM IN THE NEXUS... BUT WE DID GET KINDA STUCK HERE.
ANYWAYS! HE'S A GOOD DUDE! REALLY!
IT'S TRUE! LOOK, THAT BATTLE WAS JUST BUSINESS, MAN! I'M A HORRIFIC MONSTER, IT'S WHAT I DO, BUT TRUST ME I'VE LOST THE TASTE FOR GETTING BEAT DOWN BY HEROES. COMPLETELY.
OH. WELL
UH. THEN.
DO YOU KNOW A WAY OUT OF HERE?

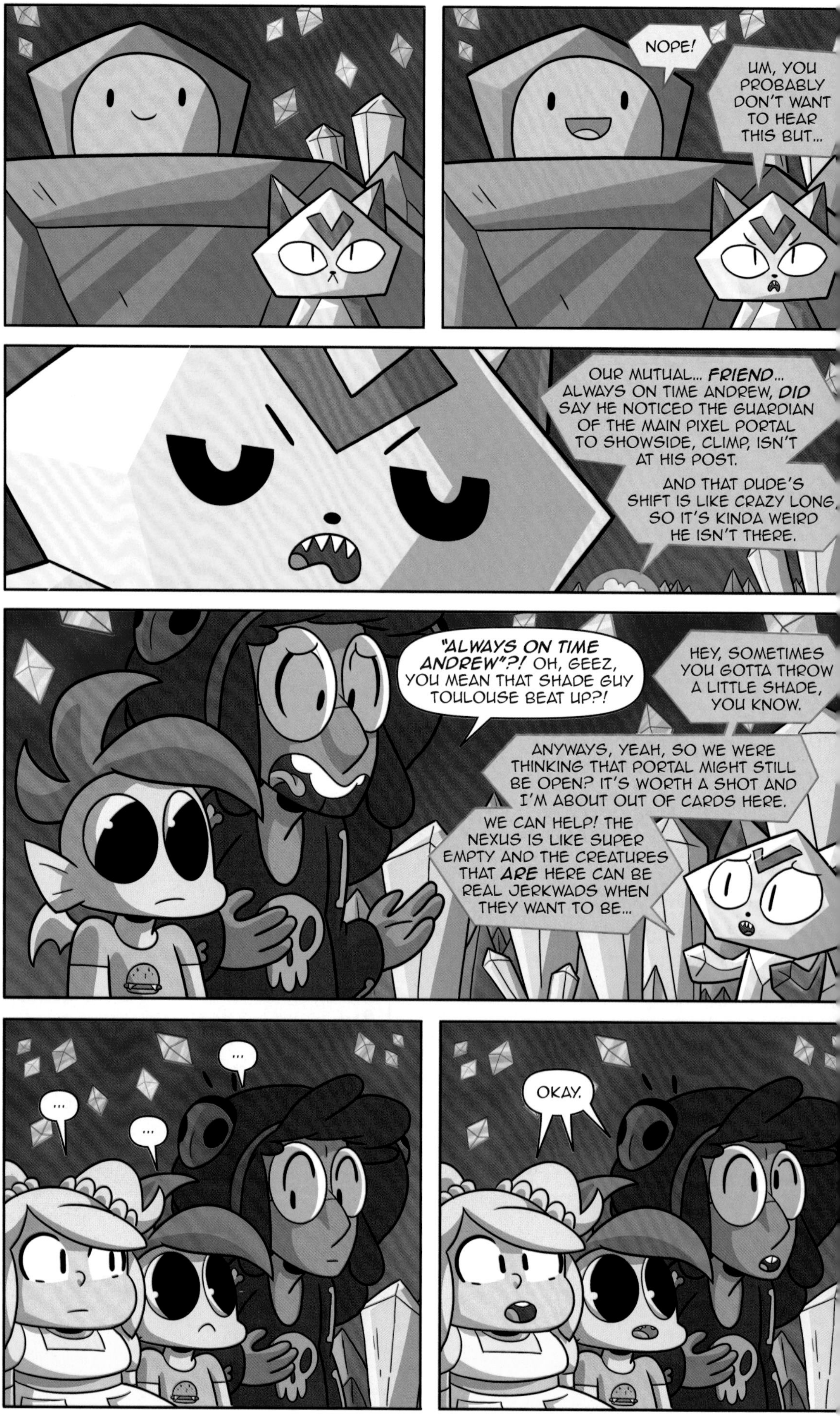
NOPE!
UM, YOU PROBABLY DON'T WANT TO HEAR THIS BUT...
OUR MUTUAL... FRIEND... ALWAYS ON TIME ANDREW, DID SAY HE NOTICED THE GUARDIAN OF THE MAIN PIXEL PORTAL TO SHOWSIDE, CLIMP, ISN'T AT HIS POST.
AND THAT DUDE'S SHIFT IS LIKE CRAZY LONG, SO IT'S KINDA WEIRD HE ISN'T THERE.
"ALWAYS ON TIME ANDREW"?! OH, GEEZ, YOU MEAN THAT SHADE GUY TOULOUSE BEAT UP?!
HEY, SOMETIMES YOU GOTTA THROW A LITTLE SHADE, YOU KNOW.
ANYWAYS, YEAH, SO WE WERE THINKING THAT PORTAL MIGHT STILL BE OPEN? IT'S WORTH A SHOT AND I'M ABOUT OUT OF CARDS HERE.
WE CAN HELP! THE NEXUS IS LIKE SUPER EMPTY AND THE CREATURES THAT ARE HERE CAN BE REAL JERKWADS WHEN THEY WANT TO BE...
...
...
...
OKAY.

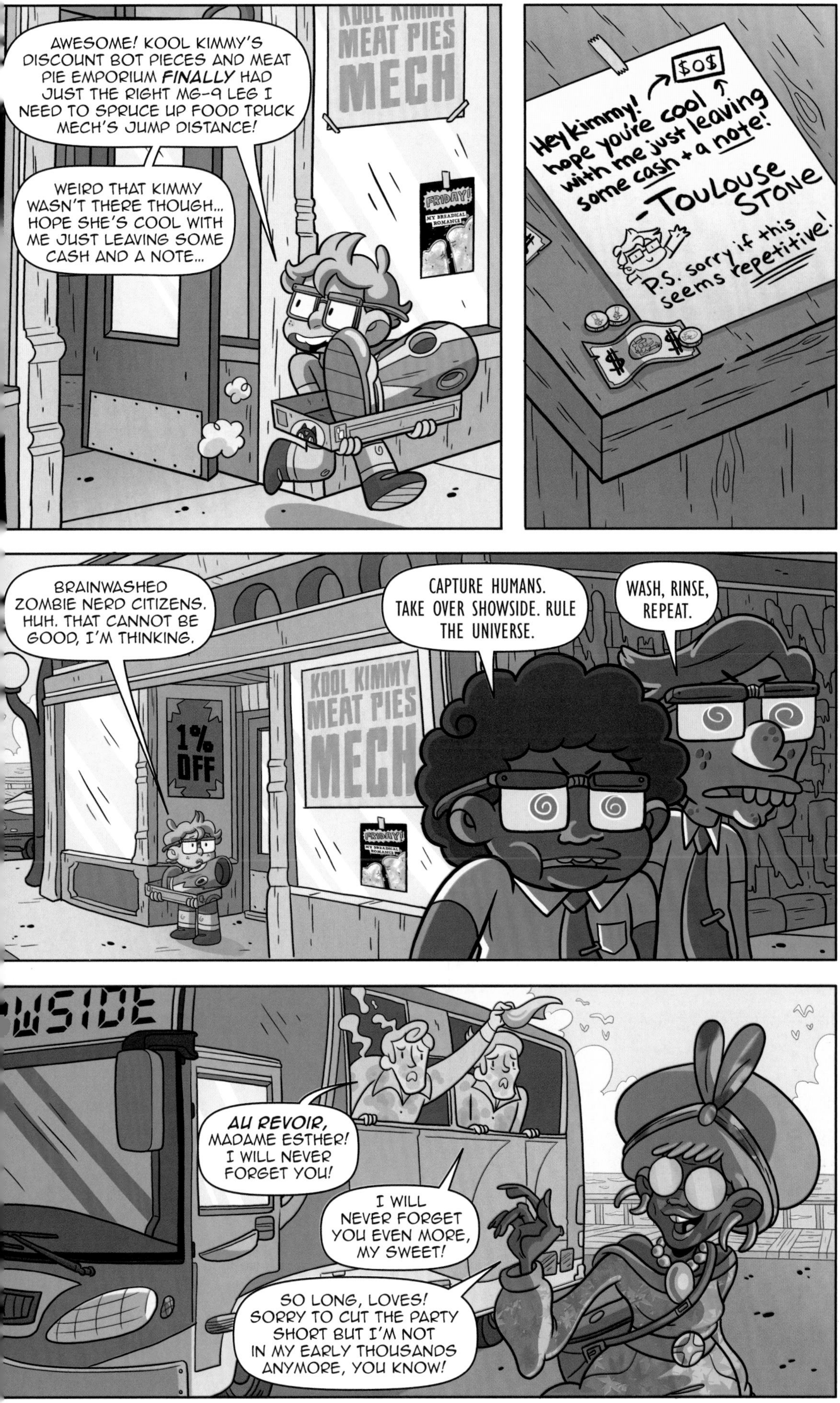
KOOL KIMMY MEAT PIES MECH
AWESOME! KOOL KIMMY'S DISCOUNT BOT PIECES AND MEAT PIE EMPORIUM *FINALLY* HAD JUST THE RIGHT MG-9 LEG I NEED TO SPRUCE UP FOOD TRUCK MECH'S JUMP DISTANCE!
WEIRD THAT KIMMY WASN'T THERE THOUGH... HOPE SHE'S COOL WITH ME JUST LEAVING SOME CASH AND A NOTE...
FRIDAY! MY BREADICAL ROMANCE
0
Hey kimmy! hope you're cool with me just leaving some cash + a note! -Toulouse Stone
P.S. sorry if this seems repetitive!
BRAINWASHED ZOMBIE NERD CITIZENS. HUH. THAT CANNOT BE GOOD, I'M THINKING.
CAPTURE HUMANS. TAKE OVER SHOWSIDE. RULE THE UNIVERSE.
WASH, RINSE, REPEAT.
1% OFF
KOOL KIMMY MEAT PIES MECH
FRIDAY! MY BREADICAL ROMANCE
WSIDE
AU REVOIR, MADAME ESTHER! I WILL NEVER FORGET YOU!
I WILL NEVER FORGET YOU EVEN MORE, MY SWEET!
SO LONG, LOVES! SORRY TO CUT THE PARTY SHORT BUT I'M NOT IN MY EARLY THOUSANDS ANYMORE, YOU KNOW!

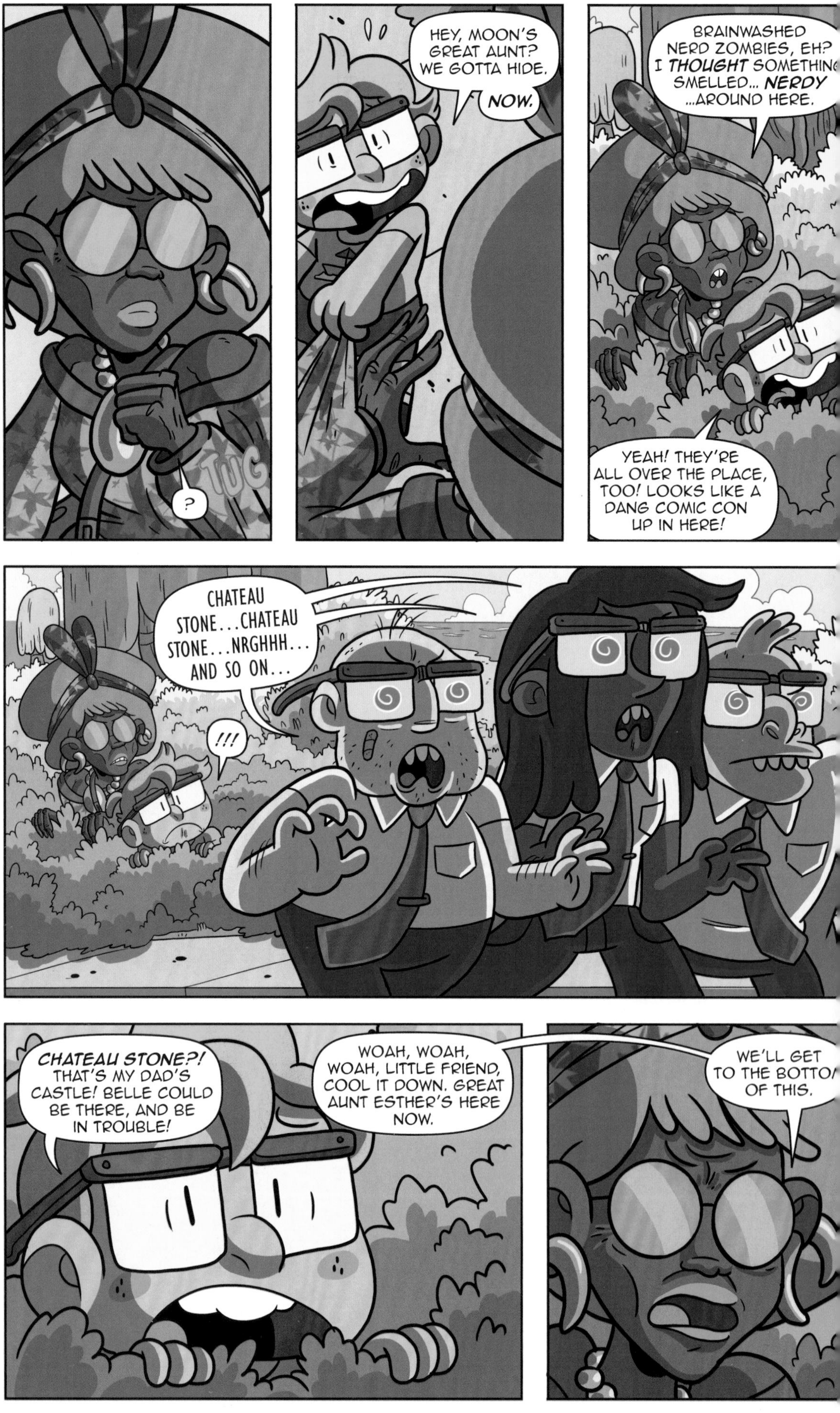
?
TUG
HEY, MOON'S GREAT AUNT? WE GOTTA HIDE.
NOW.
BRAINWASHED NERD ZOMBIES, EH? I THOUGHT SOMETHIN SMELLED... NERDY ...AROUND HERE.
YEAH! THEY'RE ALL OVER THE PLACE, TOO! LOOKS LIKE A DANG COMIC CON UP IN HERE!
CHATEAU STONE...CHATEAU STONE...NRGHHH... AND SO ON...
!!!
CHATEAU STONE?! THAT'S MY DAD'S CASTLE! BELLE COULD BE THERE, AND BE IN TROUBLE!
WOAH, WOAH, WOAH, LITTLE FRIEND, COOL IT DOWN. GREAT AUNT ESTHER'S HERE NOW.
WE'LL GET TO THE BOTTO OF THIS.

OH, YES, YES, *YES!*

SHOWSIDE'S FAMOUS CHATEAU STONE WILL DO *PERFECTLY* FOR FRANK'S FORTRESS, DON'T YOU THINK, MISTER BOO? *CLIMP?*

Quite so, Master Frank, quite so. and an excellent name choice, as well. yes, excellent and good.

...JEEZ, TONE IT DOWN A BIT, GUY.

WITH EVERY SINGLE PIXEL PORTAL SEALED OFF THANKS TO THE AMULET AND TEENOMICON, HAHA, NO FORCE IN THE UNIVERSE WILL BE ABLE TO STOP ME AND SOON NO OTHER--

US.

RIGHT RIGHT. STOP *US.* AHEM. ANYWAYS. NO OTHER DEMON WILL BE ABLE TO CHALLENGE MY REIGN! NOT HERE, AND SOON, NOT ANYWHERE!

BRAINDEAD NERDS! OPEN THE DOORS FOR MASTER FRANK! HE IS THE GREATEST!

HM, WE'LL DEFINITELY NEED TO DO SOMETHING ABOUT THE CHOICE OF *ARTWORK* ON THE WALLS...

SAYS HERE THIS STONE GUY'S A REAL TOUGH CUSTOMER, FRANKY. BEEN FIGHTING OUR KIND FOR *YEARS.*

DEMON HUNTER. MONSTER DESTROYER. LOVES SUNSETS? NOT SURE ABOUT THAT ONE, BUT, YEAH. HE'S GOT A PRETTY DANG LONG LIST OF ACCOMPLISHMENTS, JUST SAYIN'. YOU, AH, YOU THINK THIS IS A GOOD IDEA, TAKIN' OVER HIS PLACE?

Y-YEAH! BELLE'S DAD IS A *LEGEND!* THERE'S NO WAY STONE'LL LET YO--

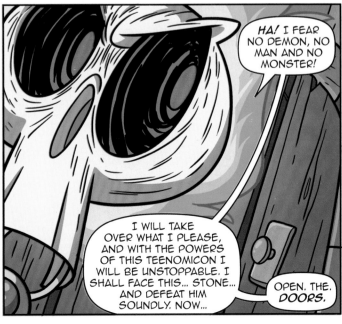

HA! I FEAR NO DEMON, NO MAN AND NO MONSTER!

I WILL TAKE OVER WHAT I PLEASE, AND WITH THE POWERS OF THIS TEENOMICON I WILL BE UNSTOPPABLE. I SHALL FACE THIS... STONE... AND DEFEAT HIM SOUNDLY. NOW...

OPEN. THE. *DOORS.*

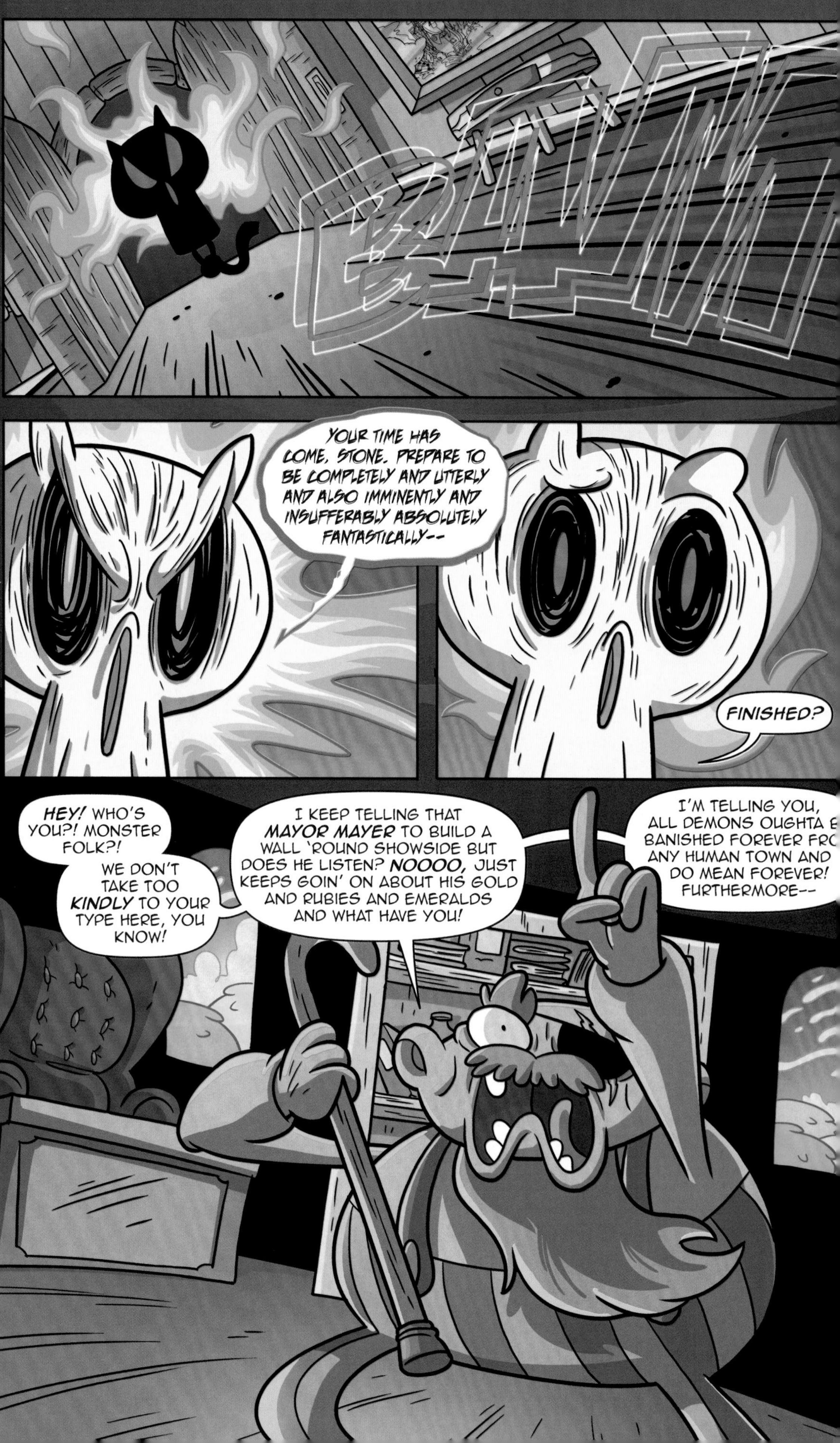
BAMM
YOUR TIME HAS COME, STONE. PREPARE TO BE COMPLETELY AND UTTERLY AND ALSO IMMINENTLY AND INSUFFERABLY ABSOLUTELY FANTASTICALLY--
FINISHED?
HEY! WHO'S YOU?! MONSTER FOLK?!
WE DON'T TAKE TOO KINDLY TO YOUR TYPE HERE, YOU KNOW!
I KEEP TELLING THAT MAYOR MAYER TO BUILD A WALL 'ROUND SHOWSIDE BUT DOES HE LISTEN? NOOOO, JUST KEEPS GOIN' ON ABOUT HIS GOLD AND RUBIES AND EMERALDS AND WHAT HAVE YOU!
I'M TELLING YOU, ALL DEMONS OUGHTA B BANISHED FOREVER FRO ANY HUMAN TOWN AND DO MEAN FOREVER! FURTHERMORE--

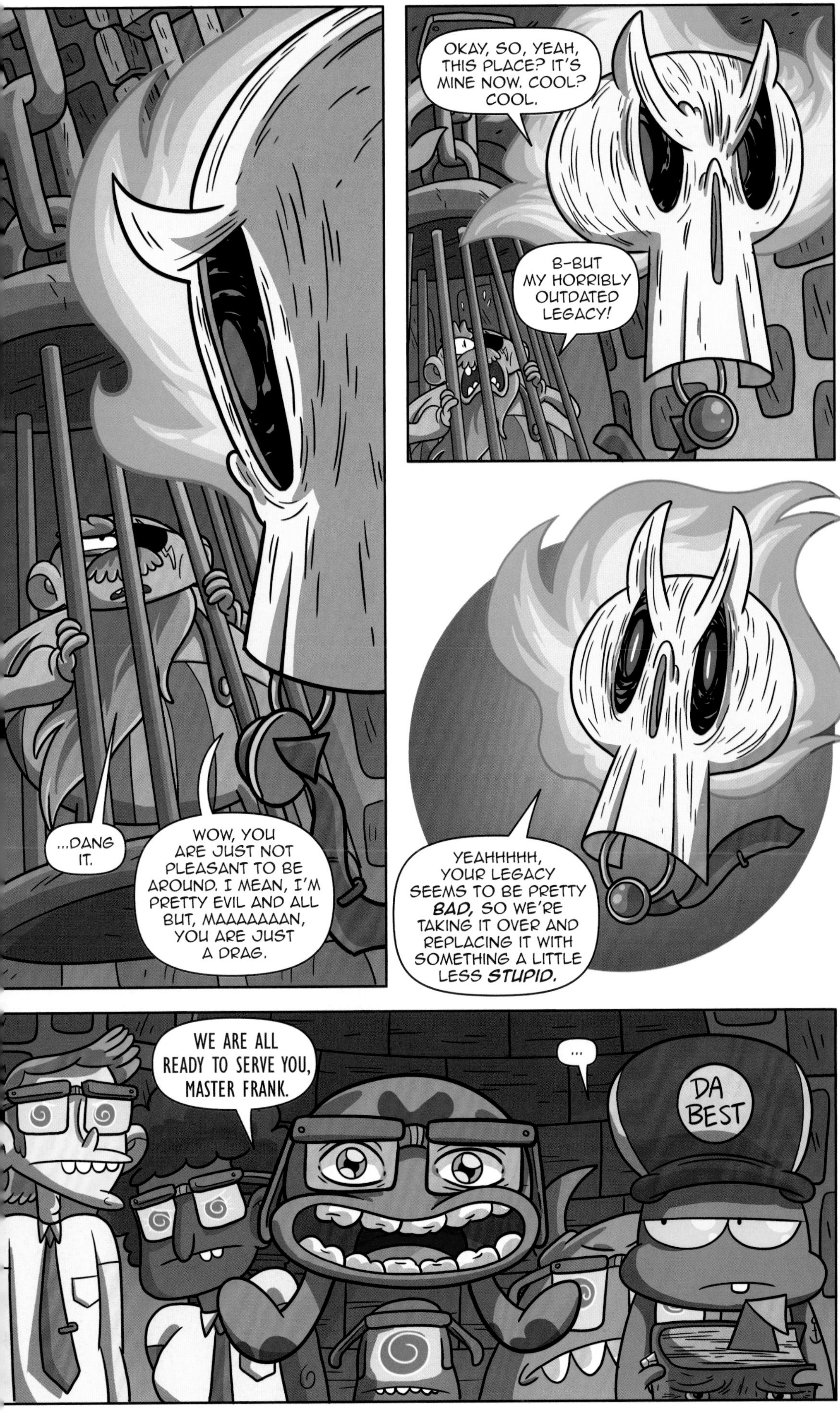
OKAY, SO, YEAH, THIS PLACE? IT'S MINE NOW. COOL? COOL.
B-BUT MY HORRIBLY OUTDATED LEGACY!
...DANG IT.
WOW, YOU ARE JUST NOT PLEASANT TO BE AROUND. I MEAN, I'M PRETTY EVIL AND ALL BUT, MAAAAAAAN, YOU ARE JUST A DRAG.
YEAHHHHH, YOUR LEGACY SEEMS TO BE PRETTY *BAD,* SO WE'RE TAKING IT OVER AND REPLACING IT WITH SOMETHING A LITTLE LESS ***STUPID.***
WE ARE ALL READY TO SERVE YOU, MASTER FRANK.
...
DA BEST

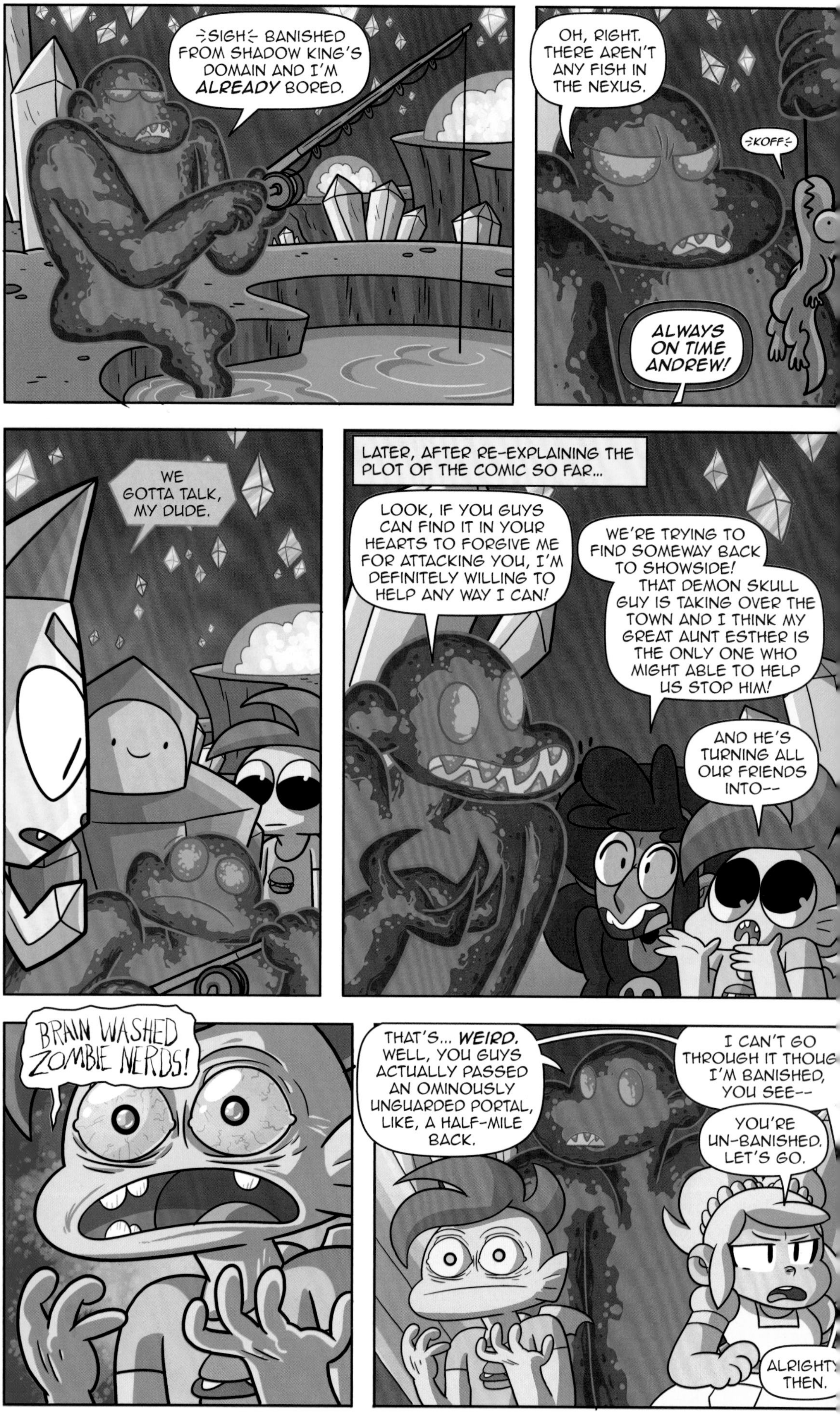

⇉SIGH⇇ BANISHED FROM SHADOW KING'S DOMAIN AND I'M ALREADY BORED.
OH, RIGHT. THERE AREN'T ANY FISH IN THE NEXUS.
⇉KOFF⇇
ALWAYS ON TIME ANDREW!
WE GOTTA TALK, MY DUDE.
LATER, AFTER RE-EXPLAINING THE PLOT OF THE COMIC SO FAR...
LOOK, IF YOU GUYS CAN FIND IT IN YOUR HEARTS TO FORGIVE ME FOR ATTACKING YOU, I'M DEFINITELY WILLING TO HELP ANY WAY I CAN!
WE'RE TRYING TO FIND SOMEWAY BACK TO SHOWSIDE! THAT DEMON SKULL GUY IS TAKING OVER THE TOWN AND I THINK MY GREAT AUNT ESTHER IS THE ONLY ONE WHO MIGHT ABLE TO HELP US STOP HIM!
AND HE'S TURNING ALL OUR FRIENDS INTO--
BRAIN WASHED ZOMBIE NERDS!
THAT'S... WEIRD. WELL, YOU GUYS ACTUALLY PASSED AN OMINOUSLY UNGUARDED PORTAL, LIKE, A HALF-MILE BACK.
I CAN'T GO THROUGH IT THOUG I'M BANISHED, YOU SEE--
YOU'RE UN-BANISHED. LET'S GO.
ALRIGHT THEN.

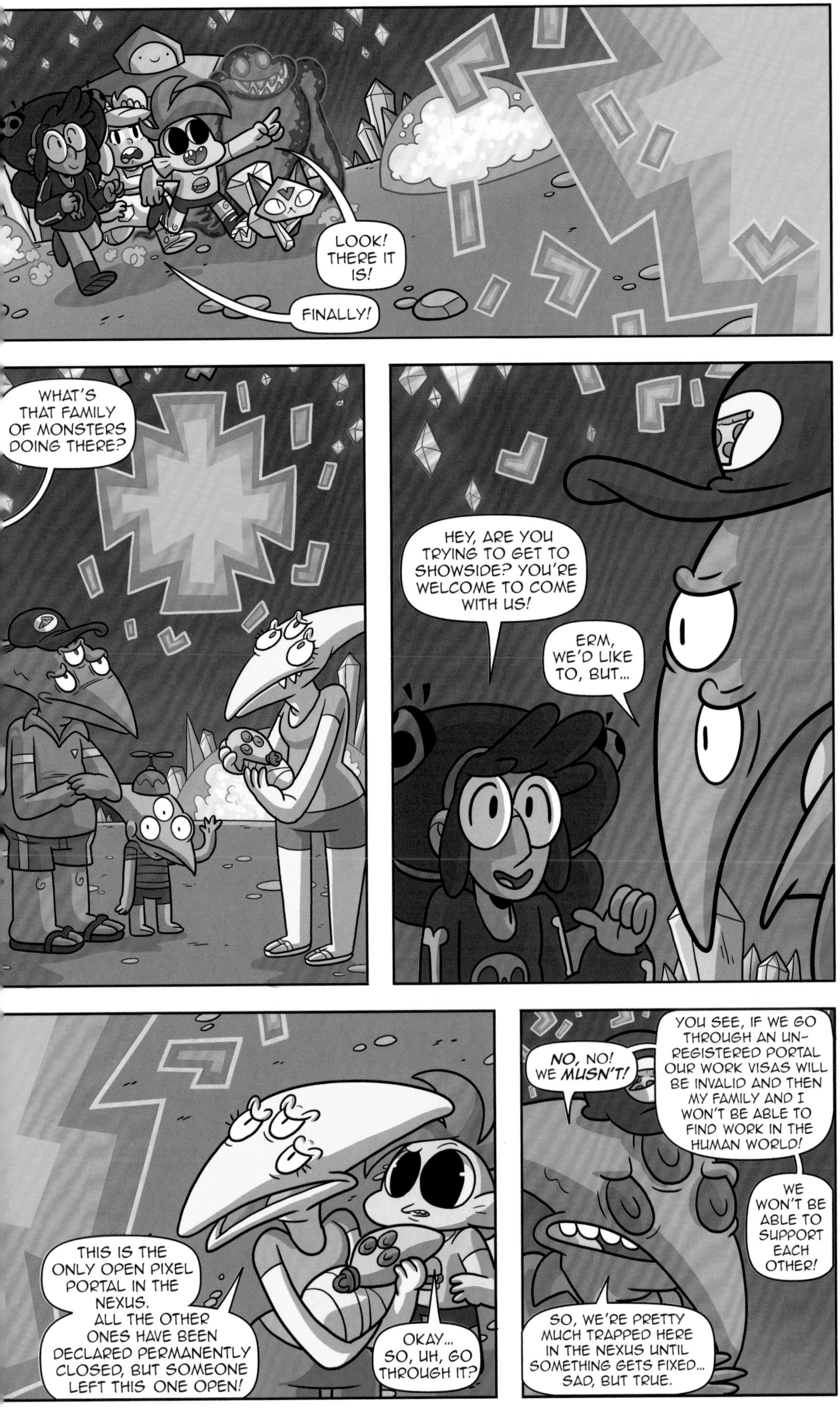

LOOK! THERE IT IS!
FINALLY!
WHAT'S THAT FAMILY OF MONSTERS DOING THERE?
HEY, ARE YOU TRYING TO GET TO SHOWSIDE? YOU'RE WELCOME TO COME WITH US!
ERM, WE'D LIKE TO, BUT...
THIS IS THE ONLY OPEN PIXEL PORTAL IN THE NEXUS. ALL THE OTHER ONES HAVE BEEN DECLARED PERMANENTLY CLOSED, BUT SOMEONE LEFT THIS ONE OPEN!
OKAY... SO, UH, GO THROUGH IT?
NO, NO! WE MUSN'T!
YOU SEE, IF WE GO THROUGH AN UN-REGISTERED PORTAL OUR WORK VISAS WILL BE INVALID AND THEN MY FAMILY AND I WON'T BE ABLE TO FIND WORK IN THE HUMAN WORLD!
WE WON'T BE ABLE TO SUPPORT EACH OTHER!
SO, WE'RE PRETTY MUCH TRAPPED HERE IN THE NEXUS UNTIL SOMETHING GETS FIXED... SAD, BUT TRUE.

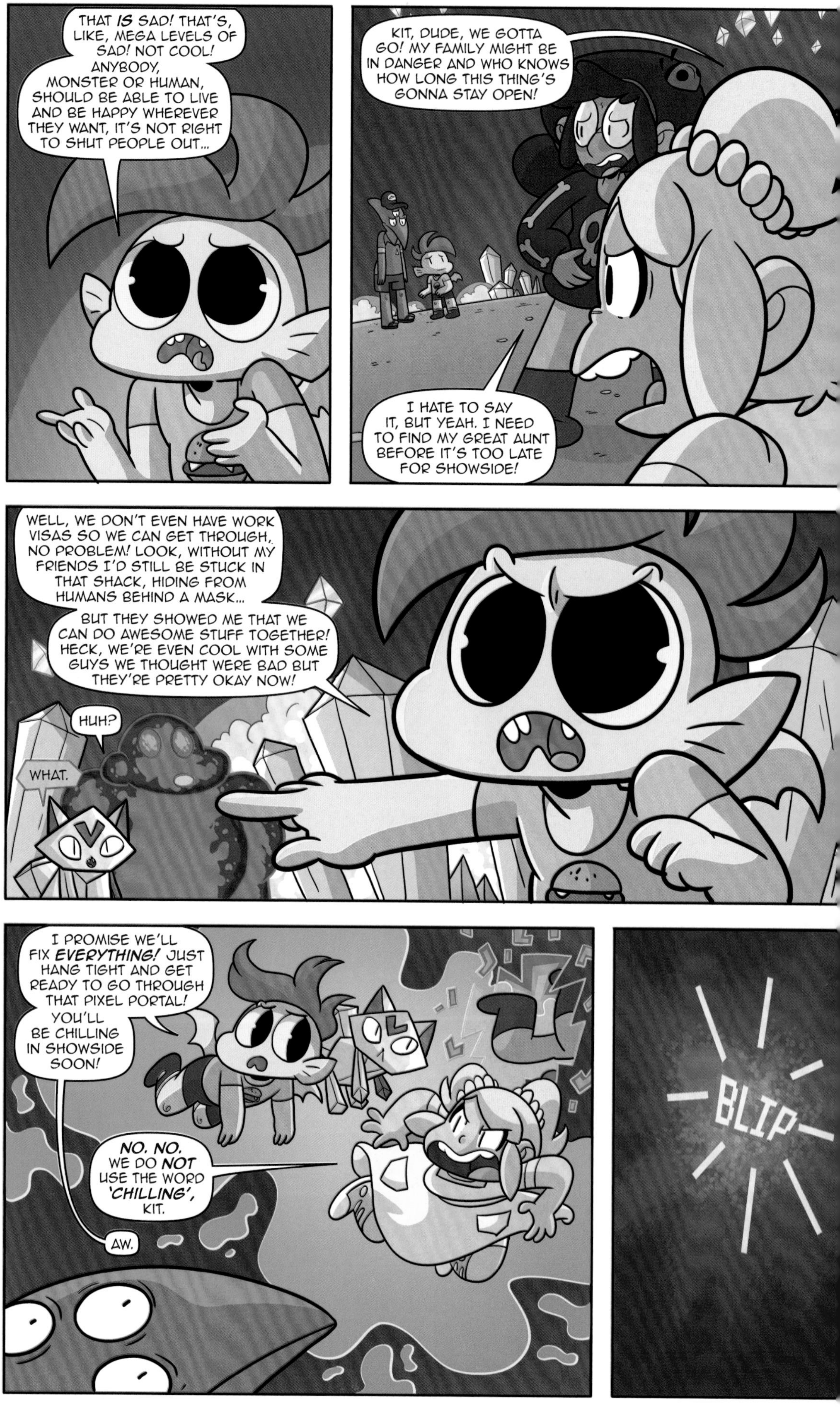

THAT *IS* SAD! THAT'S, LIKE, MEGA LEVELS OF SAD! NOT COOL!
ANYBODY, MONSTER OR HUMAN, SHOULD BE ABLE TO LIVE AND BE HAPPY WHEREVER THEY WANT, IT'S NOT RIGHT TO SHUT PEOPLE OUT...
KIT, DUDE, WE GOTTA GO! MY FAMILY MIGHT BE IN DANGER AND WHO KNOWS HOW LONG THIS THING'S GONNA STAY OPEN!
I HATE TO SAY IT, BUT YEAH. I NEED TO FIND MY GREAT AUNT BEFORE IT'S TOO LATE FOR SHOWSIDE!
WELL, WE DON'T EVEN HAVE WORK VISAS SO WE CAN GET THROUGH, NO PROBLEM! LOOK, WITHOUT MY FRIENDS I'D STILL BE STUCK IN THAT SHACK, HIDING FROM HUMANS BEHIND A MASK...
BUT THEY SHOWED ME THAT WE CAN DO AWESOME STUFF TOGETHER! HECK, WE'RE EVEN COOL WITH SOME GUYS WE THOUGHT WERE BAD BUT THEY'RE PRETTY OKAY NOW!
HUH?
WHAT.
I PROMISE WE'LL FIX ***EVERYTHING!*** JUST HANG TIGHT AND GET READY TO GO THROUGH THAT PIXEL PORTAL!
YOU'LL BE CHILLING IN SHOWSIDE SOON!
NO. NO. WE DO ***NOT*** USE THE WORD ***'CHILLING'***, KIT.
AW.
BLIP

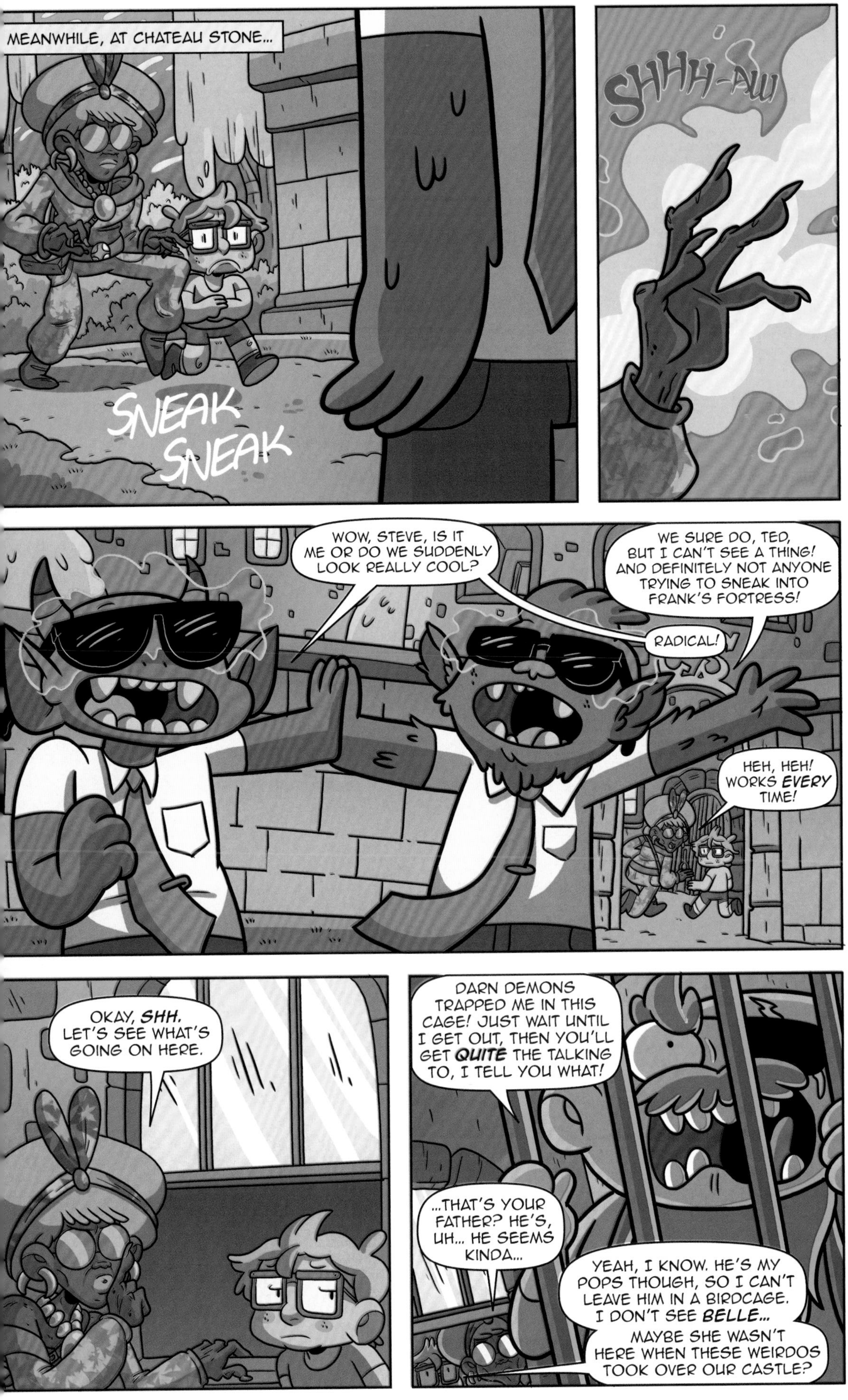

MEANWHILE, AT CHATEAU STONE...
SNEAK SNEAK
SHHH-AW
WOW, STEVE, IS IT ME OR DO WE SUDDENLY LOOK REALLY COOL?
WE SURE DO, TED, BUT I CAN'T SEE A THING! AND DEFINITELY NOT ANYONE TRYING TO SNEAK INTO FRANK'S FORTRESS!
RADICAL!
HEH, HEH! WORKS EVERY TIME!
OKAY, SHH. LET'S SEE WHAT'S GOING ON HERE.
DARN DEMONS TRAPPED ME IN THIS CAGE! JUST WAIT UNTIL I GET OUT, THEN YOU'LL GET QUITE THE TALKING TO, I TELL YOU WHAT!
...THAT'S YOUR FATHER? HE'S, UH... HE SEEMS KINDA...
YEAH, I KNOW. HE'S MY POPS THOUGH, SO I CAN'T LEAVE HIM IN A BIRDCAGE. I DON'T SEE BELLE...
MAYBE SHE WASN'T HERE WHEN THESE WEIRDOS TOOK OVER OUR CASTLE?

THE STATUE DEDICATED TO YOUR GREATNESS IS ALMOST COMPLETE, MASTER FRANK. AAAND THE LUNCH TODAY WILL BE SOUP AND SALAD, VEG-E-TABLE OF THE DAY AND WHIPPED DESSERT.

EXCELLENT, MR. BOO. WELL DONE!

SHOULDN'T WE BE BUILDING UP OUR DEFENSES N' JUNK? THIS ALL SEEMS KINDA SOON, YA KNOW?

DA BEST

CLIMP, CLIMP, CLIMP...

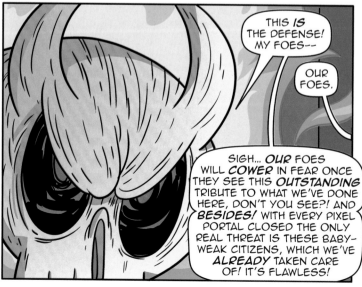

THIS *IS* THE DEFENSE! MY FOES--

OUR FOES.

SIGH... *OUR* FOES WILL *COWER* IN FEAR ONCE THEY SEE THIS *OUTSTANDING* TRIBUTE TO WHAT WE'VE DONE HERE, DON'T YOU SEE?! AND *BESIDES!* WITH EVERY PIXEL PORTAL CLOSED THE ONLY REAL THREAT IS THESE BABY-WEAK CITIZENS, WHICH WE'VE *ALREADY* TAKEN CARE OF! IT'S FLAWLESS!

ANYWAYS, I'M REALLY FEELING LIKE GAZPACHO FOR LUNCH, MAYBE A LIGHT SUMMER SALAD...

DA BEST

...

UH, OH.

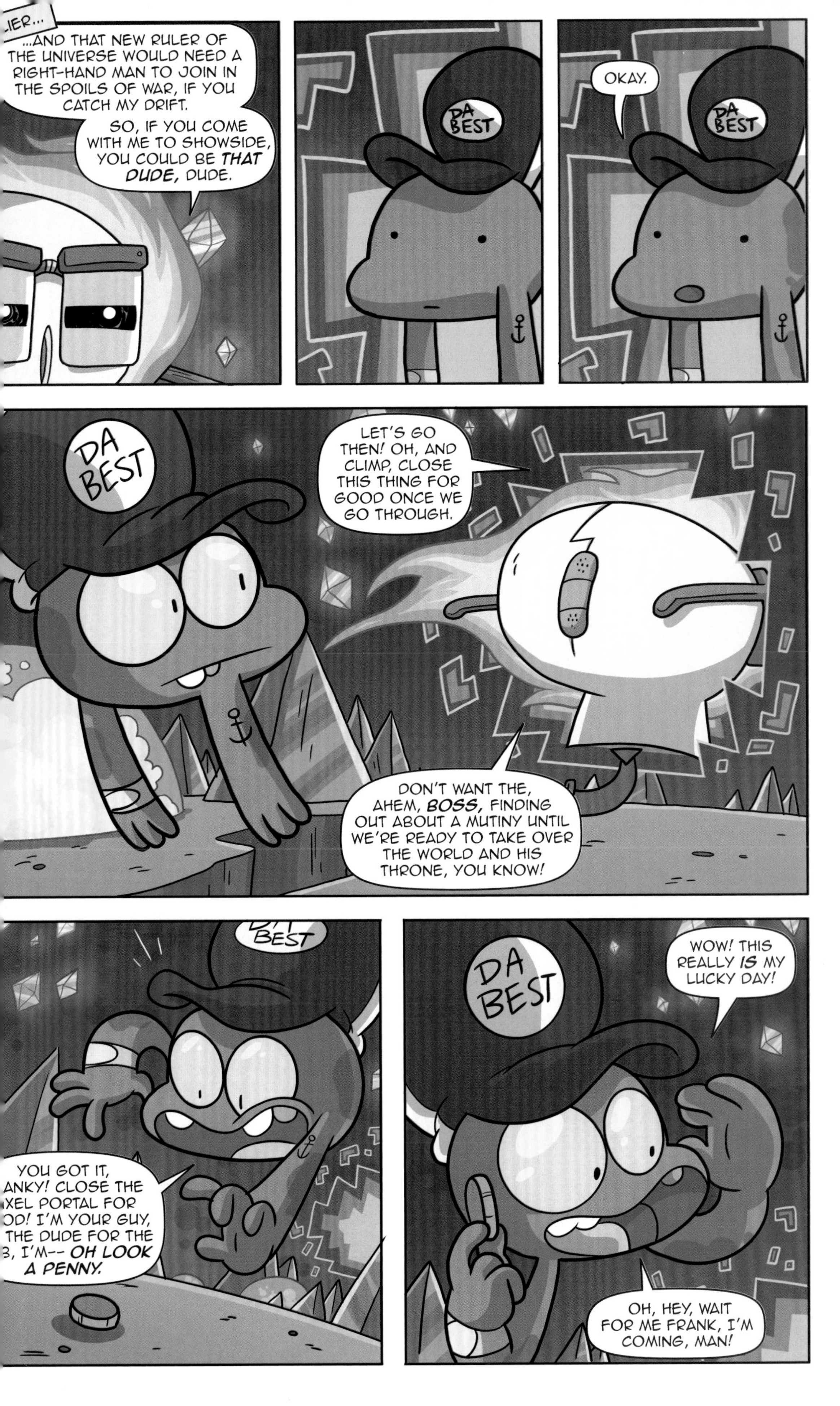

LIER...
...AND THAT NEW RULER OF THE UNIVERSE WOULD NEED A RIGHT-HAND MAN TO JOIN IN THE SPOILS OF WAR, IF YOU CATCH MY DRIFT.
SO, IF YOU COME WITH ME TO SHOWSIDE, YOU COULD BE THAT DUDE, DUDE.
DA BEST
OKAY.
LET'S GO THEN! OH, AND CLIMP, CLOSE THIS THING FOR GOOD ONCE WE GO THROUGH.
DON'T WANT THE, AHEM, BOSS, FINDING OUT ABOUT A MUTINY UNTIL WE'RE READY TO TAKE OVER THE WORLD AND HIS THRONE, YOU KNOW!
YOU GOT IT, ANKY! CLOSE THE XEL PORTAL FOR OD! I'M YOUR GUY, THE DUDE FOR THE B, I'M-- OH LOOK A PENNY.
WOW! THIS REALLY IS MY LUCKY DAY!
OH, HEY, WAIT FOR ME FRANK, I'M COMING, MAN!

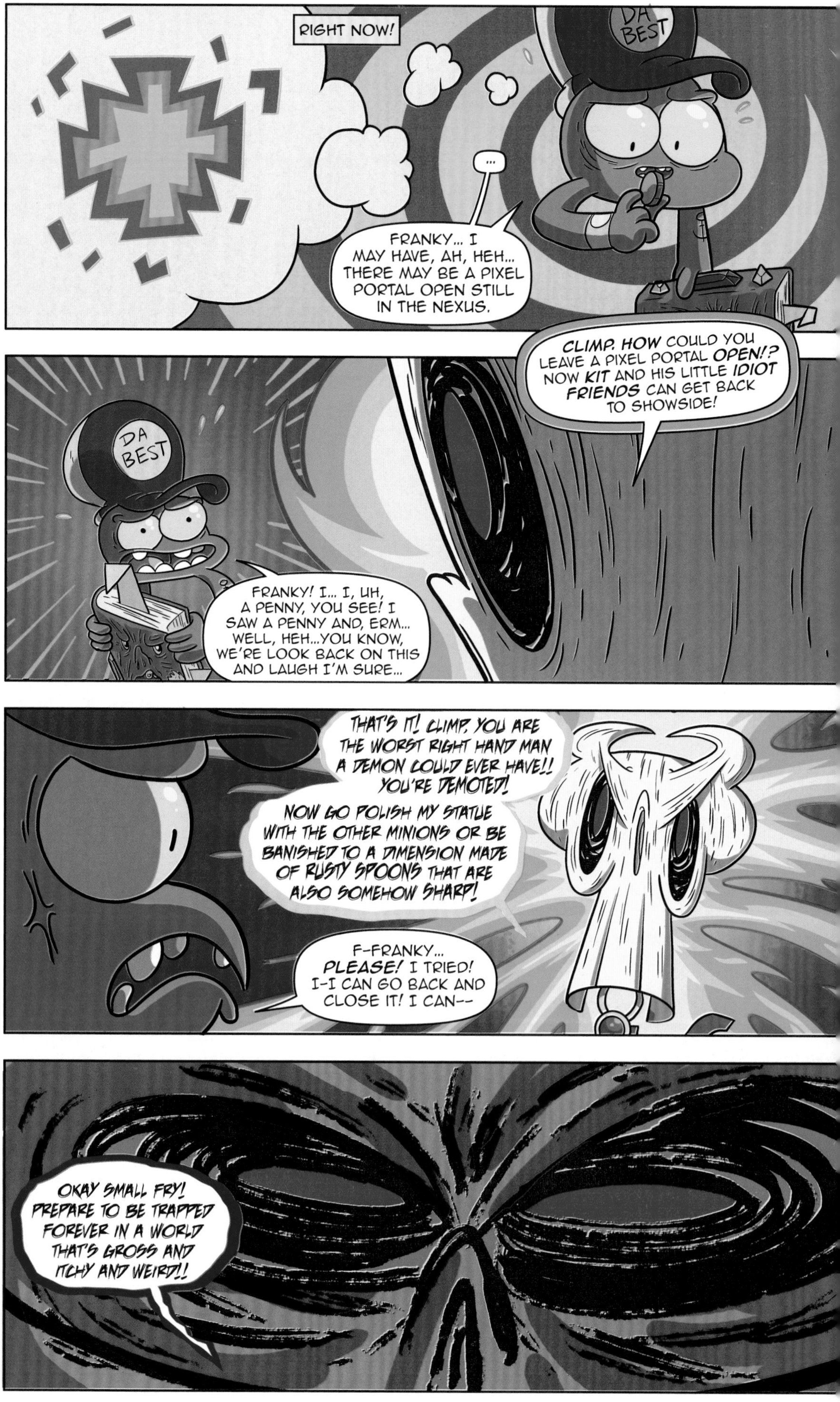
RIGHT NOW!
...
FRANKY... I MAY HAVE, AH, HEH... THERE MAY BE A PIXEL PORTAL OPEN STILL IN THE NEXUS.
DA BEST
CLIMP. HOW COULD YOU LEAVE A PIXEL PORTAL OPEN!? NOW KIT AND HIS LITTLE IDIOT FRIENDS CAN GET BACK TO SHOWSIDE!
DA BEST
FRANKY! I... I, UH, A PENNY, YOU SEE! I SAW A PENNY AND, ERM... WELL, HEH...YOU KNOW, WE'RE LOOK BACK ON THIS AND LAUGH I'M SURE...
THAT'S IT! CLIMP, YOU ARE THE WORST RIGHT HAND MAN A DEMON COULD EVER HAVE!! YOU'RE DEMOTED!
NOW GO POLISH MY STATUE WITH THE OTHER MINIONS OR BE BANISHED TO A DIMENSION MADE OF RUSTY SPOONS THAT ARE ALSO SOMEHOW SHARP!
F-FRANKY... PLEASE! I TRIED! I-I CAN GO BACK AND CLOSE IT! I CAN--
OKAY SMALL FRY! PREPARE TO BE TRAPPED FOREVER IN A WORLD THAT'S GROSS AND ITCHY AND WEIRD!!

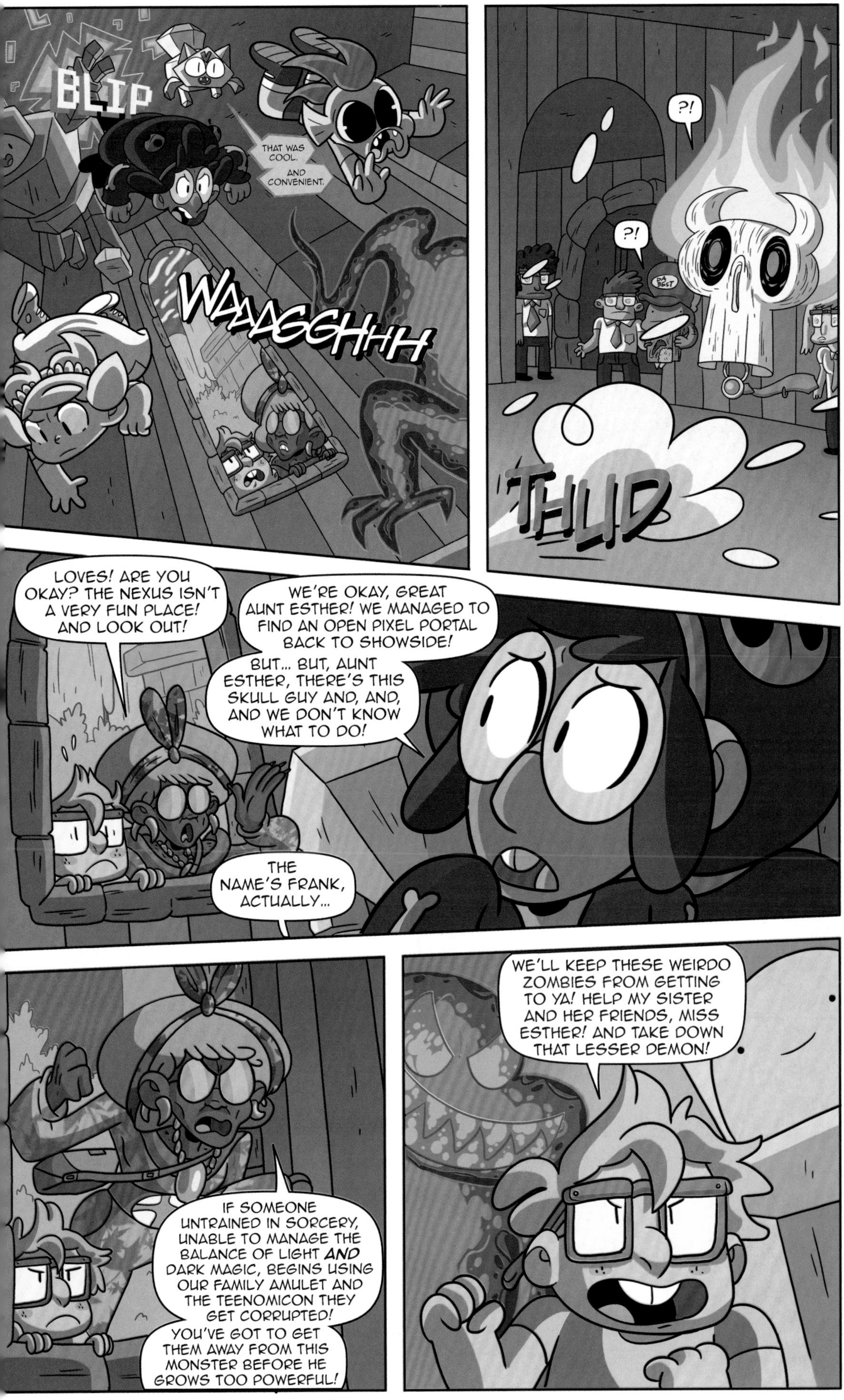

BLIP
THAT WAS COOL.
AND CONVENIENT.
WAAAGGHHH
?!
?!
DA BEST
THUD
LOVES! ARE YOU OKAY? THE NEXUS ISN'T A VERY FUN PLACE! AND LOOK OUT!
WE'RE OKAY, GREAT AUNT ESTHER! WE MANAGED TO FIND AN OPEN PIXEL PORTAL BACK TO SHOWSIDE!
BUT... BUT, AUNT ESTHER, THERE'S THIS SKULL GUY AND, AND, AND WE DON'T KNOW WHAT TO DO!
THE NAME'S FRANK, ACTUALLY...
IF SOMEONE UNTRAINED IN SORCERY, UNABLE TO MANAGE THE BALANCE OF LIGHT AND DARK MAGIC, BEGINS USING OUR FAMILY AMULET AND THE TEENOMICON THEY GET CORRUPTED!
YOU'VE GOT TO GET THEM AWAY FROM THIS MONSTER BEFORE HE GROWS TOO POWERFUL!
WE'LL KEEP THESE WEIRDO ZOMBIES FROM GETTING TO YA! HELP MY SISTER AND HER FRIENDS, MISS ESTHER! AND TAKE DOWN THAT LESSER DEMON!

TAKE DOWN *ME?!* EVEN THE SHADOW KING CAN'T TAKE ME DOWN! I'M TOO STRONG AND HANDSOME FOR THAT CHUMP! THE SHADOW KING COULDN'T HANDLE RULING THE NEXUS! HE COULDN'T EVEN HANDLE HIS OWN SON!

BRAINWASHED NERDS! *SEIZE THEM ALL!*

BA BAM!

BOO

WHO THE HECK IS THIS SHADOW KING GUY, ANYWAYS?!

Master Frank, perhaps if you decimate Kit here it will demoralize these troublesome kids and reduce the chances of the shadow king locating his prophetic child?

YES! THAT'S IT, MISTER BOO!

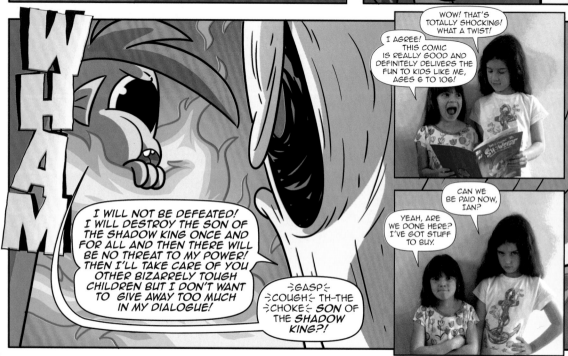

WHAM

I WILL NOT BE DEFEATED! I WILL DESTROY THE SON OF THE SHADOW KING ONCE AND FOR ALL AND THEN THERE WILL BE NO THREAT TO MY POWER! THEN I'LL TAKE CARE OF YOU OTHER BIZARRELY TOUGH CHILDREN BUT I DON'T WANT TO GIVE AWAY TOO MUCH IN MY DIALOGUE!

÷GASP÷ ÷COUGH÷ TH–THE ÷CHOKE÷ *SON* OF THE *SHADOW KING?!*

WOW! THAT'S TOTALLY SHOCKING! WHAT A TWIST!

I AGREE! THIS COMIC IS REALLY GOOD AND DEFINITELY DELIVERS THE FUN TO KIDS LIKE ME, AGES 6 TO 106!

CAN WE BE PAID NOW, IAN?

YEAH, ARE WE DONE HERE? I'VE GOT STUFF TO BUY.

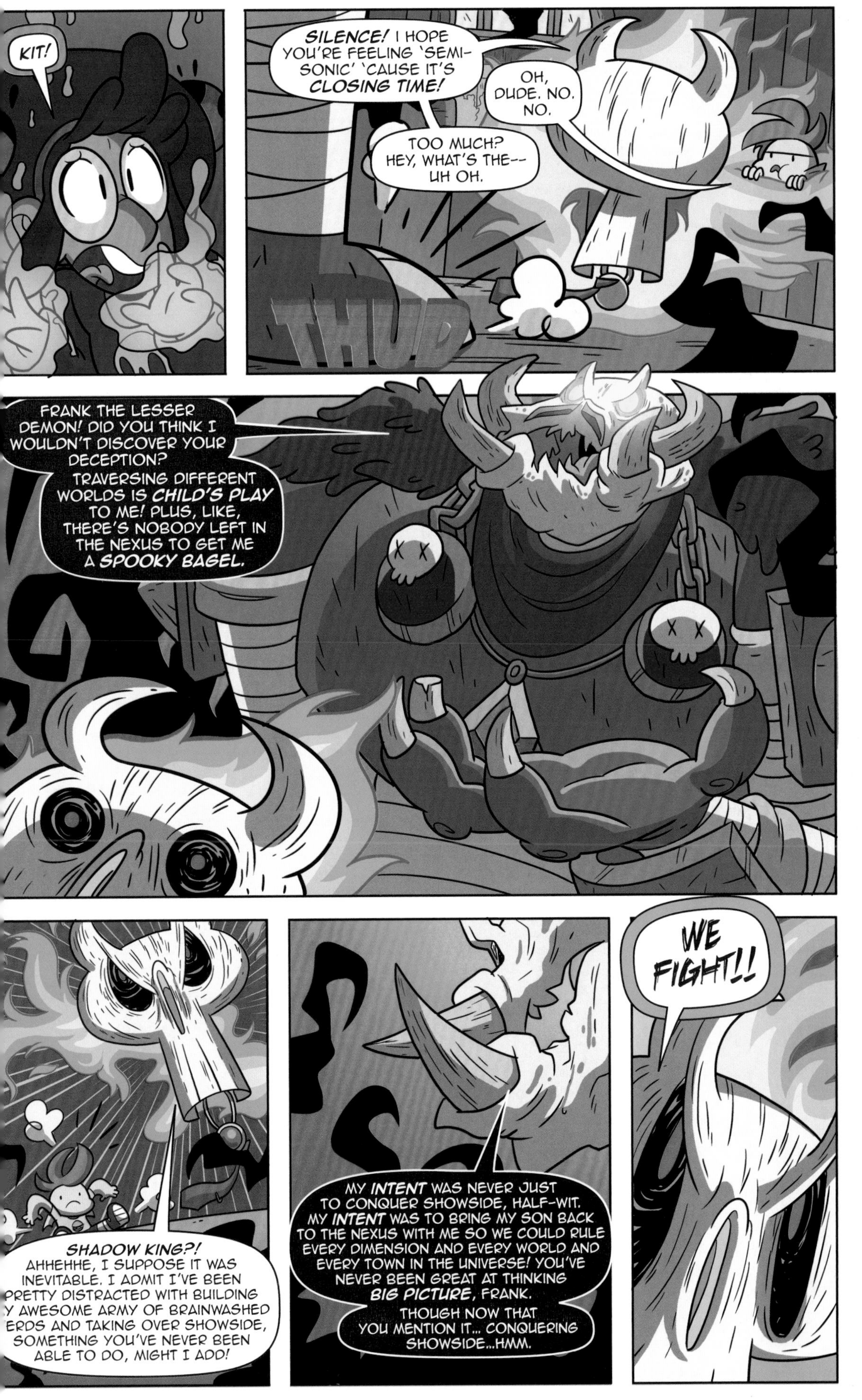
KIT!
SILENCE! I HOPE YOU'RE FEELING 'SEMI-SONIC' 'CAUSE IT'S CLOSING TIME!
OH, DUDE. NO. NO.
TOO MUCH? HEY, WHAT'S THE-- UH OH.
THUD
FRANK THE LESSER DEMON! DID YOU THINK I WOULDN'T DISCOVER YOUR DECEPTION?
TRAVERSING DIFFERENT WORLDS IS CHILD'S PLAY TO ME! PLUS, LIKE, THERE'S NOBODY LEFT IN THE NEXUS TO GET ME A SPOOKY BAGEL.
SHADOW KING?! AHHEHHE, I SUPPOSE IT WAS INEVITABLE. I ADMIT I'VE BEEN PRETTY DISTRACTED WITH BUILDING Y AWESOME ARMY OF BRAINWASHED ERDS AND TAKING OVER SHOWSIDE, SOMETHING YOU'VE NEVER BEEN ABLE TO DO, MIGHT I ADD!
MY INTENT WAS NEVER JUST TO CONQUER SHOWSIDE, HALF-WIT. MY INTENT WAS TO BRING MY SON BACK TO THE NEXUS WITH ME SO WE COULD RULE EVERY DIMENSION AND EVERY WORLD AND EVERY TOWN IN THE UNIVERSE! YOU'VE NEVER BEEN GREAT AT THINKING BIG PICTURE, FRANK.
THOUGH NOW THAT YOU MENTION IT... CONQUERING SHOWSIDE...HMM.
WE FIGHT!!

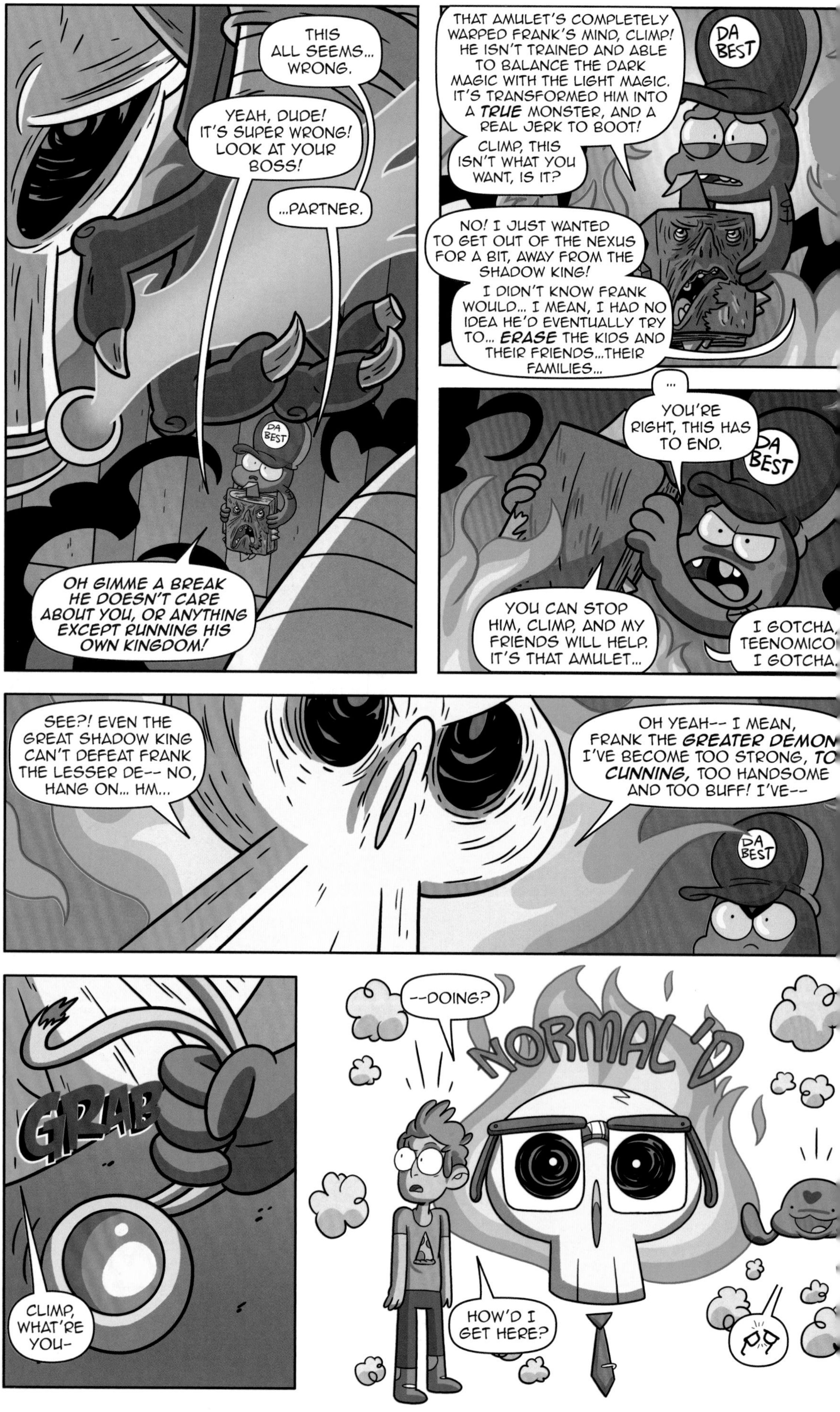
THIS ALL SEEMS... WRONG.
YEAH, DUDE! IT'S SUPER WRONG! LOOK AT YOUR BOSS!
...PARTNER.
OH GIMME A BREAK HE DOESN'T CARE ABOUT YOU, OR ANYTHING EXCEPT RUNNING HIS OWN KINGDOM!
DA BEST
THAT AMULET'S COMPLETELY WARPED FRANK'S MIND, CLIMP! HE ISN'T TRAINED AND ABLE TO BALANCE THE DARK MAGIC WITH THE LIGHT MAGIC. IT'S TRANSFORMED HIM INTO A TRUE MONSTER, AND A REAL JERK TO BOOT!
CLIMP, THIS ISN'T WHAT YOU WANT, IS IT?
NO! I JUST WANTED TO GET OUT OF THE NEXUS FOR A BIT, AWAY FROM THE SHADOW KING!
I DIDN'T KNOW FRANK WOULD... I MEAN, I HAD NO IDEA HE'D EVENTUALLY TRY TO... ERASE THE KIDS AND THEIR FRIENDS...THEIR FAMILIES...
...
YOU'RE RIGHT, THIS HAS TO END.
YOU CAN STOP HIM, CLIMP, AND MY FRIENDS WILL HELP. IT'S THAT AMULET...
I GOTCHA, TEENOMICO I GOTCHA.
SEE?! EVEN THE GREAT SHADOW KING CAN'T DEFEAT FRANK THE LESSER DE-- NO, HANG ON... HM...
OH YEAH-- I MEAN, FRANK THE GREATER DEMON I'VE BECOME TOO STRONG, TO CUNNING, TOO HANDSOME AND TOO BUFF! I'VE--
GRAB
CLIMP, WHAT'RE YOU-
--DOING?
NORMAL'D
HOW'D I GET HERE?

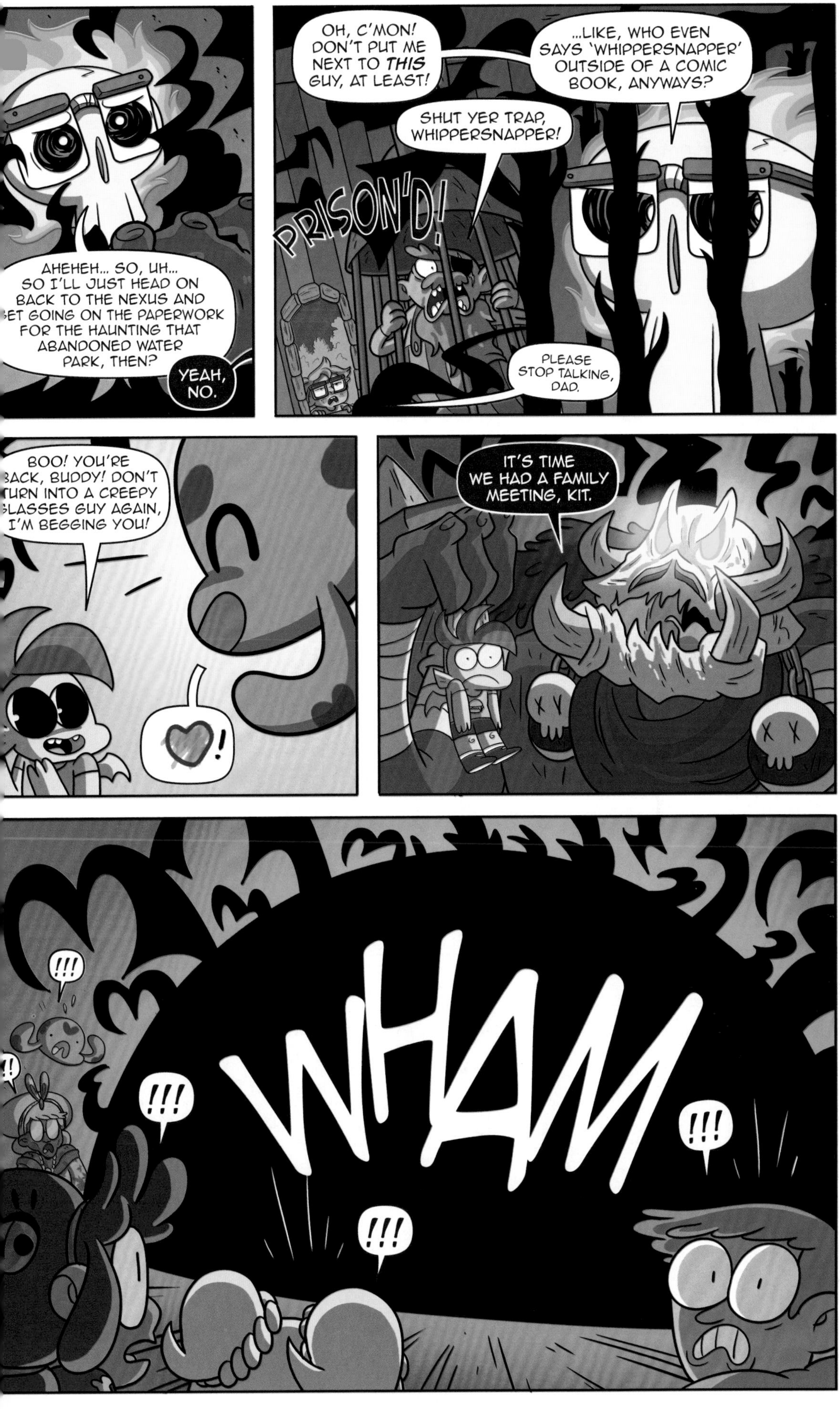
AHEHEH... SO, UH...
SO I'LL JUST HEAD ON BACK TO THE NEXUS AND GET GOING ON THE PAPERWORK FOR THE HAUNTING THAT ABANDONED WATER PARK, THEN?
YEAH, NO.
OH, C'MON! DON'T PUT ME NEXT TO THIS GUY, AT LEAST!
...LIKE, WHO EVEN SAYS 'WHIPPERSNAPPER' OUTSIDE OF A COMIC BOOK, ANYWAYS?
SHUT YER TRAP, WHIPPERSNAPPER!
PRISON'D!
PLEASE STOP TALKING, DAD.
BOO! YOU'RE BACK, BUDDY! DON'T TURN INTO A CREEPY GLASSES GUY AGAIN, I'M BEGGING YOU!
!
IT'S TIME WE HAD A FAMILY MEETING, KIT.
!!!
!!!
WHAM
!!!
!!!

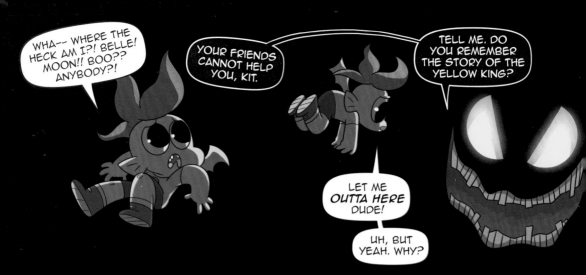

WHA-- WHERE THE HECK AM I?! BELLE! MOON!! BOO?? ANYBODY?!

YOUR FRIENDS CANNOT HELP YOU, KIT.

TELL ME. DO YOU REMEMBER THE STORY OF THE YELLOW KING?

LET ME *OUTTA HERE* DUDE!

UH, BUT YEAH. WHY?

THE FAIRYTALE, STRANGE YOU KNOW IT SO WELL, YES?

THAT'S BECAUSE IT'S ALL TRUE, KIT. I *AM* THE SHADOW KING FROM THAT FAIRYTALE. AND I'M HERE IN SHOWSIDE NOW. FOR *YOU.*

I'M YOUR FATHER, BOY. YOU ARE ROYALTY, AND DESTINED TO RULE BESIDE ME AS WE *CONQUER EVERY DIMENSION* IN THE *KNOWN UNIVERSE.*

...YOUR MOTHER... OLIVE...

...

SHE *STOLE* YOU, *HID* YOU, AWAY FROM YOUR *BIRTHRIGHT.* YOUR *DESTINY.*

IT IS TIME FOR YOU TO ASCEND THE THRONE WITH *ME,* BOY.

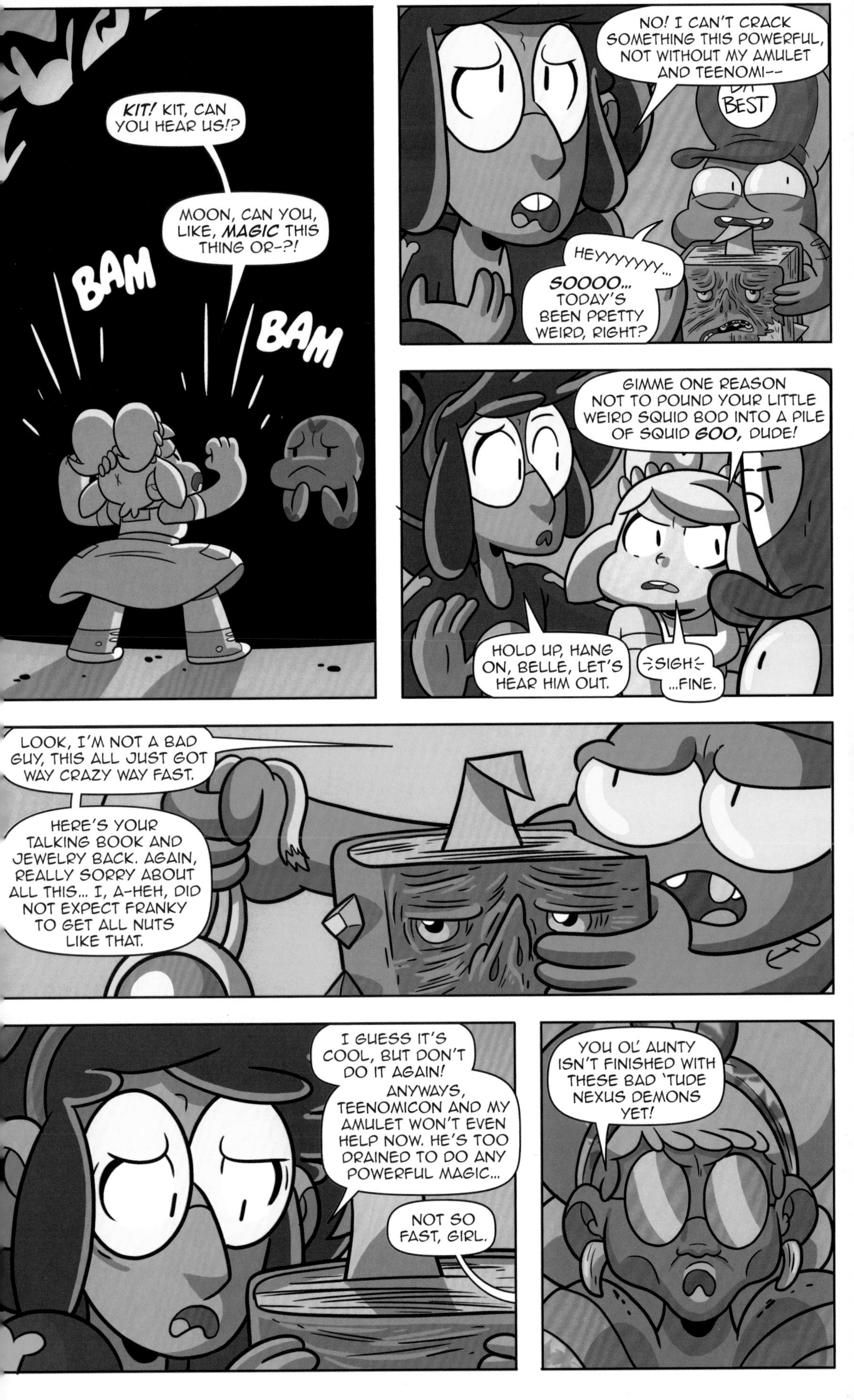

KIT! KIT, CAN YOU HEAR US!?
MOON, CAN YOU, LIKE, MAGIC THIS THING OR-?!
BAM
BAM
NO! I CAN'T CRACK SOMETHING THIS POWERFUL, NOT WITHOUT MY AMULET AND TEENOMI--
BEST
HEYYYYYYY...
SOOOO... TODAY'S BEEN PRETTY WEIRD, RIGHT?
GIMME ONE REASON NOT TO POUND YOUR LITTLE WEIRD SQUID BOD INTO A PILE OF SQUID GOO, DUDE!
HOLD UP, HANG ON, BELLE, LET'S HEAR HIM OUT.
SIGH ...FINE.
LOOK, I'M NOT A BAD GUY, THIS ALL JUST GOT WAY CRAZY WAY FAST.
HERE'S YOUR TALKING BOOK AND JEWELRY BACK. AGAIN, REALLY SORRY ABOUT ALL THIS... I, A-HEH, DID NOT EXPECT FRANKY TO GET ALL NUTS LIKE THAT.
I GUESS IT'S COOL, BUT DON'T DO IT AGAIN!
ANYWAYS, TEENOMICON AND MY AMULET WON'T EVEN HELP NOW. HE'S TOO DRAINED TO DO ANY POWERFUL MAGIC...
NOT SO FAST, GIRL.
YOU OL' AUNTY ISN'T FINISHED WITH THESE BAD 'TUDE NEXUS DEMONS YET!

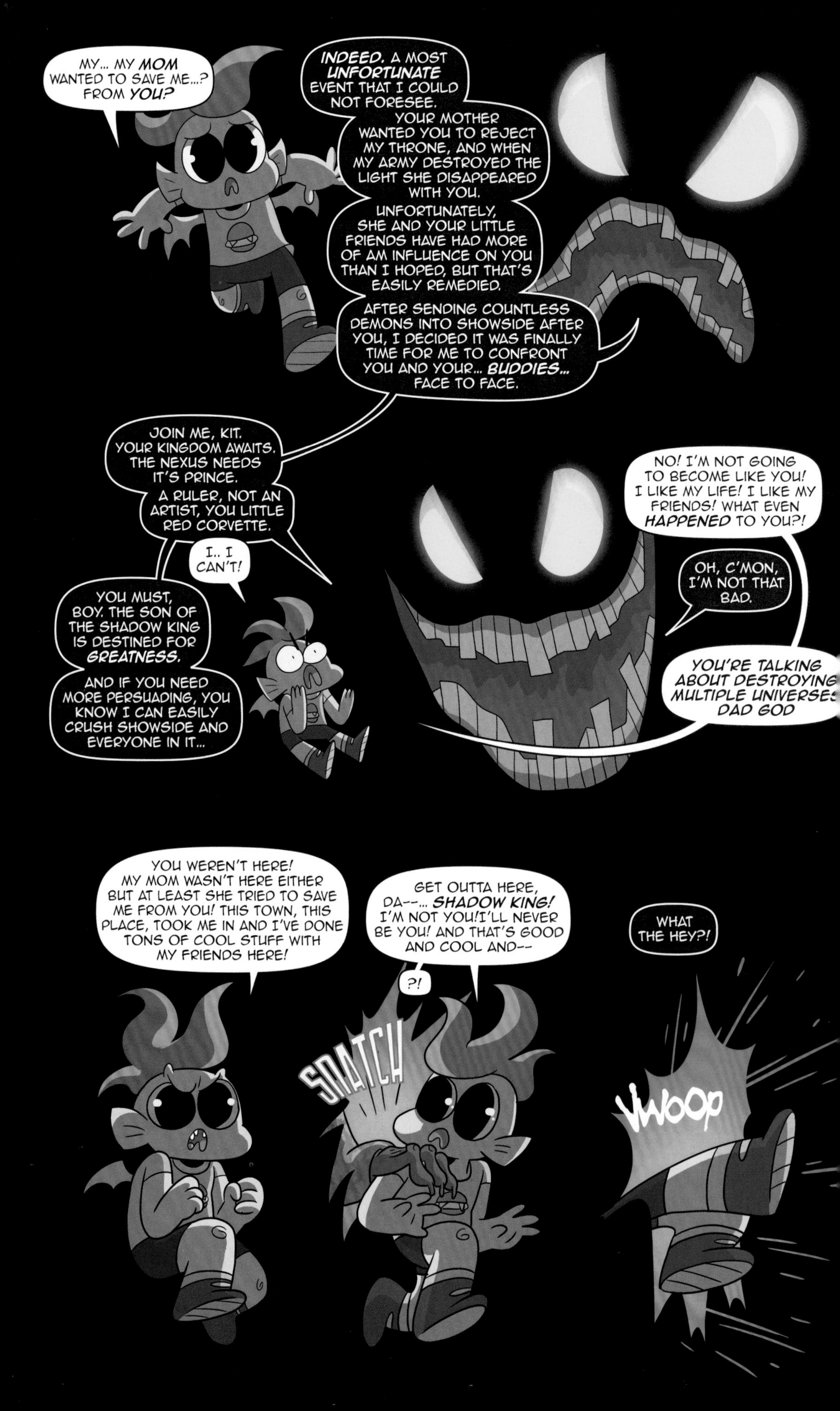
MY... MY MOM WANTED TO SAVE ME...? FROM YOU?
INDEED. A MOST UNFORTUNATE EVENT THAT I COULD NOT FORESEE.
YOUR MOTHER WANTED YOU TO REJECT MY THRONE, AND WHEN MY ARMY DESTROYED THE LIGHT SHE DISAPPEARED WITH YOU.
UNFORTUNATELY, SHE AND YOUR LITTLE FRIENDS HAVE HAD MORE OF AM INFLUENCE ON YOU THAN I HOPED, BUT THAT'S EASILY REMEDIED.
AFTER SENDING COUNTLESS DEMONS INTO SHOWSIDE AFTER YOU, I DECIDED IT WAS FINALLY TIME FOR ME TO CONFRONT YOU AND YOUR... BUDDIES... FACE TO FACE.
JOIN ME, KIT. YOUR KINGDOM AWAITS. THE NEXUS NEEDS IT'S PRINCE.
A RULER, NOT AN ARTIST, YOU LITTLE RED CORVETTE.
I.. I CAN'T!
YOU MUST, BOY. THE SON OF THE SHADOW KING IS DESTINED FOR GREATNESS.
AND IF YOU NEED MORE PERSUADING, YOU KNOW I CAN EASILY CRUSH SHOWSIDE AND EVERYONE IN IT...
NO! I'M NOT GOING TO BECOME LIKE YOU! I LIKE MY LIFE! I LIKE MY FRIENDS! WHAT EVEN HAPPENED TO YOU?!
OH, C'MON, I'M NOT THAT BAD.
YOU'RE TALKING ABOUT DESTROYING MULTIPLE UNIVERSES DAD GOD
YOU WEREN'T HERE! MY MOM WASN'T HERE EITHER BUT AT LEAST SHE TRIED TO SAVE ME FROM YOU! THIS TOWN, THIS PLACE, TOOK ME IN AND I'VE DONE TONS OF COOL STUFF WITH MY FRIENDS HERE!
GET OUTTA HERE, DA--... SHADOW KING! I'M NOT YOU!I'LL NEVER BE YOU! AND THAT'S GOOD AND COOL AND--
?!
SNATCH
WHAT THE HEY?!
VWOOP

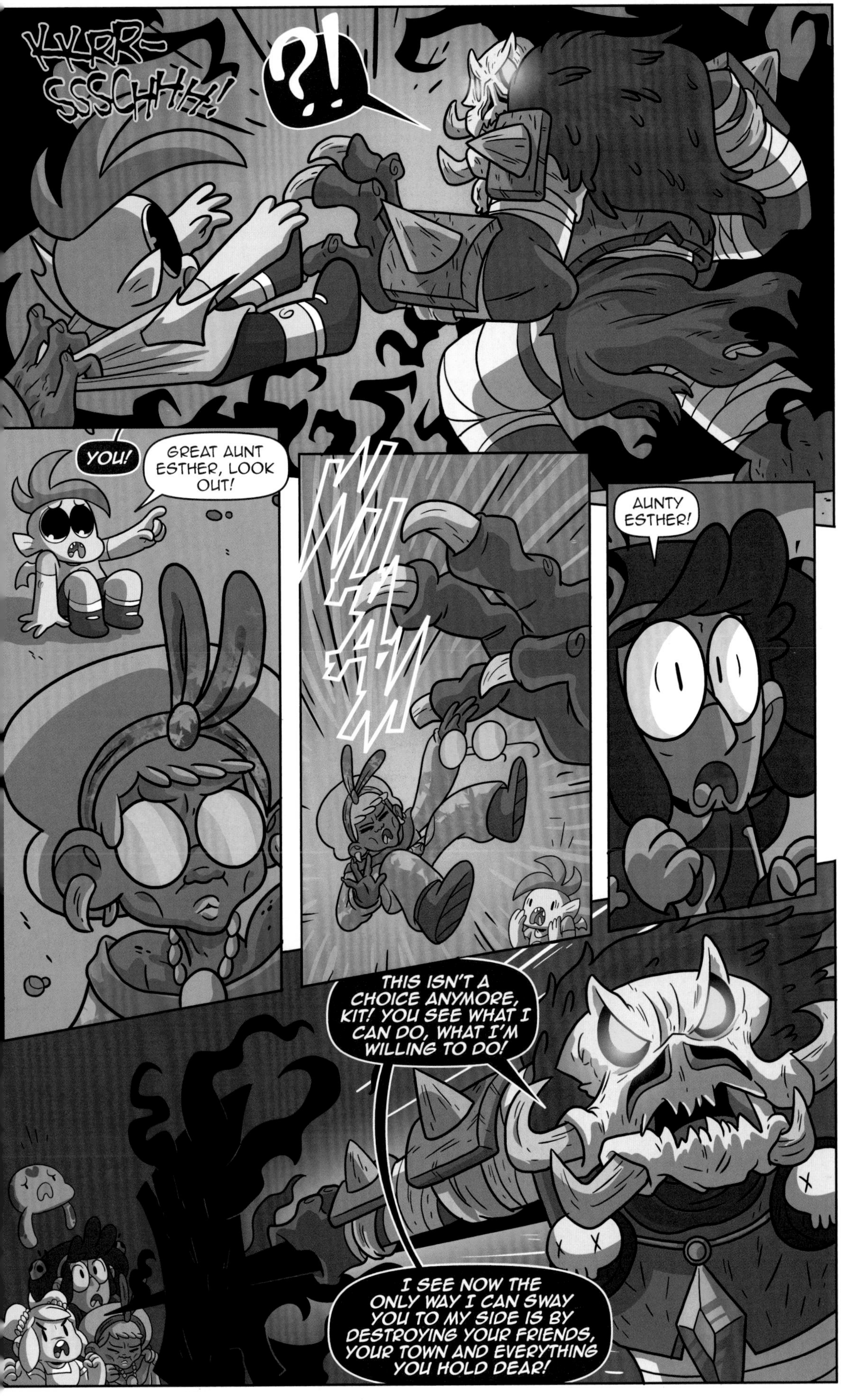

KKRR-SSSCHHH!
?!
YOU!
GREAT AUNT ESTHER, LOOK OUT!
AUNTY ESTHER!
THIS ISN'T A CHOICE ANYMORE, KIT! YOU SEE WHAT I CAN DO, WHAT I'M WILLING TO DO!
I SEE NOW THE ONLY WAY I CAN SWAY YOU TO MY SIDE IS BY DESTROYING YOUR FRIENDS, YOUR TOWN AND EVERYTHING YOU HOLD DEAR!

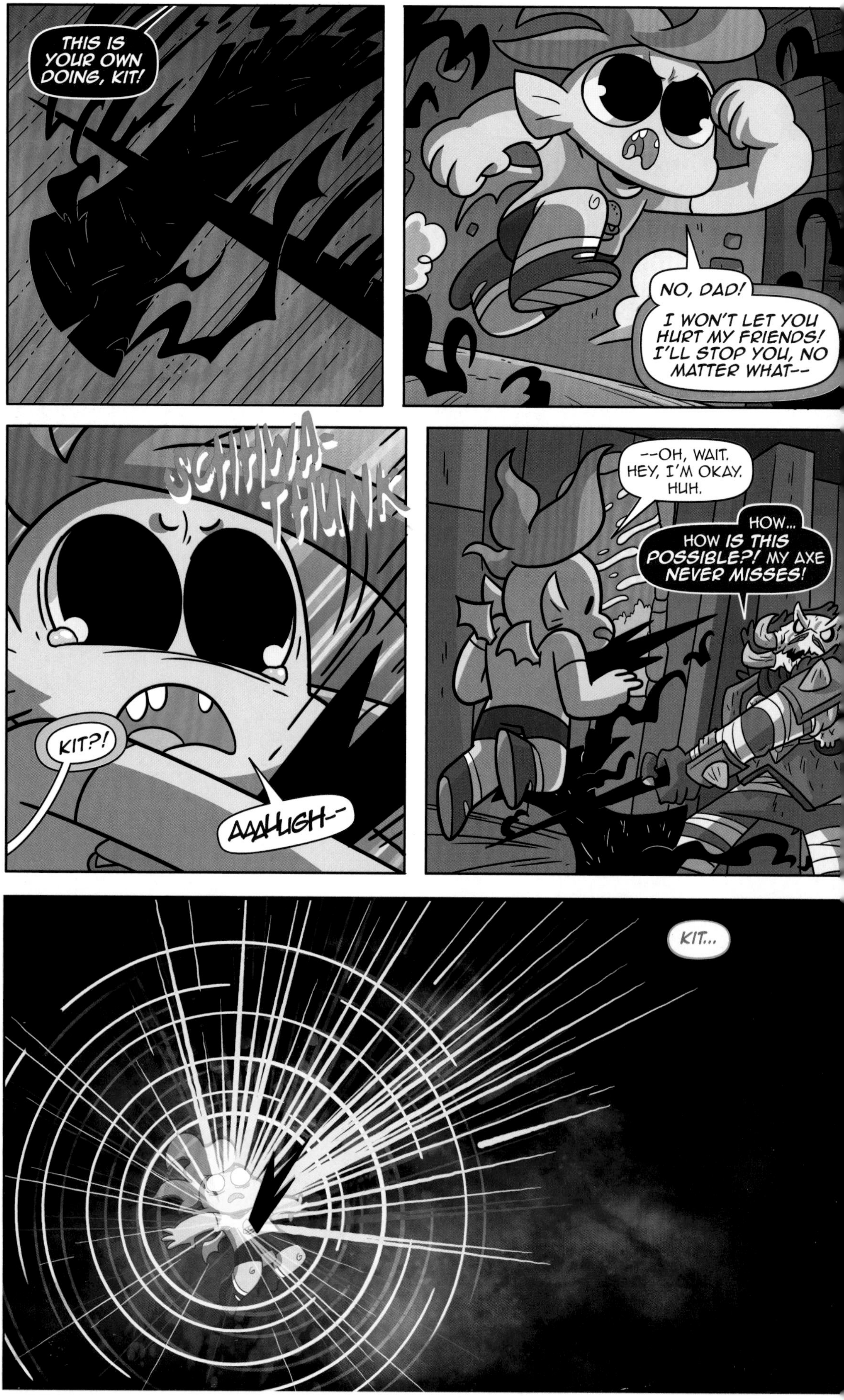
THIS IS YOUR OWN DOING, KIT!
NO, DAD!
I WON'T LET YOU HURT MY FRIENDS! I'LL STOP YOU, NO MATTER WHAT--
SCHHWA-THUNK
KIT?!
AAAHUGH--
--OH, WAIT. HEY, I'M OKAY. HUH.
HOW... HOW IS THIS POSSIBLE?! MY AXE NEVER MISSES!
KIT...

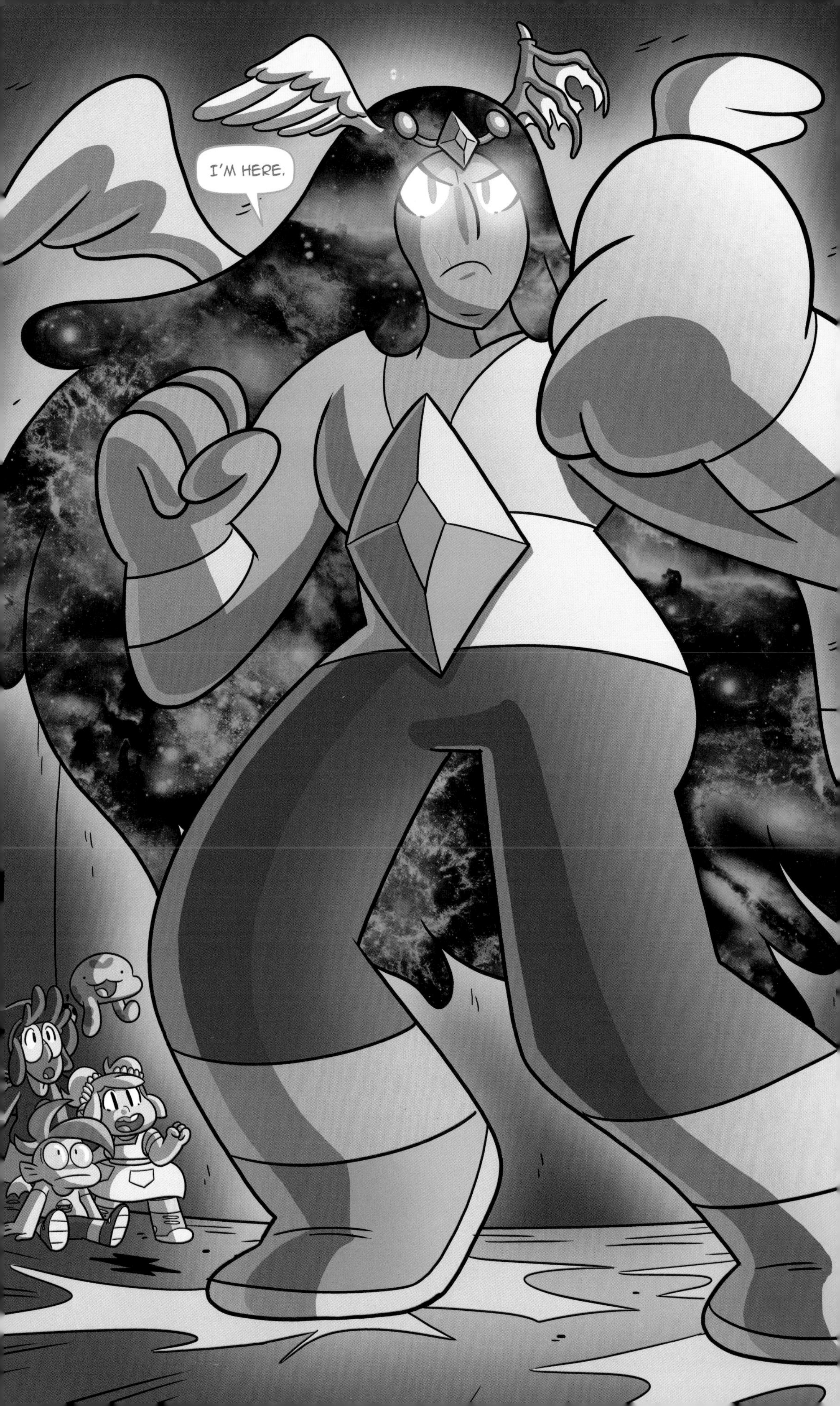
I'M HERE.

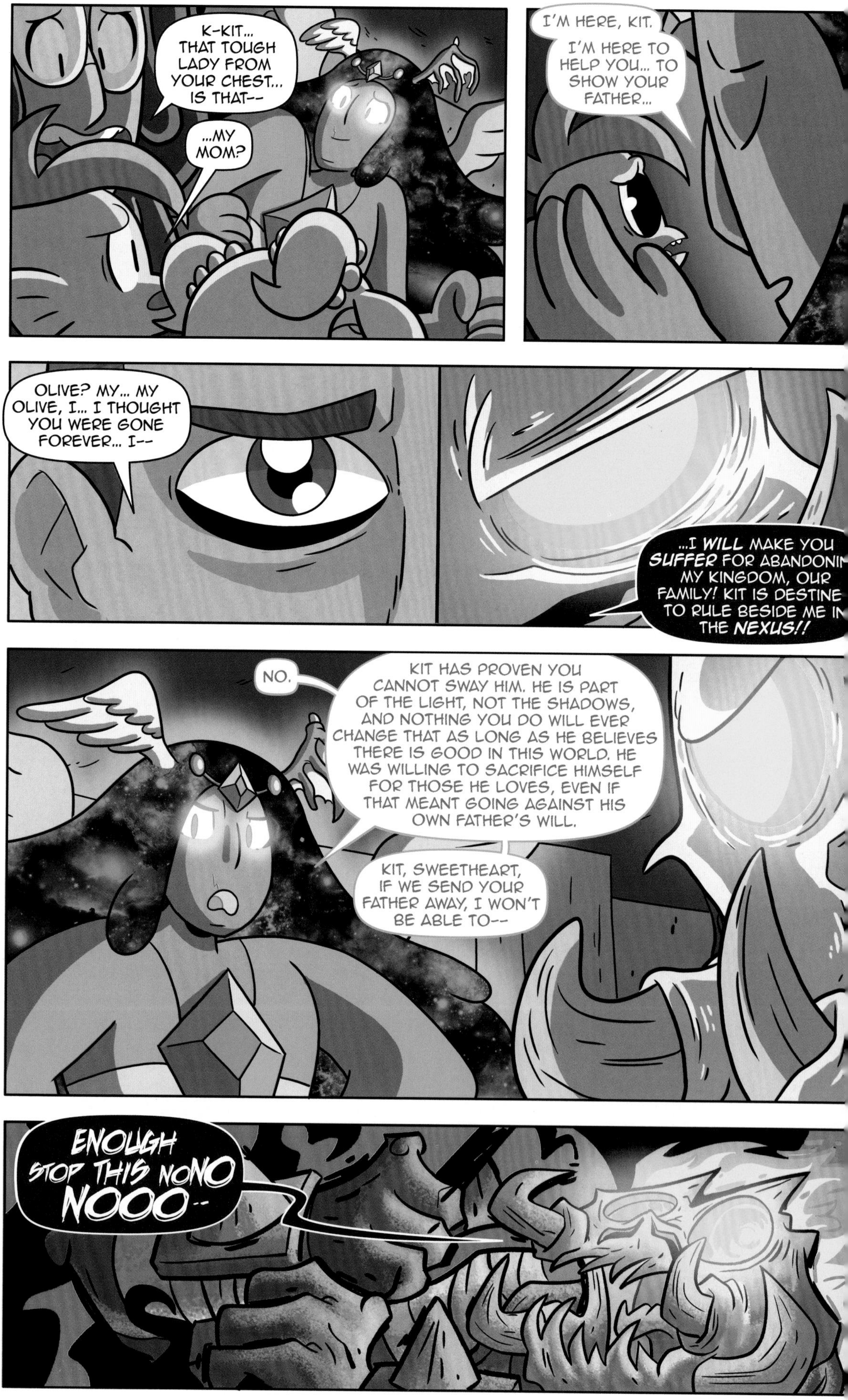
K-KIT... THAT TOUGH LADY FROM YOUR CHEST... IS THAT--
...MY MOM?
I'M HERE, KIT.
I'M HERE TO HELP YOU... TO SHOW YOUR FATHER...
OLIVE? MY... MY OLIVE, I... I THOUGHT YOU WERE GONE FOREVER... I--
...I WILL MAKE YOU SUFFER FOR ABANDONIN MY KINGDOM, OUR FAMILY! KIT IS DESTINE TO RULE BESIDE ME IN THE NEXUS!!
NO.
KIT HAS PROVEN YOU CANNOT SWAY HIM. HE IS PART OF THE LIGHT, NOT THE SHADOWS, AND NOTHING YOU DO WILL EVER CHANGE THAT AS LONG AS HE BELIEVES THERE IS GOOD IN THIS WORLD. HE WAS WILLING TO SACRIFICE HIMSELF FOR THOSE HE LOVES, EVEN IF THAT MEANT GOING AGAINST HIS OWN FATHER'S WILL.
KIT, SWEETHEART, IF WE SEND YOUR FATHER AWAY, I WON'T BE ABLE TO--
ENOUGH STOP THIS NONO NOOO--

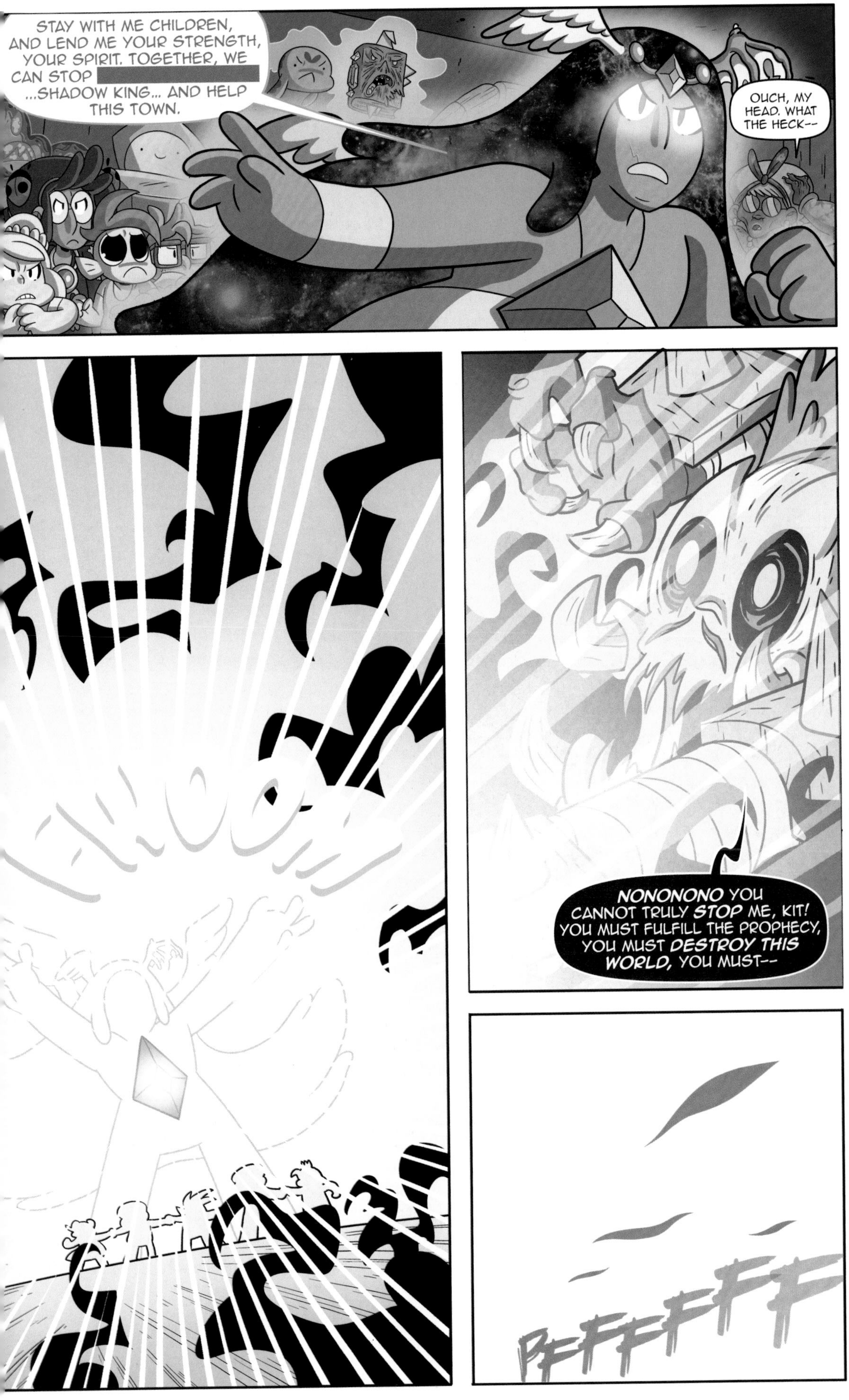
STAY WITH ME CHILDREN, AND LEND ME YOUR STRENGTH, YOUR SPIRIT. TOGETHER, WE CAN STOP [redacted] ...SHADOW KING... AND HELP THIS TOWN.
OUCH, MY HEAD. WHAT THE HECK--
NONONONO YOU CANNOT TRULY STOP ME, KIT! YOU MUST FULFILL THE PROPHECY, YOU MUST DESTROY THIS WORLD, YOU MUST--
PFFFFFF

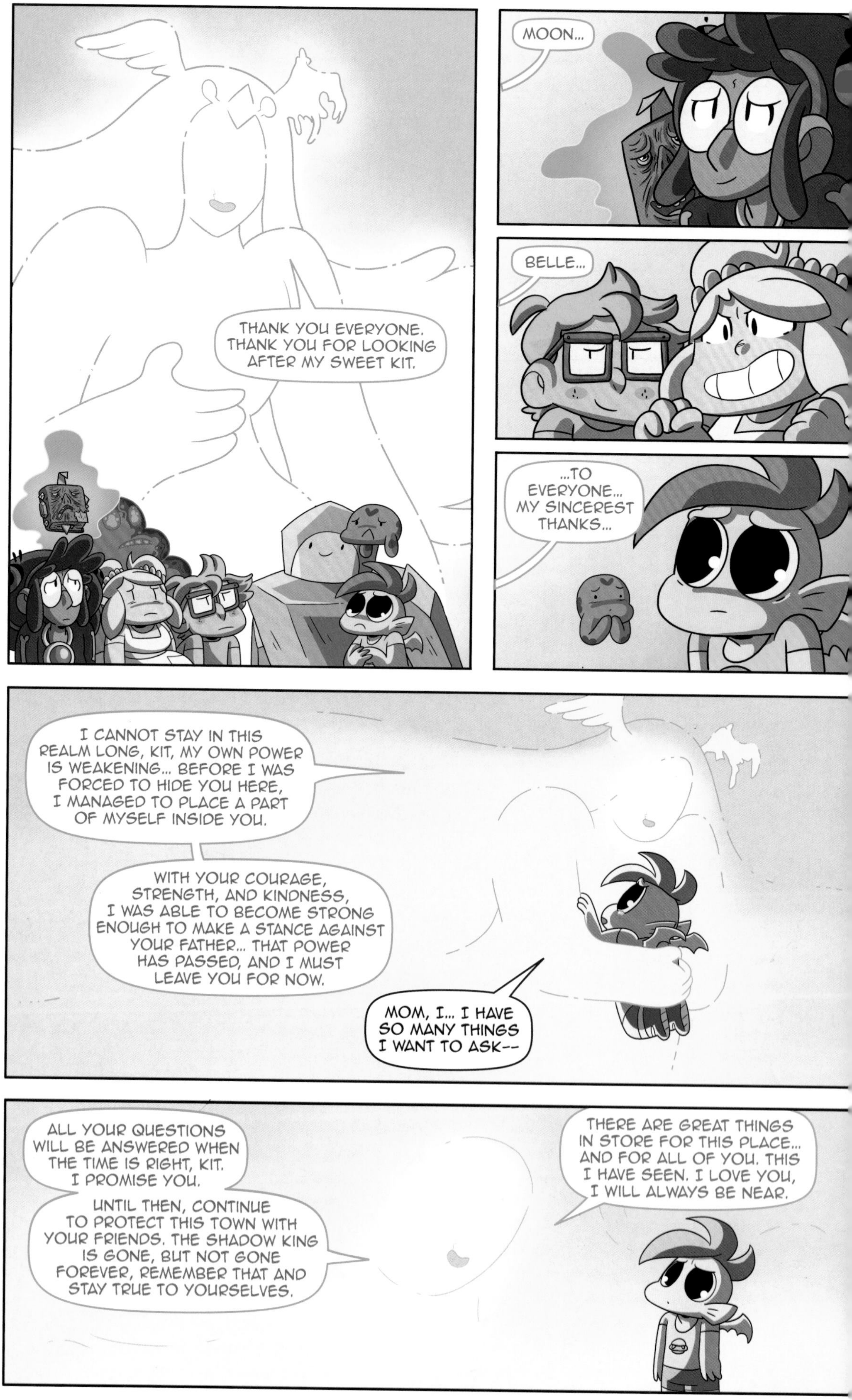
THANK YOU EVERYONE. THANK YOU FOR LOOKING AFTER MY SWEET KIT.
MOON...
BELLE...
...TO EVERYONE... MY SINCEREST THANKS...
I CANNOT STAY IN THIS REALM LONG, KIT, MY OWN POWER IS WEAKENING... BEFORE I WAS FORCED TO HIDE YOU HERE, I MANAGED TO PLACE A PART OF MYSELF INSIDE YOU.
WITH YOUR COURAGE, STRENGTH, AND KINDNESS, I WAS ABLE TO BECOME STRONG ENOUGH TO MAKE A STANCE AGAINST YOUR FATHER... THAT POWER HAS PASSED, AND I MUST LEAVE YOU FOR NOW.
MOM, I... I HAVE SO MANY THINGS I WANT TO ASK--
ALL YOUR QUESTIONS WILL BE ANSWERED WHEN THE TIME IS RIGHT, KIT. I PROMISE YOU.
UNTIL THEN, CONTINUE TO PROTECT THIS TOWN WITH YOUR FRIENDS. THE SHADOW KING IS GONE, BUT NOT GONE FOREVER, REMEMBER THAT AND STAY TRUE TO YOURSELVES.
THERE ARE GREAT THINGS IN STORE FOR THIS PLACE... AND FOR ALL OF YOU. THIS I HAVE SEEN. I LOVE YOU, I WILL ALWAYS BE NEAR.

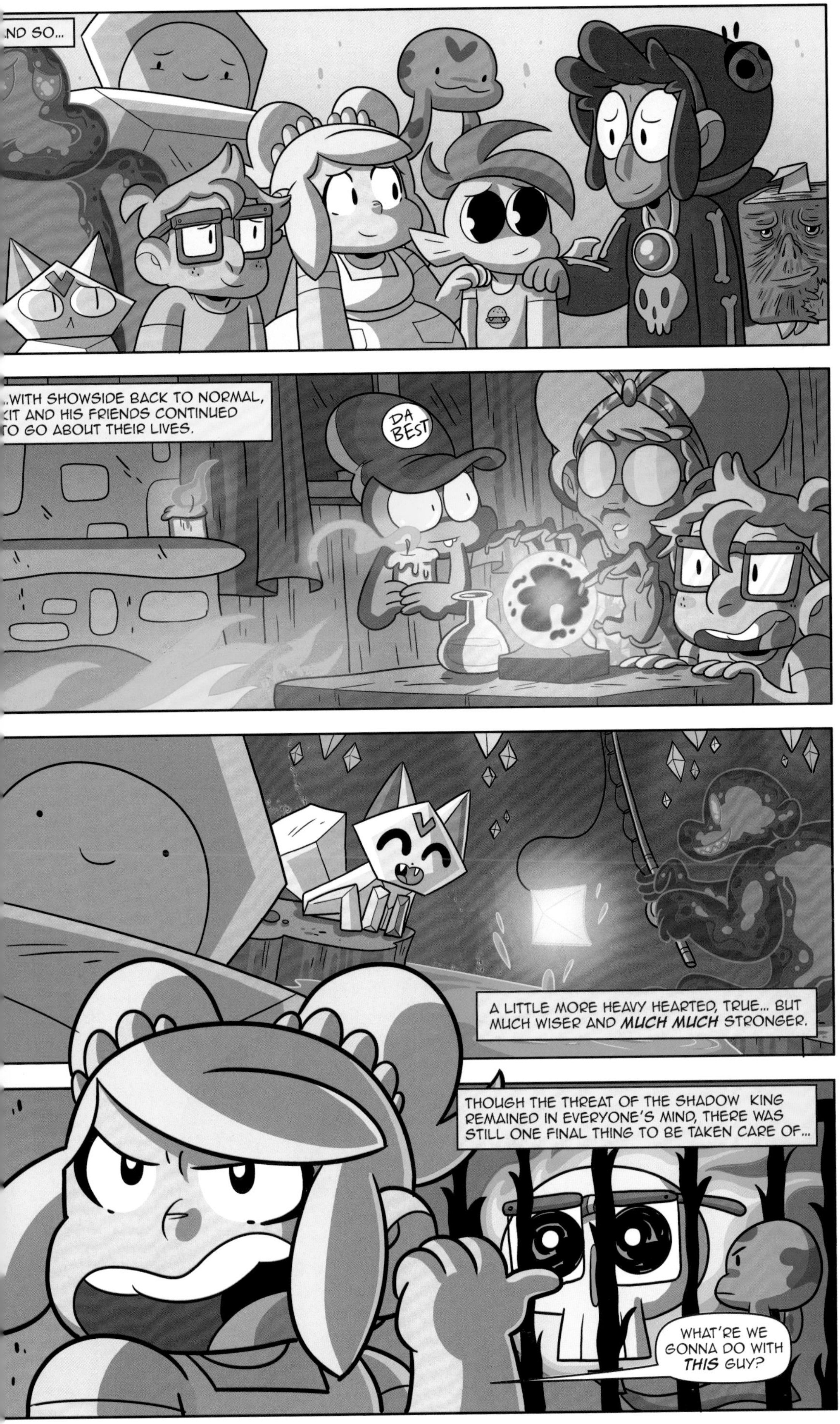
AND SO...
...WITH SHOWSIDE BACK TO NORMAL, KIT AND HIS FRIENDS CONTINUED TO GO ABOUT THEIR LIVES.
DA BEST
A LITTLE MORE HEAVY HEARTED, TRUE... BUT MUCH WISER AND ***MUCH MUCH*** STRONGER.
THOUGH THE THREAT OF THE SHADOW KING REMAINED IN EVERYONE'S MIND, THERE WAS STILL ONE FINAL THING TO BE TAKEN CARE OF...
WHAT'RE WE GONNA DO WITH ***THIS*** GUY?

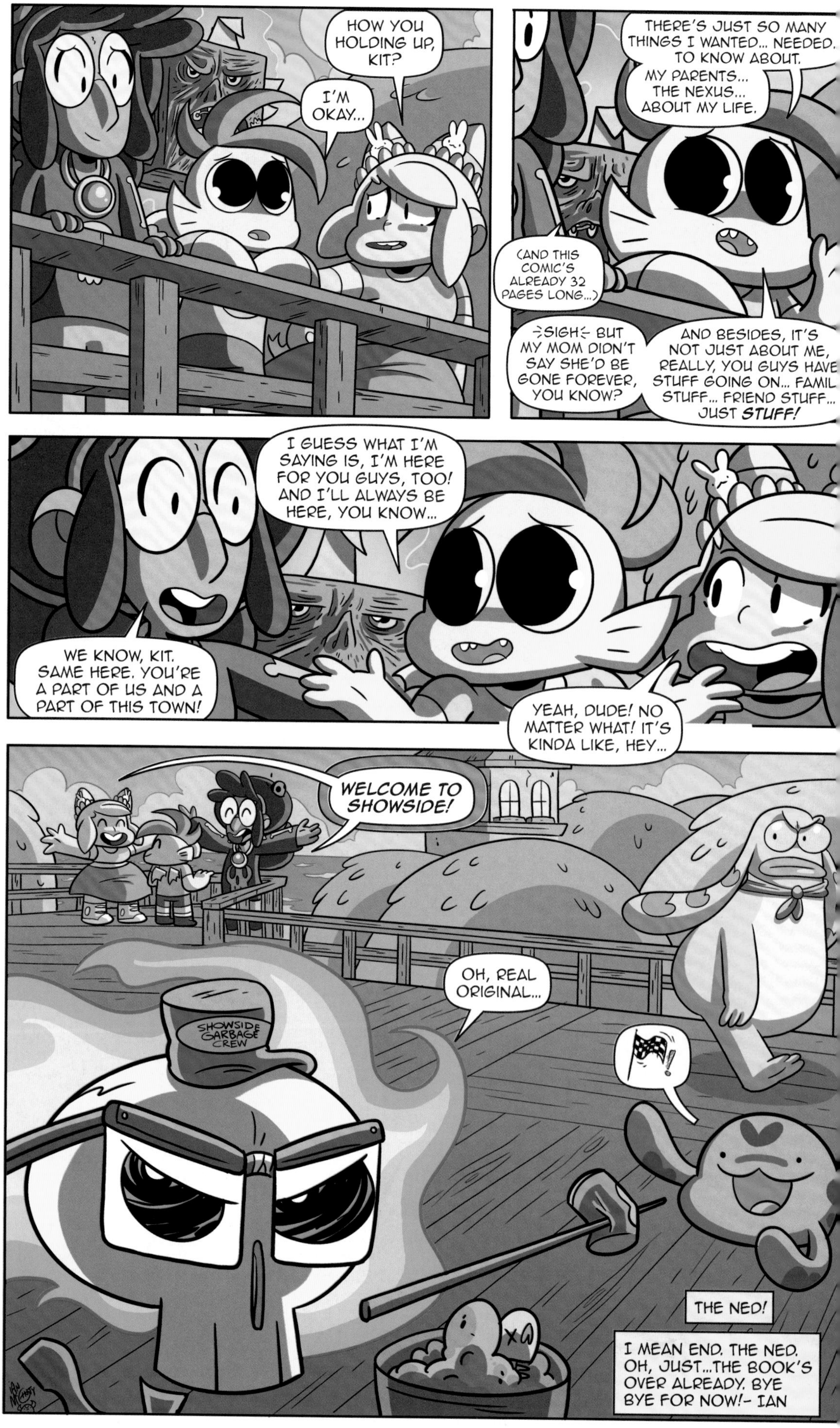
HOW YOU HOLDING UP, KIT?
I'M OKAY...
THERE'S JUST SO MANY THINGS I WANTED... NEEDED. TO KNOW ABOUT.
MY PARENTS... THE NEXUS... ABOUT MY LIFE.
(AND THIS COMIC'S ALREADY 32 PAGES LONG...)
≈SIGH≈ BUT MY MOM DIDN'T SAY SHE'D BE GONE FOREVER, YOU KNOW?
AND BESIDES, IT'S NOT JUST ABOUT ME, REALLY, YOU GUYS HAVE STUFF GOING ON... FAMIL STUFF... FRIEND STUFF... JUST STUFF!
I GUESS WHAT I'M SAYING IS, I'M HERE FOR YOU GUYS, TOO! AND I'LL ALWAYS BE HERE, YOU KNOW...
WE KNOW, KIT. SAME HERE. YOU'RE A PART OF US AND A PART OF THIS TOWN!
YEAH, DUDE! NO MATTER WHAT! IT'S KINDA LIKE, HEY...
WELCOME TO SHOWSIDE!
OH, REAL ORIGINAL...
SHOWSIDE GARBAGE CREW
THE NED!
I MEAN END. THE NED. OH, JUST...THE BOOK'S OVER ALREADY. BYE BYE FOR NOW!- IAN

THE MAYOR'S... MILLIONS?

WRITER - FRED C. STRESING
ARTIST - CAITLIN ROSE BOYLE
COLORS - MEG CASEY

AH! THE SEA! THE AIR! THE SPRAY OF SALTED WATER IN MY MOUTH! AND ALSO MY EYES!

RURWF.

STEADY ON NOW, MR. PUGSLEY. IT'S NOT SO BAD-- BESIDES! WE'RE CLOSE TO MY TREASURE TODAY.
BY MY LIP BRISTLES, I CAN FEEL IT!

HRMH.

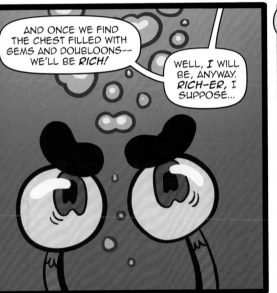

AND ONCE WE FIND THE CHEST FILLED WITH GEMS AND DOUBLOONS-- WE'LL BE RICH!

WELL, I WILL BE, ANYWAY. RICH-ER, I SUPPOSE...

AH! A KRAKEN!

BACK, YOU CRIMSON-CARAPACED CAD!

BLOOSH

HELP! MR. PUGSLEY!

STARBOARD AFT THE FORWARD MIZZENMAST! LOCK IN THE AUXILIARY POWER! AHOY THOSE MAINSTAYS! ENGAGE!

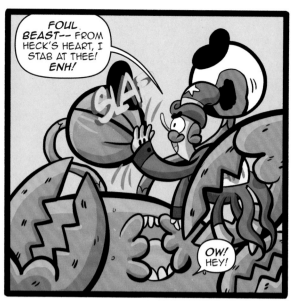

FOUL BEAST-- FROM HECK'S HEART, I STAB AT THEE! ENH!

SLA

OW! HEY!

MAYOR MAYER!

Y-YES?

YOU PROMISED MY DAUGHTER YOU'D LET HER USE THE SHIP IN FIVE MINUTES... TWENTY MINUTES AGO.

IT'S HER TURN.

...DRATBLAST IT. WE WERE SO CLOSE TO FINDING IT TODAY, MR. PUGSLEY. WE'VE GOT TO GET THAT TREASURE BEFORE-- ⇒SIIGH⇐ NEVERMIND.

I NEED TO SOOTHE MYSELF WITH SOME CHILLED DAIRY COMESTIBLES. PREFERABLY OF THE HEAVILY SUGARED VARIETY.

HELLO THERE, MICHAEL OPTICAL-LIMES. DO YOU HAVE PERCHANCE A SHERBERT TO PARCH THE SOUL OF A WEARY SEAFARER?

ALSO SOMETHING FOR ME AS WELL.

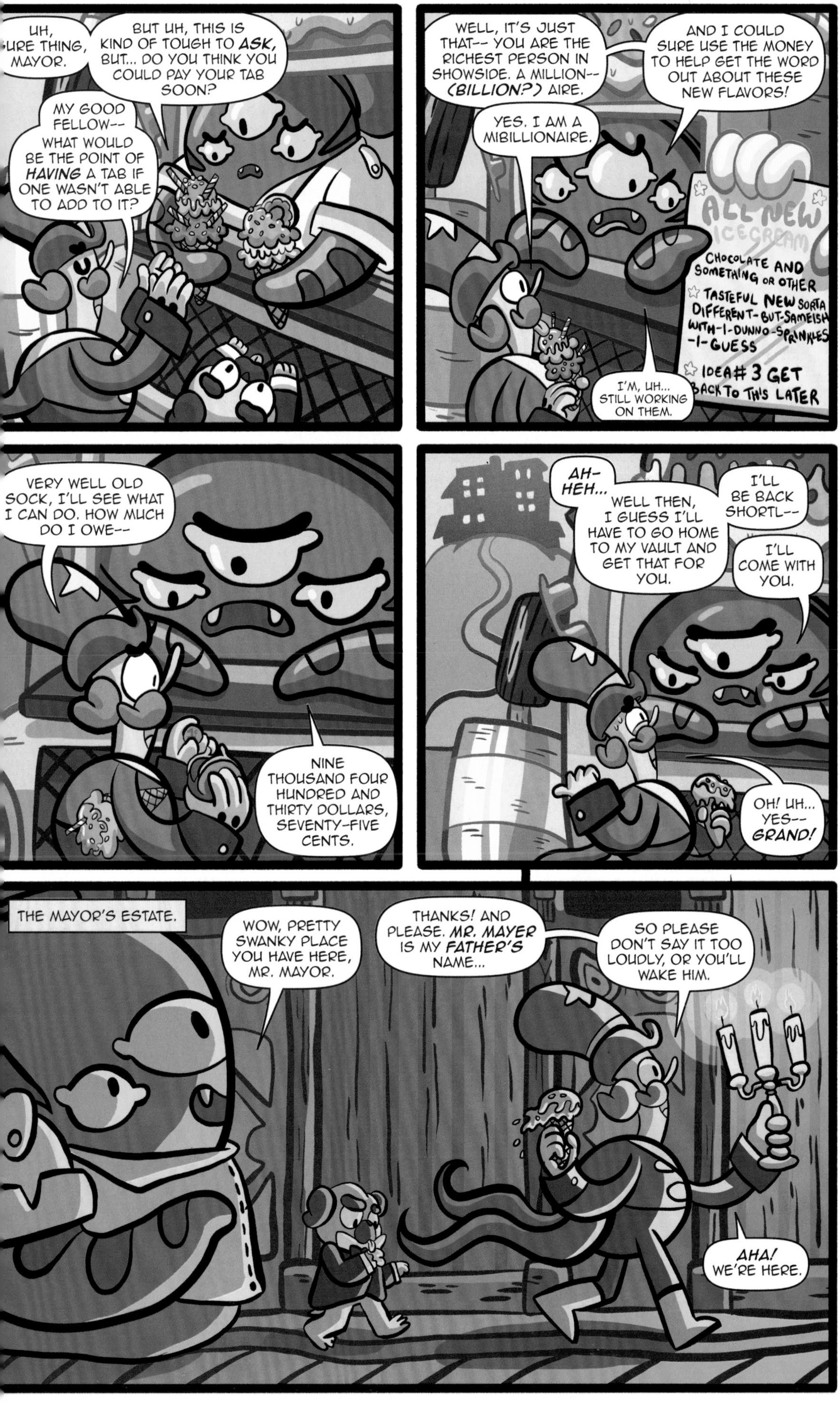

UH, SURE THING, MAYOR.
BUT UH, THIS IS KIND OF TOUGH TO ASK, BUT... DO YOU THINK YOU COULD PAY YOUR TAB SOON?
MY GOOD FELLOW-- WHAT WOULD BE THE POINT OF HAVING A TAB IF ONE WASN'T ABLE TO ADD TO IT?
WELL, IT'S JUST THAT-- YOU ARE THE RICHEST PERSON IN SHOWSIDE. A MILLION-- (BILLION?) AIRE.
AND I COULD SURE USE THE MONEY TO HELP GET THE WORD OUT ABOUT THESE NEW FLAVORS!
YES. I AM A MIBILLIONAIRE.
ALL NEW ICE CREAM
CHOCOLATE AND SOMETHING OR OTHER
TASTEFUL NEW SORTA DIFFERENT-BUT-SAMEISH WITH-I-DUNNO-SPRINKLES -I-GUESS
IDEA# 3 GET BACK TO THIS LATER
I'M, UH... STILL WORKING ON THEM.
VERY WELL OLD SOCK, I'LL SEE WHAT I CAN DO. HOW MUCH DO I OWE--
NINE THOUSAND FOUR HUNDRED AND THIRTY DOLLARS, SEVENTY-FIVE CENTS.
AH-HEH...
WELL THEN, I GUESS I'LL HAVE TO GO HOME TO MY VAULT AND GET THAT FOR YOU.
I'LL BE BACK SHORTL--
I'LL COME WITH YOU.
OH! UH... YES-- GRAND!
THE MAYOR'S ESTATE.
WOW, PRETTY SWANKY PLACE YOU HAVE HERE, MR. MAYOR.
THANKS! AND PLEASE. MR. MAYER IS MY FATHER'S NAME...
SO PLEASE DON'T SAY IT TOO LOUDLY, OR YOU'LL WAKE HIM.
AHA! WE'RE HERE.

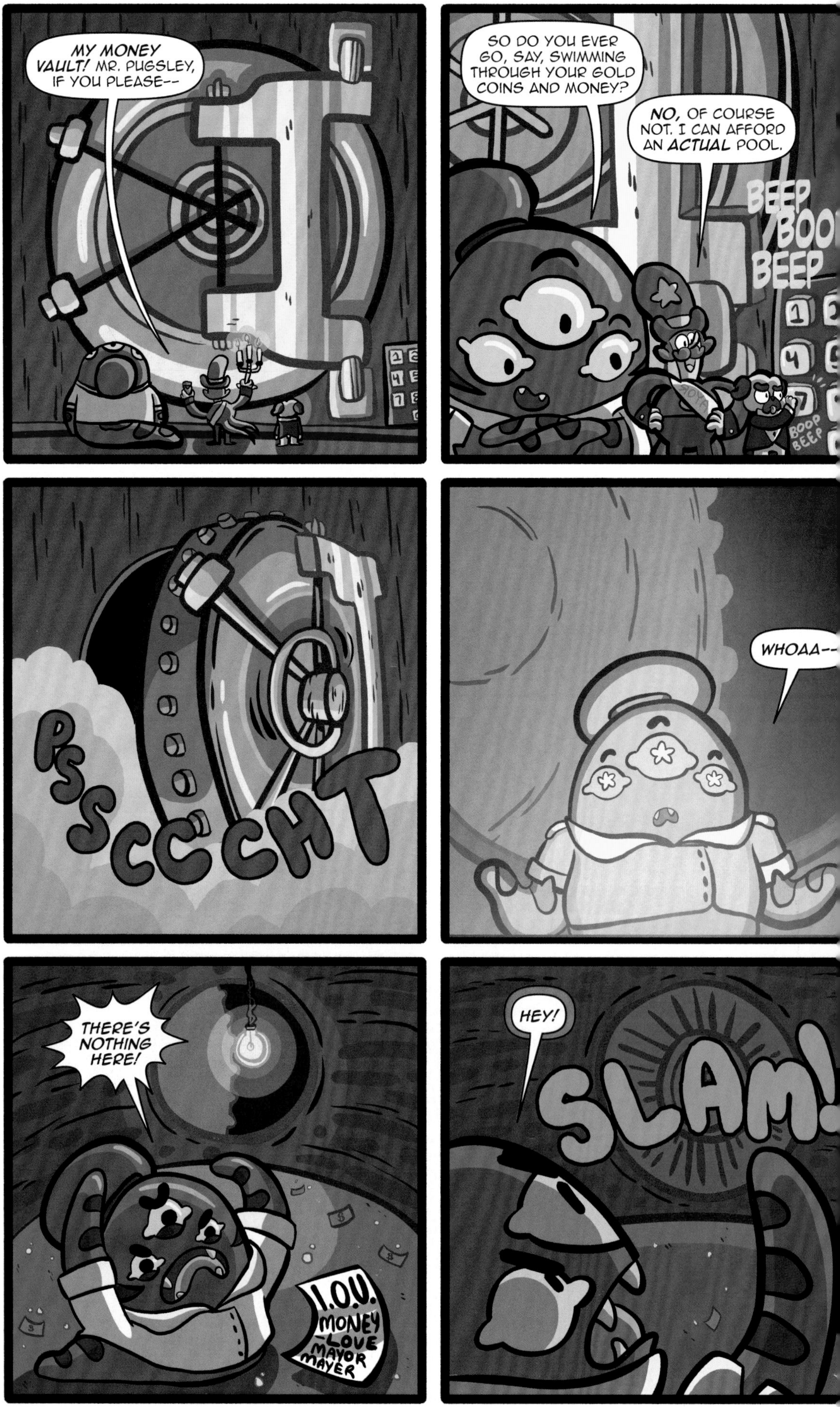
MY MONEY VAULT! MR. PUGSLEY, IF YOU PLEASE--
SO DO YOU EVER GO, SAY, SWIMMING THROUGH YOUR GOLD COINS AND MONEY?
NO, OF COURSE NOT. I CAN AFFORD AN ACTUAL POOL.
BEEP
BOOP
BEEP
BOOP
BEEP
PSSCCCHT
WHOAA--
THERE'S NOTHING HERE!
I.O.U. MONEY -LOVE MAYOR MAYER
HEY!
SLAM!

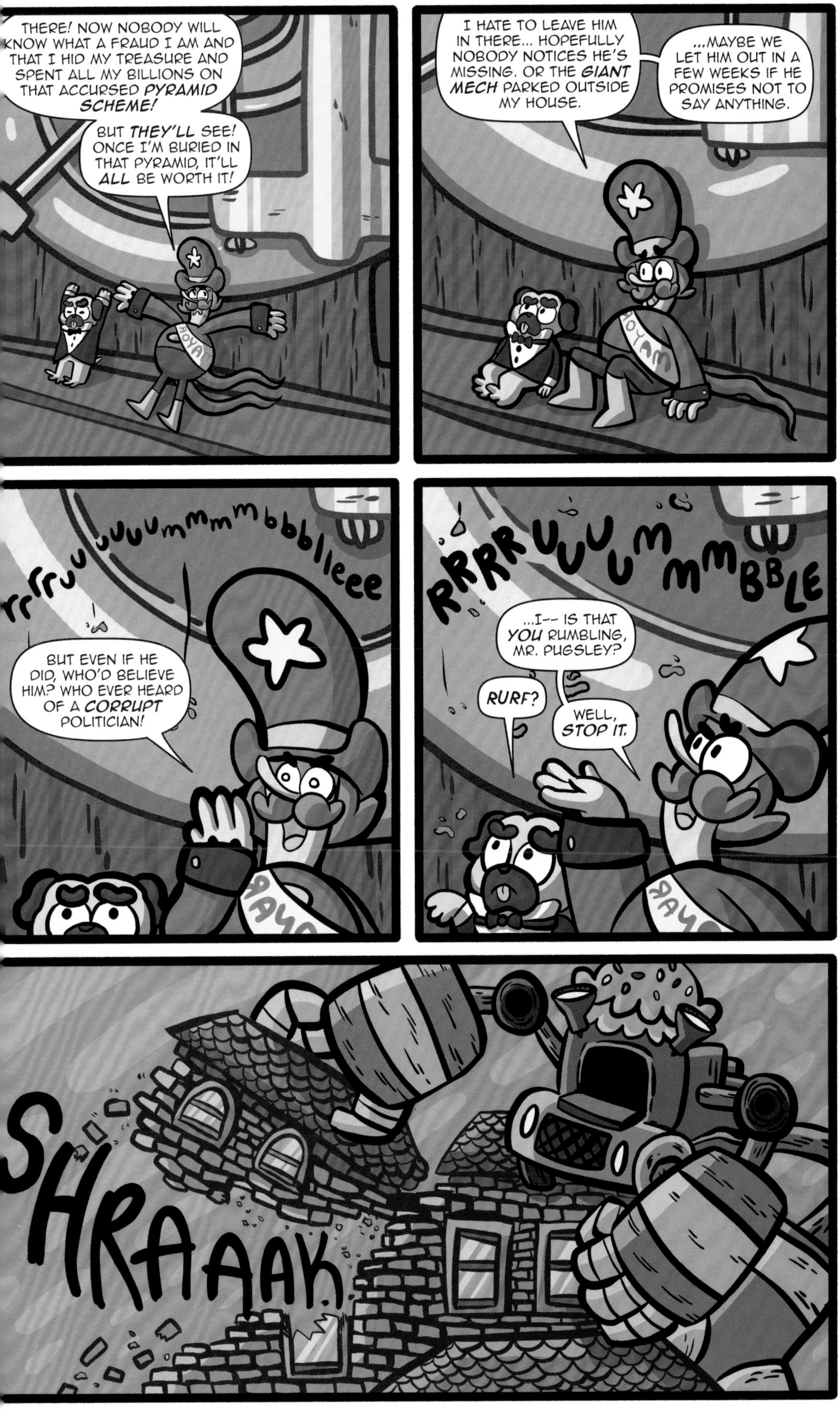

THERE! NOW NOBODY WILL KNOW WHAT A FRAUD I AM AND THAT I HID MY TREASURE AND SPENT ALL MY BILLIONS ON THAT ACCURSED PYRAMID SCHEME!
BUT THEY'LL SEE! ONCE I'M BURIED IN THAT PYRAMID, IT'LL ALL BE WORTH IT!
MAYOR
I HATE TO LEAVE HIM IN THERE... HOPEFULLY NOBODY NOTICES HE'S MISSING. OR THE GIANT MECH PARKED OUTSIDE MY HOUSE.
...MAYBE WE LET HIM OUT IN A FEW WEEKS IF HE PROMISES NOT TO SAY ANYTHING.
MAYOR
rrrruuuuuummmmbbblleee
BUT EVEN IF HE DID, WHO'D BELIEVE HIM? WHO EVER HEARD OF A CORRUPT POLITICIAN!
RRRRUUUUMMMBBLE
...I-- IS THAT YOU RUMBLING, MR. PUGSLEY?
RURF?
WELL, STOP IT.
SHRAAAK.

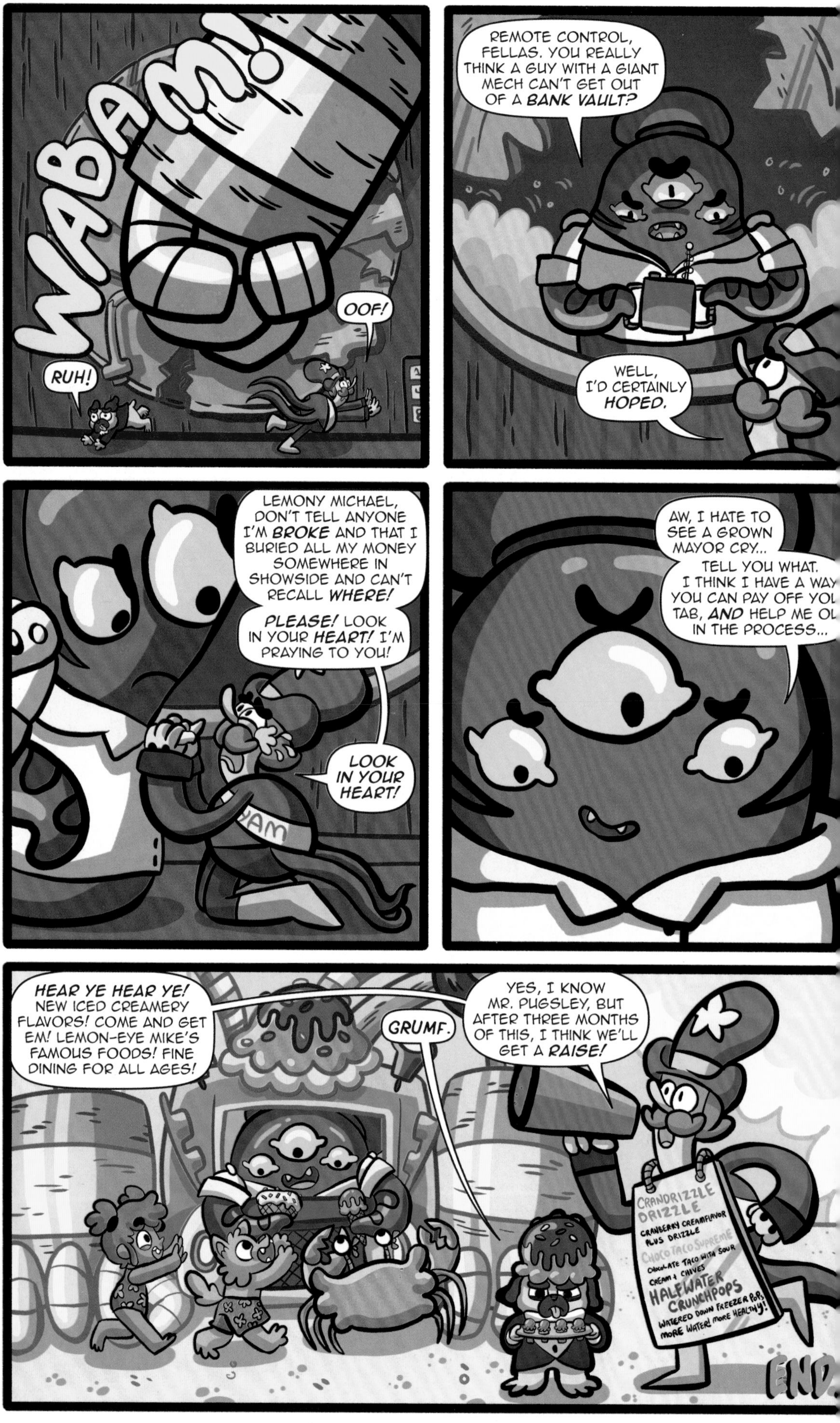
WABAM!!
OOF!
RUH!
REMOTE CONTROL, FELLAS. YOU REALLY THINK A GUY WITH A GIANT MECH CAN'T GET OUT OF A BANK VAULT?
WELL, I'D CERTAINLY HOPED.
LEMONY MICHAEL, DON'T TELL ANYONE I'M BROKE AND THAT I BURIED ALL MY MONEY SOMEWHERE IN SHOWSIDE AND CAN'T RECALL WHERE!
PLEASE! LOOK IN YOUR HEART! I'M PRAYING TO YOU!
LOOK IN YOUR HEART!
YAM
AW, I HATE TO SEE A GROWN MAYOR CRY...
TELL YOU WHAT. I THINK I HAVE A WAY YOU CAN PAY OFF YOU TAB, AND HELP ME OU IN THE PROCESS...
HEAR YE HEAR YE! NEW ICED CREAMERY FLAVORS! COME AND GET EM! LEMON-EYE MIKE'S FAMOUS FOODS! FINE DINING FOR ALL AGES!
GRUMF.
YES, I KNOW MR. PUGSLEY, BUT AFTER THREE MONTHS OF THIS, I THINK WE'LL GET A RAISE!
CRANDRIZZLE DRIZZLE
CRANBERRY CREAMFLAVOR PLUS DRIZZLE
CHOCO TACO SUPREME
CHOCOLATE TACO WITH SOUR CREAM & CHIVES
HALFWATER CRUNCHPOPS
WATERED DOWN FREEZER POPS MORE WATER! MORE HEALTHY!
END.

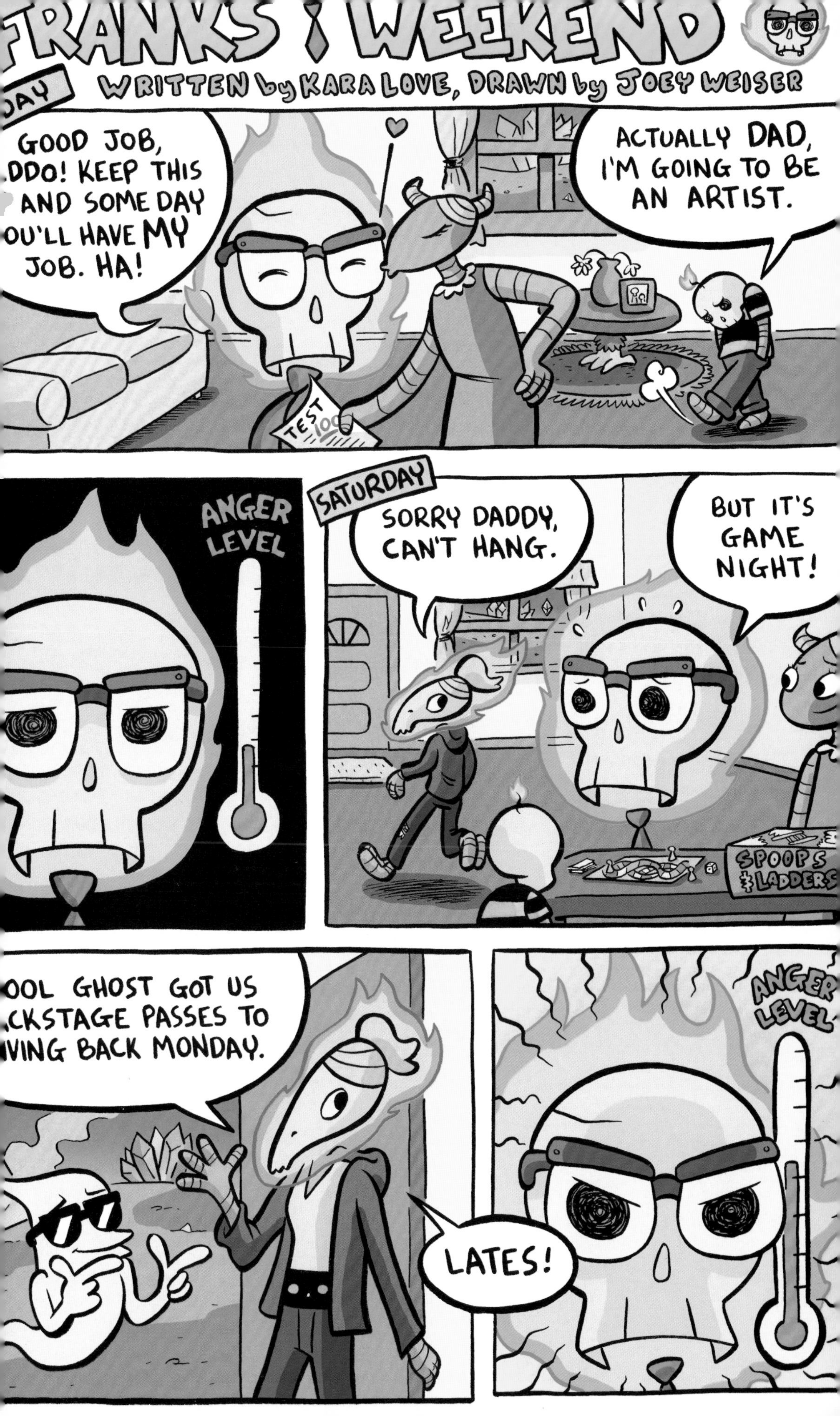
FRANKS WEEKEND
WRITTEN by KARA LOVE, DRAWN by JOEY WEISER
DAY
GOOD JOB, DDO! KEEP THIS AND SOME DAY OU'LL HAVE MY JOB. HA!
TEST 100
ACTUALLY DAD, I'M GOING TO BE AN ARTIST.
ANGER LEVEL
SATURDAY
SORRY DADDY, CAN'T HANG.
BUT IT'S GAME NIGHT!
SPOOPS & LADDERS
OOL GHOST GOT US CKSTAGE PASSES TO VING BACK MONDAY.
LATES!
ANGER LEVEL

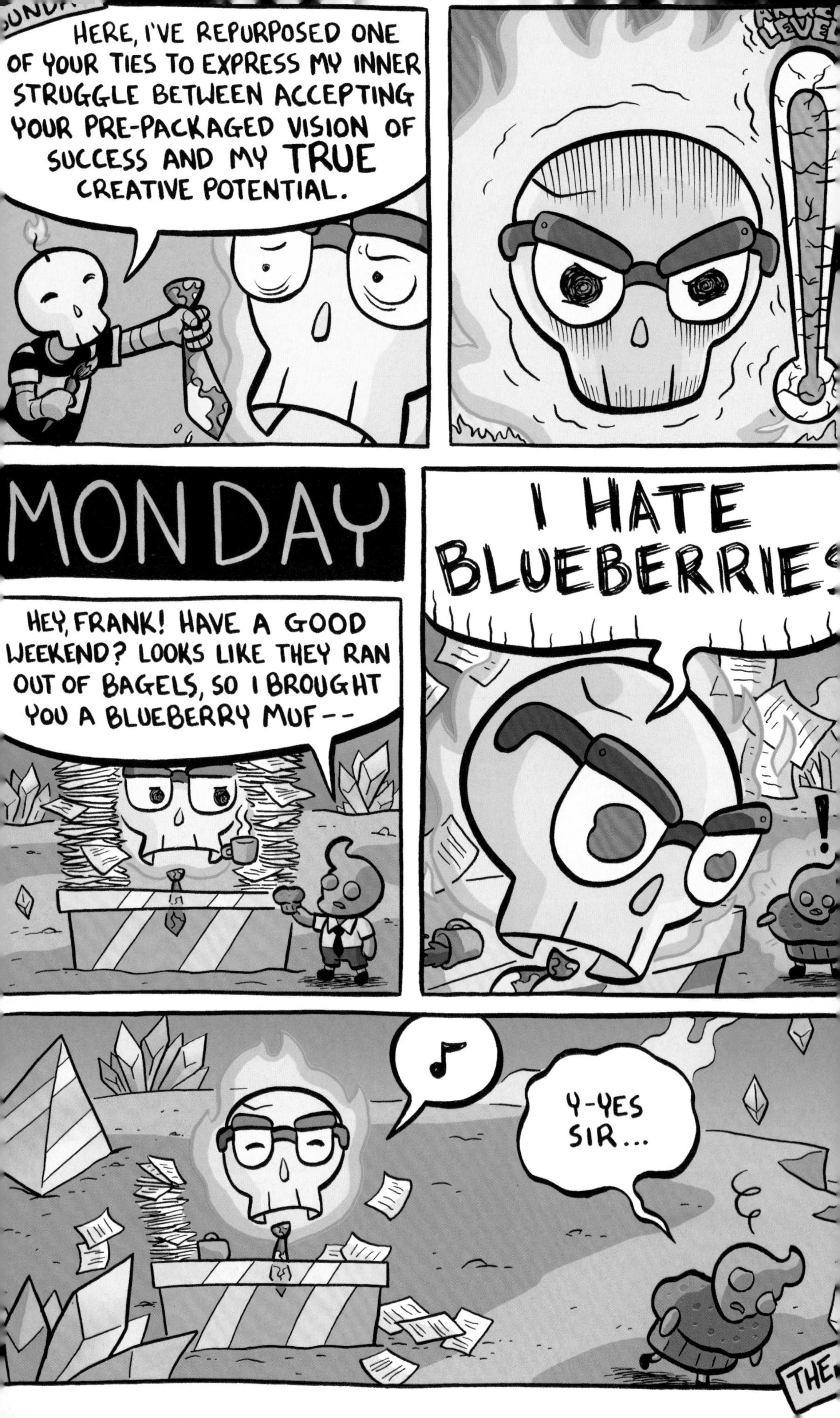
HERE, I'VE REPURPOSED ONE OF YOUR TIES TO EXPRESS MY INNER STRUGGLE BETWEEN ACCEPTING YOUR PRE-PACKAGED VISION OF SUCCESS AND MY TRUE CREATIVE POTENTIAL.
MONDAY
HEY, FRANK! HAVE A GOOD WEEKEND? LOOKS LIKE THEY RAN OUT OF BAGELS, SO I BROUGHT YOU A BLUEBERRY MUF--
I HATE BLUEBERRIES
!
♪
Y-YES SIR...
THE

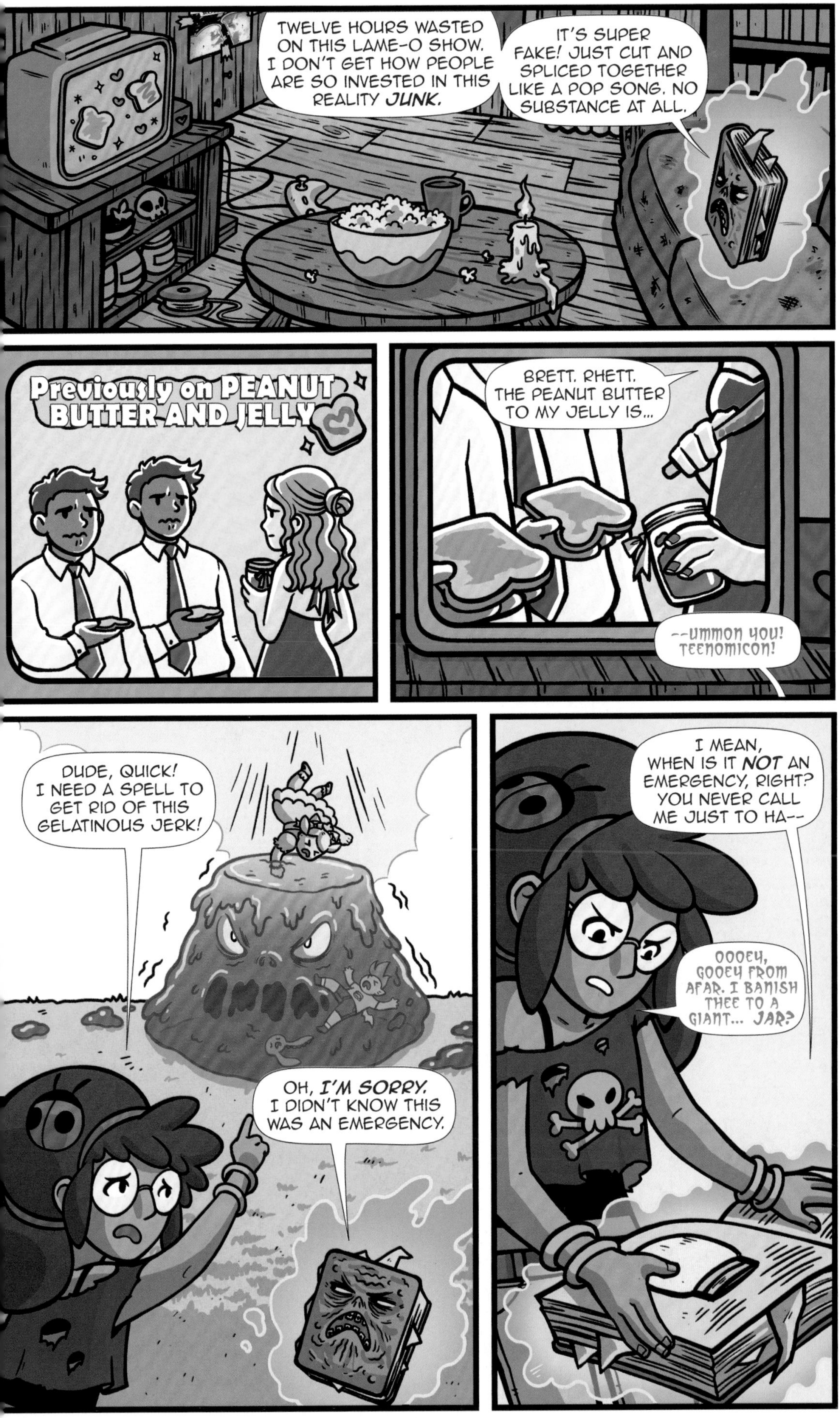
TWELVE HOURS WASTED ON THIS LAME-O SHOW. I DON'T GET HOW PEOPLE ARE SO INVESTED IN THIS REALITY JUNK.
IT'S SUPER FAKE! JUST CUT AND SPLICED TOGETHER LIKE A POP SONG. NO SUBSTANCE AT ALL.
Previously on PEANUT BUTTER AND JELLY
BRETT. RHETT. THE PEANUT BUTTER TO MY JELLY IS...
--UMMON YOU! TEENOMICON!
DUDE, QUICK! I NEED A SPELL TO GET RID OF THIS GELATINOUS JERK!
OH, I'M SORRY. I DIDN'T KNOW THIS WAS AN EMERGENCY.
I MEAN, WHEN IS IT NOT AN EMERGENCY, RIGHT? YOU NEVER CALL ME JUST TO HA--
OOOEY, GOOEY FROM AFAR. I BANISH THEE TO A GIANT... JAR?

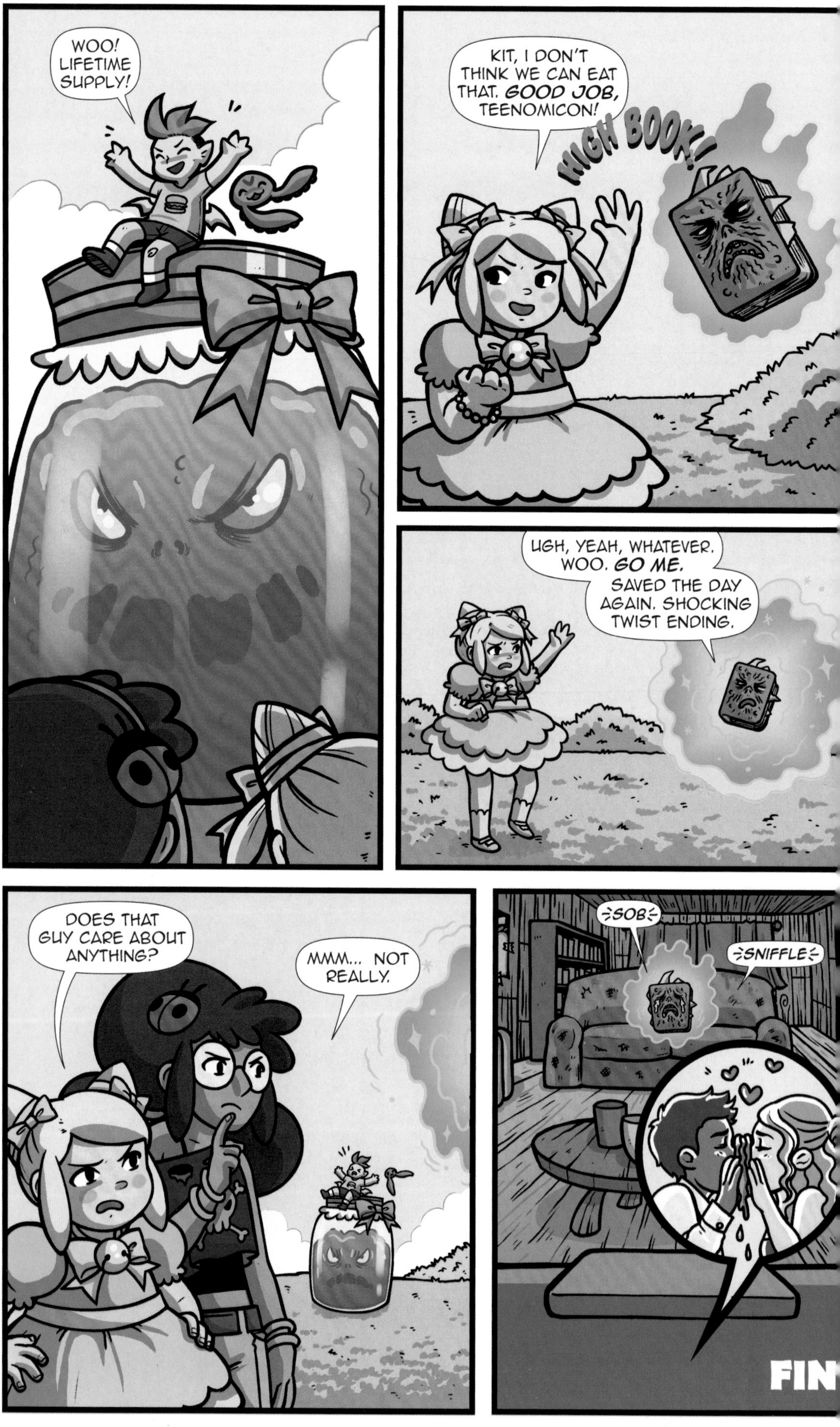
WOO! LIFETIME SUPPLY!
KIT, I DON'T THINK WE CAN EAT THAT. GOOD JOB, TEENOMICON!
HIGH BOOK!
UGH, YEAH, WHATEVER. WOO. GO ME.
SAVED THE DAY AGAIN. SHOCKING TWIST ENDING.
DOES THAT GUY CARE ABOUT ANYTHING?
MMM... NOT REALLY.
SOB
SNIFFLE
FIN

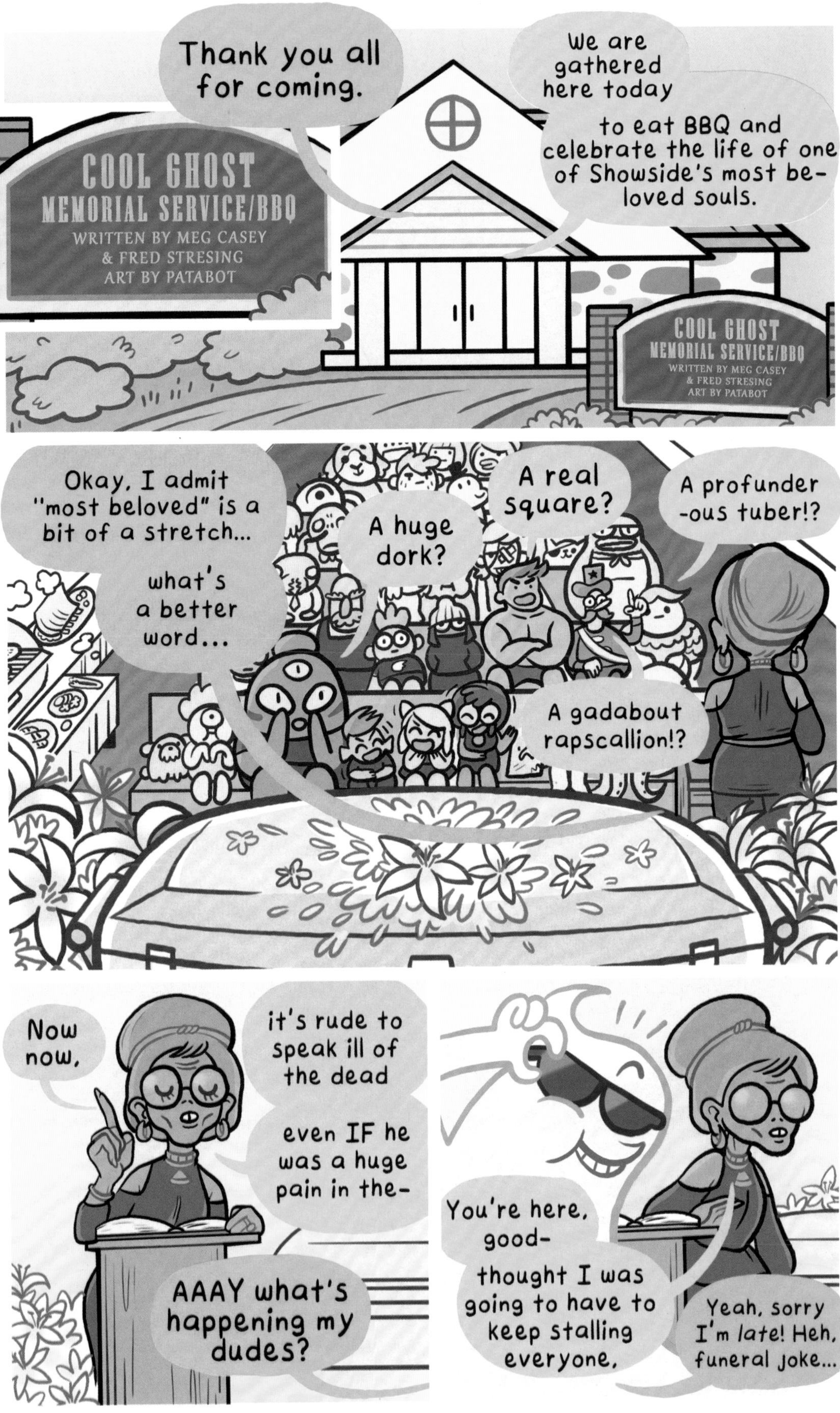
Thank you all for coming.
COOL GHOST
MEMORIAL SERVICE/BBQ
WRITTEN BY MEG CASEY
& FRED STRESING
ART BY PATABOT
We are gathered here today
to eat BBQ and celebrate the life of one of Showside's most be-loved souls.
COOL GHOST
MEMORIAL SERVICE/BBQ
WRITTEN BY MEG CASEY
& FRED STRESING
ART BY PATABOT
Okay, I admit "most beloved" is a bit of a stretch...
what's a better word...
A huge dork?
A real square?
A profunder -ous tuber!?
A gadabout rapscallion!?
Now now,
it's rude to speak ill of the dead
even IF he was a huge pain in the-
AAAY what's happening my dudes?
You're here, good-
thought I was going to have to keep stalling everyone,
Yeah, sorry I'm *late*! Heh, funeral joke...

Wow! Great to see so many of you showed up!

Well I know you all loved Cool Ghost a ton, I mean, he WAS one rad dude

I don't remember that.

Or that other time when he played hookey from school and took a joy-ride in the vice principal's Chevy?

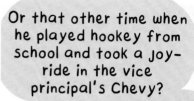

Haha! What a guy!

Like, who could forget the time he did a sweet kickflip over Lemon Eye Mike's food truck?

And that reminds me of the time Cool Ghost starred in his very own rap music video, maaaan that was great-

4 HOURS LATER

...and so I was like, "No way man!! These shades are for COOL GHOST only!!"

and my dudes, you should have seen the look on Beezlebub's face, it was TOTALLY hilarious, but I guess you had to be there. Then he sent me to he-

GEEZE, can you wrap this up already?!

I need to get home and record today's rerun of Days of Our Lives!!

I mean get home and record uh sports

yeah, I just love those sports... game...

HEY! Can we focus on the man of the hour here,

instead of some lameo antique dictionary!? JEEZ!

THUMP!!

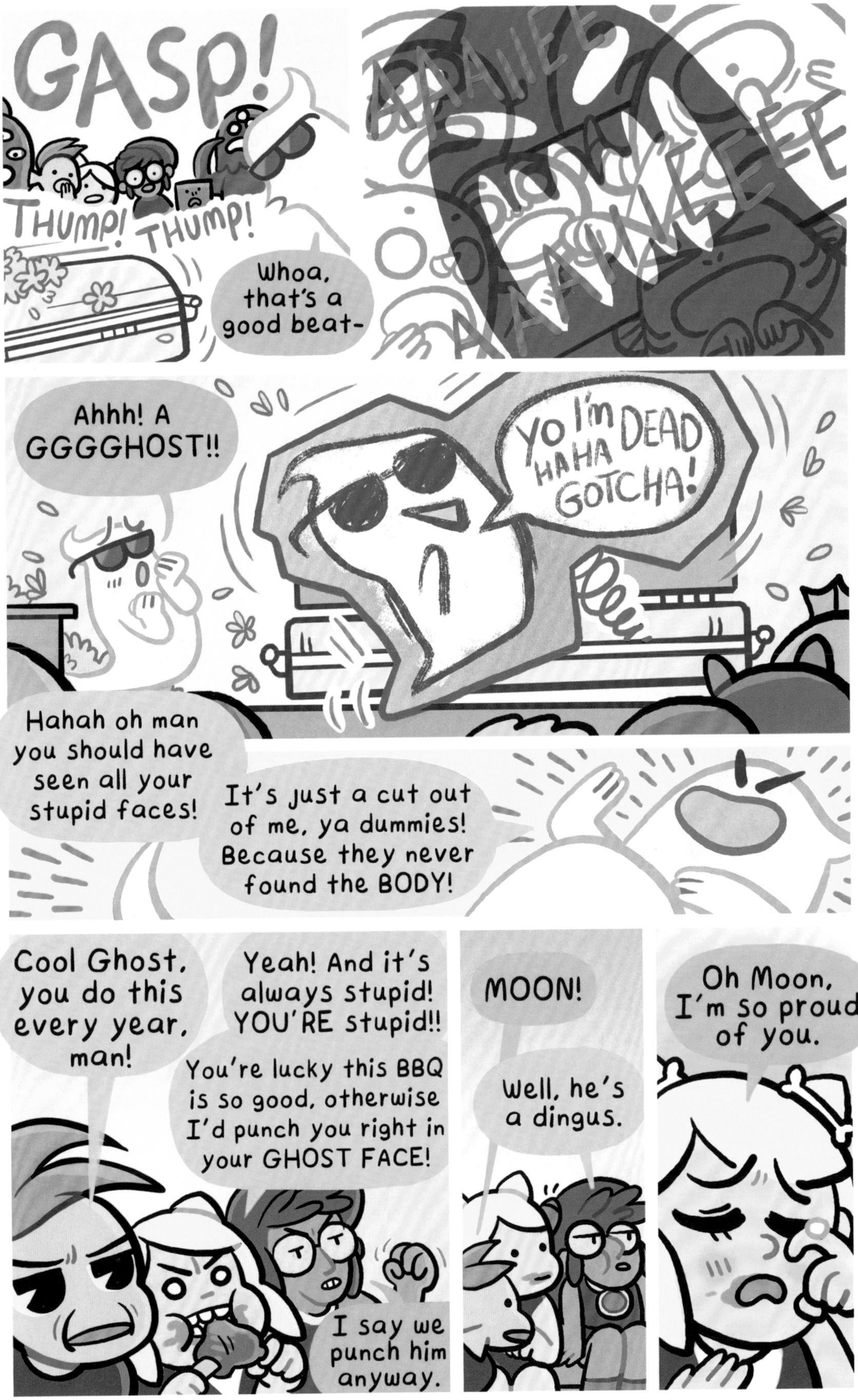
GASP!
THUMP! THUMP!
Whoa, that's a good beat-
Ahhh! A GGGGHOST!!
YO I'm DEAD HAHA GOTCHA!
Hahah oh man you should have seen all your stupid faces!
It's just a cut out of me, ya dummies! Because they never found the BODY!
Cool Ghost, you do this every year, man!
Yeah! And it's always stupid! YOU'RE stupid!!
You're lucky this BBQ is so good, otherwise I'd punch you right in your GHOST FACE!
I say we punch him anyway.
MOON!
Well, he's a dingus.
Oh Moon, I'm so proud of you.

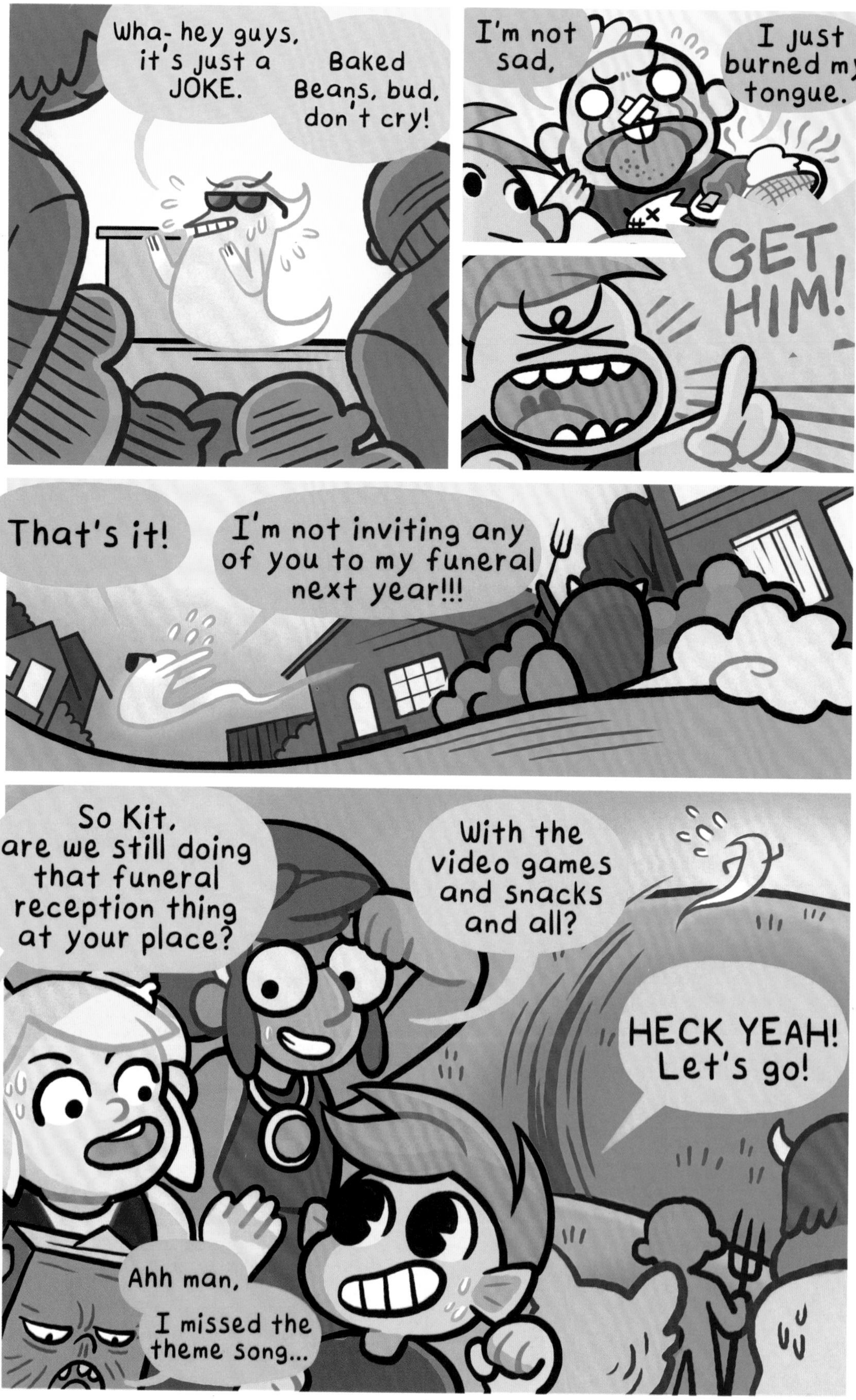
Wha- hey guys, it's just a JOKE.
Baked Beans, bud, don't cry!
I'm not sad,
I just burned my tongue.
GET HIM!
That's it!
I'm not inviting any of you to my funeral next year!!!
So Kit, are we still doing that funeral reception thing at your place?
With the video games and snacks and all?
HECK YEAH! Let's go!
Ahh man,
I missed the theme song...

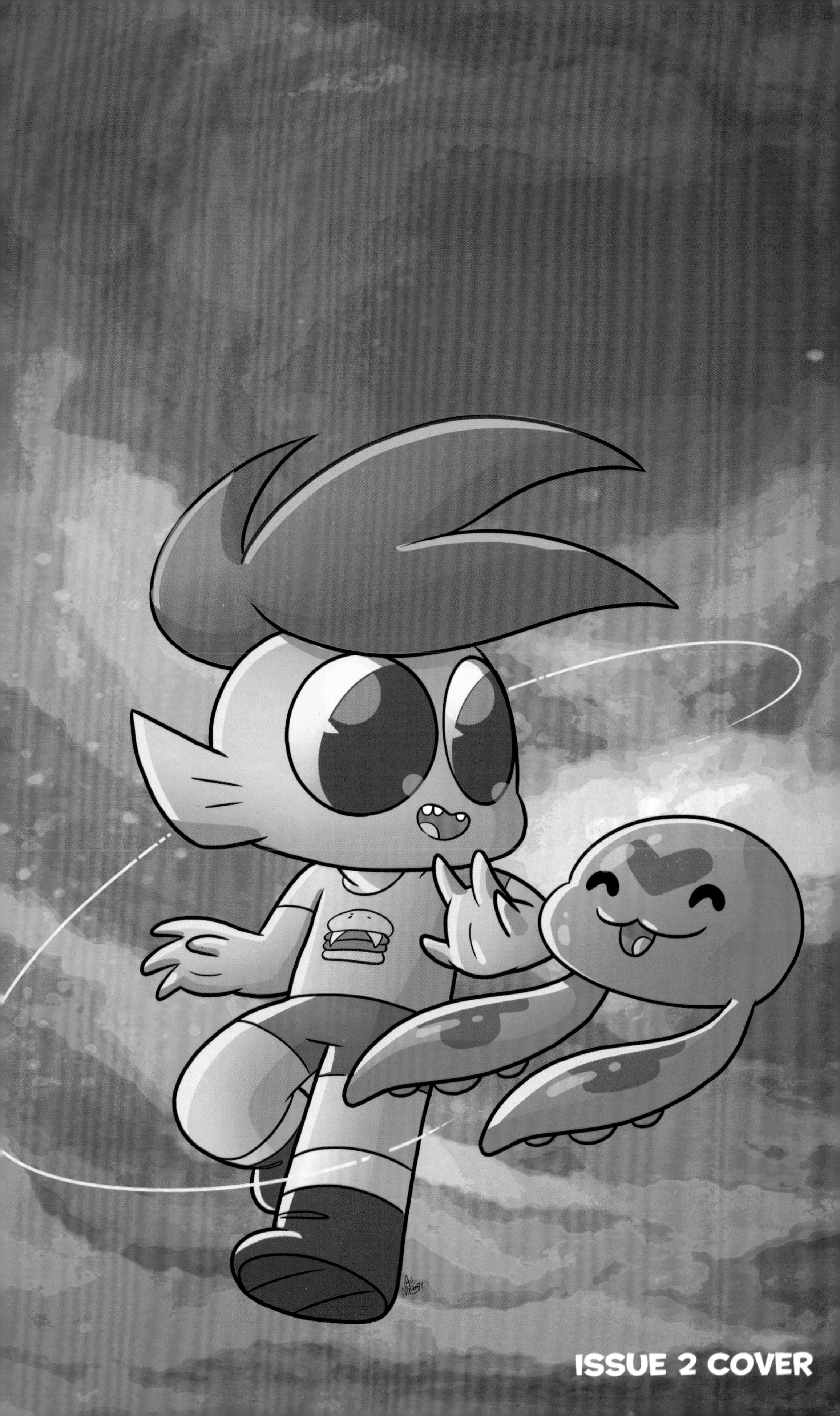

ISSUE 2 COVER

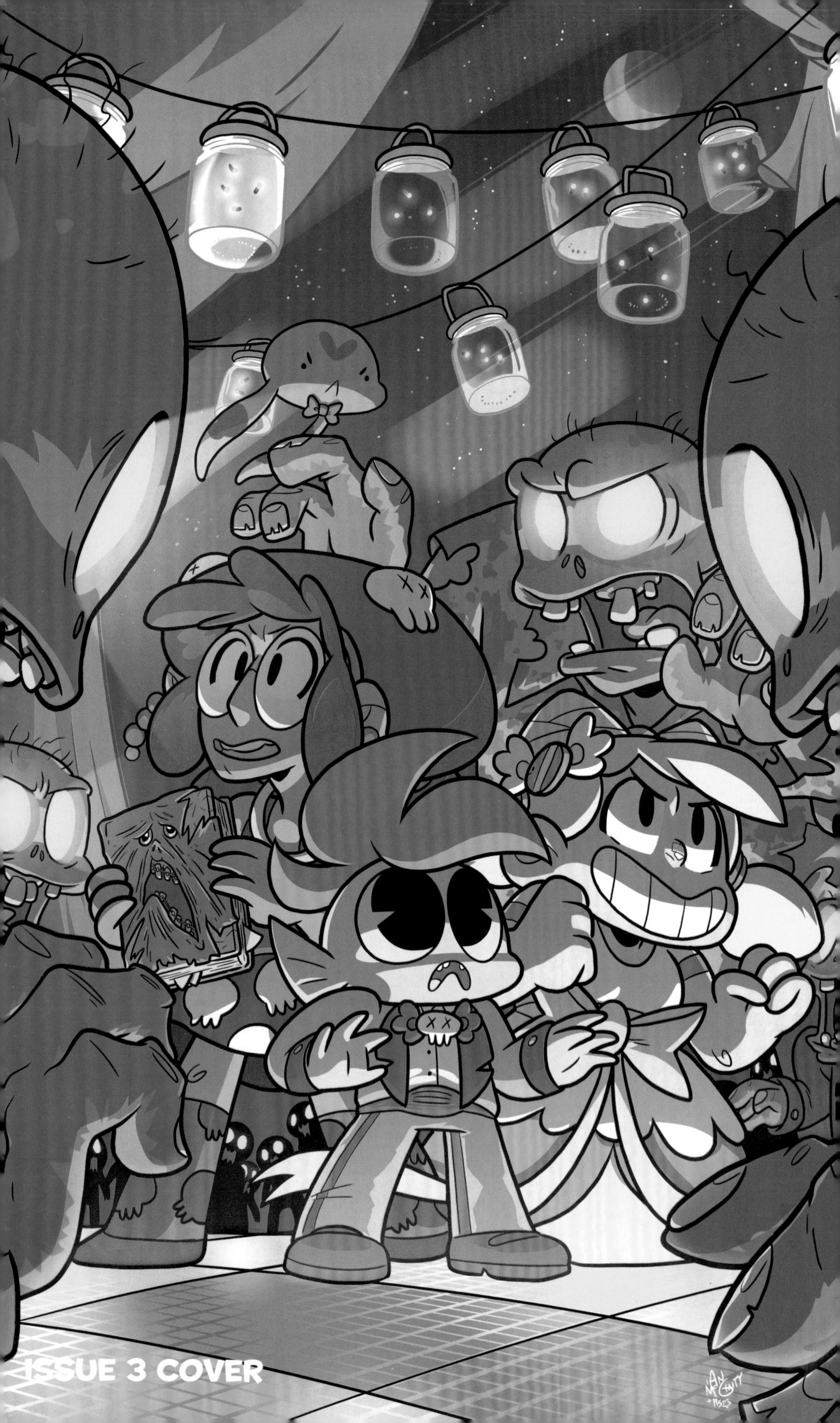
ISSUE 3 COVER

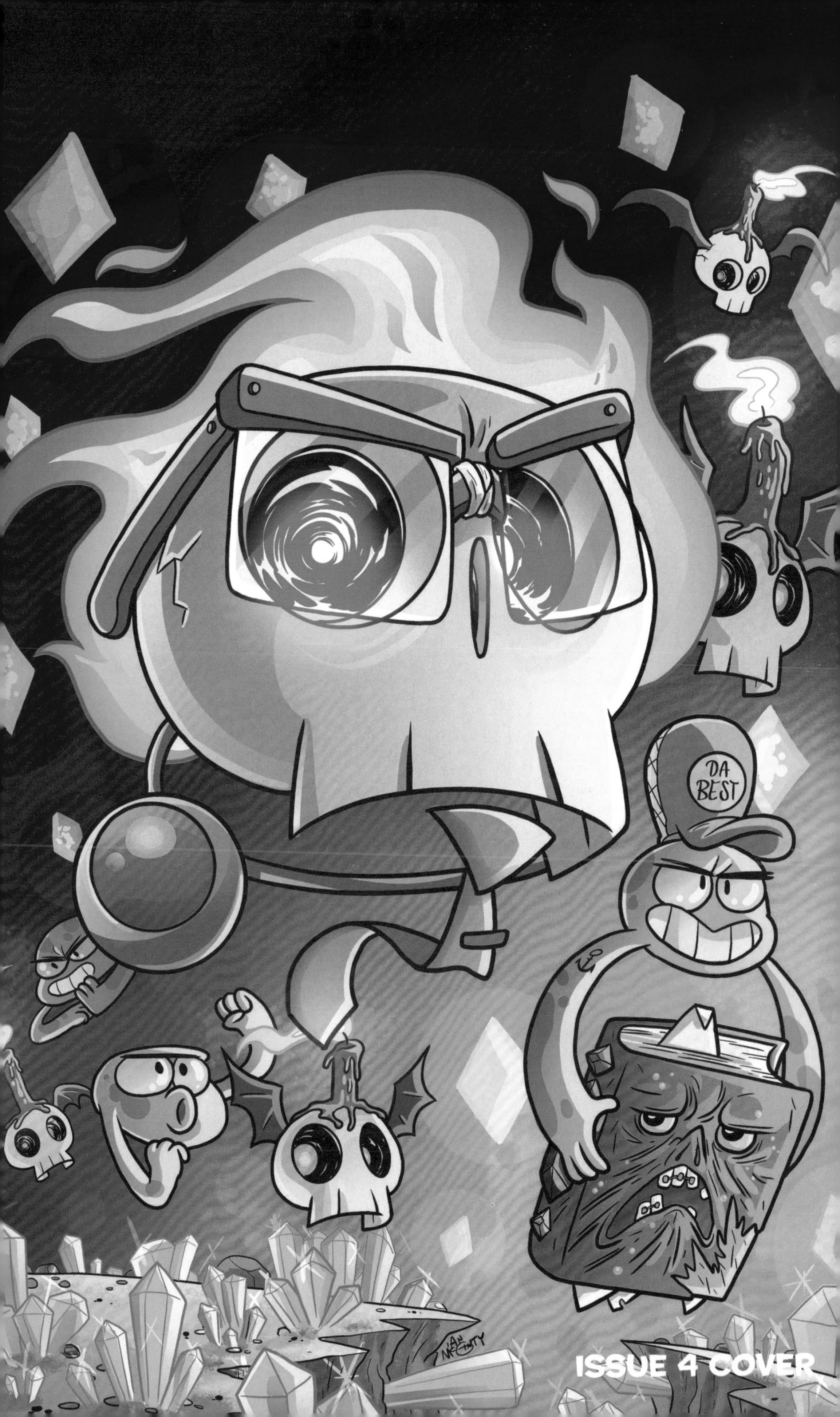
DA BEST

ISSUE 4 COVER

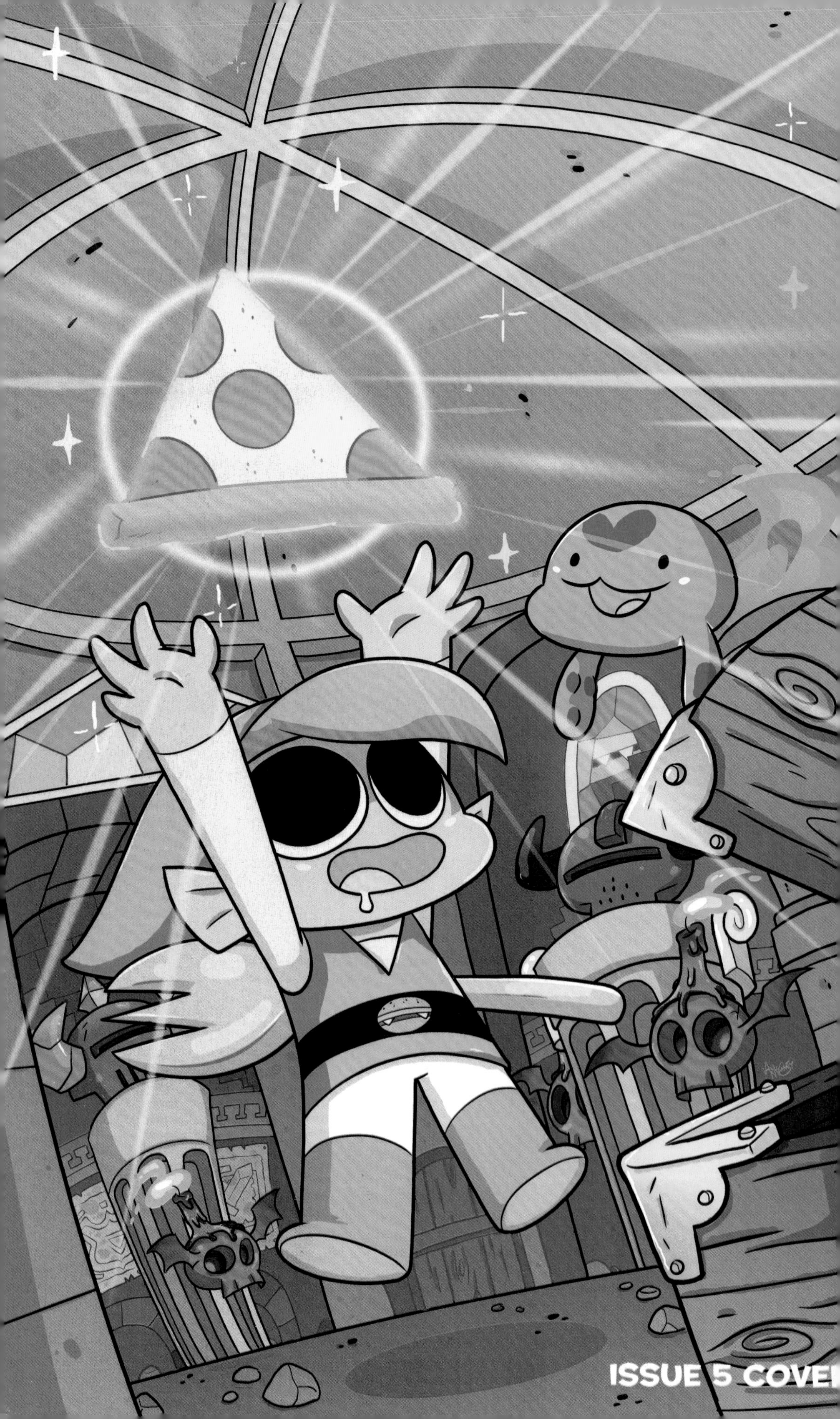

ISSUE 5 COVER

PROCESS!!!

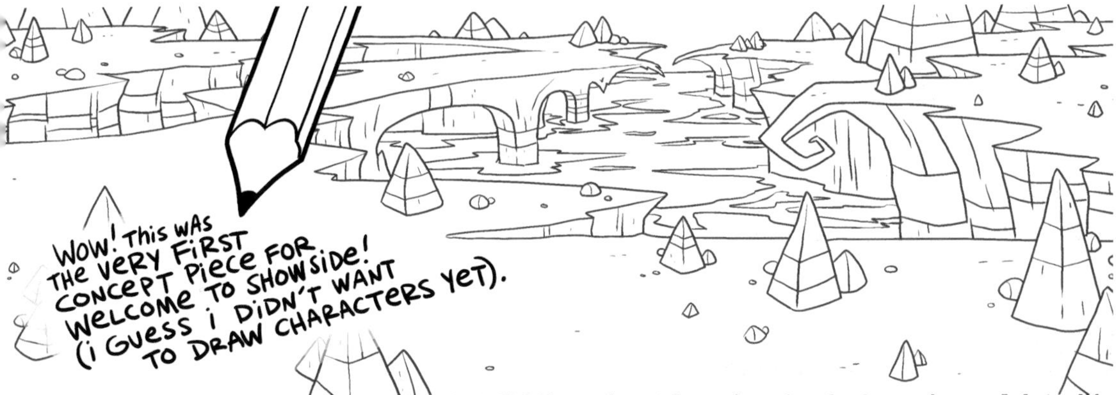
WOW! THIS WAS THE VERY FIRST CONCEPT PIECE FOR WELCOME TO SHOWSIDE! (I GUESS I DIDN'T WANT TO DRAW CHARACTERS YET).

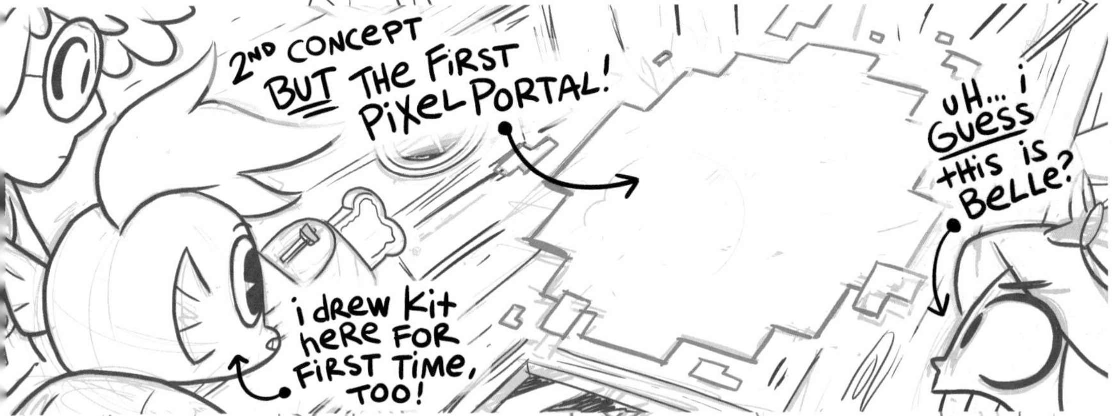
2ND CONCEPT BUT THE FIRST PIXEL PORTAL!
UH... I GUESS THIS IS BELLE?
I DREW KIT HERE FOR FIRST TIME, TOO!

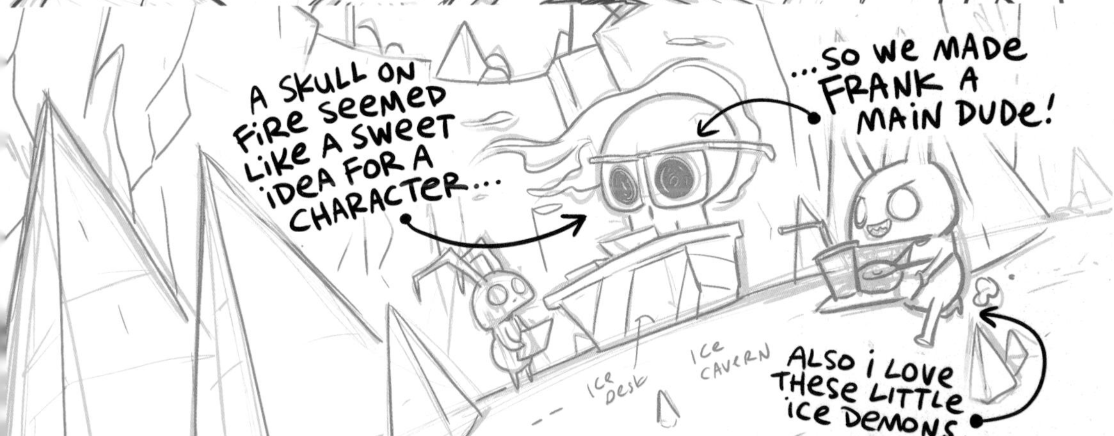
A SKULL ON FIRE SEEMED LIKE A SWEET IDEA FOR A CHARACTER...
...SO WE MADE FRANK A MAIN DUDE!
ICE DESK
ICE CAVERN
ALSO I LOVE THESE LITTLE ICE DEMONS.

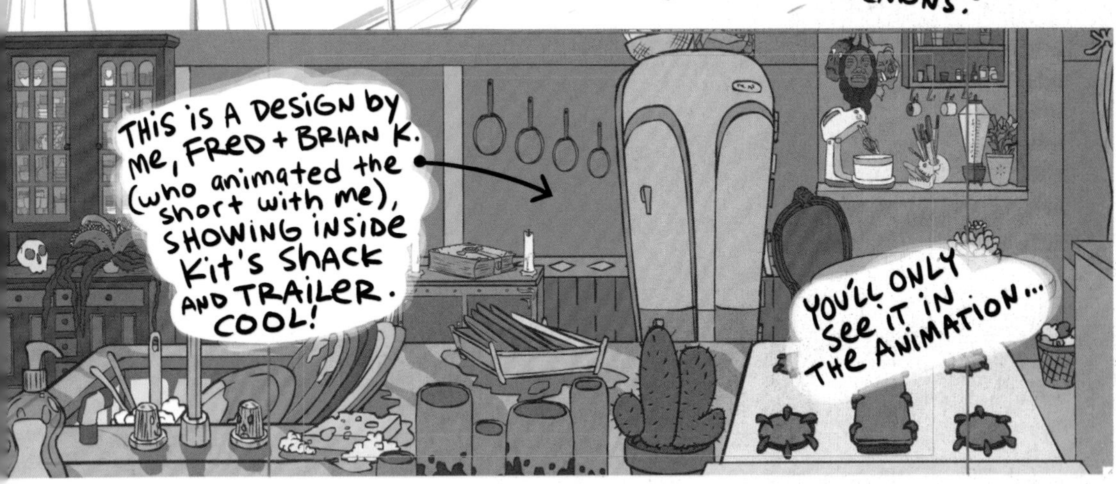
THIS IS A DESIGN BY ME, FRED + BRIAN K. (WHO ANIMATED THE SHORT WITH ME), SHOWING INSIDE KIT'S SHACK AND TRAILER. COOL!
YOU'LL ONLY SEE IT IN THE ANIMATION...

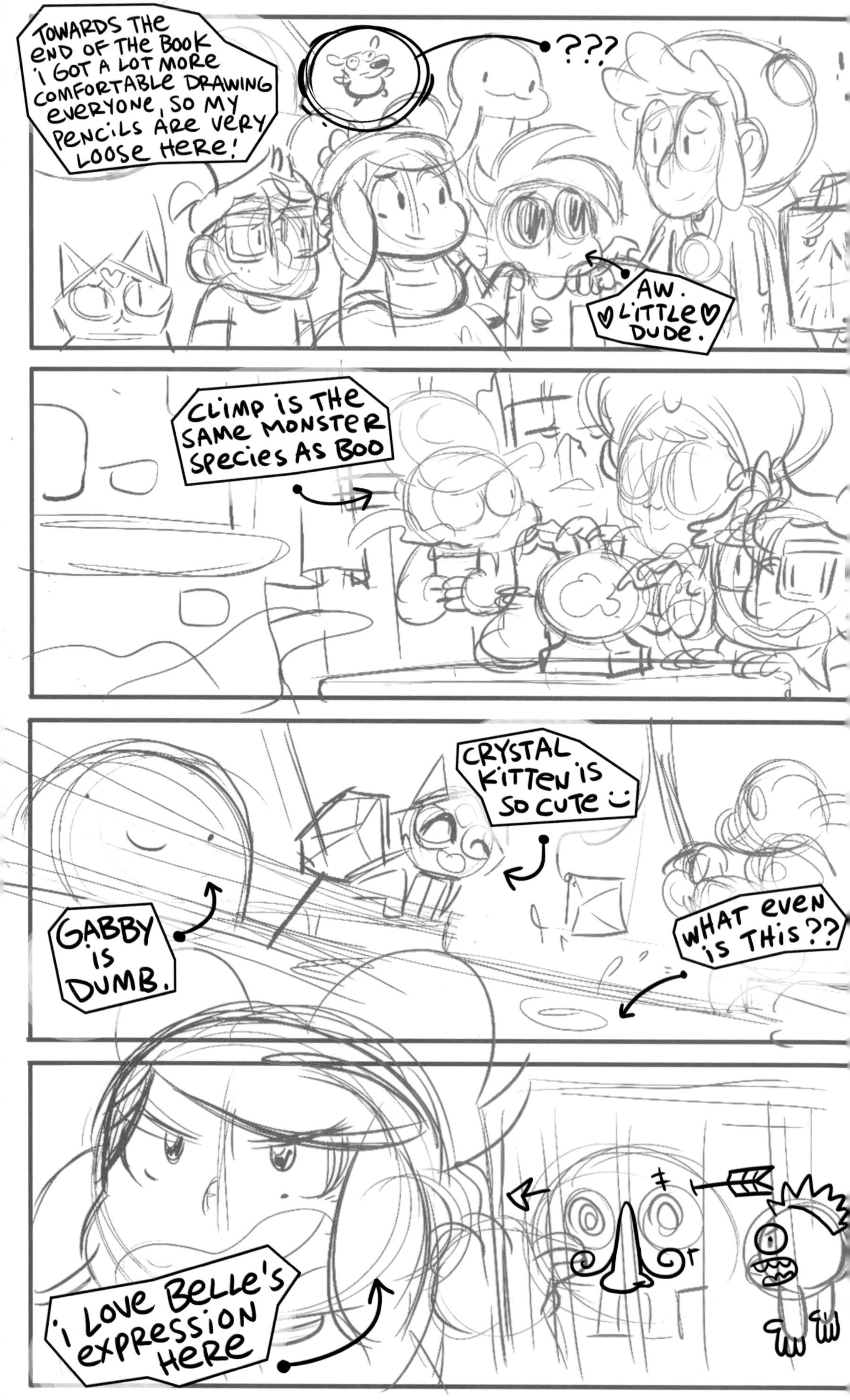
TOWARDS THE END OF THE BOOK I GOT A LOT MORE COMFORTABLE DRAWING EVERYONE, SO MY PENCILS ARE VERY LOOSE HERE!
???
AW. LITTLE DUDE.
CLIMP IS THE SAME MONSTER SPECIES AS BOO
CRYSTAL KITTEN IS SO CUTE :)
GABBY IS DUMB.
WHAT EVEN IS THIS??
I LOVE BELLE'S EXPRESSION HERE

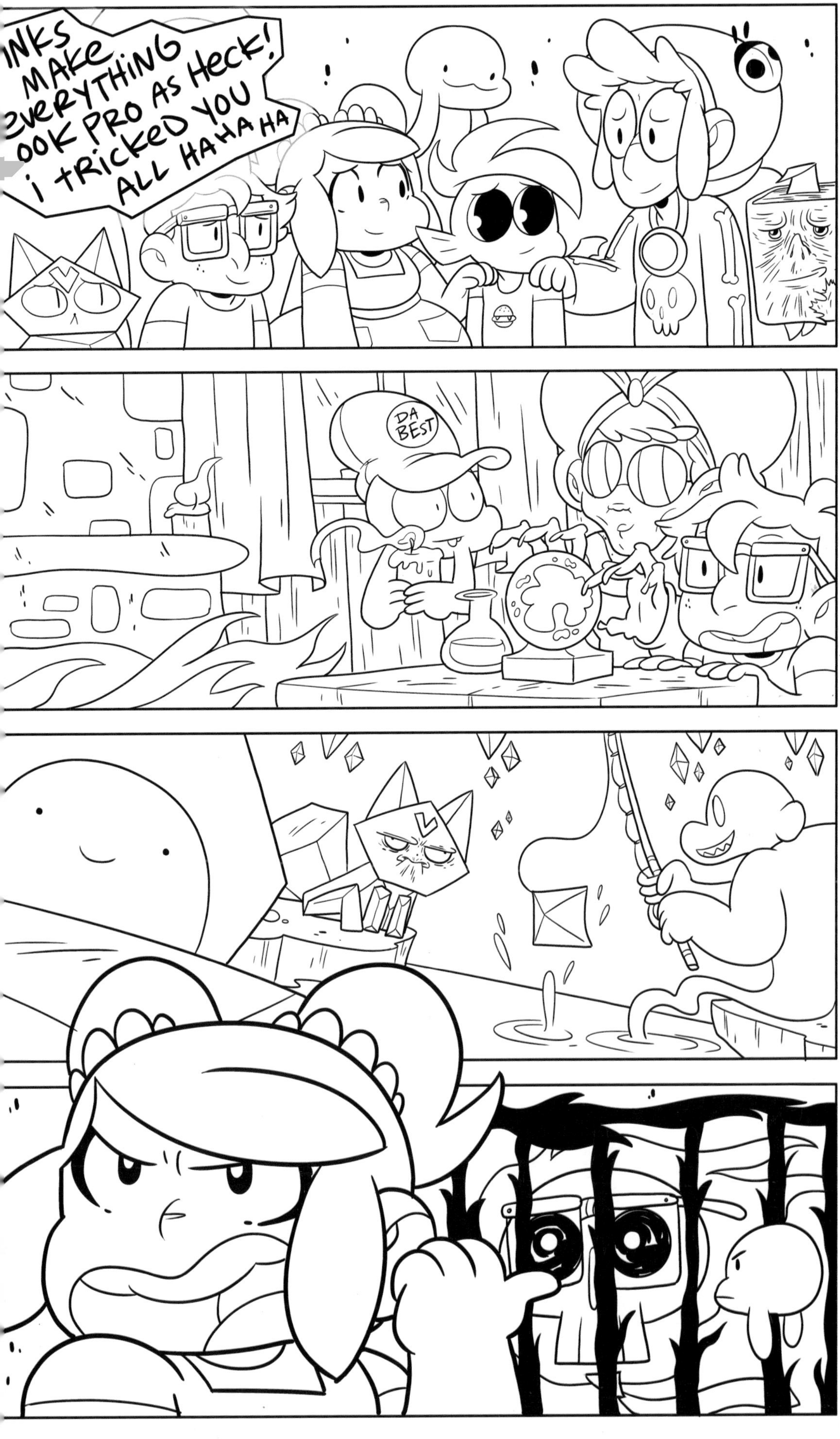
INKS MAKE EVERYTHING OOK PRO AS HECK! I TRICKED YOU ALL HAHA HA
DA BEST

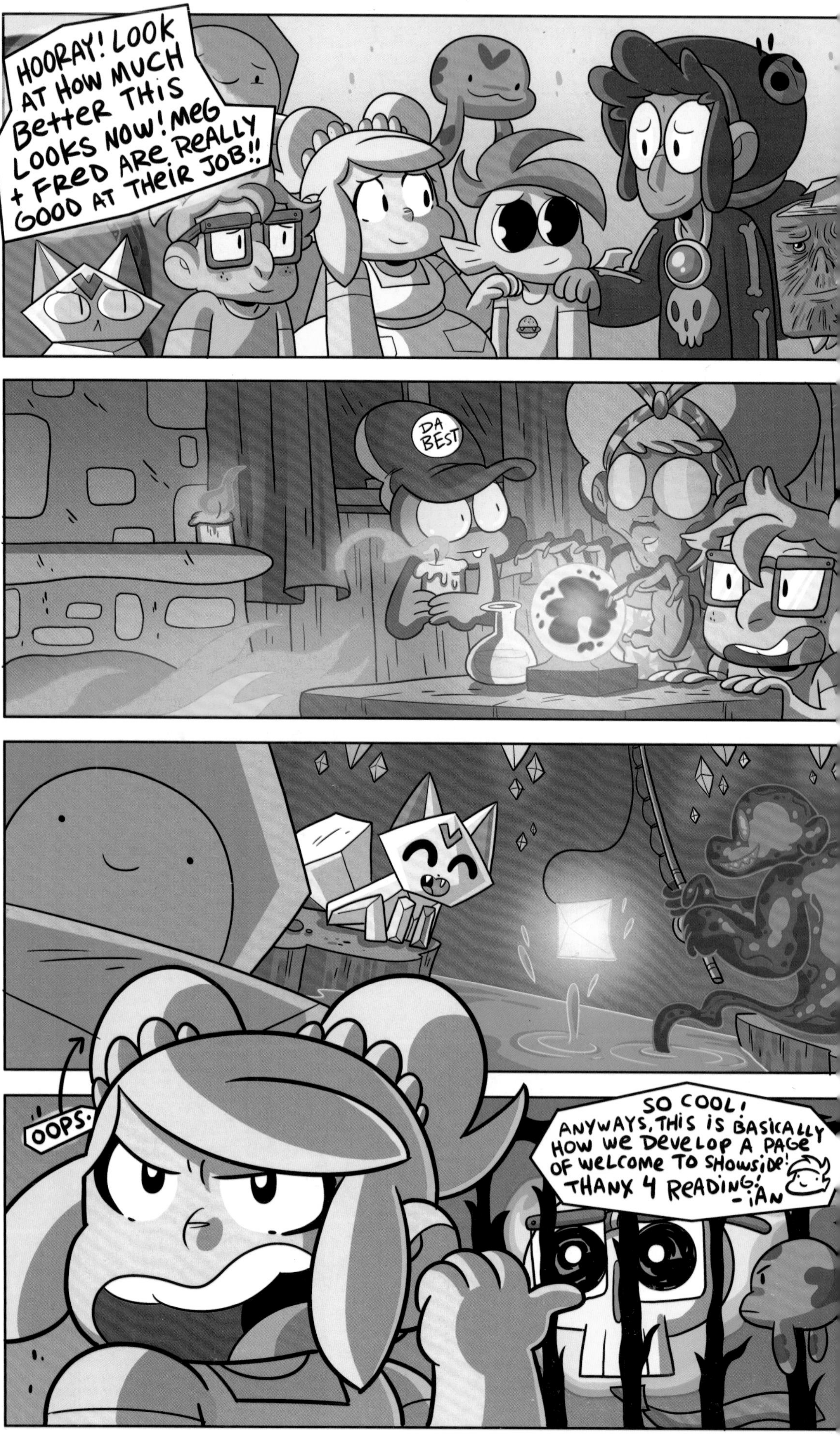
HOORAY! LOOK AT HOW MUCH BETTER THIS LOOKS NOW! MEG + FRED ARE REALLY GOOD AT THEIR JOB!!
DA BEST
OOPS.
SO COOL! ANYWAYS, THIS IS BASICALLY HOW WE DEVELOP A PAGE OF WELCOME TO SHOWSIDE! THANX 4 READING! -IAN